Rhys Bowen is the *New York Times* bestselling author of the Royal Spyness Series, Molly Murphy Mysteries, and Constable Evans. She is a recipient of the Agatha Best Novel Award and an Edgar Best Novel nominee.

Praise for Rhys Bowen

'The latest addition to Molly's case files offers a charming combination of history, mystery, and romance.' *Kirkus Reviews* on *Hush Now, Don't You Cry*

'Engaging . . . Molly's compassion and pluck should attract more readers to this consistently solid historical series.' *Publishers Weekly* on *Bless the Bride*

'Winning . . . The gutsy Molly, who's no prim Edwardian miss, will appeal to fans of contemporary female detectives.' *Publishers Weekly* on *The Last Illusion*

'This historical mystery delivers a top-notch, detail-rich story full of intriguing characters. Fans of the 1920s private detective Maisie Dobbs should give this series a try.' *Booklist* on *The Last Illusion*

'Details of Molly's new cases are knit together with the accoutrements of 1918 New York City life. . . . Don't miss this great period puzzler reminiscent of Dame Agatha's mysteries and Gillian Linscott's Nell Bray series.' *Booklist* on *In a Gilded Cage*

Also by Rhys Bowen

THE MOLLY MURPHY MYSTERIES
Murphy's Law
Death of Riley
For the Love of Mike
In Like Flynn
Oh Danny Boy
In Dublin's Fair City
Tell Me Pretty Maiden
In a Gilded Cage
The Last Illusion
Bless the Bride
Hush Now, Don't You Cry
The Face in the Mirror
Through the Window
The Family Way
City of Darkness and Light
The Amersham Rubies
The Edge of Dreams
Away in a Manger
Time of Fog and Fire

HER ROYAL SPYNESS SERIES
Masked Ball at Broxley Manor
Her Royal Spyness
A Royal Pain
Royal Flush
Royal Blood
Naughty in Nice
The Twelve Clues of Christmas

Heirs and Graces
Queen of Hearts
Malice at the Palace

The Edge of Dreams

Rhys Bowen

Constable • London

CONSTABLE

First published in the USA in 2015 by Minotaur Books,
an imprint of St Martin's Press, New York

This edition published in the UK in 2016 by Constable

1 3 5 7 9 10 8 6 4 2

Copyright © Rhys Bowen, 2015

1 3 5 7 9 10 8 6 4 2

A CIP catalogue record for this book
is available from the British Library.

ISBN 978-1-47211-889-9 (paperback)
ISBN: 978-1-47212-050-2 (ebook)

Typeset in Berthold Baskerville by TW Type, Cornwall
Printed and bound in Great Britain by CPI (UK) Ltd, Croydon CR0 4YY
Papers used by Constable are from well-managed forests and other responsible sources

FSC
www.fsc.org

MIX
Paper from
responsible sources
FSC® C104740

Constable
is an imprint of
Little, Brown Book Group
Carmelite House
50 Victoria Embankment
London EC4Y 0DZ

An Hachette UK Company
www.hachette.co.uk

www.littlebrown.co.uk

Dedicated to my fellow goddesses, Louise Penny and Deborah Crombie. Thank you both for your friendship, encouragement, and for your own fabulous writing. I am privileged to call you friends. Debs, you get an extra thank-you for coming up with the brilliant title for this book!

And as always thank you to my wonderful editor, Kelley Ragland, her assistant, Elizabeth Lacks, my publicist, Sarah Melnyk, and my goddess-agents, Meg Ruley and Christina Hogrebe. Also to John for his patient reading and great suggestions and to my many Facebook fans who tell me that they love Molly Murphy, and who gave me great input on the title.

❧ One ❧

New York City, September 10, 1905

"Don't open your eyes until I tell you." His hand gripped my forearm as he half lifted, half dragged me down from the hansom cab. If the cabby thought it strange to be transporting a woman wearing a blindfold, he had kept quiet about it.

"Open my eyes?" I exclaimed. "Holy Mother of God, Daniel, how do you think I can open my eyes? I can't see a darned thing through this."

I heard him chuckle as I was steered forward, my feet moving cautiously over cobblestones. And then suddenly I knew where I was. Familiar smells wafted toward me—baking bread from the French bakery around the corner on Greenwich Avenue, the pink climbing rose that grew beside old Mrs. Konigsberg's front door. And there were familiar sounds too—the distant clatter and rattle of barrows coming from the Jefferson Market, the bustling traffic on Sixth Avenue, the particular way that footsteps echoed back from the tall brick houses on our narrow backwater.

1

"We're here, aren't we? You've brought me home." I could hardly make the words come out.

I was in Patchin Place, returning to what had been my home before it had been destroyed by a fire, when a gang had thrown a bomb through our window. I had been staying with my mother-in-law up in rural Westchester County since I arrived back from Paris several weeks ago, and had deliberately not been back to my house, believing it to be beyond repair and not wanting to see the remnants of my former life. Not wanting to sink into despair that it could ever be made whole again. I wasn't even sure that I wanted to see it now, but Daniel must have had a good reason for bringing me here.

I had sensed his excitement when he had asked Mrs. Heffernan to watch our son, saying that he wanted to kidnap me for a little while to show me something. Then he had insisted on tying the blindfold around my eyes, saying that he couldn't trust me not to peek without it and he didn't want to spoil the surprise. I had allowed myself to be helped into the cab, utterly baffled and dying of curiosity as to what this surprise might be. Daniel was holding me around the waist now, and I reached out to grip his sleeve for reassurance. It had to be something good, I told myself. Daniel was the fairest man I had ever met. And he loved me. He would never do anything to deliberately cause me distress.

"Four more steps," Daniel said, leading me forward. "Now, stand still. Don't move."

He released my waist and I heard him walk away from me. I have never been the most patient of people so it was all I could do not to rip the blindfold from my eyes.

It was as if time stood still. I heard the pigeons that lived on the roof opposite cooing. The honk of an automobile. A baby crying far away. Then he was beside me again. I felt his warm breath on my cheek.

"Ready?" he whispered.

Then he was undoing the handkerchief around my eyes. I stood blinking in strong sunlight, looking at a newly painted green front door. This was my house as I remembered it—new windows with shining white trim, and only blackened bricks that no amount of scrubbing could clean to betray that the house had recently been a heap of ashes.

"Oh, Daniel," I gasped. "It's exactly the way it was."

"Not quite," he said. "But it's a start." He put his hand gently on my shoulder, urging me forward. "Go on. Open the door."

I walked forward. My hand gripped the doorknob and the door swung open. The smell of new paint greeted me as I took my first cautious step into the hallway. New white-painted stairs rose up on my left. Straight ahead was my kitchen, with a new pine table just like the old one and a sparkling tile floor. There was new linoleum in the hall, and to my right the parlor door was half open.

"Go on in," Daniel said, coming up behind me.

I entered the parlor. The first thing I saw was a sofa, almost like the one we had lost. I next noticed an armchair by the fireplace, and when I looked around the room, I almost jumped out of my skin. Standing behind the door were two people that I recognized—my dear friends and neighbors Elena Goldfarb and Augusta Walcott, looking as outlandishly flamboyant as ever, their faces alight with anticipation.

"Sid! Gus!" I squealed with joy as I rushed to their open arms. "I didn't even know you were back in New York." I tried to say the words as I was almost suffocated in their hugs. "I had no idea. I thought you were planning to stay in Vienna to study with Professor Freud."

"Ah, well, we decided we'd had enough of Vienna," Sid said, glancing at Gus. "And we had a parting of ways with Professor Freud. Gus couldn't agree with his interpretation of dreams."

"He insisted that every symbol in our dreams is linked to sex," Gus said. "Absolute rubbish and I told him so. He didn't like being contradicted by a woman, I can tell you, especially a foreign one, so we thought we'd better make a hasty retreat."

"When did you come back?" I asked. "Why didn't you get in touch with me?"

"We arrived back a few days ago," Sid said as I brushed away tears of joy. "But Daniel wanted us to be part of the surprise. He asked us not to contact you before the house was ready. As a matter of fact, we helped him with the finishing touches."

I looked around at the dainty end table with a white cloth and a vase of flowers, at the clock on the mantel, and beside it even a china dog like the one we'd had before.

"It's not exactly as it was," Daniel said, coming to join us. "But we tried our best to make it look the way you remembered it. I've left the things that need a feminine touch for you—the drapes and the bed linens and that sort of thing."

Until I had a baby I had rarely allowed myself to cry. Now the tears trickled down my cheeks and I threw my arms around his neck. "You did all this without breathing a word to me, and when you are so busy at work too. You're a grand sort of man, Daniel Sullivan."

Daniel gave Sid and Gus an embarrassed smile. "I had quite a bit of help from various people at police headquarters. And your friends here. Everyone has been most kind."

"So you'd no idea that the house was almost rebuilt?" Gus asked.

I shook my head. "Whenever I asked Daniel, he indicated that things were progressing slowly and I'd have to be patient."

"It was lucky that she came home in the middle of a heat wave in July and was glad to go straight to my mother's in the country," Daniel said. "If she'd been living here in the apartment with me, it would have been harder to do everything without giving the game away."

"I'm quite overwhelmed," I said. "I don't know what to say."

"For once Molly Murphy is lost for words," Sid said dryly, giving Gus a nudge. "We never thought we'd see that day, did we?"

"Come and see the rest of the house," Daniel said. "I shouldn't be spending too long away from work."

"And I shouldn't leave Liam for too long with Mrs. Heffernan," I said. "She's a little old to be minding a lively youngster."

"Who is this Mrs. Heffernan?" Sid asked.

"The caretaker at the building on West Sixty-first Street where

4

Daniel has been living," I said. "I've been staying out in Westchester with Daniel's mother but I decided it was time we came back into town so that I could look after my husband again. Not that it would have been easy in that tiny apartment with no real cooking facilities." I turned back to Daniel. "So can we really move back into our house?"

He led the way out of the front parlor and pushed open the back parlor door. "Like I said," he turned to answer, "there are still some finishing touches that only you can make. We need bedding, and drapes, and kitchen utensils. I have no idea what women need to cook with— apart from a stove. We have one of those, and some pots and pans."

I took in the back parlor with its mahogany dining table and chairs, a sturdy sideboard, and a desk like Daniel's former one tucked into a corner. The window looked onto our little square of backyard—now wild, and overgrown, and littered with builder's debris. Plenty of work to be done there. Then I went through to the kitchen—new table, new shelves holding a couple of pots and pans, and beneath them . . .

"Well, what do you think?" Daniel asked me.

"We've never had a gas cooker!" I exclaimed. Until now I'd always had an old cast-iron stove, and I'd envied those like Sid and Gus who had been able to upgrade to a more modern form of cooking.

"You'll find it so much more convenient, Molly," Sid said. "And we'll look after Liam while you go shopping for the things you still need."

Dishes and silverware, I thought. *And cheese graters, and washboards, and a meat safe*—the amount of things I needed was overwhelming. And they all cost money. I had been told that the police department was helping out with the rebuilding of our house, since it was an act of retaliation against the arrest of a gang leader that had destroyed it in the first place, but would that largesse stretch to replacing everything I had lost?

Then I had a thought that brought a smile to my face. "Can we move back here in time for Liam's birthday?"

"Oh, yes, Liam's birthday," Gus said. "We were just talking about what presents we could buy him. And we'll give him a splendid party."

I laughed. "He's going to be one, Gus. What will he know about parties?" I looked at Daniel. I could tell he was picturing what Sid and Gus's idea of a birthday party might be, with belly dancers and all kinds of bohemian folk.

"And besides," I said. "I'd like to have his birthday right here in our own dear house. A proper affirmation that we've really come home at last."

Daniel nodded his approval. "Come and see the upstairs," he said.

Our bedroom at the front of the house had a fine new bed in it, and a wardrobe, and a chest of drawers. Liam's nursery had not been furnished yet; neither had the back bedroom.

Daniel shrugged. "I couldn't quite remember what babies need," he said, "and besides, he's grown so much recently. We can bring that borrowed crib down from the apartment but I'm thinking that maybe he'll be able to go into a proper bed."

"He needs something he can't climb out of," I said. "Or the Lord knows what he'd get into. He's turned into an escape artist, Daniel. He'll be outdoing Houdini any day now."

Daniel smiled. "He's certainly become an active little tyke."

"We can't wait to see him again, Molly," Gus said as we made our way downstairs again. "He must have grown in three months."

"He certainly has, and learned to make his needs known very strongly," I replied, sharing a smile with Daniel. "His current vocabulary is Mama, Dada, and no."

Sid and Gus laughed. Daniel opened the front door and we stepped out into warm September sunshine.

"Do you have time to come over to our house for a cup of coffee and a snack before you get back to Liam?" Sid asked.

I was dying for a chat with my dearest friends, but I hesitated, glancing at Daniel. Much as I wanted to hear all their news, I knew Daniel had been working day and night on a particularly complicated case recently. He never confided much to me about his work, but he had let slip that he was having a tough time with this one. A murder case, I gathered, and more than one murder involved.

"Thank you, but I think we should be getting back now," Daniel answered, before I could say anything. "I'm sure Molly will take you up on your offer to look after our boy so that she can finish equipping the house as she wants it."

"Molly dear, you can always borrow supplies from us to get you started. It would be too overwhelming to try to shop for everything you need at once," Gus said. "We have more dishes and pans than we need, don't we, Sid."

"Absolutely," Sid said. "And spare bedclothes and pillows. Come on over and help yourself."

"You're very kind, as always." I turned to smile at them. "And I'm so looking forward to hearing all about Vienna."

"Gus is becoming quite an alienist in her own right." Sid beamed at her proudly. "Some of the other doctors working with Professor Freud were really impressed with her theories. Maybe we should have stayed, and Gus could have become an eminent scientist, a second Madame Curie . . . "

"No, we shouldn't have." Gus shook her head. "I'm not even a qualified doctor. Officially I'm not allowed to treat patients. Besides, you didn't like Austrian food—too much cream and dumplings."

"We must be going, Molly." Daniel touched my arm to lead me away. "I should be back at work."

"But you said yourself it's the first day off you've had in ages." I looked back with longing at Sid and Gus's front door. "Surely they can't begrudge you one day off."

"It's not a question of begrudging," he said. "It's a question of what is more important—my enjoyment or stopping a murderer before he kills again. I rather think the latter."

"You're chasing a murderer, Captain Sullivan?" Sid sounded excited. "You should enlist the help of your wife. She seems to have a knack for solving crimes. You should have seen her in Paris . . . "

"Oh, that was nothing," I cut in, giving her a warning frown. I had decided not to tell Daniel about that harrowing business in Paris. At the time he had had enough on his plate to worry about, and when I returned I chose not to think about what I had been through.

"What are we talking about?" I sensed that Daniel was instantly alert. "Some business in Paris?"

"Oh, an Impressionist painter was murdered by a Jewish rebel while I was there," I said in what I hoped was a breezy manner. "It was in all the newspapers."

"And Molly figured it out before the police," Gus said proudly.

"Well done." I saw Daniel exhale in relief that this crime hadn't personally affected me. "Yes, I don't doubt Molly's skills as a detective, but I'd rather she kept a good distance from my police work in New York. I don't want to put her or our son at risk, as I'm sure you understand."

"I'll bring Liam to see you tomorrow," I said as I took my leave of my friends. "You can tell me everything about Vienna."

"Sid has learned to make a mean *apfelstrudel*," Gus said. "She can make one to go with our coffee and—" She broke off as a man came running toward us. It was a police constable and he came to a halt, panting, in front of Daniel.

"Captain Sullivan, sir. I'm so glad I've found you."

"What is it, Byrne?"

"There's been another one." The young constable was still trying to catch his breath.

"Another murder?" Daniel snapped out the words.

"Another note," he said and handed Daniel an envelope, addressed in typewritten letters to him at *Mulberry Street Police Headquarters*. Daniel opened the envelope and took out a folded sheet of paper.

I could read the words as Daniel unfolded it. They were typed with a typewriting machine in the middle of an otherwise blank page. Just one sentence.

I'm saving the best for last.

❧ TWO ❧

D aniel refolded the paper. "For last?" he said.

"At least that might mean he plans to stop this murderous spree, don't you think, sir?" the constable said.

"But he plans to kill once more first," Daniel said grimly. "He does this to taunt us, knowing we can't stop him, damn his eyes." He glanced across at us, realizing he had been swearing in the presence of ladies. He cleared his throat.

"We should go," Gus said. "We look forward to seeing you tomorrow then, Molly."

I nodded and went to follow Daniel.

"Byrne—please take Mrs. Sullivan and find her a cab," Daniel said. "I'm sorry, Molly, but you must make your own way home. You have enough money with you?"

"Don't worry about me, Daniel. I'm just fine," I said. "You go and do what you have to. I can take the El. The station is quite close by. I don't need a cab."

"All right, then. I'll see you when I can." He put a hand on my shoulder and gave me a quick peck on the cheek. Then he hurried off with the constable, leaving me standing alone on a deserted Patchin Place.

I walked around the corner to Sixth Avenue and made my way to the Eighth Avenue station of the elevated railway. My insides were twisted into a knot, as they always were when Daniel was worried and possibly in danger. That note had sounded so innocent, but Daniel had obviously interpreted it as a threat to kill—another murder in what had been a growing number of them. Until now I hadn't known whether he was on the trail of one murderer or more than one. This indicated it was just one man, one twisted individual, who had kept Daniel out until all hours. There had been nothing in the newspapers warning of a fiend such as this, so I presumed the police had managed to keep it hushed up for fear of alarming the public.

I boarded the train and was soon speeding northward. I looked with interest into the second-floor windows of the tenements that we passed, where I could see lives going on almost close enough to reach out and touch. In one window I glimpsed a small child, sitting on a potty, staring up at us as we passed. In another a woman was fixing her hair, her face a picture of concentration as she stuck hairpins into her bun. I had often wondered what it must be like to live with trains passing so close outside the window all the time. I supposed the occupants got used to it. One gets used to almost anything eventually if one has to. But would I ever have gotten used to that complete lack of privacy?

I alighted at the Fifty-ninth Street station to the more genteel world of Uptown New York, and walked up to the apartment building where we'd been staying on West Sixty-first Street. From the outside it appeared quite grand—almost as swank as those new buildings along the edge of Central Park, with its Moorish-style decoration and exotic archway over the entrance. But inside it didn't quite live up to its promise. It was designed as a city residence for bachelors—each apartment a pied-à-terre with a small dark sitting room, narrow bedroom, and minute kitchen space with a gas ring. It had been hard to minister to the needs of a baby there, and to keep him from disturbing all those bachelors, so I was overjoyed at the prospect of moving back into my own home.

Mrs. Heffernan had an equally small caretaker's apartment off the marble foyer. She greeted me with obvious relief.

"Oh, you're back so soon, Mrs. Sullivan," she said. "I was just thinking about fixing the young one some food for his midday meal."

"Captain Sullivan was summoned back to work unexpectedly," I said.

"That poor man. He'll work himself into the grave if you're not careful," she said, leading me through to a cramped and overdecorated parlor. It felt uncomfortably warm and stuffy, and looked as if it hadn't been dusted too frequently, and I felt a jolt of guilt about leaving Liam there.

Liam had heard my voice and was already standing and yelling "Mama!" as I came in. When he saw me he tried to run toward me, impeded by his petticoats. I swept him up into my arms.

"I hope you've been a good boy," I said, showering him with kisses.

"No trouble at all, Mrs. Sullivan. Plenty of curiosity, I'll say that for him, but not a malicious bone in him."

I wondered what his plenty of curiosity had been trying to get into, noting the stuffed bird under a glass dome and the large aspidistra plant, but thought it wise not to ask as I thanked Mrs. Heffernan and carried Liam to the elevator. "First lunch and a nap for you, young man," I said. "Then we'll go out and get Dada a treat for his supper. I think we'll throw caution to the winds and buy him a steak. We have to make sure he keeps up his strength."

By five o'clock I had a nice sirloin steak waiting to be cooked in the pan, after I'd boiled the potatoes and beans. I had no oven, and no way of keeping things warm, but I'd just have to make do somehow. At seven o'clock I fed Liam some mashed vegetables and put him to bed. At eight I had some mashed potato myself and a fried egg. Nine o'clock came, then ten, and still Daniel didn't come home.

There was no way I could go to bed and no room for me to pace. At home on Patchin Place I'd have looked out of the window, but my window here looked onto a faceless wall of brick. I tried to read in the harsh electric light. But I couldn't concentrate.

A man who taunted the police with notes before he killed—he sounded like the epitome of evil. And he was sending those notes to my husband.

I undressed and climbed into bed, hugging my knees to myself as if it was a cold rather than balmy September evening. I was just nodding off when I heard the click of the door latch. I jumped up right away as Daniel came in.

"You should have gone to sleep, my dear," he said. He looked worn-out, his hair was disheveled and he was hollow-eyed. "Not stayed awake for me."

"I was worried about you," I said. "Have you eaten anything? I bought you a steak as a treat."

"A steak?" His eyes lit up briefly, then he shook his head. "I'm afraid I'm too tired to do justice to it tonight. I've just come from a long session with the commissioner in which I was lambasted for not doing my job."

He sank into the armchair. "We don't have any whiskey, do we? That's what I feel I need right now."

"I think there's still a drop in that bottle you were hiding under the sink." I smiled as I went to find it. I poured the remains into a glass and brought it back to him. He drained it in one gulp. "Thank you. That hit the spot."

"You have to eat," I urged. "Are you sure you won't try the steak?"

"No, really, let's save it for when I can enjoy it. Some bread and cheese will do. And did you pour the last of the whiskey?"

"Yes, I did, but just this once—I'm not having you turning into an Irish drunk, Daniel Sullivan."

He gave me a tired smile. "Not much chance of that happening. But after today . . . well, anyone would have needed a shot of whiskey."

"Really bad, was it? Your murder investigation? It's not going well?" I paused in the kitchen doorway.

He was staring down at his empty whiskey glass. "To begin with it wasn't at all clear that one person was committing these crimes, you see. Now we have to believe that we are dealing with one murderer who feels he can kill with impunity, when and where he likes."

I went through to the kitchen, cut some bread, buttered it, and added a big hunk of cheddar, then came back and placed them on the table in front of him. "You received a note today," I said. "From your conversation it sounded as if you've been getting these notes on a regular basis."

He nodded and sighed. "The first ones were only sent after he had killed someone. Now he's so confident that he sends one before and after a murder, taunting us in our inadequacy."

"And you have no idea who it could be?"

"None at all," he said. "We haven't the least little thing to go on. Nothing to tie the murders together."

"Were all of the victims killed in the same manner? In the same area?"

"Nothing," he said sharply. "Some of the deaths would have gone unnoticed as murders if we hadn't received a note boasting about them. And none of them have been in the same part of the city, the same strata of society—there's nothing to link them at all."

"Yes, there is," I said as the thought occurred to me. "There is one thing. He is sending notes to you. You are the link."

Daniel looked up sharply.

"The notes were all addressed to you, weren't they?" I said.

"Yes, they were. But I took that to mean that I'm a rather prominent member of the police force. My name and picture have appeared in the newspapers."

"So have the names of other police captains. And why not send messages to the commissioner himself, if he wants to go to the top?"

Daniel sighed again. "I don't know, and I'm too tired to think right now."

"Maybe I can help," I said tentatively, as I came to perch on the arm of his chair. "Sometimes a woman's point of view can be useful."

He shook his head firmly. "Molly, you know I can't involve you in my cases. It wouldn't be ethical and I wouldn't want to put you in any sort of danger. Besides, there's nothing you could do that hasn't already been done. I have a team of highly trained officers working with me. They have been through the circumstances of every murder with a fine-tooth comb. After at least six deaths we are none the wiser. Not one step closer to a solution." He put the cheese on the bread and took a big bite. Then after he had swallowed he looked up at me again. "For all we know they are all random killings, committed by someone who just likes feeling powerful."

"I don't think any killings are completely random," I said. "A person must have a reason for that first killing. Nobody suddenly decides one day to go out and just kill somebody, anybody. Someone has upset him, or thwarted him, or he's decided he hates all women, or black people, or Italians . . . but there has to be some kind of rationale behind the first murder."

Daniel shook his head. "The first murder that we know about was a simpleminded old woman who lived in a small house in Brooklyn. Who would want her out of the way?"

"The other possibility, of course," I said tentatively, "is that only one of the murders is important. The real murder is hidden behind the smoke screen of random killings."

He frowned, considering this. "You think so? Yes, I suppose that is possible. All right. I'll go through the list again, although I've been through it a hundred times already."

"So who were the rest of the victims? Were they also in Brooklyn? Also feebleminded?"

Daniel smiled and shook his head. "I'm sorry, Molly. I really don't want to involve you in this. Besides, I'm too tired to talk." He pushed his plate away. "I'm even too tired to eat. Come on. Let's go to bed."

I helped him up from the chair and he held my hand as we walked through to the bedroom.

I slept fitfully that night, unable to shake the worrying thought that out of all the policemen in New York, a violent and disturbed person had selected my husband as the recipient of his notes. As I lay awake, listening to Daniel's rhythmic breathing, I longed to help—not just because of my incurable curiosity, but because I hated to see my husband so tired and worried. We had come a long way, Daniel and I. At the beginning of our relationship he had dismissed my detective skills as sheer female luck, but over the years he had come to admit, grudgingly, that I was actually a good detective. But that had never extended to asking for my help on a case. Pride, I suspected. Daniel Sullivan was a proud man.

But that didn't stop me from toying with the information he had shared with me. *Why send cryptic notes to a particular member of the police?* I asked myself. Because our murderer wanted to feel clever. He enjoyed stumping the police and making them appear stupid. But why Daniel? Was it as simple as seeing Daniel's picture in a newspaper, after he had solved a crime or arrested a criminal, and feeling animosity toward him? Or had this to do with some time he and Daniel had crossed paths—a criminal Daniel had put behind bars, maybe, now out of prison again and bearing a grudge?

I decided to mention this to Daniel in the morning, but I was still sleeping when I sensed he had gotten out of bed, and I came to consciousness fully only to hear the front door slam behind him. Liam awoke and demanded to be fed. We breakfasted. I bathed him and we were ready to visit Sid and Gus just after eight o'clock. But they lived a civilized and childless existence. They were not used to receiving visitors at such an ungodly hour. Still, I didn't want to linger in that cramped and airless little apartment. I'd take the elevated railway down to Greenwich Village and if we arrived too early, I could amuse Liam by letting him watch the people and pigeons in Washington Square, or even buy some fresh fruit in the Jefferson Market.

It was an overcast morning, rather uncomfortably warm, with a heaviness to the air promising rain or even thunder later. Ninth Avenue was busy with early-morning activity—people hurrying on their way to work and shopkeepers winding out awnings, putting out trays of vegetables, bric-a-brac, flowers, books. Smart carriages and hansom cabs raced past. Delivery drays lumbered along and there was even an occasional automobile, dodging in and out of slower traffic and impatiently tooting its horn, which delighted Liam. I should have been enjoying the scene but I couldn't shake off a feeling of uneasiness. I found I was glancing over my shoulder as if someone was watching me—which of course was absurd, since nobody knew I was in this part of the city.

When we reached the Fifty-ninth Street station I realized my folly at coming out so early. The platform was jam-packed with business people, traveling down to the commercial center of the city at the southern tip of Manhattan. I was half-minded to go back down the stairs and hail one of those cabs. But that would have been an extravagance we couldn't afford, especially with the added expense of furnishing our house looming. I still hadn't had time to ask Daniel where the money was going to come from to buy those bed linens and kitchen supplies. That was one of the problems with being a policeman's wife—there was never time just to sit and talk. And there was too much time to worry, alone.

A train came rumbling down the track toward us, the bright disk on the front of the locomotive revealing it to be a Sixth Avenue local. Just what I wanted. But apparently so did everyone else. The crowd surged forward and I saw to my dismay that the carriages were already full. A portly man with muttonchop whiskers, wearing a derby hat, saw me carrying a baby and stepped aside for me to get on board, but just at that moment a man came hurtling past, nearly knocking me over as he ran down the platform. My protector in the derby hat leaped to my aid, muttering curses at the unchivalrous lout, and as he did so the doors slammed, the whistle blew, and the train pulled out.

"No matter," my portly protector said. "See, another train is right behind it. They come thick and fast at this time of the day, and I'll wager this one is less crowded too."

As it rattled into the station and pulled up with a squeaking of breaks, I saw that it wasn't a Sixth Avenue train this time. It was a Ninth Avenue train. I hesitated as the doors opened and others climbed aboard. I could take this train to Christopher Street, but it would mean a longer walk at the other end. Then it struck me that it would also mean that I would walk past Sid and Gus's favorite French bakery. I could stop off there and bring them croissants for their breakfast. Thus encouraged with the idea of buying my friends a little treat, I was about to climb aboard the second car when I heard the sound of a hacking cough. *No, thank you,* I thought. I was forever mindful that summer diseases can linger into September in New York. Every year had its share of cholera and typhoid, and consumption was ever present. I wasn't going to expose Liam to that risk. I backed away and pushed through the crowd to the third car instead. Passengers were packed like sardines behind the first two doors. I wrenched open the third door and heaved Liam and myself up the step. This part of the car was just as crowded. Two round middle-aged women, immigrants from somewhere, dressed in black dresses and black headscarves, were sitting on the seats nearest the door, leaning across to each other, deep in conversation and oblivious to me, continuing to talk around me as if I wasn't there. A man across the aisle tried to offer me his seat, but I couldn't get past a large lady with a round shopping basket on her arm, so I was forced to stand with Liam in my arms.

This was not wise, I told myself. No wonder I couldn't shake off the feeling of unease that had gripped me since I left the apartment that morning. I tried to hang on to the leather strap above my head but Liam was now too heavy to hold with one arm, and besides he was wriggling and complaining at being squashed like this.

I'd get out at the next station and take the Broadway trolley instead, I decided. It took longer but at least there would be fresh air and Liam could see out as we rode. I was swung from side to side as the train picked up speed. Then I was pressed to the door of the carriage as the train started to round a curve. I remember thinking that we were traveling much too fast for such a curve. And surely there was no steep curve on the Ninth Avenue El? It was the Sixth Avenue train that went around that sharp bend. But even as these thoughts were flashing through my mind, suddenly there was a tremendous jolt. I was flung violently against the carriage door. The large woman and her basket slammed into me. Liam cried out. People were screaming. The screams were deadened by the sound of screeching metal, of splintering wood. The life was being squeezed out of me as more people piled into me. I tried to yell, "Liam!" as he was wrenched from my arms.

And then we were falling. Plunging down toward the street below.

❦ Three ❦

I must have passed out because I opened my eyes to a scene of hell. I couldn't breathe. I couldn't move. As I came back to consciousness I realized I was lying, pressed against a door that miraculously held fast, with a jumble of people across me. The air was full of acrid smoke and through it there came moans and screams. Someone very close to me was whimpering, "Help. Somebody help me."

For a moment I couldn't remember where I was and how I had come to be in this predicament, then the full realization came back to me. The train going too fast around a steep curve. Squeal of metal. Awful jerk. Plunging. Falling. I tried to push away the weight that was pinning me down and saw it was the large woman with the basket. She seemed to be unconscious. And the second I tried to shift her weight from me I remembered I had been holding Liam. She must be lying on him. Suffocating him. I struggled desperately and got a hand free, then pushed with all my might.

"Liam!" I yelled. "Where's my baby? Somebody help me find my baby."

Other people stirred, shifted, moved. My other arm came free. And there was no Liam in it. No Liam pinned to the door or on the floor at my feet. In my panic I struggled to stand upright, but I tee-tered and couldn't get my balance. Then I looked out of the window and saw why. I was in a train car that was dangling at a crazy angle, suspended from the elevated track above. I had no idea whether we were hanging in midair or the other end of the car was resting against something solid. Any minute now we could continue our plunge to destruction. And my child was nowhere to be found. I scrabbled around like a mad thing through the smoke-filled car—pushing aside God knows whose limbs to look under seats, under bodies, growing more and more frantic every second. It hurt me to breathe and I couldn't tell whether it was because of the acrid smoke or whether I was injured. I saw there was blood on my hands and couldn't tell if it was mine or someone else's.

Then through the chaos I heard a cry.

"Liam!" I screamed and clambered down the steep angle of the car, over seat backs, people's backs. There were shouts, complaints. Then I heard his wailing again, his little voice full of fear, and another voice saying calmly, "Don't worry, son. Your mama's here somewhere. We'll find her."

A gentleman, dressed in smart business attire—his dark suit now covered in dust and debris—was holding my son, who was squirm-ing and bawling like a mad thing. Liam's new white sailor suit was streaked with black and the matching sailor hat was missing.

"Liam. My precious." I grabbed him and held him tightly to me, rocking him, crying with him. I could feel his little heart pounding against me and a searing pain in my chest with each breath.

"Thank you." I looked up at the man.

"He was quite fortunate," the man said. "He must have slid down under the seats and landed at my feet. Come on. We must see if we can get out of here before this car catches on fire too."

I glanced down and could make out a crushed and burning heap below us. It was hard even to recognize it as a former railway car-riage, and I realized it was the second car, the one I hadn't taken because of the man who was coughing. *On such minute details hangs our fate*, I thought.

There was movement below us. Shouts through the smoke. More shouts coming from outside the car.

"Careful," someone warned. "Don't shift the weight or we might fall down to the street."

"No, it's all right," a man's voice shouted back. "We're resting against the wall of a building, and if I can get this window opened enough we can climb out onto a window ledge."

One by one people were helped through the carriage window. Hands came out from the building to pull them to safety. The smart gentleman called out, "Lady with a baby here. Take her next." And I was passed down to the window. Liam screamed as he was wrenched from my arms again and handed through to waiting arms. I had to hitch up my skirts as I squeezed through the window and then take a large step, through the black and swirling smoke, across to the nearest window ledge. But frankly, concern about who might see my bloomers was the last thing on my mind at that moment.

Then I was in a small kitchen that reeked of garlic and onions. Several dark-eyed children huddled behind the table, eyeing us with fear and fascination. Liam was handed back to me. I was assisted through the apartment, onto a landing, and down a flight of steep wooden stairs before coming out to join the throng on the street below. I could hear the sound of fire truck bells jangling as an engine approached. Police were yelling "Stand back. Let them through."

As the smoke swirled and parted I felt that I was looking at the aftermath of a battle. In front of me was the twisted, smoldering wreckage that had once been a train carriage. It appeared to have landed on top of a truck, which was now burning. People were crowding around the wreckage, still trying to extricate those trapped inside. Those who had managed to escape now sat on the curb, holding up handkerchiefs to blood-spattered faces. Others staggered around in a daze, their clothing bloody and burned, while still others lay silent.

I couldn't tell whether they were unconscious or dead and I turned away, shivering.

Find a cab, I told myself. Take a cab to Sid and Gus. They'll know what to do. They'll take care of me. I jumped as a hand touched my arm. "Are you all right, ma'am?" a uniformed constable asked me. "You're as white as a sheet."

"I was in that carriage that's still hanging," I said. "I couldn't find my baby."

"Are you sure you're not hurt? And the little boy?"

"He seems to be unhurt, thank God. I think I'm all right. It hurts me to breathe."

"I'm thinking we should maybe get you to the hospital," he said. "Just to be on the safe side. People don't always recognize that they are injured in an accident, and you're clearly suffering from shock."

"Oh, no. I'm sure there are people who need help more than me," I said.

"Best to have the little guy checked out too," he said and led me to a waiting ambulance in which several people were already sitting. I didn't have the energy to argue with him at that point and besides, I did want to make sure that Liam was all right. He was quiet now, his thumb in his mouth as he snuggled against me. I put my hand down to my side and tentatively felt my ribs. A shot of pain made me gasp. A broken rib then, maybe?

The ambulance doors were closed and we lurched as the horses started forward.

"Not exactly doing much to help if we've broken bones, is it?" the woman next to me said. She was holding her left wrist and I could see a bone jutting out through the flesh. I shuddered and turned away. The ride seemed to take forever, with bone-shaking jarring and rattling as the horses galloped over cobbles. Then thank God we came to a halt. There were voices outside. The back door opened and we were helped down.

"Where are we?" I asked, hoping to hear that we were at St. Vincent's, just around the corner from Patchin Place.

"You're at Roosevelt Hospital, my dear," said a nurse.

I almost laughed at the irony. Roosevelt Hospital on Tenth Avenue, just down the block from the apartment building where I had started out that morning. Well, at least I could go back home when they released me. The waiting room was full and we sat on hard benches, breathing in the carbolic, antiseptic hospital smell. Finally I'd had enough. I went up to a nurse sitting at the desk. "Look, I'm not at all badly injured," I said. "And my baby seems to be fine. I think we'll just go home."

She looked at me, frowning. "If you really think you're well enough, of course you can leave. God knows we've got enough to do right now."

"Right. Thank you. I'll be on my way then," I said.

I headed for the bright light coming from the doorway, and the next thing I knew my legs buckled under me.

When I opened my eyes I was lying in a cold and narrow bed at one end of a long ward of identical beds. The beds around me seemed to be occupied by other women. Two nurses were standing at the foot of my bed, deep in whispered conversation. I raised my head to look around me. "Liam?" I called out. "What's happened to my boy?"

"Just lie back and take it easy." One of the nurses came over to stand beside me. Beneath the white veil she had a fresh red-cheeked face. "The doctor is examining your son right now." She picked up my wrist and started to take my pulse.

"What happened? Why am I here?"

"You fainted, that's what. You went into shock, my dear. Quite common after an accident. I've sent the orderly for a nice cup of hot tea for you. That's what you need for shock. Get that down you and you'll feel a lot better."

The tea arrived and I drank it, gratefully. Then a doctor came into the ward. "Another accident victim?" he asked, coming up to my bed.

"There's nothing much wrong with me. I can go home," I said.

"I'll be the judge of that, young woman," he said firmly. "Now, let's take a look at you." He took out his stethoscope and listened to my heartbeat. Then his hands moved skillfully over my body. I winced as he touched my side.

"Ribs hurt, do they?" He pressed a little harder making me wince even more. "Possible broken rib on this one, Nurse. Get her out of her street clothes and into a gown."

"But I don't want to stay here." I tried to sit up. "And where's my baby? I want him with me."

"You'll do as Doctor says." The nurse wagged a firm finger at me. "I'll go and find out about your baby. Is there someone who could take him if you're kept in here overnight?"

"Not really. My husband is a policeman. He can't stay home."

"No relatives?"

"Not in the city."

"Well, we'll sort that out later. Screen around this bed, nurse. Let's get you out of those clothes."

Two of them undressed me carefully. Even though it hurt me to raise my arms, I was relieved to find no obvious wounds. And even more relieved after the doctor came back and examined me more thoroughly.

"I don't think you've broken your ribs. You may have cracked one, but I think it's just a bad bruise. We'll strap you up, which will make breathing easier."

"I can go home then?"

He shook his head. "We're keeping you overnight, just in case. You've a bad bump on your head, so you might have experienced a concussion. You did black out in the waiting room, remember. And you're definitely in shock. No condition to go home and take care of a baby."

"Where is my child?" I asked. "He's all right, isn't he?"

"He's in the infant's ward at the moment. Bawling his head off, but

I gather he's perfectly fine. He can go home as soon as there's someone to take care of him."

I let out a sigh of relief. Liam was unharmed. That was the main thing. I turned to the nurse as the doctor left. "Can someone send a message to my husband? He'll want to know where I am and that I'm all right."

"I'll find you some paper," a young nurse said, "and we'll have a messenger deliver it. Is he nearby?"

"I don't know where he is at this moment." Suddenly I was near to tears. "But if you deliver it to police headquarters, they'll find him."

"Oh, a policeman, is he?" The young nurse nodded with understanding. "There's every chance he's already at the scene of the accident. Half the New York police seem to be there, from what I've heard." She had a gentle voice with a tinge of Irishness to it.

"He's a captain," I said, "and he's working on an important case. I hate to worry him with this, but he'll want to know."

"Of course he will." She came back with writing paper and I wrote, *I'm in Roosevelt Hospital. Survived the train wreck with only a scratch or two but they won't let me go home tonight. Liam's fine too. In the children's ward.*

The young nurse took it. "We'll have a messenger take it to the nearest police station," she said. "They'll be able to contact your husband, I'm sure. They'll know where to find him and he'll be here in no time at all." She put her hand on my arm. "Now, why don't you get some rest?"

"Can't I go to my son first? He'll want to know his mother is safe and nearby."

She shook her head. "You're not going anywhere without doctor's orders. Know that your boy is safe and being looked after for now. Now shut your eyes."

I tried to do as she had said, and in truth, my head was beginning to throb. I put my hand up and touched a painful lump. *Why did this have to happen now?* I thought angrily. Just when I was ready to move back to my own home, to get it furnished and to start life again. But then I reminded myself that I was better off than many poor wretches. I had survived the train crash with only minor injuries. I wasn't lying still and pale on the street, waiting to be covered by a shroud, nor was I still trapped inside the mangled wreckage of a smoldering carriage. And my son was safe and well. I had a lot to be thankful for.

❧ Four ❧

I n my dream I was in a narrow, confined space. I tried to move but
I couldn't. I couldn't even turn my head to see what was going on
behind me, although I could hear a familiar voice, cutting through
the layers, demanding, "Where is she?"

"I'm here, Daniel," I tried to say. "Come and rescue me."

Then the voice, right above me now. "My God. What's wrong with
her? Is she badly hurt? Is she unconscious?"

I forced myself back to consciousness and Daniel's face swum into
view, his eyes full of fear.

"Hello, Daniel," I forced my lips to say.

"Thank God." He breathed a sigh of relief. "You were lying there
so still and peaceful that I thought for a second . . ."

I reached out and took his hand. "I'm fine, really. Just a bump on
the head and some bruised ribs. They've strapped me up, which helps
with the breathing, but they won't let me go home."

"And what about Liam? Where is he?"

"The doctor says he's fine, Daniel. He's in the children's ward until someone can take him."

27

"He's not hurt? Are you sure?" His eyes were still darting nervously as he perched on the bed beside me.

"Don't worry. He's perfectly all right. Obviously he was terrified but I don't think he was hurt in any way. We were so lucky, really. When I was thrown backward a woman fell into me and must have knocked him from my arms. And he slid under the seats until a man picked him up. A miracle, really, when you think of it. All those heavy people could have fallen on him."

"Thank God," he said again, and his voice cracked this time. "What a terrible business. I came past the site of the accident. When I saw that twisted metal I found it hard to believe that you had survived. What on earth went wrong?"

"I don't know," I said. "It was a Ninth Avenue train and it was traveling quite fast and then suddenly it was going around the curve that the Sixth Avenue line takes. Someone must have failed to switch the points back after a Sixth Avenue train went through right before us."

"There will be hell to pay when we find out who is responsible," he said. "And it could have been much worse too. The whole train could have fallen. Which car were you in?"

"The one that was hanging in midair, suspended."

"Oh, my darling. How terrifying that must have been." He squeezed my hand.

"But I was so lucky, Daniel. I was about to get into the second car, the one that crashed to the street and killed the people inside. It was only because I heard someone coughing, and I didn't want to risk Liam catching some disease, that I changed my mind at the last second. I could have been still lying in that mangled wreck."

Daniel's hand was warm as he continued to hold mine and a spasm of pain crossed his face. "I almost told you to take a cab when you traveled today. Then I thought that the train was just as easy, with stations near either end of the journey. Now I'll never forgive myself."

"Daniel, there's nothing to forgive. How many years have we traveled on the elevated railway, and nothing bad has happened? And we're

28

both more or less unscathed. I'll be as right as rain in the morning. I just need to know what to do with Liam today. I don't like to think of him in a ward full of crying and sick children, but I know that you have an important job to do."

"I could send a telegram to my mother to come and get him and take him back to her place," he said. "If I send it now she could be here by this afternoon. It's a pity she can't stay with us yet. We don't have room in the apartment and we don't have a guest bedroom yet at the house."

"I don't think she could manage to take him alone on a train, Daniel. He's quite a handful and awfully heavy now. Besides, I don't want to be parted from him." .

"It would only be for one night, Molly. And if they release you in the morning, then you can also go straight up to Westchester and let my mother look after you. You'll need to rest and recover, you know."

I was torn between wanting to stay in New York to move back to my own house, and having someone take care of me for a few days until I was back on my feet. Then I decided that the last thing I wanted right now was to be fussed over by Daniel's mother. I wanted to get on with my own life and be back in my own home as soon as possible.

"You could take Liam down to Sid and Gus's," I said, cheering up as the idea occurred to me. "I know they'd love to look after him."

"What do they know about babies?" Daniel said testily. "They'll probably feed him frog legs and curry, and let him smoke a hookah or play with their knife collection."

I had to laugh at this. "Daniel, they looked after him a lot when I was in France."

"Yes, but with you there with them, surely," he said.

I was about to say that I'd been running around all over Paris, but then I remembered that I'd been on the trail of a murderer and had wisely kept the information about this from Daniel.

"There were times when I was out alone, and they entertained Liam," I said cautiously.

"Yes, but keeping him entertained is not the same as knowing when to change his diaper, put him to bed. I'm sure my mother would be glad . . . "

I touched his hand again. "Daniel, they are expecting to see us this morning, looking forward to seeing Liam again. They'll be wondering what's happened to me. Liam and I can both stay with them. And I'd be happier in their house, knowing I was just across the street from my own place. Really I would."

He frowned. "Very well, I suppose, although I still think it would make more sense to send you both up to Mother's. I'll take Liam down with me when I go back to Mulberry Street."

"Thank you, Daniel." I smiled at him and he nodded.

"Have there been any developments in your case?" I asked. "Any more notes? Another murder?"

"Not when I left," he said. "We're taking any extra precautions we can, because of his threat."

"You mean 'saving the best for last'? Is that what he said?"

Daniel nodded. "We've got our men guarding prominent people in the city—but it's hopeless, really. We don't know who might be important to a warped mind like his—maybe a member of his own family?"

"Do you have any reason to believe that any of the murder victims might have been his own family members?"

Daniel shook his head. "No, absolutely not. In each case, those closest to the murder victim couldn't think of anybody who might have wanted to harm him or her."

"Have the crimes escalated in violence since the first one?"

Daniel paused, then said, "None of them was particularly violent. But don't you worry yourself about it now. You need to rest and recuperate. And I'm afraid I have to get back to work. If we can be on hand the moment a murder is reported, we might stand a better chance of finding evidence. Each time we've been notified about a death so far, it's been too late, and any evidence there might have been has been lost. But he'll have to slip up eventually. They usually do when they become too cocky. Or sometimes, they actually want to be caught."

He patted my arm and stood up. "But none of this is your concern. Get some sleep. I'll go and find Liam and report back to you as soon as I can."

Then he leaned over and kissed me tenderly on the lips. "I said long ago that you were like a cat with nine lives, Molly Murphy Sullivan. I rather think that was the eighth you've just used up. I'm going to wrap you in cotton from now on."

Then he smiled and strode out of the ward.

I lay back and tried to sleep again, but my mind was alert and now that I knew that Liam was safely with his father, I found myself considering Daniel's baffling case. I wished he'd have shared more details with me because I actually had time, lying here with nothing to do, to think through them in detail.

Saving the best for last. That certainly did sound like it could mean the killing of a prominent person, didn't it? I wondered if all the murders had been leading up to this one—honing his skills, seeing what he could get away with, so that he could finally kill his intended target. But from the little Daniel had told me, they had found no clue about the circles the killer moved in, or whether his intended target might be rich or political or even religious. No wonder Daniel looked so worried. This case made searching for that proverbial needle in a haystack seem easy.

I shifted uncomfortably on the hard mattress. Now that the shock had worn off I was horribly aware of my various aches and pains. My head was throbbing and it hurt me to breathe, in spite of the bandage around my ribs. The woman in the next bed was asleep, snoring loudly and moaning in her sleep. At the other end of the ward, orderlies were changing the bed linen, chatting as they worked. It had started to rain and there was the sound of drumming on the roof.

It felt so strange and alien here, as if I'd been transported to another world where I didn't belong. All I wanted was to be safely home with my husband, my child, my friends. Now that I had time to consider it, my mother-in-law's elegant country home seemed inviting, and I realized that I had been foolish to reject Daniel's suggestion to take us there to recover. It wasn't that my mother-in-law was a monster or anything like that. Of course I'd be well looked after with Mrs. Sullivan, her housekeeper, Martha, and young Bridie, her Irish ward, to wait on me. And the pleasant country air wafting in through the windows and fresh fruits and vegetables from the garden to eat would be lovely. It was only because I was too thin-skinned about Daniel's mother's subtle criticisms of my child-rearing and housekeeping skills—her hints about what good matches his friends had made, and her constant litany of all things connected to high society— that had made me decide that even this hard hospital bed was a better option. Now, after only a few hours, I had reversed my opinion.

A meal cart was wheeled into the ward and an unappetizing stew was sloshed onto plates. I tried to sit up without letting the watching nurse know I was in pain. I was extremely hungry but could manage only a couple of mouthfuls of the glutinous mess in my bowl. This would be a quick way of killing off the patients, I wanted to say, but I could not see a glimmer of humor in any of the faces around me. The woman who had been snoring was now being fed and dribbles of stew ran down her chin, like Liam when I was feeding him, but far less appealing.

Only one day, I told myself. Tomorrow I'd be safely with Sid and Gus and they'd be making me laugh and spoiling me. Then, of course, I began to worry. Sid and Gus led very active lives. They were always attending meetings with their suffragist sisters, salons with fellow painters and writers. What if they couldn't or wouldn't take Liam today? What would Daniel do then? And would I feel well enough tomorrow to look after a lively and curious one-year-old?

I must have drifted off to sleep again because I awoke, instantly alert, to a feeling of danger—the same feeling that had accompanied me to the train station that morning. I sat up with some difficulty and looked around. The ward lay silent, with most of its occupants sleeping. Light was fading, but I couldn't tell whether it was because it was approaching evening or the rain clouds had made the day even more gloomy. A nurse walked through the ward, her feet clacking on the linoleum floor. She nodded when she saw me. "Oh, you're awake. Doctor left you some medicine to take away the pain and help you sleep."

"Thank you, but I'm sure I can sleep without taking anything," I said.

"Best do what the doctor prescribes," she said. "But you don't need to take it until after you've had your dinner. Don't want to fall asleep and miss that delicious food, do we?" And she gave just the hint of a smile.

I propped a pillow behind my back and looked around me. How quiet everything was. Unnervingly quiet, as if I was lying in a morgue. I shuddered and thought of the bodies I had seen lying on the sidewalk. And then I saw someone coming toward me—her black smoking jacket and emerald green pantaloons an amazing contrast to the starched whiteness of the ward.

"Here you are," Sid said, hurrying over to my bed. "I've had a devil of a time. Some awful old crone tried to tell me that visiting hours were over. From two to four only, she said. So I went around the corner and waited until she'd gone, then slipped inside. But I didn't know which ward you were in. I went into the men's ward by mistake—imagine the look on their faces when they saw me." And she laughed. I tried to laugh too but my side hurt. Sid noticed. "Are you in pain? Daniel said you only had bumps and bruises."

"The doctor thinks I might have cracked a rib. I've only just discovered that laughing hurts. I hadn't had a chance to laugh all day in a place like this."

"I should think not. It's like a morgue in here, isn't it?" She looked

33

around, then gave a guilty grin as she realized her voice echoed from tiled walls.

"How's Liam doing?" I asked.

"Absolutely splendidly. Delighted to see his aunts again, and of course we have such interesting things to play with."

"Daniel was afraid it might be your knife collection or hookah." We exchanged a smile.

"We're saving those for tomorrow," she said. "But my dear, we can't leave you in this house of horrors overnight. Why don't I take you home with me right now?"

"I haven't been given leave to go," I said.

"Nonsense. There are ways around things like that. Hold on a minute." She opened the briefcase she carried instead of a purse, pulled out a pad of paper, and sat down on my bed to write. I had no idea what she was writing and couldn't see over her shoulder. But when she had finished, she handed it to me.

"That should do the trick," she said.

I read what she had written. *I am Mrs. Sullivan's personal physician and give my permission to discharge her to my care in a private nursing home.* I looked up at her twinkling eyes. "Sid, you are wicked."

"Well, do you want to come or don't you? We've a feather mattress waiting, and I believe Gus is cooking duck breast in orange sauce."

"If you put it like that, help me up. But I've no idea where they put my things, or what we're going to say if they summon the doctor who examined me."

Sid was scrabbling in the small bedside cabinet. "Your things appear to be in here. Oh, dear—your dress is rather the worse for wear, I'm afraid. We'll have to go and retrieve a change of clothing for you and Liam from your flat in the morning, but in the meantime Gus has a host of pretty nightgowns and fluffy slippers, so you'll be quite comfortable."

I tried to stand up and felt woozy. I had to be able to walk out of here.

"Do you carry smelling salts?" I asked Sid.

"Certainly not. Never having worn a corset in my life, there has been no need for smelling salts," she said. "Are you feeling faint?"

"Just rather unsteady. I've hardly had a thing to eat all day."

"Then let me see what I can do. You sit down and start getting dressed and I'll be back." She set off down the ward. I was just wrestling with getting my dress over my head when I heard an angry voice beside me saying, "Mrs. Sullivan. What do you think you are doing?"

I pulled the dress down from my face. "My doctor learned about my accident and has sent someone to take me to a private nursing home," I said. "There's a letter here on the bed."

She picked it up, sniffed, and said, "I see. I don't know what Dr. Harrison will say about this. It's really up to him to discharge a patient. But I have to suppose you are going to good care."

"The best," I said.

"Nice for those who can afford it." She sniffed again. "Didn't you say your husband was a policeman?"

"We have connections," I said, trying to sound breezy. "Could you help me get into this dress? I can't lift my arms."

She helped, rather roughly, I thought. And I was just having the buttons done up when she looked up and exclaimed, "What the devil?"

Sid was coming toward us, now wheeling a wheelchair that rattled across the floor.

"How do you do?" Sid said. "I'm here on behalf of Dr. Goldfarb and Dr. Walcott. We've a cab waiting outside for Mrs. Sullivan."

"Very well, then." The nurse looked stunned and lost for words. "I'll leave you to it, then. Will you take your medicine before you go?"

"I don't think so, thank you," I said. "Dr. Goldfarb will prescribe a sleeping draft if I need one."

Sid helped me into the chair and wheeled me to freedom. Once we were safely in the cab we both burst out laughing. It was a brief moment of triumph.

❦ Five ❧

Soon I was safely tucked into Sid and Gus's spare bed, with Liam lying beside me, peacefully sucking his thumb and clearly relieved to have his mother back at his side. I had asked Sid to send a message to police headquarters to let Daniel know I had joined Liam at their house, and I lay back, content that I was safe, relatively unharmed, and in a few days would be back in that house across the street.

Sid and Gus looked after Liam like old hands. I heard his delighted squeals of laughter, and then they brought him up to see me, saying they had fed him chicken soup with dumplings and he had eaten like a horse. Gus cooked the promised duck breast with orange sauce for our dinner and served it with crispy potatoes and a green salad. She even insisted on a glass of wine to accompany it. "It will help you sleep. Better than any of those sleeping drafts they force on you in the hospital," she said.

I nodded. "They had some kind of noxious mixture they wanted me to drink, but I turned them down. How lucky, or I might have been fast asleep when Sid arrived and wouldn't have been able to be rescued."

I was lying back, feeling pleasantly drowsy, when there came a thunderous knock at the front door. I heard barked words in an angry voice and footsteps thundering up the stairs, before Daniel burst into my room.

I saw his face and attempted to sit up. "Daniel, what's the matter?" I asked.

"What's the matter?" he demanded. "I go to the hospital to visit my wife, only to find her bed empty and some strange story about a doctor moving her to a private nursing home."

"Hold your horses." I raised my hand. "I wrote you a note. I sent it to headquarters with instructions that it was to be given to you immediately. Didn't you get it?"

"I didn't go anywhere near headquarters," he said. "I had a long meeting with the commissioner and the mayor—at which I was soundly chewed out yet again, by the way—and then I rushed straight over to see you. Only to find you gone and hear a garbled story about who had taken you."

"I'm sorry, but I did try to let you know."

"You were supposed to stay in that hospital until tomorrow, weren't you?" He was still blustering. "How could you countermand a doctor's orders like that?"

"Daniel, calm down," I said. "You're shouting and you'll wake your son—to say nothing of upsetting my hostesses. They were keeping me overnight for observation, that's all. And I was highly uncomfortable. The bed was hard, the woman next to me was snoring and moaning, and I wouldn't have fed the slop they call food to my dog. I couldn't have been more overjoyed when Sid came to rescue me."

Daniel sank onto the bed beside me. "Do you know what I thought? I thought you'd been kidnapped."

"Kidnapped?" I couldn't help grinning. "And who was likely to burst into a hospital ward and kidnap me?"

"It's no joke, Molly," he said quietly. "I haven't shared the details of this case I'm working on with you until now, because it didn't concern you. Now I'm afraid it does concern you—at least to a certain degree. We received another note today."

"What did it say?"

"It said, 'If at first you don't succeed. Better luck next time.'"

"Which meant he'd tried to kill somebody and had been thwarted by your increased police presence?"

He shook his head. "He enclosed a clipping from the early edition of the evening newspaper. A clipping about the train accident."

"The train accident—but surely, it was just that. He can't be trying to claim that he caused it, can he?"

Daniel was still staring at me. I shook my head. "Impossible, Daniel. The man is delusional. Someone forgot to switch the points and sent a Ninth Avenue train around the curve on the Sixth Avenue route."

"We'll know more when we've questioned the man in the signal box and the locomotive driver," he said. "Of course it's not unheard of that someone claims credit for a spectacular accident, or even comes forward to confess to a murder he couldn't possibly have committed. But in this case he had promised to kill on a certain day, and he tried to keep that promise."

I stared at the silk counterpane with its swirls of bright flowers and tried to make sense of what he was saying. "So you think he arranged this train to crash, knowing that a particular person was on board, only not all the carriages came off the rails, and the person he had in mind was not killed?"

"It's a possibility," he said.

"So that might have been what he meant by 'saving the best for last,'" I said. "Not a prominent person, but a spectacular event. It must have seemed rather spectacular to him if he was watching—the train racing around that curve and then jumping the tracks and plunging downward." I looked up to meet Daniel's gaze. "Do we know if any prominent people were on that train?"

He cleared his throat. "You were on that train," he said.

I gave an uneasy laugh. "Me?"

He nodded. "You said something to me the other night that made an impression. You said the one thing linking all the deaths was me. All the notes were sent to me, not to other officers."

"So you think it might be someone with a grudge against you?"

"It's a possibility," he said. "And what better way to get back at me than killing you."

I thought for a moment, then shook my head again. "That's rubbish, Daniel. He could not have known which train I would take. In fact, I was going to board the Sixth Avenue train that came right before it. Only . . . " I broke off.

"Only what?" Daniel asked sharply, reading my expression.

"A man came running past and bumped into me, knocking me backward. By the time I had righted myself the doors had closed."

"Did you happen to see what this man looked like?"

"No, it was all a blur. The platform was horribly crowded. I had Liam in my arms. I was most concerned about holding onto him and not falling. But it was a young man, I think. Slim—at least not portly. Wearing some kind of dark suit, dark hat." I paused, frowning. "That's all. As I said, it was all a blur."

Daniel sighed.

"But how could he . . . " I began.

"He made you miss the Sixth Avenue train, Molly. Knowing that a Ninth Avenue was following it."

"But he didn't know I'd take the Ninth Avenue train. I might well have waited for the next Sixth Avenue—after all, that station was much more convenient for me. That is what I was planning to do actually, until I decided to stop at the French bakery and bring Sid and Gus their favorite croissants. And if he was on the platform, having bumped into me, he could hardly be in the signal box, changing the points, could he?"

"It does all sound rather far-fetched, I agree. And maybe I'm reading too much into this, because it was my wife and child in danger. But the man is an opportunist, Molly. He has taken tremendous risks before, and we know he didn't succeed in killing the person he wanted to kill today."

"If at first you don't succeed," I said. "The rest of that phrase is 'try, try again.' That's not very encouraging, is it?"

"You stay put right here. I'll have a man stationed to keep an eye on you, and you are supposed to be resting and recuperating anyway. The murderer won't know where you are now."

"I still can't believe this, Daniel. If someone wanted to kill me, he could have hidden in the bushes when I was up in Westchester County and shot or stabbed me when I went out for a walk. He could have strangled me in the apartment when you were out."

"True," Daniel nodded. "And I may just be clutching at straws, Molly. There may have been someone else on that train—someone who took that very train to work every day—whom he wanted to dispose of. It's just that I've been a policeman long enough that I don't like coincidences. And this was a pretty big coincidence."

"If it is someone with a grudge against you—why try to kill me and not you?"

"Maybe he wants to punish me. And what could be worse punishment than killing my wife and son?"

I was finding this conversation more and more disturbing, but I tried to sound detached and professional as I continued, "And the other people he has killed so far? Is it possible they have any connection to you? Have their murders been to punish you?"

He shook his head. "No connection to me at all. No connection to each other, as far as we can tell. At least none of the family members whom we have questioned has ever heard of the other victims."

"Maybe you should give me the details," I said. "If I'm to lie here and recuperate, I'll have time to ponder. Perhaps I'd come up with some kind of connection you'd overlooked."

"Oh, no, Molly," he began. "You know how I feel about involving you in my cases."

"You're not involving me. You're just adding the perspective of a woman—a woman detective, and though I say so myself, a darned good one."

He looked at me long and hard. "Very well," he said. "You should rest tonight, but I'll come and see you tomorrow and have one of the clerks write out a list of the various murders for you. That way you can take notes."

"Speaking of notes," I said. "What do you know about the notes that he sent? Any telltale features?"

"None at all. They were typewritten by an ordinary Remington typewriter on the sort of onionskin paper you'd find in any office."

"No damaged keys on the typewriting machine?"

"Nothing unusual."

"Have your men asked who might have purchased a typewriting machine recently? I shouldn't imagine too many people buy such things."

"It's fairly easy to get your hands on a typewriter these days," Daniel said. "Our murderer could work in an office or bank."

"How about fingerprints on the paper?"

"None. Which is interesting in itself, isn't it? He's meticulous. Not making any errors. Of course there were several on the envelopes, but one would expect that—sorters at the post officer, delivery men, even the constable manning the front desk."

"So they were mailed? Not hand-delivered?"

"Only today's was hand-delivered."

"And nobody remembers what the person who delivered it looked like?"

"It was a small boy. That's all they could tell me. One of the street urchins given a coin to run an errand. He handed it to a woman coming into police headquarters to make a complaint and ran off. She couldn't remember what he looked like. We've little chance of finding the right one again."

"So your man was close by—close enough to engage the services of a street urchin."

Daniel sighed. "Who knows? He may have been following my every move."

"Then he may know you are here right now."

"Hardly likely. I took a cab from City Hall. We went at a hell of a lick too, and I could swear there was no one following us."

"So what about the postmark on the letters? Were they all mailed from the same place?"

"The first few were mailed from Grand Central Terminal," he said. "There is a mail drop in the main station area. As you can imagine thousands of people pass it all the time. But we set a man to keep watch there day and night and the next note was posted at the main post office."

"He's one step ahead of you all the time," I said.

"It certainly seems that way."

"When did these notes start coming, Daniel?"

"The first one came in May, right after you'd sailed for Europe. Right before the first murder."

"And what did it say?"

"It said 'When I was alive I was unjustly accused of a crime I didn't commit. Now I am dead I can exact retribution with impunity.'"

"Holy Mother of God!" I exclaimed. "We're dealing with a ghost."

I stared at Daniel not knowing what to say.

"Now you see why this is complicated." Daniel said. "I can't help feeling that someone is having a good laugh at our expense. Obviously I don't believe in ghosts and I certainly don't think that they can mail letters from Grand Central Depot. Or use typewriting machines, for that matter."

"So it has to be a living person claiming to be someone else, someone who has died," I said slowly, considering each word as it came out. "Maybe someone who feels a relative or friend was punished unjustly and wants revenge on his behalf?"

"That's possible, I suppose," Daniel said.

I was warming to this idea. "And he feels you were responsible for the wrongful conviction and death of this person. That should be easy enough to trace, Daniel. You need to come up with a list of people who were executed based on your investigation and evidence. There can't be that many."

"I've been in the police department for fifteen years, Molly. I've been involved in quite a few murder investigations."

"But not hundreds, surely. How many murder trials are there each year, for the love of Mike? And how many result in a death sentence?"

He nodded. "Yes, I suppose it's not an overwhelming number. But it may not necessarily have been a murder trial followed by an execution. It may have been as simple as someone dying as a result of a disease he caught while in prison, or being murdered by another inmate. Or even someone who died of shock or grief after a trial. How could I ever check on those?"

"You could start with what I suggested," I said, quite animated by the challenge now and forgetting the twinges in my side. "A list of all your murder trials, especially the ones that resulted in a death sentence. That gives us somewhere to start. I'm surprised you haven't done that before."

A spasm of annoyance crossed Daniel's face and I realized I shouldn't have said this. Daniel liked to think of himself as the superior detective, with me as the lucky amateur.

"To be fair, Molly," he said, "it was only today, after this last note, that I began to take seriously the notion that these killings could have anything to do with me in particular, rather than the police in general. I still don't know that to be true."

I was about to say that I had been the one who suggested that he might be the link between the crimes, but this time I wisely kept quiet. Men are easily upset over such matters, I've noted.

"We do know a couple of things about him, don't we?" I went on.

"And those are?" He still sounded testy.

"We know that he's an educated person. He knows how to use a typewriting machine and he uses words like 'retribution' and 'impunity.' That is not the vocabulary of a man in the street."

"And the other thing?"

"He is right here in New York City. On the spot, ready to hand a note to a street urchin. That's something I could do for you when I'm a little better—"

"What?" He was looking at me warily.

"I could question some of the street children in the area around Mulberry Street. They'd never talk to the police but they might see me as less of a threat. And the man may have paid the boy well—something he'd have boasted about to his friends."

Daniel shook his head firmly. "Molly—what have we just been talking about? It's quite possible that the train wreck today was caused because someone wanted to kill you." He held up his hand. "I know it's far-fetched. It could well be that our killer is deranged and delusional and gets a thrill from claiming responsibility for such a dramatic accident, but really had nothing to do with it. Nevertheless, we have to take his words seriously and consider the fact that you may be in danger. So the last thing I'd want you to do is to blunder into the middle of the spider's web."

"I could disguise myself," I said. "I've done it before—I've even dressed as a street urchin myself."

He laughed now. "I don't expect you fooled anybody for more than a second," he said.

"I'll have you know that some boy was ready to fight me for taking over his patch as a crossing sweeper," I said.

Daniel snorted. "Molly, listen to me. I am sharing some details of this case with you because you've got a good head on your shoulders and you seem to bring a fresh perspective—and because it appears you might be personally involved. But I am not allowing you to go looking for trouble. You are to stay put and heal from your injuries. And that is an order."

"An order?" I sat up straight now. "You think you can order me around, Daniel Sullivan?"

I was staring him straight in the eye.

"You're wanting to do field investigation on my case, and I give the orders to my team of officers," he said. "And as your husband, I'll do anything within my power to keep you safe." He reached out and stroked my hair, which was hanging loose over my shoulders. "I don't want to lose you, Molly. I nearly lost you and Liam earlier this year. I want to be able to get on with my work, knowing that you are both out of harm's way. Don't you understand that?"

His hand caressing my hair had a disturbing effect. All the fight evaporated from me. "I do understand, Daniel, and you're right. It would be like offering myself as bait, and I can't do that." *At least not yet*, I added silently.

"Did I mention recently that you have lovely hair?" he said, look-ing at me with a sparkle of desire in his eyes. "You're a very attrac-tive woman."

"Don't get any ideas, Daniel. I've ribs that are all strapped up and hurt me to breathe."

"And a minute ago you were suggesting running all over town talk-ing to street urchins," he said. "But don't worry. I'll save the thought for later, when we're back in our own home." He stood up. "I should be going. I haven't had a thing to eat since God knows when."

"I'm sure Sid and Gus could find you something."

He shook his head. "No, thanks. I'm not in a mood for small talk and politeness. I'd rather pick up a pint and a sausage in a bar." He bent to kiss me. "Stay put and stay safe, my love. Don't do anything foolish. I'll stop by in the morning with the details I promised you on the vari-ous notes and murder victims, and you can ponder them at leisure."

"Maybe Sid and Gus would have some brilliant thoughts," I said. "Three heads are better than one, and they are both highly educated women."

"Oh, no, please." Daniel held up his hand. "I must insist that you mention none of this to your friends. This is an ongoing police investigation, Molly. I am only including you this once as I feel I owe it to you to be as informed as possible. But it cannot be discussed with anyone else, especially not with your friends. It could jeopardize our operation."

"I hardly think that anything my friends do could damage your investigation, Daniel," I started to say, but he cut in.

"Molly, I must have your word on this. It is not to be discussed or even mentioned. Do you promise?"

"If it's so important to you, then I suppose so," I said grudgingly. Daniel had never really taken to Sid and Gus, thinking them to be outlandish and frivolous, which they were in some ways. But he had never come to appreciate their kindness and generosity and their great love of life that was infectious to all those around them. I looked upon them as the sisters I had never had, and I couldn't picture life without them.

After Daniel had gone, I realized, of course, that he was right. Sid and Gus did tend to look upon detective work as an exciting game. And if they knew that someone had tried to kill me, I wouldn't put it past them to shadow me everywhere I went. At least I knew I was safe in their house for now, and if a deranged man in New York City had really tried to derail a train to kill me, he would think I was still in the women's ward in Roosevelt Hospital.

❧ Six ❧

Gus put her head around my door. "The lord and master has departed, so it seems. I heard the front door slam. I take it he was not pleased that we had sneaked you away from your hospital bed. At least that's what we guessed from the way he came barging in and stormed up the stairs."

I gave an apologetic smile. "I'm sorry for my husband's rudeness, but in his defense he was more frightened than angry. He had not received the message I sent him and arrived to find my hospital bed empty and a vague rumor about my having been taken off to a private clinic. He deals with some pretty ruthless characters, as you know, and was terrified I'd been kidnapped."

"Oh, I see. Then we'll forgive him this time. I was about to ask him to stay for dinner."

"I suggested you'd be able to rustle up a bite to eat for him, but he was in no mood to be sociable. He has a lot to contend with right now, Gus. A difficult case and the commissioner of police on his back."

"He mentioned it, remember, when you came to see your house. And we volunteered your services."

"Not much chance of anyone in the New York police inviting me to help," I said guardedly. "Besides, in my current condition I'm not much use for anything. I was so looking forward to moving back in across the street, but now I don't know when I'll be able to go shopping for all the things I need to make the house habitable."

"Don't think about that for now. As I said, we can supply you with linens and dishes enough to keep you going. Then you can choose your own at leisure."

"You're always so kind," I said.

"Nonsense. You and Liam are the closest thing we have to family these days." She plumped up the pillow on my bed, not wanting to betray emotion. "Do you want anything more to eat, or maybe a glass of milk to help you sleep?"

"Nothing, thank you. I always sleep so well in your house."

"Sid has some wonderful sleeping powders if you need one," Gus said. "You might find the pain in your ribs wakes you up during the night. Why don't you take one tonight, just to be sure?"

"I want to hear Liam if he cries," I said. "He's been through the same traumatic event as I have. He might well have nightmares about it."

"We'll listen for Liam," she said. "And we'll come and wake you if he's inconsolable. I'll bring you the sleeping draft, all right?"

"All right," I agreed.

She soon returned with the promised cocktail. "Sleep tight. Don't let the bedbugs bite," Gus whispered as I drained the glass. I lowered myself onto the pillows as Gus turned out the electric light.

The next thing I knew I heard Liam crying and woke with a start to find birds chirping outside my window and the sky streaked with early-dawn light. I had slept a dreamless night and felt clearheaded and ready for anything, although I still experienced twinges of pain as I tried to sit up, and more pain as I lifted Liam from his bed, indicating that I wasn't ready to be on my own yet. When I went to change him I realized, of course, that his clothes were all back at the apartment, and I didn't want to ask either Sid or Gus to make the journey to the Upper West Side. Maybe Daniel would have time to fetch what we needed later in the day.

I need not have worried. Sid sat beside me, as I fed Liam a boiled egg, with a notebook and pencil in her hand. "Now," she said. "List of what you need. Your clothes. Liam's clothes and the door key."

"I can't ask you to do that," I said. "Daniel can . . . "

"Daniel's involved in a tricky case. We know that," Sid said. "How much trouble is it to collect a few clothes?"

"But the El won't be operating, after yesterday's crash."

"So I'll take a cab. More pleasant anyway."

"But expensive."

"Don't be silly." Sid patted my hand as if I was a child. "Where do I find the key?"

I directed her to my purse. An alarm was sounding inside my head. If someone was watching my apartment building he might be able to follow Sid to this house. Then I told myself I was worrying too much. She'd be in a cab. He wouldn't be able to follow. And besides, why would he be watching our building? He'd think I was still in the hospital. And if he found out I'd left, he'd think I was in an undisclosed private clinic.

Sid departed. I played with Liam and kept an ear open for Daniel. He didn't come all morning, but then I'd learned that I could never count on his appearing when he said he would. Sid returned with bags of clothing, and I had just gone upstairs to change my clothes when Daniel arrived.

"She's just getting dressed," I heard Sid say. "I've been to your apartment to bring clothes for her and Liam."

"Oh, it was you. Thank God," he said. "I went to the apartment myself and was told by the caretaker that someone had just been there. You had me worried."

"Worried that someone might have broken into your apartment?" Sid asked. "You're not still afraid that the Italian gang is out to destroy you, are you? I thought that matter was all settled."

"No, nothing like that," I heard him say as he came up the stairs. "I thought Molly might have been foolish enough to have attempted the journey herself."

"No, she's been resting like a good girl," Sid said. She tapped on my door. "Molly, dear, are you decent? I've a young man to see you."

Daniel came in, saw me sitting at the vanity putting pins into my hair, and nodded with satisfaction. "Well, you're certainly looking much better," he said. "Well rested?"

"Perfectly, thank you. And it feels good to be in clean clothes. Did Sid tell you she was kind enough to go and retrieve some of our things?" I wasn't going to let him know I had overheard the whole conversation and the worry in his voice.

"Yes, she did. Mrs. Heffernan gave me a shock when she said someone had been up to our place. I thought for a moment . . . " He broke off, then managed a smile as he came across the room to me.

"You thought that the killer had come looking for me?" I had lowered my voice in case Sid or Gus was still within earshot. "Aren't we reading too much into this, Daniel? Do you have any reason to believe that he was responsible for yesterday's crash, or that I was a target?"

He sighed and sank onto the small upright chair by the window. "We are none the wiser, as usual. The signalman has been questioned and swears that he saw the disk on the front of the locomotive indicating a Sixth Avenue train, and the engineer swears that the train bore the correct disk, that he put it on himself."

"He's right. The train definitely said Ninth Avenue when it came into my station. No question about it. What disk is on the engine now?"

"None," he said. "That's the interesting part. There is no disk to be seen. And the locomotive didn't come off the track."

"So that adds fuel to your belief that your killer orchestrated this. Somehow he changed the disk while the train was in the station and then removed the disk before there could be any investigation."

"It does seem that way."

"And was there any person of note on board that we know of?"

"Persons of note rarely travel in crowded El carriages," he said.

"And speaking of 'of note'—no more notes have arrived, I take it?"

"Not as far as I know. But then I wouldn't expect one." He held out a large envelope. "I've had one of our men write out a list of the various victims for you. This is for your eyes only, remember. Your friends should not be privy to this." I noticed that he tried to avoid calling Sid and Gus by their nicknames, as if they were too shocking to be spoken out loud. It was another small way of displaying his disapproval of their unacceptable lifestyle.

I opened the clasp on the envelope and took out several sheets of typewritten paper.

"They are in chronological order," Daniel said.

I was already reading the first sheet. "'May 10: Dolly Willis. 285 Flushing Avenue, Brooklyn. (Feebleminded woman of sixty-two. Lived with her sister. Pushed into the path of a speeding trolley.)

"'Note said: "Trolley and Dolly rhyme. A fitting end this time."'"

I looked up. "'This time'? Does that mean there might have been other times before that you don't know about?"

Daniel frowned. "Now, that's an interesting thought. There are always unsolved homicides in the city, and in cases like this one, deaths that might never have been ruled a homicide. If we hadn't received the note it might never have been established that she had been pushed under a trolley."

"You mean that she was a feebleminded woman and could have stepped into the path of a trolley without assistance?"

"Quite possible. And people were intent on waiting to cross the street themselves so no one would have noticed the well-timed push. It was hard to come up with witnesses a few days later, and only one person said that the old woman seemed to have suddenly gone pitching forward."

I paused, digesting this. "So this man may have been perfecting his methods for ages before the first death we know about?"

Daniel sighed. "It's possible. Yes. But we'd have no way of knowing if the deaths were ruled accidents, or if he didn't manage to kill the first times."

I read on down the page: "'May 31: Simon Grossman. Age twenty. Lived with parents, Dr. and Mrs. Grossman, 258 Fifth Avenue. Student at New York University. Drank a cup of coffee laced with cyanide in Fritz's, a crowded coffee shop frequented by students on MacDougal Street.

"'The note said: "Simon says good-bye, or would if he could speak."'"

I looked up at Daniel. "A student at New York University. And I take it not in any way related to poor old Dolly?"

"Not in any way. He was the son of a well-respected doctor, and she lived with her sister who was a former housemaid."

"And she had never been employed by the doctor, I take it?"

"She had not. She worked for a prominent banker, was given a little legacy when he died, and went home to take care of her mother and sister in Brooklyn. The mother passed away a few years ago, and the two sisters lived happily together until this."

"How sad," I said. "And how senseless. A feebleminded woman couldn't have been a threat to anybody, could she? Why choose her, I wonder."

Daniel shook his head. "I wish I could tell you."

"I see what you mean when you say there's no connection. A simpleminded old woman and a university student, and such different methods of murder. In your experience, does a poisoner normally resort to a more violent crime?"

He shook his head. "I'd say no. Poisoners are usually secretive, quiet, reserved types. If you poison, you don't have to be present when the murder takes place."

"So the only thing these murders have in common is that they were terribly risky," I said. "Pushing someone under a trolley on a crowded street and putting cyanide in a coffee cup in a crowded café both come with a strong chance of being observed."

"That's true. He does like to take risks."

"Maybe he gets a thrill out of taking risks," I said. "Were the other murders equally risky and public?"

"Risky, yes. Public, no," Daniel said. "Read on."

I turned to the next page: "'June 21: Maud Daughtery, age sixty-three. Widow. Lived with her only son, 485 10th Avenue. Chelsea.

"'The note said: "Mother didn't always know best."'

"What did that mean?" I asked, looking up from the paper.

Daniel shrugged. "We took that to mean that she did not lock her bathroom door when taking a bath. There was a table lamp on the dresser beside the bath, and someone dropped it into the water, thus electrocuting her."

"She lived with her presumably grown-up son," I said.

"She did. Terrence, aged forty-two. A studious and reserved young man who is employed as a tutor to an Upper East Side family."

"And might have had reason to hurl a lamp into his mother's bathtub?" I asked.

Daniel smiled. "We looked into that, believe me. From what we learned of the mother, she was an overbearing and unpleasant woman who bossed everyone around and probably made her son's life miserable. However, he was in a schoolroom with three children at the time his mother was killed, and he seemed genuinely distraught at her death."

"And I also take it that this woman was in no way related to either simple Dolly or the university student?"

"That's right. In no way related. Never lived in the same part of the city or moved in the same circles. And the same is true for the other victims."

"This murder did take a good deal of nerve, as you say," I commented. "To break into a house, wait until someone took a bath, and then electrocute her. That would take observation of the family's habits and a good deal of planning. That is not the same kind of crime as pushing someone in front of a trolley."

"And they become progressively more daring. Read on."

I turned to the next sheet of paper. "'July 12. Marie Ellingham. Age seventy. Address 352 East Fifty-second Street. Died of arsenic poisoning. Police not able to determine when and how it was administered.

"'The note we received said, "Judge not that ye be not judged."'

"What could that mean? Was she judgmental by nature?" I asked.

"Her husband was a retired judge."

"And presumably you've checked into whether he might have had a motive for poisoning her?"

"We went through the whole household thoroughly. He was visibly upset by her death. Devastated, actually. It seems they were a devoted couple. There was no trace of arsenic to be found in the kitchen, on the utensils, anywhere. The cook and maid had been with them for years. The only thing of interest was that the bedroom window was at the rear of the house, facing a small garden, and it was open."

"So someone could have climbed in, administered the poison, and departed again."

"Exactly, except it was quite a climb to the window, and he would have risked being seen from the windows of the houses behind."

"And no ties to the other three victims, I assume?"

"None." He leaned closer. "And the interesting thing, Molly, is that this death would have been ruled as natural causes if we hadn't received the note. Marie Ellingham was prone to gastric troubles, she had a delicate stomach, and her own physician was quite willing to say that the bout of vomiting had been too much for her heart at her age."

"Fascinating," I said. I looked at the papers. There was only one more.

"'August 22. Herman Hoffman. Age forty-five. Lower West Side.

Twenty-nine West Street. Owned a small meat-processing business. He was found in his meat safe on Monday morning, dead.

"'The note said: "Frozen, packed, and ready for delivery."'"

I shuddered. "How horrible. Poor man. What an awful way to die. And that note—it shows a character completely devoid of human feeling, wouldn't you say? Pleased with his own cleverness."

"I'm afraid you're right. A warped and twisted person who delights in killing. All I can hope is that he meant what he said when he talked about saving the best for last—that he really intends to stop this killing spree."

"Going back to the meat packer—what do we know about him? He didn't supply meat to the judge or any of the others, I take it?"

"He had married and moved to the city about a year ago. Until then he ran a butcher's shop in the Catskills. From what his wife tells us, it was an extremely happy marriage, a second for him after his first wife died. A first for her, somewhat late in life, but they were both looking forward to a bright future."

"If he was locked in the meat safe all weekend, didn't she report him missing?" I asked. "Isn't that suspicious?"

"That's the thing. He had told her he was going up to Woodstock to visit his mother. She didn't want to come, not being too fond of his mother. So she thought she knew where he was."

"And she hadn't recently taken out a life insurance policy on him?" I asked.

Daniel laughed. "What a gruesome little thing you are. Most women would have reached for the smelling salts at the very start of this conversation, not discussed it as calmly as if it concerned the price of sugar."

"You know I'm not most women." I turned back to the mirror to put a final pin in my unruly hair. Then something struck me. I put down the hairpins and leafed through the papers.

"There's one missing," I said, waving them triumphantly.

"What do you mean? You've read them all."

I shook my head. "The murders are all about three weeks apart, right up to yesterday's train crash, if we include that. But there wasn't one in early August. Why not? Could that have been one murder he couldn't pull off, or a note that somehow didn't get delivered to you? Or was he off on vacation at the seashore?"

Daniel took the papers from me and examined them, frowning. "That's an acute observation, Molly. But if there was one murder he couldn't commit, how would we ever find out about it?"

"I don't know, but it seems that's your best chance of solving this," I said. "Because at the beginning of August, somebody might have lived to tell the tale."

❧ Seven ❧

Downstairs a clock chimed with a sweet, melodious *ting*.

Daniel stood up. "I should be going. The commissioner wants me at today's briefing and will no doubt be annoyed that I've come up with nothing new."

"Apart from the missing date in August," I pointed out.

"That may have a perfectly simple explanation," Daniel said. "It was devilishly hot. There were the usual summer epidemics in the city at that time. Our killer could have caught some disease and been too sick to carry out his planned murder. Or he could have decided to let the early-August victim live. Or it could be that he hadn't actually planned these murders to be three weeks apart, and the dates were purely circumstantial."

"I think he sounds like the sort of meticulous individual to whom dates would matter. It's also important that several of these deaths, if not all, could have been ruled as accidents. Feebleminded Dolly stepping out in front of a tram; the overbearing mother accidentally knocking her lamp into the bath; the judge's wife dying of gastric trouble; the butcher accidentally locking himself into the safe. Only your university student's cyanide would have shown up as a deliberate murder." I looked up at Daniel. "This is a game to him, Daniel. A game of cat and mouse, and he wants to make sure you stay on his trail."

"You can say that again." Daniel sighed as he walked toward the door. "He is enjoying taunting me, showing up my inadequacies."

"All the more reason to figure out who might have a personal grudge against you. I think you should do as I suggested, and make a list of criminals who were convicted and executed thanks to you. My guess is that this is someone's brother or best friend, seeking revenge on behalf of a dead prisoner."

"But why is he including innocent people in his revenge?" Daniel lingered with his hand on the door handle. "Why would anyone gloat over pushing a simple old woman under a trolley?"

"That's what you need to find out," I said. "Either they are all random killings, or all but one are random killings, meant to hide the one instance in which he wanted a person dead. Or . . . he is enjoying sending you off on fools' errands, or . . . " And I paused, considering this, "Or he has some kind of agenda and reason for wanting these particular people dead."

"And me with no way of finding out why." Daniel frowned, turned to go, then remembered something. "Oh, Molly, I meant to tell you. I did accomplish something positive this morning," he said. "I stopped by Sloane's and ordered two beds—one for the spare room, and a single one for the maid's room upstairs. That way my mother can come to stay right away to take care of you, and she can help you look for a new servant. Perhaps you'd feel strong enough to make a list of the various sheets and pillows and things that we'll need, and I can ask Wanamaker's dry goods to deliver. The sooner our life is back to normal, the better for all of us."

Then he gave me an encouraging smile and closed the door behind him. I sat at the vanity, looking at my reflection in the mirror and trying not to feel annoyed. I suppose he genuinely thought he was doing me a kindness by bringing his mother down to look after me, but I took it to mean that he wanted me out of Sid and Gus's clutches as soon as possible. I finished my toilette and went downstairs, easing myself down step by step, as walking was still painful. I came into the drawing room to find Sid on the floor, creeping around on all fours and growling as she chased a delighted Liam.

"I'm a bear," she said, looking up as I came in. "A very fierce bear." And she growled again, making Liam shriek, half in delight and half in terror.

"Don't be too realistic," I said. "I don't want him having nightmares."

"He likes it," she said, standing up and brushing off the dust from her black silk trousers. "It's good for children to be scared from time to time. How about some luncheon—the delicatessen had a fine-looking ham this morning, and we've tomatoes as an extra treat?"

"Oh, that's nice," I said. Having grown up without ever meeting a tomato, I still hadn't really developed a taste for them, but I did know they were a luxury item, and there was a hot debate going on as to whether they were a fruit or a vegetable.

"And you'd like some lunch, wouldn't you, young man?" Sid swept up Liam and carried him through to the kitchen. It had rained during the night, leaving the air bright and fresh with just a hint of fall about it. The windows of the conservatory behind the kitchen had been opened, letting in a refreshing breeze. I sat Liam on my knee and fed him soup and mashed potato, both of which he ate with relish in spite of the garlic I could taste in the former. Clearly he'd grow up to be a young man of cosmopolitan taste.

"Do I gather that Daniel was annoyed I had been to your apartment?" Sid asked as she bustled about the kitchen, retrieving items from the meat safe. "He certainly seemed put out when I told him."

"He wasn't angry with you. He was frightened. He thought someone might have come to kidnap me," I said.

"He seems obsessed with your being kidnapped, Molly." Sid undid wax paper and laid slices of ham on a plate as she spoke. "Does he have reason to fear for your safety? Are you keeping something from me?"

I wasn't sure what to say. I had promised Daniel that I wouldn't mention his investigation. I managed a bright smile as she brought the plate across to the table. "I'm afraid Daniel is overreacting at the moment. I think my being involved in the train crash yesterday has really unnerved him, especially after what happened to us earlier this year."

"I can certainly understand that." Sid put a plate of spring onions and tomatoes next to the ham. "But this Italian gang is no longer making threats to you personally, is it?"

"No. That's all settled," I could say with honesty. "The moment all charges were dropped against their leader a sort of truce was established. I don't think we're ever going to be able to subdue them completely, with new Italian immigrants pouring into the city all the time. Daniel thinks that we'll have to learn to live with them."

"I'm glad I'm not in his position," Sid said. "Wanting to do the right thing but always having to compromise. It can't be easy."

"No," I said. "His mother wants him to leave the police and go into politics."

"Senator Sullivan. It has a certain ring to it, and he'd garner the Irish vote," Sid said with a smile.

"Oh, and speaking of Daniel's mother," I went on, as I reached to put a slice of apple in front of Liam. "Daniel dropped another little bombshell as he was leaving. He's been to Sloane's and ordered a couple of beds so that his mother can come to stay immediately and help me hire another maid."

"Perfectly sensible, given the circumstances," Sid said.

"Whose side are you on?" I demanded.

"Nobody's side, just seeing Daniel's rationale in doing this. He knows you aren't in any fit state to go to Sloane's and buy beds yourself, so he's saving you the trouble. And it would also make sense to have your mother-in-law around for a while as you get the house up and working again. You can't go shopping at a department store with a wriggling baby on your hip. And we might not always be available to babysit. Gus has been asked to give a lecture on Professor Freud's interpretation of dreams and the latest research in Vienna, so she'll need to prepare for it."

She leaned closer to me, lowering her voice. "Between ourselves I rather think she sees herself as an expert in diseases of the mind and hopes to be invited to lecture in more academic circles. Some of Dr. Freud's colleagues in Vienna were clearly impressed by her forward-thinking, you know."

"Wouldn't she require some kind of academic credential before she could lecture at a university?"

"Oh, definitely. But where would she find anyone qualified to teach her over here, and who is likely to accept a woman to study as an alienist? If she ever tried to present a thesis it would most likely be rejected. Doctors in this country completely reject the notion that the inner workings of the mind can be unlocked through dreams."

I thought privately that it was unlikely Gus would study long and hard enough to become a doctor of anything. Sid and Gus usually tired of their latest enthusiasm quite quickly. Wisely I kept quiet. Maybe she really did have a calling to become an alienist. She certainly had a lively enough mind for it.

"It's a constant struggle for us women to be taken seriously, isn't it?" Sid said, now speaking in a normal voice again as she put bread on the table. "Yet another state has rejected a woman's right to vote even in local elections. It seems as if our suffrage movement is making no progress at all. I've been trying to get our suffrage sisters back into the saddle after the summer to plan our next campaign. The problem is that most women are either at the mercy of a husband or their family. If the family goes to Newport for the summer, they have to go along. I've been trying to round our group up and set them back to work. It's like herding cats, Molly. They're all in favor of the idea of women's suffrage, but they can only dedicate themselves to it when it fits in with their social schedules."

I recalled that Sid and Gus had abandoned the cause so that Gus could paint in Paris earlier this year and then so that Gus could study with Professor Freud in Vienna. Again I said nothing and nodded agreement as I spread butter on a slice of bread.

"It hasn't been easy, Molly," Sid said, aware of my silence.

"No, I'm sure it hasn't been," I said. I retrieved Liam's apple and handed it back to him.

"Sometimes I feel that we're going nowhere. Do you know there is even a thriving Anti-Suffrage League now?" Sid didn't look up from slicing a loaf of bread. "Actively working to block our every move. Disgusting, I call it. Our movement will only succeed if we all dedicate ourselves to the cause, not when it suits us, but wholeheartedly. Anyway, I've finally managed to round up enough women to hold a meeting here tomorrow night. I hope you'll attend if you feel up to it."

"I fully intend to," I said. "However much my husband is against the idea."

"Most men are." Sid sighed. "Many women too, unfortunately. They think we should allow ourselves to be guided by the superior intellect and worldly ways of our menfolk. Utter rot, of course. I'll put my intellect and worldliness up against that of a man any day." She looked up, realizing she was waving the bread knife in a dramatic manner and chuckled.

"How convenient that I'll be here tomorrow night and not have to invent a reason to attend your meeting. However shortsighted Daniel can be, I don't like to deceive him or go behind his back." I paused, then added, "Even if he did go behind mine by inviting his mother and buying beds without consulting me."

Gus joined us and we had a lively discussion over lunch on the frustrations of the suffrage movement and the shortsightedness of most men. Afterward Sid carried Liam upstairs for his nap and insisted I take one too.

"We're going shopping this afternoon, Molly," she said. "Is there anything we can get for you?"

"Nothing, thank you," I replied. "Unless you'd like to pop into Wanamaker's and buy linens for my house."

"Of course. Give me the bed sizes and I'll be happy to do it."

"I was only joking, Sid," I said. "Daniel told me to make a list and he'd have Wanamaker's deliver. I'd rather like to have bed linens in place before his mother arrives or she'll be buying what she wants."

"Well, sheets are no problem, are they?" Sid said. "But you'll need pillows. Feather pillows. And do you have mattresses for the beds? Make sure you get a feather mattress for your bed. Your mother-in-law and the maid can sleep on horsehair." And she grinned.

"It seems rather overwhelming at the moment," I said.

"I told you we can lend you enough sheets to start you off. But you should select your own blankets and quilts. Choose your color and then tell Daniel that Wanamaker's can send over several for you to choose from."

"Can one do that?" I asked.

"Of course. If they want your business, they have to be amenable," she said.

How different it was to have grown up privileged, I thought. In my childhood quilts were made and beds were stuffed with whatever odds and ends of fabric could be retrieved from cast-off garments. I don't think my mother ever bought bed linens from a store in her life. Not that there were any stores close to our cottage on the wild west coast of Ireland.

I made my way slowly up the stairs and took off my dress before I lay down. I had opened the bedroom windows and lay there listening to the gentle cooing of pigeons on the rooftops, the roar of the city muted and distant. *How peaceful it was here*, I thought. And yet my house across the street had always seemed a peaceful haven too, until somebody had hurled a bomb through my window. Could it be true that at this moment someone was plotting to kill me? It seemed hard to believe. I had been one of several hundred passengers on a train that had somehow been diverted to the wrong route. Someone had made a mistake. It had to have been an accident, because there was no way that one man could have orchestrated and carried out such a complicated feat.

Thus reassured I lay back, letting my mind drift over Daniel's complicated case. Unrelated victims from such different walks of life. Crimes that would never have been considered murders without the notes to Daniel. And at the beginning of August, someone might have lived who should have died. Fascinating. Had the killer slipped up once? Had that annoyed him? Or had he once decided to show mercy? If Gus really had studied long enough to have become an expert in diseases of the mind, maybe she could have come up with a profile for a man who would behave in this way. But I, with no such training, felt completely in the dark.

Then an idea came to me. My mind had wandered on to Sid's impassioned speech about the suffragists and how she was trying to make them all work together. A group of people working toward a common cause. . . .Was it possible that Daniel was not looking for one man, but a group? Surely not politically or religiously motivated, since the victims were so diverse and so seemingly random. But what about a club, a secret society for which the initiation was to commit a murder? It was a horrible thought, but that might explain why the crimes were so different.

Secret society. I toyed with the words. One of the victims was a student at the university here. Wasn't that the sort of thing with which rich young boys might amuse themselves? If I were looking into this investigation myself, I'd start with Simon Grossman. I'd find out whether he came from an affluent family and what circles he moved in. Because his death was the only one that was clearly a murder. Perhaps he had been part of the secret society but had objected to the killings—had threatened to go to the police and so had to be silenced in a hurry.

A group such as that could work together to derail a train. But then the question arose as to why they'd send their notes to Daniel. Still, I felt a glimmer of excitement as I lay back to sleep. It was that old feeling of being the hound and catching the first scent of the fox. And as soon as I was able, I'd go to that café, just south of Washington Square, and ask a few questions for myself.

❧ Eight ❧

It was not a restful sleep this time. I was in a dark and confined space, hanging over a cliff.

"Let go of the baby or we'll all plunge to our deaths," someone was shouting.

"I'm not letting go of my baby," I screamed back, but he was wrenched from my arms. I awoke sweating, my heart pounding. It was a grim reminder that I wasn't going to get over the train crash in a hurry.

When Daniel stopped by to visit later that evening, he reported that he had sent a telegram to his mother, asking her to come as soon as possible. And I, in turn, was able to tell him that I had arranged for Wanamaker's to bring a selection of bedding to Sid and Gus's house for my approval.

"What?" Daniel demanded. "Have you lost your senses, Molly? Has living with rich friends gone to your head?"

"I don't see why you're so upset," I replied, feeling my own hackles rising. "You said you'd left it to me to select things like linens that women supposedly know about. Well, I'm about to select. And since I can't go to the store, the store has to come to me."

"Yes, but . . . " Daniel spluttered. "Asking a store to bring you a selection? You know they'll only send their most expensive items. We are not rich, Molly. You know that. Besides, I've already asked my mother to bring any extra bedding she might have. My mother never throws away anything. I'm sure she has the quilt I had on my bed as a child among the many items stashed away in her attic."

"Daniel Sullivan!" I stood up, glaring at him. "If you think I am going to begin my new life in my new house with the castoffs from your mother's attic, you can think again."

"Only until we have time to make proper choices, and to budget what we can afford, Molly. And you know my mother has very good taste."

"Oh, I see." I was pacing now, oblivious to the twinges of pain in my side. "You come in here, announcing that you've selected beds at Sloane's. You choose all the furniture for our house, without consulting me, but you begrudge me the selection of the sheets for my own bed?"

He took a step back, surprised by this outburst. "Whoa there." He held up his hand. "I tried to re-create our house exactly as it was. I thought you'd be pleased. I wanted to surprise you."

A small voice in my head whispered that he had done a nice thing for me, but I couldn't let go of the anger that surged up whenever I felt powerless. "Maybe I didn't want our house exactly as it was," I said. "Some of that furniture was yours. Your choice, your taste. Well, I've been through a lot this year, Daniel, through no fault of my own. You should want to make it up to me."

"Some people would give their eye teeth to spend a summer in Paris," Daniel said. "I don't think we can consider a sea voyage and a summer in Europe a hardship."

"Yes, a summer in Paris is a wonderful thing, but not when I had to go through—" I stopped short, remembering once again that I had never told Daniel the true details of what had happened to me in Paris, not wanting to upset him at such a difficult time.

"Had to go through what?"

"Worrying about you," I said quickly. "Trying to recover from losing my home, nearly being killed, nearly losing my child, and not knowing if you were dead or alive. Not knowing if the gang would seek me out in Europe. It was hardly a carefree time for me, Daniel."

"I see." He nodded. "Of course you have been through a lot this year. Which was why I wanted to make it up to you. I tried to bring back your house as you remembered it. I worked hard at it, Molly, traveling all over the city in my spare time, having friends keep their eyes open for various items of furniture. And I think I did a pretty darned good job too."

He was yelling now too. We were facing each other like two dogs meeting unexpectedly, fur bristling. That small voice was louder now, telling me not to go on with this.

"You did, Daniel. I'm sorry." I put a hand on his shoulder. "But I don't want to feel that you've taken over everything. I'm trapped here with painful ribs. You've invited your mother without consulting me. And now you tell me she's going to be bringing her sheets and quilts with her and you don't want me shopping for my own. It's no wonder I'm upset."

Daniel shook his head. "I'll never understand women," he said. "When I think I'm taking care of you and protecting you, you explode."

"Then let me explain one thing about women that you should know by now." I folded my arms as I faced him. "If you want to please your wife, do not tell her you are letting her mother-in-law furnish her house because she has good taste."

I saw a smile twitch at his lips. "I didn't say that."

"No, but you implied it. How do you think I feel if I have no say over my own life?"

"Point taken," he said. "But truly it was nothing to get worked up about. I did say it was only until we could make a proper selection. No sense in rushing into things."

"There's also no harm in seeing what Wanamaker's has to offer," I said. "I don't have to buy any of the things they bring."

"I suppose not," he admitted grudgingly. "I'm sorry. I should not have reacted so strongly. After what happened to you yesterday, I wanted to make sure you were safely settled in your own home as soon as possible. And you will need help, won't you? You're not up to taking care of a house and Liam on your own—which is why I invited my mother."

"Yes, I'll need help," I agreed. "But I'm choosing my own bed linen, Daniel Sullivan."

He laughed and took me in his arms. "I'm glad your fiery nature is back, my darling. You've been so subdued since you came back from France. I've missed my old Molly."

And he kissed me, gently at first and then with increasing passion.

"No more, Daniel," I warned. "You have to handle me carefully. Remember I'm injured."

"Of course. We'll save that for later, when we're back in our own house. I've never felt comfortable making love to you in that apartment with Liam in the same room." He ran a hand over my shoulder. "You get some rest, and I have to go back to work."

"Again? It's almost dinnertime."

"Afraid so. Another briefing with the rail people."

"They work you too hard, Daniel."

"I do what has to be done. And if I think that a monster is still at large in this city, someone who feels he can murder at will, then I have to keep working until we stop him."

"There is one thing, Daniel," I said as he headed for the door. "I had a thought. What if we weren't looking for one person, but for several?"

"A gang, you mean?" He shook his head. "This doesn't have the stamp of gangland killings."

"I didn't mean a gang. I was thinking more of a secret society. What if their initiation requires them to kill? That might explain why these murders were so very different."

Daniel frowned, then shook his head. "A secret society? This is the twentieth century, Molly. And New York City."

"One of the victims was a student at the university. Students have been known to do such things."

"He was a victim, not a perpetrator."

"He was the only one whose death was immediately recognized as a murder. What if he was a member of such a society, but decided he wanted no part of what they were doing?"

Daniel shook his head again. "An interesting theory, but I can't take it seriously. Obviously we have looked into the backgrounds of the various victims. We have a good idea of his character, his friends, and his family. He was an easygoing, outgoing, likable young man with a bright future ahead of him." He paused, then added, "Of course, he wasn't a saint. He liked to go out drinking with his friends. He found it hard to live within his means, as many students do. His father said that he'd gotten into debt, and the father had to give him a severe talking to. But he was not the sort to be involved in anything underhanded."

"Parents don't always know what their sons are capable of getting up to," I pointed out.

"I can have one of my men make discreet inquiries, I suppose," Daniel said. "But I don't see how we're going to flush out a secret society. Besides, I feel in my gut that we're dealing with one person who is waging some kind of personal vendetta."

"Against you," I said.

"I don't want to believe that, but you may be right. We're no farther ahead with the cause of the train crash. My superiors want the locomotive driver to be prosecuted. They think this is something to do with a looming union strike. But he swears he is innocent and feels terrible about what happened. He also swears there was a Ninth Avenue disk on the front of his train when he set off."

"I can attest to that too. So can the other passengers," I said.

Daniel shook his head. "If only one thing made sense, I'd know where to start," he said. "But keep coming up with your suggestions. If nothing else, they cause me to reexamine my own theories."

He closed the door behind him. I couldn't resist a small smile of satisfaction. Who would have thought, a couple of years ago, that Daniel Sullivan would ever have admitted that my suggestions were useful to him? We had come a long way together!

Sid and Gus were in earnest discussion at dinner, over the best way the suffrage movement should move forward. Sid thought the time had come for more desperate measures. Suffragettes in England were chaining themselves to the railings outside the Parliament buildings. They were attacking policemen and their horses. Gus heartily disapproved of this.

"If we want to have the average housewife on our side, we have to behave in a way she can admire," she said. "We have no hope of succeeding until every woman in the country realizes that it is her right to vote, and that she is being denied her full participation in society."

"So how do we win over the housewives of New York, let alone Kansas and Alabama?" Sid said. She turned to me. "You're a married woman, Molly. You have to keep the peace with a typical male. What do you suggest?"

"I wish I knew," I said. "It's part of allowing women control over their own lives, isn't it? We're raised to be told that men are wiser and more experienced and that they know what's best for us. I suppose it's the education of girls that must be changed. For myself, I ruled the roost over my younger brothers after my mother died. I refused to wear a corset then, and I leap at Daniel now anytime he tries to lord it over me."

Gus laughed. "Yes, well, I wouldn't class you as the average housewife. You've run your own business. You've moved in a man's world. You've faced danger many times. Most women are content to stay home. They want to be protected and cosseted."

"Do you think that's really true?" Sid asked. "Is it perhaps that nobody has offered them alternatives?"

"Look at the other girls who were at Vassar with us," Gus said. "They were receiving a first-class education, but most of them couldn't wait to be married and become mistress of their own homes."

"Not all of them have given up the cause, Gus," Sid said. "I've been mining the Vassar alumnae list and have rounded up four of them for our meeting tomorrow night. Two were before our time, one after, but one of them will be familiar to you. Does the name Minnie Bryce ring a bell?"

Gus looked up, frowning. "Minnie Bryce. Wasn't she a senior in our dorm when we were freshmen? Tall, and rather imposing-looking." Gus's eyes lit up as a memory came to her. "I remember now. She was the one who gave us a talking-to after we climbed the ivy to get in that open window one night."

"Of course. I'd forgotten that." Sid chuckled. "She threatened to report us to the house mother, but she never did. Must have been a good sort at heart." She took a swig from her wineglass. "Well, she's now Minnie Hamilton, married with four sons. She's just the sort of person we need in our sisterhood. She can influence the next generation of young men."

I must have yawned. Gus glanced across at me. "Molly, you're looking tired. You've been sitting up too long and we've been boring you with our diatribes. Off to bed with you."

I stood up. "I'm not at all bored, but I really am feeling like a limp rag at the moment, so please excuse me. I must accept that it will take a while to get over what happened yesterday."

"Of course it will," Gus said. "There is the matter of delayed shock, as well as the bump on your head and your poor ribs. Do you need me to bind them for you again before you sleep?"

"I'll be just fine, thank you," I said. "I'm leaving the doctor's binding in place as long as possible. But perhaps I will take another of the sleeping powders you offered me. It helped me to sleep well last night, and I am aching all over at the moment."

Soon I was lying in the comfortable bed and fell asleep. But this second night was not as successful. In my dreams I was back in that confined, dark space, trying to get out, searching for my baby, and when I awoke my head was throbbing. I lay there in the dark, listening to the night noises of the city—cats yowling on some distant rooftop, the revving of an automobile engine, a police whistle. They were unsettling noises, reminding me that I was in a city of danger, that even in my friends' house I could never feel truly safe.

❧ Nine ❧

I n the morning I felt hollow-eyed and groggy as Sid brought Liam in to see me. He, in contrast, seemed remarkably healthy and happy, giggling when Sid pretended to bite his toes.

I forced myself to get up and dress in preparation for the visit from the representatives of Wanamaker's. They came around noon—two of them, a very superior-looking young man in a black frock coat and a harried young woman, who was carrying the parcels. Actually I was not enthralled with anything they had brought, and I told them that I'd come to the store with my husband as soon as I felt better.

I had a nap in the afternoon, in preparation for the evening meeting, and heaved a sigh of relief when Daniel came to visit me around five o'clock, before the suffragists arrived. I could only imagine his feelings if he'd found me surrounded by militant women making inflammatory banners.

"Well, that's settled then," he said, looking pleased with himself. "I received a telegram from my mother. She will be with us tomorrow. It's very good of her, isn't it?"

"Oh, yes. Very good," I tried to say with all sincerity.

"And no doubt you've ordered enough linens to furnish the most splendid beds?"

I shook my head. "There was nothing that really took my fancy. The quilts and eiderdowns were rather too ornate for my taste. So let's hope your mother arrives with enough sheets and blankets for both beds."

Daniel shot me a questioning look. I could tell he was wondering whether I was trying to play games—to make sure we had nothing to sleep on, because he had expressed his disapproval of Wanamaker's coming to the house. Now that I thought about it, I was rather pleased with this unplanned outcome. But I maintained a serene expression.

"Don't worry," I said. "Sid and Gus have already kindly offered to lend us anything we need until we have time to go shopping together. We'll be fine."

He managed a smile and reached out to squeeze my arm. "How are you feeling?" he asked.

"A little hollow-eyed," I said. "I didn't sleep well last night. Bad dreams."

"That's to be expected, isn't it?" Daniel said. "You were in a severe accident. You've probably had a concussion."

"It's also the underlying worry," I said. "When you tell me that it's possible a train crash was orchestrated to kill me, it's hardly reassuring, is it? It means that I could be in danger at any moment, anywhere in this city."

"Perhaps I exaggerated the danger, Molly. I went too far," he said. "You were the one who pointed out that the only thing linking all the murders together was me. And then you were on the train that crashed, and I got the note saying it was too bad he hadn't succeeded. I'm afraid I thought the worst."

"There could have been any number of people he wanted to kill on that train," I said. "My own belief is that he's enjoying claiming responsibility just to upset you. It will probably turn out to be a simple accident after all—a disk that flew off in the breeze, or a signalman who was not paying proper attention and misread." Then I held up my hand, excited. "I've got it, Daniel. If the disk wasn't attached properly, and it somehow slipped or twisted, a nine upside down is a six."

"You may have hit on something there," he said. "I'll have to see how these disks are attached, and if that's a possibility. But then why wasn't the disk found?"

"It could have blown off and landed in somebody's window for all we know. Or maybe a child took it as a souvenir after the train crashed."

"You're right." He leaned across and took my hand. "I can't wait until we're back in our own house living a normal life again, can you? It's been hard going home at night to that narrow, dingy apartment and wishing you were there to hold in my arms."

"You'll be able to hold me in your arms tomorrow night," I said. "But carefully. I'm fragile. I might break."

He laughed. "I tell you what, I'm devilishly hungry, Molly. Do you think there's a chance your friends would invite me to dinner tonight?"

"They would, but you wouldn't want to come," I said. "They've a whole band of women coming for a meeting."

"Oh, God. No thanks. Well, it better be the pie shop again." He got up, squeezing my hand before he let it go. "Until tomorrow then. I'm meeting Mother at the station, if my work allows me to escape for that long. If not, she'll have to take a cab. You'll make her welcome, won't you?"

"Of course," I said. "What time is she expected?"

"Not until about four thirty."

"I'll be in the drawing room and keep an eye out for her."

"Splendid. Well, good-bye then, my darling."

"Good-bye." I blew him a kiss.

As soon as I heard his footsteps going down the stairs, I felt bad that I had turned him away the one time he had wanted to have dinner with us. But truly I was doing him a kindness. Women suffragists would not have helped his appetite!

I sat in the kitchen while Sid and Gus made sandwiches and pitchers of lemonade.

"One has to be careful about offering wine," Sid said. "Sometimes these women are also ardent followers of the temperance movement."

"It's a warm evening," Gus said, as she wrapped a stack of dainty sandwiches in a damp serviette. "We were thinking it might be more pleasant to sit in the conservatory, rather than the more formal atmosphere of the drawing room."

"Good idea." I nodded agreement.

"And since we won't have time for a proper meal, Sid has made a cold soup," Gus went on. "And there is salad left from luncheon. Help yourself whenever you feel like it, Molly."

I took some cold cucumber soup, fed Liam, and by the time I had put him to bed I heard a knock at the front door, followed by women's voices in animated conversation. The first of the ladies had arrived. I spruced myself up and came downstairs to find four women seated in the wicker chairs in the conservatory. Two of them were earnest young women I had met before on a similar occasion. The other two were older women and unfamiliar to me. They both looked like solid and affluent matrons, and it was quite a surprise to find them at such a subversive meeting. While we were exchanging pleasantries, more women kept arriving, until there were ten of us.

"That's all, I think," Sid said, looking around with satisfaction. "A good number at such short notice, don't you think?"

"It's hard for so many of the sisters to get away," one of the older women said. She had an air of authority to her, as if she had once been a schoolmistress, and I thought that I wouldn't like to cross her. "If they are married, their evenings are devoted to serving dinner to their husbands and putting the children to bed. You might have better luck if you schedule the next meeting for the morning or afternoon. No husband objects to his wife attending a coffee morning with friends, but they are highly suspicious of a woman who wants to go out at night alone."

"I suppose you're right," Sid said, "but I was thinking of our young unmarried women who work during the day. At least five of us are gainfully employed."

"Really?" the older woman asked. "As what?"

"I work in a bank," one of them said.

"And I in a flower shop."

"I'm a teacher," the little redhead I had met before added.

"And I am a typewriter for a firm of lawyers."

"Mercy me," the older woman said. "I had heard that those typewriting machines were simply too strenuous for young women to handle."

The girl laughed. "That falsehood was spread by men who fear that women are encroaching on their jobs and don't want us in the workplace."

"Well, good for you, I say," the other older woman said loudly. She was rounder and jollier looking, like a friendly grandmother. "It warms my heart to see young women taking up such varied positions. When we can add lawyer and senator to that list, I'll be well satisfied."

"Not in your lifetime, I fear, Mrs. Mitchum," Sid said.

"Mrs. Sullivan was a detective, if I remember correctly," the earnest, dark-haired young woman said. I tried to remember her name.

They all looked at me in astonishment, making my cheeks turn red. "That's right," I said. "I ran my own detective agency until I married."

"And her husband forced her to give it up," Sid added, with a sideways glance at me.

"Isn't that always the way," one of them muttered. "Men can't abide the thought of a woman with a career, especially a successful one."

"To be fair to Daniel," I answered, "he is a captain in the police department, and a wife who worked as a private investigator would not be tolerated. Besides, he wants to protect me and keep me safe. It's a natural male instinct."

"Not all of us want to be protected," the dark-haired girl said. "I'm perfectly capable of standing on my own two feet."

"How about you, Mrs. Hamilton?" Gus asked as she came in with a tray of sandwiches. "Sid and I remember you as a rather terrifying senior in our dorm. We always tiptoed past your room."

"You were at school together?" Mrs. Mitchum asked.

"At Vassar. We have several alumnae in this group." Gus indicated the redhead and two others.

"Yes, I was a senior when these two were obnoxious little freshmen," Mrs. Hamilton laughed. "Always trying to sneak out of the dorm at night, I remember. How wonderful that your friendship has lasted all this time."

"Yes, it is wonderful," Gus said, glancing across at Sid.

"And neither of you has married?"

"No. Neither of us has married," Gus replied evenly. "Another cucumber sandwich, Mrs. Hamilton?"

"Sometimes I think we all would have been wiser not to," Mrs. Hamilton said. "I find the raising of four sons quite taxing, and I have almost no time for my own pursuits. And now I have the care of my young niece as well, which is not easy. But it is the path I have chosen, I suppose." She pushed back an imaginary strand of hair from her face, as if in annoyance. Then she turned back to Gus. "Did I not hear that you spent the summer in Paris?"

"We did," Sid said. "Miss Walcott pursued her art. Her painting was much admired."

This was a slight exaggeration, and Gus had the grace to blush, muttering, "Oh, no, not really."

"I hope your painting was of pleasant subjects, and not this dreadful rubbish that is being produced in Paris these days," Mrs. Mitchum said. "How they have the nerve to call it art. Flying cats and blue faces, indeed. Whatever next?"

"I envy you being able to spend a whole summer in Paris." Mrs. Hamilton sighed. "It was always my dream to travel. But I said yes to Joseph and next thing I knew I was the mother of four boys." She laughed.

"We were also in Vienna," Sid said. "Miss Walcott was studying with Professor Freud."

"Freud?" Mrs. Mitchum exclaimed. "Isn't he that dreadful man who claims that we are entirely driven by sexual impulses?" And she fanned herself with her gloves.

"I'm afraid he does," Gus admitted. "But he has done wonderful work in unlocking the subconscious of the human mind and in treating mental illness. And he has written a brilliant treatise on the interpretation of dreams."

"Dreams?" one of the women asked. "Can dreams be interpreted? Surely dreams are just our minds wandering aimlessly when we are not present to direct our thoughts."

"Some dreams are just that," Gus said, "but Dr. Freud and his colleagues have discovered that dreams are also a conduit through which our deepest fears and angers and longings can be expressed. Sometimes these feelings are so strong, or so traumatic, or so deeply suppressed, that we don't even want to name them, so our subconscious self expresses them as symbols or metaphors."

"I remember going to a carnival when I was a girl, and there was a fortune-teller who told us what our dreams meant," one of the women said. "But I thought it quite silly even then. I was going to marry an important man and travel the world, if you please. So far I have only been to Boston."

"So your mentors in Vienna dismiss the notion of prophetic dreams, like Joseph in the Bible?" someone asked. "Dreams sent to warn us? Surely there are documented cases?"

"I don't think they'd want to believe in them," Gus replied with a smile. "Because it would be hard to offer a scientific explanation."

"When I was growing up in Ireland folks were hot on interpreting dream symbols," I chimed in. "If you dreamed of a white cow you were going to come into money. If you dreamed of a black bird it meant an impending death . . . that sort of thing. I never put much store by it myself, but the older women swore by it."

"I'm not talking about the sort of dream interpretation that fortune-tellers use," Gus said. "This research has a serious scientific basis. I didn't completely agree with Professor Freud's interpretation. To him most dream symbols are related to sex. If you dream of a tower it's a male symbol, and a gaping cave might relate to a female."

"Mercy me." The older women exchanged horrified looks.

"I didn't go along with that," Gus said hurriedly.

"I should think not. Most decent people are not preoccupied with sexual function," Mrs. Mitchum said. "And talk of it should not go beyond the confines of the married bedroom."

"I agreed with the opinion of some other researchers, that there are dream symbols that seem to be common to all dreamers throughout the world," Gus went on, warming to her subject now. "For example, if you dream of a house, it's usually a symbol for how you see yourself. If you dream of a fine, solid house, then you have a good self-image. If you dream of a house with dark, gloomy rooms you don't want to enter, then there are parts of yourself you are afraid to face."

"Interesting," the red-haired girl from Vassar said. "I often dream that I'm in a large house, and I'm surprised to find I own it."

"You see!" Gus pointed at her excitedly. "You are just realizing your full potential."

The girl beamed. "How exciting. I must tell Mama. She claimed I'd never amount to much."

"What other symbols are there?" one of the women asked.

"A runaway horse, for example. If you're in a buggy with a runaway horse, it signifies an aspect of your life you can't control."

"I've dreamed that, many times," Sid said.

"And another fascinating revelation of this research is that we are sometimes so afraid to admit to a fear that we skirt around it even in our dreams, and create puns or rhyming words to express it. If we think our child is too pale and we are secretly worried he is sick, we might dream of him carrying a pail." She looked around the group. "But a trained alienist has ways to unlock the most enigmatic of symbols to get to their real meaning. You should see the wonderful cures that Professor Freud and his colleagues have achieved for those with severe mental problems or those who have experienced traumatic shocks. I really wished that I could have stayed longer and become an expert myself."

"Why didn't you?" one of the older women asked.

"We decided we missed New York too much, and there was considerable resistance to a woman wanting to be part of such a man's world. Several of the men there still believe that women are prone to hysteria and are incapable of serious discussion. Professor Freud himself was upset when I questioned his theory that lucid dreams are produced mainly by sexual impulses. It seemed like a good time to leave Vienna." Gus looked across at Sid and smiled.

"You had the most marvelous insights, Gus," Sid said. "Even some of the professors were impressed. They realized you brought a fresh new perspective to their research—an American woman's perspective."

Gus looked highly embarrassed about all this praise. "That's kind of you to say, but shouldn't we be concentrating on the reason for which we are here?"

"We should," Mrs. Mitchum said. "You have heard, I take it, that the suffragist movement has a new leader. Mrs. Catt has had to step down, or has been forcibly replaced, I'm not sure which, by Mrs. Anna Howard Shaw. Although I can't say I'm overjoyed by this choice. I think her approach will be too cautious, and the time for caution is past."

"That's just what I've been saying," Sid said. "We have tried to persuade gently and it is not working. We have to shake up society and make people listen to us."

"Quite right," Mrs. Hamilton said.

But that was about as far as the group could agree. One person's idea of forceful behavior was another's idea of militancy. I sat there while the arguments raged across me and was suddenly overcome with weariness. I stood up and begged to be excused.

"Of course, Molly dear," Gus said. "I think it's very courageous of you to be with us at all after your ordeal." She turned to the others. "Mrs. Sullivan was in that terrible train wreck yesterday, can you believe."

There was instant sympathy. "Not in that carriage that plunged to the ground, surely?" Mrs. Mitchum said.

"No, luckily I was in the one behind it. We came off the rails but were left hanging over the side, lodged against an adjacent building."

"Even so she was taken to hospital with cracked ribs and a bump on her head the size of an onion," Sid said.

"My poor dear young woman, then off to bed at once with you," Mrs. Hamilton said. "You should not be up and around at all. It's important to rest after an ordeal like yours. It's not just the physical injury; it's the matter of shock. The damage from shock can be quite profound, as I've just found out. We have our niece with us who has been through a trauma of her own and is still not fully recovered."

"I'm sorry to hear that," Mrs. Mitchum said. "What sort of trauma was it?"

"A house fire. Her parents were burned to death. She was lucky to get out alive." She shook her head. "But she is young, she is resilient. She will recover with time and loving care."

I left them and dragged my aching body up the stairs. I found myself feeling overwhelmed with tonight's chatter, with the imminent arrival of my mother-in-law, and with what had happened to me. I lay there, listening to the animated voices floating up from the open windows of the conservatory. Much as I agreed with their cause, I found it hard to be an active participant when I had more serious things occupying me. I wouldn't be able to rest properly until the man who was sending notes to Daniel was finally apprehended.

I lay back and tried to sleep, but Gus's words on dreams kept buzzing around my head. Were my dreams of a dark and confined space only reflecting what I had experienced in the train crash yesterday, or did they mean something deeper? Could they mean that I felt confined by my marriage? On such disturbing thoughts I finally drifted off to sleep.

❈❊ Ten ❊❈

T he next day when I awoke, my first thought was that it was
Liam's birthday. My son was now a one-year-old. Then I
realized I had no present, no cake, nothing to celebrate with.
I told myself that Liam didn't know when his birthday was, so it
would make more sense to wait until we were safely moved back
into our house and . . . "Holy Mother of God," I muttered, sitting up
so rapidly that I felt a shot of pain from those ribs. Today my mother-
in-law arrives. I'd have no time for birthday plans, even if I felt well
enough to bake a cake. I knew she was coming to look after me, but
there was still so much to be done to make the house fit for a guest.
I washed and dressed with rapidity and went across the street to my
house. The beds had been delivered from Sloane's, and Sid and Gus
brought over armloads of sheets, pillows, and counterpanes to make
up beds for Daniel's mother as well as for Daniel and me. Liam's crib
was being brought down from the apartment, along with the other
items we'd been using, but I was leaving that to Daniel.

"Poor old Liam," I said, watching him sitting and playing with Sid's
stuffed bear. "It's his birthday and we've nothing for him."

"I thought you agreed we'd have a proper celebration when you were feeling better and installed properly in your house," Gus said. "And we haven't had time to buy presents yet either."

"I know. I'm just being silly," I said. "It's just that every setback reminds me of what we've lost, and that we're not quite back to being a normal family yet."

Gus put her hand on mine. "It will come, Molly. Just be patient. You've got Daniel and you have us too. And we're going to give Liam the best birthday ever soon. You'll see."

I felt tears coming to my eyes again. Really I was turning into a dreadfully weepy woman these days. I blinked them away and gave Gus a bright smile. "Right. Let's finish that list of things I'll be needing."

Sid and Gus then disappeared back to their own house, only to return with an amazing assortment of sundry dishes, knives and forks, kitchen utensils, and dishcloths.

"I really don't need all this," I said, eyeing items that I could hardly identify—a garlic press, a French coffeemaker, and some kind of slicing machine. "And I couldn't deprive you of so much."

"We hardly ever use these things, Molly," Gus said when I tried to protest. "It will be good to give them the light of day."

"And you'll need a bedside lamp," Sid said, as she came down from the second floor. "We could bring down the one in the guest room. I'll go and get it."

She went to the front door, then stopped and called out, "There's someone at our door, Gus."

"Can I help you?" she called out. We then heard her say, "Mrs. Hamilton. I hadn't expected to see you again so soon."

The tall, severe-looking woman spun around at the sound of Sid's voice coming from across the street. "Oh, Miss Goldfarb. You startled me. I'm so sorry to disturb you."

"We were just helping Molly move back into her newly renovated house," Sid said.

"I've obviously come at an inconvenient time." Mrs. Hamilton turned to leave. "It was a foolish impulse on my part to call without an invitation. Please excuse me."

Sid went over to her. "Not at all. We were about to stop for a cup of coffee or tea. Won't you join us?"

"No, it wouldn't be right when you're obviously so busy." She sounded flustered, and I was surprised. At last night's meeting she had seemed like a woman who is always in command of herself.

"But we insist, don't we, Gus?" Sid took Mrs. Hamilton's arm and steered her toward their front door. "Come along, Molly. You've been working too hard and need a break too, and Liam should be waking up from his nap by now."

We followed her back across the alley, and Mrs. Hamilton was shown into the conservatory while Sid put on a kettle. I went to retrieve Liam and brought him down to join us. Mrs. Hamilton made a great fuss of him.

"Enjoy him while he's this age, Mrs. Sullivan," she said. "Soon it will be ripped trousers and skinned knees and all kinds of trouble, I promise you. I find myself wishing that I'd had girls. So much easier."

"I took care of three young brothers, so I know a bit about little boys and what I'm in for," I said.

"And where are your brothers now? Still in Ireland?"

"Two of them are dead, I'm afraid. The youngest is still in Ireland." I turned away, not wanting her to see my expression at the mention of this painful subject.

"It seems we all have our personal crosses to bear, doesn't it?" she said. "Life was not meant to be easy."

"Coffee, Earl Grey, or Japanese tea?" Sid poked her head through the doorway.

Life is easy for them, I thought, and then I remembered that life had not been so easy this summer. Mrs. Hamilton was right. We all have our personal crosses to bear.

When the tea tray was brought in, Sid and Gus handed around cups and then seated themselves facing us. Liam was given his favorite kind of hard gingersnap and lay back on my knee, sucking it contentedly.

"So what brings you back again so soon, Mrs. Hamilton?" Gus asked. "Did you perhaps want to reminisce over old times at Vassar when there weren't so many strangers present?"

Mrs. Hamilton shook her head. "Nothing like that, Miss Walcott, although recalling old times is always pleasant. I came to ask you a favor. I tried to pluck up the courage to talk about it last night, but the moment never seemed right." She paused and looked from one face to the next. I don't think any of us had an idea what might be coming next. Mrs. Hamilton had appeared to me to be the kind of woman who is completely in command of her life and not prone to asking favors. "It's my niece, you see. Young Mabel Hamilton."

A spasm of pain crossed her face and she closed her eyes as if trying to blink it away.

"You said she was in a house fire that killed her parents?" Sid said gently. "How very sad for her and for you. I presume you lost a sister or a brother?"

"It was my husband's brother who was killed, so no blood relation of mine, but he was very dear to us—a jovial, likable sort with a big laugh. He and Joseph came from a close family."

"And Mabel's mother?" Sid asked.

Mrs. Hamilton spooned sugar into her teacup and stirred it before she answered. "I developed a true affection for her over the years," she said. "When she first married my husband's brother, Albert, she was a shy and withdrawn little thing. She'd come from a very sheltered background, you see. Sheltered, and pampered to the point of being spoiled. Only child of a rich banking family—Susan Masters, she was." She looked around for signs of recognition. "You've presumably heard of Deveraux and Masters, the merchant bankers?"

"Oh, yes, of course," Gus said. I couldn't tell whether she really had or was just being polite. I certainly hadn't, but then I'd never moved in such elevated circles.

"As I said," Mrs. Hamilton went on, "she had come from a privileged and sheltered background, and it was quite a step down for her to have married our Bertie. She was only eighteen years old when she married him. He'd seen her at a dance and been quite smitten but never thought he stood a chance. But he proposed and she said yes, and I think they've been happy enough, although quite different in their tastes. She's all for reading and music and quiet pursuits, and he's all for company and the outdoors and sports." She paused, again closing her eyes. "I meant 'was.' I must now refer to them in the past tense."

"A great tragedy," Gus said.

"Susan became quite attached to me over the years," Mrs. Hamilton continued. "I believe she saw me as the big sister she never had. And now they are gone, burned to death in their beds."

"But their daughter managed to escape," Gus said. "That was a small miracle, I suppose. Was she an only child?"

"She was."

"And you said that Susan was an only child of a rich banking family," I interjected, without really thinking whether it was wise. It's often been a fault of mine. I say something when it comes into my head, without thinking of the consequences. "Does that mean that Mabel is now a rich heiress?"

Mrs. Hamilton looked startled. "Well, yes. I presume that she is. We have been so engulfed in our mourning that the question of money has not arisen."

I could tell immediately what she was thinking—that I had been implying they only took in their niece in the hope of financial gain, because she was an heiress—but that wasn't what I'd meant at all.

"You said you brought Mabel to live with you," Sid said. "That was a kind gesture."

"It was either us or her grandfather, and he keeps a bachelor establishment after the death of his wife," Mrs. Hamilton said. "And Mabel was such a poor, devastated little thing that we couldn't say no. I must say she's no trouble at all, compared to the boys. She's quiet and retiring like her mother was. Hardly says a word unless spoken to. But then after what she has been through, it's little wonder."

She broke off and there was a moment of silence in the room. The day was cooler than yesterday, with a brisk breeze that came in now though the open window, making the leaves on the potted palm rattle.

"So how do you think that we can be of help to you, Mrs. Hamilton?" Sid asked cautiously. "You said you came about your niece."

Mrs. Hamilton nodded. "She was found sometime after the fire, curled up in the back garden, apparently asleep, but unharmed. When she came to herself she had no memory of what had happened. Didn't know there had been a fire. Asked about her mother and father."

"It must have been the shock of what she went through trying to get out," I said.

"That was another strange thing," Mrs. Hamilton said. "She showed no signs of having been in a fire. Two of the servants also made it out safely, but they were blackened, with minor burns and singed hair. The third servant was not so lucky. Her room was in the attic, above Susan and Bertie's room. They found her charred body later."

"Very sad," I said. "We also lost a servant girl in a house fire earlier this year."

"But to get back to Mabel," Sid said. "She was found unharmed in the back garden with no memory of what had happened."

"That's correct. The police have been investigating the fire, naturally, and they find it suspicious that she came out of it quite unscathed."

"Do they suspect that she might have started it?" I asked.

She took a deep breath, then nodded. "That is certainly what the lieutenant has been hinting. An odious young man, keen on promotion, if you ask me."

"Did Mabel dislike her parents? Had she any reason for wanting to do away with them?" I asked.

Mrs. Hamilton shook her head again. "She is a sweet child. There is no guile about her and she adored her parents. It makes no sense at all."

"Had she shown any signs of mental instability before the fire?" Gus asked carefully. "It has been noticed that puberty can bring on such things."

"Again I have to reiterate what I said. She is a sweet child, a little shy, but completely lovable."

"Mrs. Hamilton," I said, the detective in me now taking over. "You said she remembers nothing of the fire. Would you say that is true, or is that just what she is claiming? Has she ever tried to bluff or cover up something she has done in the past?"

"No, no." She was animated and sounded distressed now. "I told you. There is no guile in her. Now, one of my boys—Winslow—he is a master at coming up with excuses and tall tales to cover up his transgressions. You know—the dog managed to open the cookie jar and stole the cookies. That kind of thing. But I can see through them right away. I'm sure I'd be able to tell if Mabel was lying. But her grief on finding out that her parents were dead and her home burned was real, I'd swear to that."

"So why did you come to us, Mrs. Hamilton?" Sid asked. She was never one for preamble and liked to get to the point.

"It was what Miss Walcott said yesterday, about her study into the interpretation of dreams," Mrs. Hamilton said. "You see, since the fire Mabel has been plagued with the most awful nightmares. She wakes screaming. I once found her cowering in the corner of her room shouting, 'Keep away from me. Don't touch me.'"

"I see," Gus said. "So you believe that in her subconscious mind she remembers what happened that night, and it expresses itself in her dreams?"

"That's exactly what I believe," Mrs. Hamilton said. "The possibility only occurred to me when you were speaking last night, but it must be true. So I wondered if you'd come and see her. Let her tell you the content of these nightmares, and then see if we can come to the truth."

Gus glanced at Sid before she spoke. "Mrs. Hamilton, I should tell you that I'm not a qualified alienist. I have only touched the surface of the study of dreams. Maybe you should look for a true specialist."

"But, Gus," Sid interrupted. "You have said yourself that America is far behind in the study of mental illness. I am sure there is nobody over here who has made a study of dream interpretation. You told me that American doctors scorned Professor Freud's theories."

"That's true," Gus agreed. "Very well, Mrs. Hamilton. I will come and see Mabel. I will do what I can."

Mrs. Hamilton reached out and took Gus's hand. "Thank you. I can't thank you enough. The thought of that sweet child locked away in a prison or mental institution by an overzealous policeman is breaking my heart."

"I presume a thorough investigation of the fire has been carried out," I said. "Do they know how and where it started? Because there is something that strikes me as odd."

"And what is that, Mrs. Sullivan?" Mrs. Hamilton asked.

"That the parents were burned to death in their beds. Why did they not at least try to escape?"

The other three women around the table stared at me suspiciously.

"What are you suggesting, Mrs. Sullivan?" Mrs. Hamilton said. "The fire started in their bedroom. They did not have electricity in their house. The windows were open, and it is thought that a breeze blew over an oil lamp on the bedside table."

"They slept with the lamp still burning?"

She nodded. "Susan did not sleep well on hot nights. Sometimes she liked to get up and read by the window."

"Even so," I went on. "If a fire started in the room of a normal, healthy person, they would be woken by the smell of burning and the crackle of flames before the fire had a chance to engulf the room.

So why were they both found lying in their beds? Do you know if they took sleeping drafts to help them sleep on hot nights?"

Mrs. Hamilton shook her head. "I'm sure they did not."

"And was an autopsy ever conducted?"

She looked confused now. "An autopsy? Mrs. Sullivan, my brother-in-law and sister-in-law were burned to death. Their charred bodies were found lying on the iron frames of their beds. It was quite clear what killed them."

I wonder, I thought, but did not say.

❧ Eleven ❧

W ell, that's a rum do, isn't it?" Sid asked, as she returned
from escorting Mrs. Hamilton to the front door. "Poor
woman. Poor child. I hope you'll be able to help her, Gus."
"I hope so too," Gus said. "Now it's come to an actual case, I'm
questioning my skills and wondering if we shouldn't write directly
to Professor Freud to ask for his recommendation. He may know of
a qualified alienist who is working in America." She looked from Sid
to me. "This is something really serious we're dealing with. Not just
the sanity of a young girl, but a possible criminal case. It's not for my
amusement any longer."

Sid turned to me. "What do you think, Molly? You clearly read
more into this from the beginning, with the questions you asked. You
think it's possible that Mabel killed her parents, don't you?"

"I haven't met the girl yet, so I can't make a judgment on that," I
said as I rescued the sugar bowl from my overcurious son. "But I do
think there is something fishy about the whole thing. The parents
burned to death in their beds while the girl is found completely unharmed and apparently asleep in the garden below. It doesn't add up,
does it?" I put Liam down on the tiled floor and he promptly began

to totter toward the open back door. I saw what Mrs. Hamilton had meant about boys being a handful. I leaped up and grabbed him before he could go down the step headfirst.

"I'll tell you one thing," I said. "There was a reason why those people didn't leave their bed when the fire started. I'll talk to Daniel and see if he can look into it."

"And will you come with us when we go to see the girl?" Gus asked. "With your background as a detective you might pick up things that neither Sid nor I would find suspicious."

"I'd very much like to," I said. "I admit to being curious. Although it might be difficult now that Daniel's mother is arriving."

"Au contraire," Sid said. "You'll have your babysitter, and you'll need to be shopping for the hundred and one things she'll point out that you lack."

I laughed. "You're even more devious than I am. But it is true. She will be able to look after Liam—if anyone can," I added as he squirmed to get down from my lap and almost launched himself into midair. "Speaking of which"—I stood up with him—"I had better get back to my task across the street. And I'll need to do something about food for tonight. There's nothing in the larder yet, and I've all my staples back at the apartment. Let's hope Daniel has had time to pack and arrange for everything to be delivered. But I'll still need something for tonight's dinner and tomorrow's breakfast."

"Give me a list of what you need right now," Sid said. "I'll pop down to Gambarelli's and have them deliver."

"Delivered?" I said. "Well, just this once, I suppose." I laughed. "I better not get into the habit of having things delivered. Daniel will think I've picked up expensive habits in Paris."

Then I had another thought. "Actually, why don't I go to Gambarelli's? It's only just across the square. A short walk and fresh air might do me good."

"Molly, it's no trouble," Sid said. "We're here at your disposal, you know."

"Then could I ask another big favor, and have you dust the living room before my mother-in-law arrives? She is bound to notice every particle of dust. I just tried, and the act of reaching up to dust is still quite painful for me."

"Of course it is," Sid said. "We're happy to do it, and the shopping too."

"I'm sure a short stroll will be good for me, and it's a lovely day," I said. "But I will take your advice and have them deliver, just this once."

"One of us should come with you," Gus said. "In case you suddenly feel faint."

I smiled. "I'd rather you kept an eye on my son, if you don't mind," I said. "I'm sure I'll be just fine. And if I feel wobbly on my pins, I'll just turn around and come home."

I put Liam down for a nap, then set out down Patchin Place. The warm sun on my shoulders felt good and I tried to breathe in the smell of Mrs. Konigsberg's roses before another jolt of pain shot through me. I'd just have to accept the fact that I could not make myself heal quickly just by willing it. Maybe I had been foolish to go out for this walk. But as I reached the end of Patchin Place and headed for Washington Square, my confidence returned and I strode out quite briskly.

Gambarelli's was just on the far side of MacDougal Street. As I went into the dark interior of the store, the familiar smell of spices and pickles and garlic sausages rose to greet me. I handed Mr. Gambarelli my list and paid the bill. "My boy is just out on an errand, but I will send him straight to you when he returns," he said. "It is good to see you back in the neighborhood, Mrs. Sullivan."

I realized then that everyone must have heard about the fire that destroyed our house.

"Thank you," I replied and found myself blinking back tears.

As I headed back toward the square I had to negotiate gaggles of university students, loitering on the street corner or coming out of the bookshop. Their attire ranged from smart blazers and boater hats to the sort of European student costume I had seen in Paris—the baggy pants and a worn jacket with patched elbows, and on the head a cloth cap. They talked earnestly in small groups and I imagined they were discussing philosophy or literature. This was one of the occasions when I truly envied Sid and Gus their experiences at Vassar.

Then I heard one of them say, "She's a corker, all right. Best little barmaid in Greenwich Village," which dispelled my illusion immediately.

Then, of course, I realized with a jolt that on the other side of the street was Fritz's café, where Simon Grossman had drunk a cyanide-laced cup of coffee. I crossed the street toward the café and stood outside, looking and thinking. This was one of those places that had been started by an Austrian to mimic the elegant café scene of his native Vienna. But alas, the location was not right for an elegant clientele, being surrounded by students and immigrants and more recently by starving artists and writers. So it had become a place that served soups and sandwiches as well as little cakes, at prices students and starving artists could afford. I had been in there myself a couple of times since I moved to Patchin Place and had always found it lively and inviting.

It was crowded now, with students clustered around its marble-topped tables, drinking big cups of milky coffee or dunking rolls into it. I realized I hadn't been told what time of day Simon Grossman had died, but he had been drinking coffee, so it had probably been in the morning, just like this. I stood in the doorway looking around. The owner, presumably Fritz, sporting an impressive mustache that curled up at the sides, saw me, recognized I wasn't one of his usual customers, and came out from behind the marble-faced counter to me. "You wish coffee, madam?" he asked.

Why not? I thought. It would give me an excuse to stay and observe.

"Thank you," I said. "It seems rather crowded."

"It is always crowded in here. These young layabouts, they would rather sit here and drink my coffee than go to their classes. Wait, I find a table for you." And before I could stop him, he ejected two boys who were sitting in a corner.

"Oh, no really," I protested.

He shook his head. "They have been here over an hour, nursing one cup of coffee. Not good for business." He raised his voice to them. "Go on. Off with you. Your papa expects you to be studying, not wasting time here."

"But we were discussing a philosophy paper, Fritz. Working hard, I swear," one of them said, although I could tell from his grin that this hadn't been the case. I decided that their corner table would be an ideal site to observe, and I took a seat at it as they gathered up their books. As Fritz departed to get my coffee, I gave them a friendly smile.

"Tell me," I said. "Do you come here every day?"

"When we can afford it," one of them said.

"I don't wish to sound morbid," I said, "but were you by any chance here when that student was killed?"

"You mean the duel last year?" one of them said, his face lighting up. "Wasn't that something?"

"Ye Gods. I half expected to have my head slashed off," the other agreed. "Those guys were insane."

"No, I meant Simon Grossman, the young man who drank the poisoned coffee," I interrupted before they got carried away by their description.

Their eyes opened wider then. "So it was poisoned!" one of them said. "We often wondered, didn't we, old sport?"

The other nodded. "They never said anything. Let us think that he'd had a fit or something, but I always thought there was something fishy."

"Did you know Simon Grossman?"

"Saw him around from time to time, but didn't have any classes with him. You'd often see him here or in a tavern, usually with a young lady, of questionable virtue, one might say."

"He liked to enjoy life, that's for sure. That's why it was such bad luck that he croaked like that. And you say it was deliberate? Or did he take his own life?"

"If he enjoyed life, why would he want to take it?" I asked.

They looked at each other before one of them said, "Well, one did hear," the chubbier one began, glancing around to see who might have been in earshot, "that Simon had run up gambling debts. He didn't want to tell his old man, naturally. His father thought the sun shone out of Simon's head, you know. Anyway, Simon tried to cadge money from a couple of our friends, but they were broke themselves."

I shook my head. "I don't think someone who loves life would kill himself over debts. And certainly not with cyanide. It's a beastly painful death."

"Cyanide, was it?" The two boys exchanged a horrified glance.

"So I understand," I said.

One of them was looking at me cautiously now.

"That's right, it was utterly beastly," the other boy said. "We were sitting at our usual table in the corner here and there was suddenly this tremendous fuss—table knocked over, broken crockery, coffee everywhere, and someone thrashing around on the floor."

"Someone said, 'He's having a fit,' and then someone else said 'He's dead. My God, he's dead.'"

"Tell me," I said, "was the café really full at that time? Did you notice anyone who wasn't usually here, anyone hanging around the tables, or anyone who left as soon as all the commotion started?"

"Why this morbid curiosity?" the one who had been eyeing me curiously now asked. "Are you a newspaper reporter? Because it's old news now, isn't it?"

"No, I'm a friend of Simon's family," I said, "and they are still angry that his killer hasn't been apprehended."

"I presume they've checked with the Italians?" the chubby one said. "The ones who run the tavern with the gambling parlor in the back, down on Bleecker Street? They're a wild lot, and if Simon owed them money . . . "

"I don't think cyanide is their chosen method," I said. "A knife in the back, perhaps?"

The two young men were now looking at me with horror, and I realized that respectable women don't usually go in for this type of conversation.

"So you didn't notice anyone behaving suspiciously, or anyone leaving in a hurry? You didn't see someone who might have been a member of the Italian underworld?"

One of them shrugged. "To tell you the truth, we were chatting with some other fellows and only turned around when we heard the crash. And it was pretty crowded at the time—fellows coming and going and waiting for tables."

"But in answer to your question," the other said, "I didn't see anyone who stood out, I'm sure. Everyone looked like a regular student. I think we'd have noticed, just the way we noticed you come in, if there had been someone unusual."

The chubby one nudged his friend. "We have to go or we'll be late for class again."

"Excuse us." They nodded to me. "I hope they find the guy who did this. Everyone seemed to like Simon Grossman, even if he did enjoy his vices. Who'd do a foul thing like that?"

I wished I knew. I tried to chat with Fritz after that, but he hadn't seen any suspicious strangers, and he told me he had been so busy pouring coffee that he too had only looked up when the table crashed over. I did take from him the names of the students who were sitting with Simon, but was told they were his regular group of pals, with whom he met at the café every morning. I suspected that Daniel would already have grilled them and discovered nothing, and I didn't think that they'd reveal to a strange woman any incriminating facts about Simon Grossman. As I paid my bill and walked out, squeezing between tables, I saw how incredibly easy it would be to drop poison into a coffee cup while the occupants of the table were engrossed in conversation. But I had also learned that an outsider, an Italian gang member, for example, would have been noticed in the café. So whoever did this was likely one of them.

And it was only when I was crossing the street on my way home that I realized I might have been reckless to go out like this. Not because of my delicate health, but because the killer might have been watching my house and caught sight of me.

Daniel would not be pleased, and I decided to say nothing of my visit to the café, at least for now.

❦ Twelve ❦

There was no sign of Daniel all day. The delivery boy brought the food, and I had just finished stacking it in the pantry when a hansom cab turned into Patchin Place. It stopped only a few yards into our little backwater. Drivers didn't like to come any farther, as it was hard to turn and even harder to back up the horse. I had been watching from the parlor window—a real lace-curtain twitching Irishwoman for once—and saw the cabby helping down my mother-in-law from the seat. Then my heart gave a leap of joy, because I saw the cabby swinging down young Bridie. She was the child I had brought from Ireland when I came to New York, and she had been abandoned by her father and brother when they went to work on the building of the canal across the Isthmus of Panama. No news had come from them in quite a while, making me wonder whether they were still alive. One heard awful things about the conditions and the diseases down in that hellhole.

My mother-in-law had taken in Bridie to train her as a maid, but had grown fond of her and now seemed to be raising her to be a young lady. Either way, she had blossomed into a sweet young girl, almost twelve years old, and I was delighted to see her. I went to the front door to meet them.

"Mother Sullivan, how good of you to come," I said. "And Bridie too. What a lovely surprise."

"I thought she might be useful minding the baby," Mrs. Sullivan said. "And it's lonely for her up at the house with just Martha to talk to. And of course she pestered me until I agreed she could come."

Bridie gave me a sheepish smile. "I didn't pester. I asked nicely. I didn't want to miss out on seeing Liam."

"Only Liam, I notice." I grinned as I ruffled her hair. "You'd no real desire to see me then?"

Bridie came over and hugged me fiercely.

"Careful, child. Molly's been injured." Mrs. Sullivan touched my shoulder as if I was made of porcelain as she leaned forward to kiss my cheek. "But you, my poor dear girl. What a terrible thing to have happened to you. When we read about it in the newspaper I said to Martha 'I just hope nobody we know was riding on that train.' And then we got Daniel's telegram. It's a miracle you're still alive, saints be praised."

"Yes, it is a miracle," I said. "I almost got in the car ahead, but there was a man coughing and I didn't want Liam to catch a disease. That was the car that plunged down and so many people were killed. I was in the car that hung down over the edge. We would have fallen all the way to the street as well, but we came to rest against the side of a building."

"Awful!" she exclaimed again. "And Daniel says you've broken ribs?"

"Either cracked or bruised, not broken," I said. "But they certainly hurt enough when I try to do anything like pick up Liam."

"Of course they would. Well, I'm here now."

Mrs. Sullivan turned to the cabby who was struggling with a large trunk. "Bring that up to the house, will you?" she said. The cabby gave a sigh as he heaved it onto his shoulder and followed us. I opened the front door.

"I can't tell you how grateful I am," I said. "Please do come in. I'm afraid the house isn't quite ready yet, but Sid and Gus have lent me some items so we'll get by for now."

"They are still living across the street then?" She shot a disapproving glare at their house. "Last thing I heard they were off gallivanting in Europe."

"Yes, they just came home recently from Vienna. Miss Walcott has been studying with Professor Freud."

Her eyebrows shot up. "Not that awful man who says that all we think about is . . . " She lowered her voice and said, "S-e-x."

"I can spell, you know," Bridie said. "But you never told me what sex is."

"Later, dear," Mother Sullivan said. She turned back to the cabby. "You might as well take that upstairs to my room."

"I'm a cabdriver, not a footman or a delivery boy," he said. "I'll leave it in the front hall. You can do what you like with it after that."

"And I was going to give him a good tip too," Mother Sullivan said as the cabby stomped away and I closed the front door behind him.

"Now, where's that adorable grandson of mine?" she asked.

"He's asleep on my bed. His crib is still at the apartment where Daniel's been staying. He's supposed to pack up our stuff and have it delivered, but the Lord knows when he'll find time to do that. He's been awfully busy lately."

"When is that poor boy not busy?" she said. "Working himself to the grave, that's what he's doing. You must persuade him to leave the police, Molly. I've told you we have friends who would be only too glad to help him get into politics."

"But he loves what he does, Mother Sullivan. He's not designed for a life of leisure, you know that."

She sniffed. "You're right about that. Just like his father."

I showed her the newly furnished parlor and then took her upstairs to the bedrooms. She didn't seem particularly impressed, but then I realized that everything looked just as it once was to her. She had never seen my house burned and in ruins. She had no idea of the work it had taken to bring it back to how it was. And as I looked at it myself I felt ashamed that I had criticized Daniel for doing it all without me. It had been a mammoth task for him and one undertaken with love. I'd tell him that as soon as he got home.

At our bedroom door Mother Sullivan stopped short, as Liam lay blissfully asleep on top of the eiderdown. "Oh, I see you already have the bed made up," she said. "Daniel told me you'd no bed linens. That's why I brought the trunk with me."

"Oh, these are only borrowed from my neighbors, in case you'd not brought the bed linens with you but had them sent by a carter service," I said quickly. "And we'll need to make up a bed for Bridie, since I didn't know she was coming. There's a bed up in the old maid's room, Bridie, love. You can have a room to yourself."

"You can get the linens you'll need from the trunk and make up the bed yourself, Bridie," Mrs. Sullivan said. As soon as Bridie was out of the way she turned to me. "She's getting to an age when I'm wondering what to do with her, Molly."

I glanced out of the door to hear Bridie rummaging around in the trunk. "Why, she's not proving to be difficult, surely?"

"Quite the contrary," Mrs. Sullivan said. "She's turned into a grand little helper. I'm concerned about her future, that's all. I've taught her to read and write and do sums, but I'm thinking she needs more education if she's going to make her way in the world. She's as smart as a whip and the local school only goes up to sixth grade. Besides, it must be boring for her with only Martha and me for company. So I was thinking maybe she might stay with you for a while, and attend a proper school. Meet children of her own age. And to pay for her keep she can help you out around the house, until you find yourselves a new maid. She's good with Liam, isn't she?"

"She is, and there would be no need to pay for her keep. I'd be delighted to have her with me. But what about you? Won't you miss having her around?"

"I'll miss her, all right. But I have to think of her, not me. I may not be around forever and I want her to be able to make her way in the world. Maybe she can become a teacher. She'd like that, I know."

"I think it's very sweet and generous of you," I said, and gave her a kiss on her cheek. "I'll need to talk to Daniel and see what he says, but surely he couldn't object."

"We won't mention it to Bridie until it's all settled," she said, "and she can come up to me in the vacations, can't she?"

"Of course." I turned back to the bed, where Liam was now gazing at us sleepily. "Oh, look, Master Liam has finally woken up. It's your grandmother come to visit us, young man."

"Isn't he the birthday boy today?" she asked. "I could have sworn it was the fourteenth? I've a little something for him in the trunk— Martha's made him a new sailor suit and we've bought the hat to go with it and proper little leather boots now that he's walking."

"That's grand. How kind of you," I said. "And we've decided to have a proper celebration when I'm well and we're properly set up in the house."

Mother Sullivan looked around. "It seems as if you have most things you need here. Enough for me to get started on dinner anyway. What had you in mind?"

"My supplies haven't arrived yet from the apartment so I thought we'd keep it simple tonight with ham and mashed potatoes. I'm sure you're tired after traveling and I can manage," I started to say but she held up a hand. "Enough of that. You've been in a terrible train crash," she said. "I'm here to make sure you have a chance to heal. Now, let's see to dinner."

She had dinner on the stove and Bridie had fed Liam by the time that Daniel arrived home. He looked around the kitchen and beamed. "Well, isn't this nice? My family and my home back together. I can't think of anything that would make me more happy."

"Your wife has been doing too much, Daniel. Trying to get the dinner herself with her poor ribs all bandaged up. I told her she's to rest and let Bridie and me take care of the house."

Daniel seemed to have noticed Bridie for the first time. "Oh, so you brought young Bridie too. That will be nice company for Molly and Liam."

We sat down to the simple meal of ham, mashed potatoes, and pickles. Daniel ate with such relish that I had to believe it was his first decent meal in days. I watched him as he ate, noticing how his hair still curled boyishly across his forehead and how handsome he was. And how tired he looked. I wondered if Mother Sullivan was right and this job was killing him, and I wondered what I should do about it.

"You seem quite glad that my mother is here after all," Daniel said as we undressed in our new bedroom. "I have always sensed that you resented her and didn't want her to interfere."

"I truly am glad she's here this time, Daniel. And Bridie too."

"Yes, she's a good little helper now, isn't she? My mother has trained her well. But I can't see her ending up as a maid, can you?"

I laughed. "No, it won't happen. More likely your mother will marry her off to a local landowner and brag to her friends about the good match she has made." I was about to say something to him about Bridie staying on with us after his mother had gone home, so that she could attend school, but I decided this wasn't the moment. Let him become fond of her and enjoy having her around the place first, I thought. So I went on, "I simply couldn't have managed on my own. It still hurts me to breathe, let alone pick up Liam, and I'm sure my ribs will heal more quickly if I don't have to do too much work."

"Of course. And far better for you to heal in your own home than with those friends across the street. All that coming and going and painting and women's meetings is not conducive to rest and recuperation, I'm sure."

"They are very kind and look after me well, Daniel, but as it happens they have a lot on their plate at the moment."

"Oh, really? What are they up to now?" He sounded amused.

I couldn't mention the suffragist meeting, but I said, "You remember Gus told us she had been studying the interpretation of dreams with Professor Freud in Vienna."

"A lot of bunkum if you ask me," he interjected.

"We'll have to see about that. Personally I thought it made sense as Gus explained it. But anyway, she's been asked to help a young girl who has been through a tragedy and is now having horrible nightmares." I climbed into bed, enjoying the feel of clean sheets and a new soft mattress.

"Your friend believes she is qualified to help in such a case?" Daniel asked.

"No, she expressed the belief that she should not try to help, because she was not qualified. She intends to write to Dr. Freud to ask for his recommendations, but in the meantime the child's guardian begged her to come. It's a very strange and sad case, Daniel. Perhaps you've heard about it—one of the men in your department is handling it." And I briefly gave him the facts as they had been told to me.

"I believe I did hear something about it," he said. "About a month ago, wasn't it?"

"That's right. When Mrs. Hamilton told us the story, nobody else seemed to think it strange that the parents were both found dead in their beds, while the girl and most of the servants escaped safely. But surely that raises a red flag, doesn't it, Daniel?"

"The investigating officer obviously thinks so. Do you know which officer is handling the case?"

"No, we weren't told his name, but apparently he thinks the girl started the fire and then got out."

"And you think she might have killed her parents first, and then started the fire to cover up the crime?"

"It did cross my mind, I confess. I asked if there had been an autopsy and Mrs. Hamilton got quite shirty with me. She said the bodies were charred beyond recognition, and it was quite obvious how they died. But I was wondering, what if they had been drugged or poisoned first?"

I looked up at him as he lowered the gas and climbed into bed beside me. "Is there any way you could order an autopsy?"

"I can't interfere in another officer's case," he said, "and besides, they will have been buried long ago. An exhumation order is something that is never taken lightly." He slipped an arm under my neck and drew me toward him so that my head rested on his shoulder. "You mustn't worry at the moment, or get involved in such things, Molly. Your job is to heal."

"But what if the police are trying to accuse this child of something she didn't do?"

"Molly," he whispered. "If this girl is deranged and wanted to get rid of her parents, what does it really matter whether she drugged them first or not? This is out of your league, and Gus Walcott's as well, if you want my opinion. You should let the police do their job and stay well away."

"But you wouldn't object if I went to see the girl with Gus? We have been invited by the aunt. And it would satisfy my curiosity."

"Your insatiable curiosity," he said, stroking my hair. "But please warn your friend that she is playing with fire if she acts in the capacity of a qualified alienist when she is not. If it turns into a case of criminal insanity, she may find herself in the witness box, and she would be torn apart by a prosecuting attorney. She could even be prosecuted herself for practicing medicine without a license."

"I think she knows that, Daniel. But we've been asked to meet the girl, and Gus values my opinion, so I think we should go."

Daniel sighed. "I'm finally back in my own bedroom with my beloved wife, and all we do is talk about criminal cases. I should have opted for a young miss who embroidered samplers."

"You'd have been bored with her in ten minutes." I went to give him a mock slap and he caught my wrist, holding me close to him. I felt my pulse quicken at his nearness, then reminded myself rapidly about the state of my ribs.

"But it is lovely to finally be back here. I was ungrateful the last time we spoke, Daniel. You did a tremendous job and it's all perfect. I'm so glad to be home and in bed with you beside me."

"It's a pity you have damaged ribs or I'd take that as an invitation," he said with a smile, "but given the circumstances, I think a kiss will have to suffice."

And he planted his lips firmly on mine. I waited for the usual arousal I felt in such circumstances, but my head was still buzzing with too many worries. As Daniel draped an arm over me and fell asleep, I found myself thinking about Bridie, and a brilliant idea came to me. Bridie's father's family lived somewhere in the Lower East Side. Her father's cousin Nuala was one of the most unpleasant women you'd ever meet, and her sons were the worst sort of ragamuffin. There was even a rumor that they were now affiliated with one of the street gangs. Not the sort of relatives you'd want. But it came to me that these boys might be ideal for getting information out of a younger child. If I paid them well enough, perhaps they could do what Daniel thought impossible, and find out who gave a note to a street urchin to be delivered to police headquarters.

I gave a little smile of satisfaction at the thought of delivering such news to Daniel. Then I snuggled up against him, feeling the comforting warmth of his body against mine, and fell asleep.

❦ Thirteen ❧

M rs. Hamilton lived in a comfortable neighborhood just east of Gramercy Park. I looked out of the hansom cab with interest as we passed that square, with its gardens surrounded by elegant homes, and fond memories came back to me.

"I was once locked in the gardens here," I said to Sid and Gus.

"When you were working on a case and chasing a criminal?" Sid asked, her eyes lighting up.

"When I was pushing an old woman in a bath chair," I replied. "I worked for a while as a companion to a crotchety old woman, Miss Van Woekem. She lives in that house over there. I grew quite fond of her, after that rocky start. I hadn't realized you needed to bring a key to let yourself out of the gardens. She wasn't at all amused at being locked in there for hours."

Sid and Gus chuckled. "You've had a colorful life, I'll say that for you," Gus said.

"Oh, I've had a colorful life? I like that," I retorted. "What about you two? I've never turned my living room into a Mongolian yurt."

"We just play at things," Gus said. "We've never taken anything too seriously, until now. I think what we went through in France rather shook us up and sobered us a little. I took my studies in Vienna seriously enough, didn't I, Sid?"

"You did. I rather wish you'd stayed on. You might have made a major contribution to the study of diseases of the mind."

"There is still time to pursue my studies over here," Gus said. "I'm now realizing how little I actually learned in such a vast field. I have to confess I'm having serious misgivings about seeing this young girl. I'm not a doctor. Could I be doing more harm than good?"

"I mentioned it to Daniel. He was concerned that if it ever came to a court case, you could be called as a witness, and even prosecuted for practicing medicine without a license, he said."

"A court case?" Gus said. "I'd hate to think of a young girl being dragged into court, especially after what she's already gone through."

"We don't know the circumstances yet, do we, Gus?" I said gently as the cab passed the square and proceeded along Twentieth Street. "We have to consider that she could be guilty of setting the fire. I'm sure we'll make a better judgment after we've spoken with her."

"We've written to Professor Freud asking for advice," Sid said. "Gus will meet the girl and is certainly capable of making a preliminary assessment as to whether she has deep-seated mental problems that are beyond her capabilities."

The cab came to a halt outside a row of well-kept brownstones. To me they epitomized comfortable middle-class prosperity, and the thought crossed my mind that Mrs. Hamilton hadn't done too badly for herself. If she hinted that her deceased sister-in-law had taken a step down in the world by marrying Mr. Hamilton's brother, then Susan must indeed have come from the realms of the Four Hundred.

We were helped down from the cab and mounted the flight of steps to a green-painted front door. It was opened by a maid, and we were led through into a front parlor. Here the air of elegance and obviously good furniture was spoiled by subtle hints that this was a household of four boys. The carpet and sofa were a little the worse for wear. There were lead soldiers lying under one of the chairs. Before we could take a seat Mrs. Hamilton herself appeared. She looked flustered, with wisps of hair escaping from her bun.

"Miss Walcott, Miss Goldfarb, Mrs. Sullivan. How very good of you to come, and so rapidly too. I must apologize about the state of the place. The boys were playing at war and I've just had to banish them to the nursery with threats of dire consequences if they dare to make a noise or show their faces."

We smiled with understanding as she went on, talking quickly and with agitation. "Mabel had another of her nightmares last night and I insisted that she keep to her bed today. So perhaps you wouldn't mind coming upstairs to see her?"

"Does she know we are coming, and why we are here?" Sid asked.

"I informed her that some ladies wanted to see if they could help her with her bad dreams and she put up no resistance. In fact she has been no trouble since she came here. She has always struck me as such a sweet child, which is why . . . " She broke off as her voice choked up.

We went up a broad flight of carpeted stairs, then a second flight, narrower and not carpeted. Mrs. Hamilton went ahead of us. "I'll just make sure she is not sleeping," she said in a low whisper. She tapped on the door, then put her head around it. "Mabel, dear, are you awake?"

"Yes, Aunt Minnie," we heard a little voice say.

"I've brought some ladies to see you," Mrs. Hamilton said gently and ushered us into the room.

My first impression of Mabel was that I was looking at a French bisque doll with enormous blue eyes and corn-colored hair. She was so pale that she almost merged into the whiteness of the pillows behind her head. She sat up and looked at us with apprehension as we crowded into her small bedroom.

"Hello, Mabel." Gus took the initiative. "I'm Miss Walcott, and these are my friends Miss Goldfarb and Mrs. Sullivan. Your aunt asked us to come because of the nightmares you've been having since the awful tragedy. Your aunt wondered if I could help you, as I've been learning how to interpret dreams."

"My aunt told me," Mabel said.

"May I sit down?" Gus said, pulling up a chair beside the bed. "And my friends can sit on the window seat in the sun, unless you'd prefer that they wait in another room while we have our talk?"

"It's all right. They can stay," Mabel said in a resigned voice.

We sat. Shafts of sunlight painted stripes on the flowered wallpaper, highlighting the only color in the otherwise white room.

I could tell that Gus didn't know how to begin.

"Mabel," I said. "We were so sorry to learn about your parents. What an awful thing to have lived through. It's no wonder you are having bad dreams. I did too, after my house burned down."

She turned to look at me, trying to sum up whether my words were genuine.

"Your house burned down too?" she asked.

I nodded.

"Did anyone die? Anyone not get out?"

"Our little servant girl," I said. "She died protecting my son. It still haunts me. I think I know a little how you feel."

She sat in silence for a while and then said, "I can't believe they are gone. I just didn't believe it when Aunt Minnie told me. I mean, not my papa. How could it be? He was so big and strong. I keep expecting to hear the front door slam and his big voice yelling, 'Where's my Princess Mabel?'"

She looked down at her sheet, smoothing it with a tiny white hand. "I keep asking myself how I could get out when he didn't."

"You don't remember getting out?" Gus said. "Maybe there was a fire escape outside your window and not outside theirs?"

She shook her head. "It was the other way around. The fire escape was outside their window, not mine. And I don't remember anything at all. Not the fire. Not getting out. Nothing, until I woke up and these faces were over me and someone said 'She's alive. God be praised.'"

"So how do you think you got out?" Gus asked.

"I've no idea. Unless I walked in my sleep."

"Do you walk in your sleep sometimes?" Gus asked.

"Sometimes. I used to more when I was little. But how could I not have woken up if there was a fire and flames all around me?"

"Mabel, is it possible that you walked in your sleep and . . . " I started to say, then shut up again. "No, never mind. It's not important." I had been going to ask whether she might have knocked over her parents' oil lamp by accident, or even lit a match, tried to light a fire, and all without knowing it. But I realized as I said it that this was a burden I couldn't lay on her. She was already carrying enough guilt because she had lived and they had not.

There was another awkward silence that seemed to go on forever.

"Tell me about your mother, Mabel," Sid said. "You must miss her dreadfully."

Mabel pressed her lips together and I could tell she was willing herself not to cry. "Mama was so soft and gentle. She always used to braid my hair for me. Aunt Minnie never does it right and she jerks my head with the hairbrush. Mama never did. And she let me come into her room and sleep on the daybed when I had bad dreams."

"Have you always had bad dreams?" Gus asked.

"I've had them sometimes, you know, the way one does. But not like this. These are so vivid and horrible, and when I wake up I don't know whether I'm awake or asleep, or what is real and what is not."

"Can you tell me about any of them?" Gus asked.

"It's hard." Mabel looked flustered now. "They are so real at the time, but when I try to remember, it's all so unclear."

"Tell me about the first one," Gus said gently. "What is the one thing you remember—the one thing that made you afraid?"

"The snake," Mabel said firmly. "There is always the snake."

"You dream of a snake?"

"A giant snake," Mabel said. "So big that it fills the room and looms over me."

"What does this snake look like?" Gus asked.

Mabel shuddered. "It's shiny and it has eyes like slits and it rises up over me, and . . . "

"Is it red?" Gus asked.

Mabel shook her head. "It's all black, and I see these eyes looking down at me, and it bends nearer and nearer and . . . " She stopped, shuddering. "I don't want to go on," she said. "It's too horrible."

"Does the snake try to bite you?" Gus asked.

"I said I don't want to go on," Mabel said, more firmly now.

"I know this is upsetting for you, Mabel, but I am trying to help. So tell me, is the snake always in the nightmares?" Gus asked.

Mabel frowned. Then she said, "I think so. Yes, but I don't want to talk about it anymore. I can see his eyes. They are just slits, but they glint when he looks at me, as if he is pleased."

"I would like to help you," Gus said, "but I can't unless you describe the dreams in detail to me."

"No." She was shaking her head violently. "No. I don't want to remember."

"I'm afraid the nightmares will continue until we can decipher what they mean," Gus said gently. "Usually once we unlock the symbols in such dreams, they go away. You want that, don't you? You want to be free of them."

"Yes, but I can't . . . "

"I have an idea," Gus said. "Why don't you write down what you remember of the dreams, at your leisure, when we're not here? When you have another dream, write it down as soon as you wake up, when it's still real and vivid to you. Because, you see, we now think that our dreams are symbols. So any small detail that you can remember may be the key."

"The key to what?" Mabel asked.

"To what happened on the night of the fire."

"We know what happened," Mabel said. "There was a fire. My parents got burned up. I escaped and they didn't."

Gus stood up. "We should go now," she said. "But I'd like to come back again, if I may, to see what you've remembered and written down. It might be very helpful, Mabel. I suspect you'll go on having the dreams until we can figure out what they mean."

We were about to leave when we heard heavy footsteps coming up the stairs. Mrs. Hamilton came in, looking rather flustered. "Mabel, dear, you have another visitor," she said. "I tried to tell him that you weren't well enough to receive visitors today, but . . . "

And a big, blond-haired man wearing the New York police uniform pushed past her into the room. He looked absurdly young to be a policeman, like a chubby, overgrown schoolboy.

"Hello, Mabel," he said. "I'm back again for another little chat. Wanting to see if you've anything more to tell me. If your memory has returned."

He looked around, suddenly taking in the three of us. "Hello, what have we got here?" he said. "Having a little party, are you? And your aunt saying you were too weak to receive visitors." He smirked. I took an instant dislike to him.

"I think she meant outsiders," Sid said, glancing across at Mrs. Hamilton. "That doesn't apply to family and friends." She went across to him, extending her hand. "I am Elena Goldfarb. Mrs. Hamilton was at Vassar with us. We are old, old friends."

"Lieutenant Yeats," the blond man said. "New York police. And I'm glad to see that Mabel is now well enough to receive old, old friends of the family. Being among old friends may well have jogged her memory, eh, Mabel?" He looked from one of us to the next. "So has she decided to confide in any of you what happened on the night of the fire?"

"Lieutenant Yeats," Mrs. Hamilton said severely. "How many more times do I have to tell you that the child remembers nothing?"

"Conveniently for her, so it would seem," he said. "So your memory hasn't returned yet, Mabel? You still don't know how you came to be lying on the ground, apparently asleep, while your house was burning?"

"I told you, I don't know." Mabel's voice trembled. "Why don't you believe me? Why do you keep coming back like this? Make him go away, Aunt Minnie."

"You only upset her," Mrs. Hamilton said angrily. "After all that she's been through, do you want her mind to snap completely?"

Gus stepped out between the policeman and the girl. "Officer Yeats," she said. "I am Augusta Walcott, a friend of the family. I have also just returned from Vienna where I have been studying the problems of the mind with Professor Freud. I can tell you quite categorically that it would not be at all unusual for someone to experience complete amnesia after such a traumatic event. If you want Mabel to remember what happened that night, I suggest you let her recover in complete peace and tranquility. In her own time, she may be able to tell us more. But she certainly won't if she's being bullied and threatened."

"Listen," Yeats said. "I can have her taken down to the Tombs and kept there until her memory returns, if I like."

"On what charge?" It was my turn to step forward now.

"A charge of arson, ma'am. Setting fire to a house with the intention of doing away with her parents."

"And what proof do you have of this, other than the fact that she escaped and they didn't?" I tried to control my anger.

"I don't need proof," he said. "Let's just call it a gut instinct. Oh, and the fact that everyone else in the house, even the ones who escaped, had blackened clothing and faces and singed hair. And Mabel showed no sign of having been in a fire at all. So this leads me to believe that she got out before the fire started. The question then would be why? And how did she know there was going to be a fire?"

I glanced across at Mabel, who was looking away, her eyes screwed tightly shut. I took a deep breath. "I don't think we should be discussing this in front of the child. We are only causing her more distress. Miss Goldfarb has just told you that she has been studying with leading alienists in Vienna. If anyone can break through the girl's amnesia, she can. Why don't we give her time to do her work, and then we might know the truth, rather than stabbing at it in the dark?"

He heard my Irish accent and frowned. "And are you another old friend of the family?"

"Actually no," I said. "I am an old friend of these two ladies, who invited me to come with them today. They thought I might be useful because my husband is a colleague of yours in the police force."

"Oh, yes?" There was that hint of a smirk again.

"Captain Sullivan," I said, and I noticed with great satisfaction that his smirk vanished.

"What an obnoxious man," Sid said as we rode home in a cab. "It was all I could do not to hit him."

"I felt the same way," I said. "I was so delighted to tell him that my husband was his superior in the police department."

"That probably saved that child's bacon," Sid said. "You heard what that policeman said. He was all ready to haul Mabel off to the Tombs. Such barbaric behavior. One wonders how someone like that ever got promoted to lieutenant."

"I'm afraid the police department rather rewards aggressive bullying," I said. "Daniel is one of the exceptions, but then you should see him when he's dealing with a gang member. He's quite frightening. I hardly recognize him as my husband."

"Yes, but Daniel would never bully a frightened child," Gus said. "The poor little thing is so fragile to start with."

"Of course he does have a point," Sid said.

We looked at her sharply.

"Well, if you were in his shoes, you would have to wonder, wouldn't you? Why was she the only one who showed no signs of having been in the fire?" When we didn't answer, she continued, "You think she has buried the horror of that night deep in her subconscious, don't you, Gus? But if she got out before the fire, would she have experienced any horror? She would never have seen her parents burned."

"Unless something had happened to her parents first," I said slowly. They both turned to me. "I suppose we have to consider that it's just possible she did kill her parents, then set their room on fire, exiting down the fire escape outside their window." I shook my head quickly. "I don't want to believe that, and I find it hard to believe, but we do need to find out what made her leave the house unscathed by the fire."

"But she loved her parents," Gus said. "You could tell from the way she talked about them. Her father called her his Princess Mabel. Her mother braided her hair. She is devastated by their death."

"What if it was a horrible accident, and she's dealing with deep-seated guilt?" Sid said. "What if she went into their room and by mistake knocked over a lamp? Then the flames went up between her and the door, so she escaped the only way she could, down the fire escape?"

"Which still doesn't explain why she didn't wake her parents and let them escape too," I said. "If she'd knocked over the lamp she'd have screamed. They'd have awakened. All would have escaped safely, even if the fire couldn't be extinguished." I paused, letting them digest this. "No, there's something not right here. There was a reason her parents burned in their beds. I think it's possible they were killed first."

"By Mabel?" Gus asked.

"I hope not, unless she's got some kind of demonic possession or evil other self, like one reads about in books."

"Dual personalities are apparently a documented phenomenon," Gus said.

"So were you able to make anything of her dream, Gus?" Sid asked. "A black snake that filled the room."

"I'm afraid I'm in the dark about that," Gus said. "Unless the nameless monster we all have in our dreams takes on the form of a snake for her, and just symbolizes danger."

"Why did you ask her if the snake was red?" Sid asked.

"Because I thought she might be using it as a symbol for the fire—tongues of red reaching out for her, rising to fill the room. But she was quite definite that it was black. And it had frightening slit eyes that looked down at her."

"I noticed something interesting," I interjected. "She said 'his' eyes. She talked of the snake as 'it' to begin with, but then she made it masculine."

"That is interesting," Gus said. "Let's hope she is able to write down more details of future nightmares. I feel very strongly that they may unlock the mystery for us."

"Professor Freud would probably say that the snake was a symbol of masculinity," Sid commented. "That dreaming of a snake was normal at the time of puberty."

"He probably would say that," Gus agreed. "But Mabel wouldn't be terrified by it unless she had reason to fear her awakening sexuality. And we know she's been sheltered."

"There is always her father," Sid said.

There was a sudden silence in the cab, and the rhythmic *clip-clop* of the horse's hoofs sounded unnaturally loud.

"You don't think her father tried to . . . " I said, not able to finish the sentence.

"It does happen," Gus replied.

"So he tried to interfere with her and she killed him?" Even as I said the words I dismissed them in my own mind. Mabel had loved her father; that much was evident. There had been no hesitation when she spoke of either of her parents. It struck me that we were looking for an unknown factor, but at this moment I had no idea what it was.

❦ Fourteen ❦

By the time we reached home my ribs were aching from the constant jolting over cobbles. My mother-in-law took one look at me and ordered me up to bed.

"I told you it was too soon for you to be running around," she said. "The only thing that can heal ribs is rest. Now, you go and lie down and I'll bring you up some of the soup I've just made."

For once I allowed myself to be bossed like this.

"Where is Liam?" I asked as I hauled myself up the stairs. "Has he been good?"

"Like a little angel. He's just fallen asleep, but Bridie's been amusing him all morning, and you should hear him laughing and cooing. It delights the heart to hear such sounds. He needs company, now that he's growing up. It's time you gave him a little brother or sister and stopped running around with those women across the street."

"He's only a year old," I said.

"That's right. Eighteen months between babies is ideal, that's what they always used to say, and you're already running a bit late on that."

I almost asked why she was giving me advice on going forth and being fruitful when she had only managed to produce one child herself. But I remembered Daniel had said it was a sore subject for her, and she didn't like to talk about it.

"Your friends across the street," she said, following me into the bedroom and peering out of the window. "No doubt they are still into championing votes for women and that kind of thing."

"Yes, they are," I replied.

She sniffed, then gave me a long hard stare. "I'm wondering if your friendship with them may not be the best thing for your husband's career."

"What on earth has our friendship got to do with Daniel?" I demanded.

"If he were to run for office some day, such a friendship could well be held against him."

"But Sid and Gus are wonderful people. They are kind, and caring, and amusing, and cultured. You couldn't want for better friends," I said, trying to check my rising anger.

She patted my hand. "You've led a sheltered life, my dear, and you probably don't realize the full implications, but such friendships are not natural. When I was young, romantic friendships among young women were accepted, even encouraged. But that was only until a suitable match could be made. Two women living together like that . . . it's just not right. What will your children think, when they are old enough to notice?"

"They'll think that Auntie Sid and Auntie Gus seem to have a lot of fun at their house," I said. "Which is what I think too. And if they choose not to marry, that's up to them." I sat on the bed and started to unbutton my shirtwaist. "You mentioned something about soup?" I added, closing the conversation.

I got up after a long nap and had tea in the kitchen. Sid and Gus were not mentioned again. I knew that Daniel was not thrilled about my association with them, but this was one area where I chose to ignore all criticism. Sid and Gus were my dear friends, and that was all that mattered.

Being Friday, Mother Sullivan cooked cod with a white sauce for dinner, and miraculously Daniel arrived home in time to join us. It seemed that having his mother here was a good influence on him.

"How's my invalid?" he asked.

"Not improving through rushing all over the place this morning," Mother Sullivan said before I could answer, as she brought the pie to the table. "You should have seen her earlier. Pale as death she was, and clearly suffering."

"You exaggerate," I said. "I went out for an hour with Sid and Gus to visit friends. Hardly exhausting, and I'm feeling just fine now."

"Take it slowly, Molly," Daniel said, giving me a long look. "These things can't be rushed."

"I'm fine, really I am," I said. I spooned food onto a plate and passed it to Daniel, then to Bridie. "How is the case coming along? Have they discovered any clues about the train crash yet?"

"Nothing at all." He shook his head, but there was a warning look in his eyes that said we should say nothing more in front of his mother. "I take it your little jaunt with the neighbor ladies today was to visit the young girl you told me about."

"Yes, it was. It was rather disturbing, as a matter of fact. The girl claims to remember nothing but is having horrendous dreams, dreams that upset her so much that she was shaking and couldn't even talk about them. Gus has asked her to write them down as soon as they happen, as that might be less distressing than having to recount them."

"And Gus thinks she can analyze the dreams and thus cure the girl?"

"That's what she hopes," I said.

"What's all this? Your friend has turned into a fortune-teller now, has she?" Daniel's mother asked.

"No, remember I told you that she's been studying in Vienna with Professor Freud?"

Mother Sullivan sniffed. "Professor Freud! Smut merchant Freud, if you ask me. Mrs. Hennessy at church was saying that he's trying to make out we're all depraved, with unnatural desires. I'm afraid it only goes to confirm my opinion of your friends, Molly."

"So you think it's a better idea to lock mad people away in asylums, rather than try to find out what's ailing them and try to help them?" I asked. "I've been in one of those places. They are the closest thing to hell you could find."

"You were in an asylum?" she asked nervously. "For what reason?"

"I was trying to trace a missing girl, back when I ran my detective agency," I said. "I discovered her there, quite sane but put there by evil people."

"Mercy me," she said.

"Anyway, Professor Freud might have some strange ideas, but a lot of good will come from the study of the mind, I feel sure. And lately he's turned his attention to the study of dreams. He's written a treatise on dream interpretation. Gus has been telling me about it. It sounds fascinating."

Mother Sullivan laughed. "The old Irishwomen were always interpreting dreams when I was a girl. Dream of a black cow and you were going to come into money or get married or something. That kind of rubbish."

"They did the same where I come from," I said. "They reckoned some people could dream the future—and maybe they were right and some people could. We always prized ourselves on our second sight. But this is different. Gus says that we sometimes express what is troubling us in our innermost souls through symbols in our dreams."

"I dream that I'm flying," Bridie chimed in. "I'm flying and I'm looking for water and I'm going really fast because I know it's a long way, but if I can only spot the water, I'll be all right."

"I think even I can interpret that one," I said. "You're looking for the Panama Canal and hoping to see your father and brother."

"Looking for Da and Shamey? Maybe you're right, Molly," Bridie said. "I'm that worried about them. I do wish they'd write to me. Just once."

"I'm sure they will, when they get somewhere they can post a letter," Mrs. Sullivan said kindly, but she shot me a look telling me to leave this subject alone.

I thought about suggesting to Bridie that we pay a visit to her disreputable relatives in case they had any news, but it didn't seem the right moment to do so. I was sure Daniel would forbid such an outing at the moment and besides, I hoped to pull off a satisfying little coup. Even as I said this, I felt ashamed of myself. I'd be using Bridie to score a point and prove to Daniel that I was just as good a detective as he. *Why must I still see myself in competition with him?* I wondered. Shouldn't I be content to be a wife and mother?

"So Augusta has been analyzing this girl's dreams, has she?" Daniel asked. "Any luck?"

"No, Mabel wouldn't tell us much. Just something about a large snake, and its eyes, and how it loomed over her. She was terrified."

"Do you think there was an element of insanity there? You thought before you saw her that perhaps she'd killed her parents."

"I wondered how she managed to escape from a fire when they didn't. Now I'm even more confused. Apparently she showed no signs of ever being in the fire—no blackened face or singed garments, nothing. And the fire escape was right outside her parents' bedroom. So I have to think that something must have happened to them to make them unable to climb out of their window. But as to Mabel killing her parents—I find that hard to believe. She seems like such a sweet, gentle creature, and she clearly loved them both."

"During my fifteen years in the department," Daniel said as he reached out for another slice of bread and began buttering it, "I have found it impossible to tell who looks like a murderer and who doesn't. Little old ladies who calmly poisoned their siblings or their lodgers. And seemingly sane young people who did away with their parents, then absolutely denied it against irrefutable evidence. What do the police think?"

"Don't get me started on the police," I said angrily, as I held my fork poised in midair with a mouthful of fish on it. "An unpleasant young lieutenant is in charge, and he's convinced that she killed her parents and is only feigning amnesia. But he was such a bully that I'm afraid I took an instant dislike to him."

"Really? What is his name?"

"Yeats," I said. "He looks awfully young, and he seems to possess no skills when it comes to dealing with the general public. He was rude to each of us."

Daniel smiled. "Ah, yes. Yeats. I know about him. His father is a big wheel at Tammany and the boy is destined for politics. I agree. He is an unpleasant little toad, far too keen to make his mark quickly. But then I suppose I was that way myself when I first started. The desire to get that first conviction in a murder case is very strong, as you remember, Mother."

"I do indeed, both with you and your father. Remember how furious you were whenever one of yours got off on a technicality, or pleaded insanity?"

Daniel nodded. "It's only when you witness an execution for the first time that you realize what a terrible power you have, and a glimmer of doubt creeps in. Right before they pull the switch to turn on the current, you find yourself wondering if you've made a mistake and are killing an innocent person."

"I'm sure Yeats would have no such qualms," I said. "He seemed really pleased with himself. He threatened to have Mabel locked up in the Tombs to make her remember. Can you stop him from doing that, Daniel?"

"It's not my case and he doesn't report to me," Daniel said. "But I can have a little chat with him and suggest that he needs to make sure of his facts before he talks about wilful murder. He'd need some kind of proof, not just a hunch."

"You mean some kind of evidence in the bodies? But they'll have been buried for a month or more. Will anyone give permission to have the bodies exhumed?"

"If it's a question of someone being arrested for murder. Yeats would have no case without physical evidence."

"Can you find evidence in burned and charred bodies?" I asked. "I know you might be able to see a gunshot or a stab wound, but what about poison?"

Daniel considered before speaking, staring out past the kitchen door. "I think a good pathologist could detect something obvious like arsenic in the tissue."

"But if someone had turned on the gas while they slept? Or if they had been smothered, for example?"

Daniel gave a half snort, half chuckle. "I can't answer that one, Molly. We can tell a person has been smothered by the broken blood vessels in the eyes and the flush on the face, but if the face is badly charred?" He shook his head. "I'd think not. But you're not suggesting that a young girl could smother both her parents? They'd struggle. The other would wake up. You need considerable strength to smother someone."

Mrs. Sullivan gave a little grunt of what I took to be disapproval.

"I'm sorry," I said. "Do you have everything you need? Some more beans?"

"No, thank you," she said stiffly. "Sit up straight, Bridie."

We sat for a moment in silence. But I couldn't leave well enough alone. I had to make the most of having Daniel to talk to, for once. "Well, I'm thankful you're going to put pressure on that obnoxious Yeats person to exhume the bodies. At least then we'll know more."

Daniel drained his beer glass and put it down. "You realize that might not go well for your young girl," he said. "If it transpires that her parents were killed or drugged first, it will be assumed that she did it. It will be taken as proof that she's guilty."

"Unless the form of death was impossible for a young girl to carry out."

Daniel's eyebrows raised. "You are now talking of killing by person or persons unknown? That has never been mentioned before, has it?"

"No, it hasn't," I said.

"So you're now suggesting that a stranger managed to gain access to a house that had servants in it, made his way upstairs, and killed two people in their beds, before setting fire to the house? What would the motive be, Molly, since this possibility has never come up before?"

"I don't know," I said. "But maybe I should have a talk with Mrs. Hamilton, the girl's aunt. She might know of a family feud, or another reason that someone might have wanted Mabel's parents dead."

Daniel shook his head. "It would take a significant family feud to cause someone to kill two people before setting fire to their house. That sort of thing doesn't normally happen to respectable middle-class people."

"It happened to us," I said. "I would never have believed it either, but it did happen to us."

"My circumstances are rather different," Daniel said. "I was dealing with a ruthless gang at the time. They were trying to teach me a lesson. What did Mabel's father do? What was his profession?"

"I don't know, but it was something respectable and middle class, I expect. Mrs. Hamilton didn't mention it. But Mabel's mother came from a wealthy banking family. Her name was Susan Masters. Does that mean anything to you?"

"Masters?" He paused. "Of Deveraux and Masters? Yes, I'm familiar with that firm. Merchant bankers on Wall Street, I think. But banking is usually only a dangerous profession if one is the clerk behind the counter at the time of a robbery." He grinned. Then his face became serious again. "I think you should leave well enough alone, Molly," he said. "And besides, this speculation does not address the primary piece of evidence—how did the girl escape without any signs of having been in a fire?"

Daniel's mother put down her fork with a clatter. "Is the dinner table conversation in this family always to be about murders?" she asked. "It's most unhealthy for young Bridie, and not too good for my digestion either."

"I don't mind," Bridie said. "I think it's exciting."

"It's quite unsuitable for a young girl like you," Mother Sullivan said firmly. "In my day dinner table conversation centered on socially acceptable subjects like balls, and parties, and . . . "

"And scandals, Mother," Daniel said. "Don't forget I've been at enough of your dinner parties to know that the conversation often touched on infidelity and other delicate topics."

"Really, Daniel." Mrs. Sullivan sniffed in indignation. Daniel and I exchanged a knowing grin and went back to our food. Later, when we were alone in the privacy of our bedroom, he said to me, "I really want to warn you about getting involved in your friends' problem. You have no experience with insanity and the forms it can take. I have seen people who appear to be quite normal one moment and raging demons the next. It is out of your league and your friends' too. And from what I know of young Yeats, you might well find yourself locked in the Tombs for obstructing justice."

"He's a horrid man, Daniel. I just hate to see that young girl bullied by him," I replied. "The very least you could do is to suggest the exhumation. Then Mabel couldn't be arrested until the results are known. And by then, Gus may have found a qualified alienist, who would be taken seriously in court, to treat her." I pulled my nightgown over my head and slid into bed.

"Enough about murders and courts," he said. "I come home to let the cares of the day slip away, not to discuss them into the night." And he climbed into bed beside me.

"I'm sorry," I said. "But you know me. I can't help being interested."

"You can't help wanting to stick your nose into any criminal case." He laughed. "You are still not prepared to stop being a detective. I know you too well, Molly Murphy."

"I only want to see justice done," I said. I smoothed down the covers and turned to look at Daniel. "And speaking of criminal cases," I went on, "have you started making a list of your own cases—ones that ended with the death penalty and might have made your note writer seek revenge against you?"

"I have started, yes, but frankly I don't see where it's going to help. Most of the cases I've come up with were clear-cut. A man killed his wife with an ax. Found with blood all over his clothes, even admitted his guilt. That sort of thing." He sat up in bed, propping a pillow behind his head. "But I've been giving some thought to what you said about some of the murders being random, to hide the real one for which the killer had a motive. That might make sense, Molly."

"It might well," I agreed. "That first victim, the simple old woman. He could have seen her and decided that she was of no use to society, and therefore her death wouldn't matter. If he was testing himself, trying out how easy it was to kill someone, then she'd have been a likely target. She was too simple to know she was being followed, and probably not as aware as other people of the approaching streetcar."

"So you're saying that he killed her simply to see how easy it is to kill someone?"

I nodded. "And the second murder might have been for the same reason. How easy was it to walk through a crowded student café, and drop cyanide into a coffee cup without anyone noticing?"

"But then your system breaks down," Daniel said. "The murders after that are no longer opportunistic, or in public places. He had to gain access to private homes. He poisoned. He even entered a bathroom where a woman was taking a bath. Surely her screams must have been heard? And what about the man in the meat safe? Wouldn't it have taken brute strength to force him in and lock the door? If only one of those killings has a clear motive, then why are the others so unnecessarily complicated? Why flirt with failure like that? Servants could have apprehended him in the judge's house. The woman's screams could have been heard when a man entered her bathroom. And he might not have been strong enough to force the butcher into the meat safe."

I sat up now too and wagged an excited finger at him. "I've just heard one word that might make sense of this. Judge. I asked you about your trials that led to execution or death. What if he's also taking his revenge against a judge? You can narrow down your search, Daniel. Have you ever brought someone to trial who was then sentenced by that particular judge?"

"I believe I have, but it would have been early in my career. He's almost eighty. He retired from the bench some time ago. Let me think about it. . . ." He paused, frowning. At the end of our quiet little street, I heard the bells of a fire truck as it left the Jefferson Market fire station. In the city, there was a constant reminder that danger was never far away.

Daniel shook his head as he reached to turn down the gaslight. "I do remember a couple of trials, but neither one resulted in the death penalty. And I also remember that this particular judge was known to be soft. A kind-hearted old man who would avoid sentencing someone to death if he could."

We both lay back against the pillows.

"We don't seem to be getting anywhere, do we?" Daniel said. "And there is still the threat of his last note—he still wants to kill one more time." He turned to me and kissed me gently. "But it's not your worry, Molly. Go to sleep, and sweet dreams."

But I didn't have sweet dreams. Instead I was in that dark, confined space again, lying there unable to move, listening to the drip of water and a strange rumbling. And I knew I had to get out before it was too late.

Fifteen

The next morning I awoke with a headache. Daniel's mother appeared at my door with a cup of tea.

"Daniel said you had a bad night, moaning in your sleep," she said. "He told me to tell you to stay home and rest. You could be suffering from delayed concussion after your accident, you know. And shock. One can't be too careful with these things."

She insisted I have breakfast in bed. I sat up, eating my boiled egg and looking out of the window at the deserted street. Doing nothing did not come easily to me, especially when there were so many questions to be answered. I was itching to find out whether anyone could have had a motive to kill Mabel's parents, and how easy it would have been to gain access to their house. But I told myself I could wait until the bodies were exhumed and an autopsy was performed. If it was confirmed that they died as a result of the fire, then there was no more to be done. It could never be proved that Mabel started that fire deliberately and then got out.

I lay back in bed and thought about the dream that had been troubling me. The dark, confined space. The drip of water. The strange rumbling. And the awful feeling of doom. Were they taking me back to that train crash, when I was trapped in the car, or did they mean something more? In the dream, I definitely felt trapped. I knew I had to escape before something terrible happened. In Ireland we'd take such a dream as a warning, a portent of something bad about to happen. At home we believed very strongly in psychic powers and the sixth sense. I'd often thought that I had it myself, until it let me down and didn't warn me of the worst thing that had happened in my life. But Gus would say that the symbols in my dream represented deep-seated fears from my own life. The fear of being trapped? Of no escape? I shook my head. But I didn't feel trapped. I loved my life and my husband and child. Was the dream maybe a flashback to a time when I had been trapped somewhere? I tried to go over my many adventures as a detective. Yes, there were times I had been in danger, but they no longer haunted me. I'd have to ask Gus and see what she could tell me.

I lay back and tried to sleep, but sleep wouldn't come and my head throbbed. So I got up and held a hot washcloth to my temples. I actually felt better when I was up and moving around, so I dressed and went downstairs to find Bridie and Liam rolling a ball to each other down the length of the hallway. "Ba!" Liam said excitedly. "Ba!"

It seems he was learning new words almost every day now, and I beamed at him with pride.

"Yes, it's a ball, isn't it? You like playing with Bridie, don't you?"

"Ba!" Liam said again, impatient for her to roll the ball back to him.

How nice it would be to be a child again, I thought. Not a care in the world except playing, eating, and sleeping. Then I remembered that Mabel was little more than a child, and she carried a terrible burden around with her. I wondered if she would ever be free of it.

Mrs. Sullivan looked up from the kitchen, her hands and apron white with flour. "I thought I'd make a stew and dumplings today. It was always one of Daniel's favorites." Then a frown crossed her face. "But what are you doing out of bed? Daniel said you were supposed to rest and do nothing until you recovered from the accident."

"I feel better when I'm up than when I was lying down," I said. "Can I help?"

"No, you cannot. You go through to the parlor and put your feet up. All that rushing around and excitement yesterday was clearly too much for you. Fires and murder, indeed. I never let my husband bring his work home with him. If he ever tried to mention a case he was working on, he got a black look from me, and he hushed up again quickly."

"But I enjoy discussing Daniel's work with him," I said. "Remember I was a detective myself once. I might even be able to offer him some insight when he's dealing with a difficult case."

"You've a young child to think about now," she said, glancing at Liam chasing the ball. "Do you want him to grow up thinking that the world is full of murders and crimes? He's a right to think that the world is a safe and lovely place. It's up to a mother to create that kind of haven for her children."

She was right, of course. I certainly didn't want Liam growing up thinking that the world was full of danger. But then he'd been in danger himself already and didn't seem any the worse for it. Certainly no sign of the sort of bad dreams Mabel was experiencing. But I did take Mrs. Sullivan's point. From now on, any discussion of Daniel's cases would be when Liam was safely in bed.

My headache lingered through most of the morning, even after I'd drunk a cup of coffee. I had a suspicion that Sid's strong Turkish coffee might well do the trick. Normally I could hardly bear to swallow it, and the spoon almost stood upright in the cup, but today I needed it. However Mother Sullivan was so adamant that I lie and rest that I didn't want to risk creating a scene and incurring Daniel's wrath when he came home. I suppose I must have become meeker since my marriage.

I didn't feel like reading, and I never felt like sewing. I couldn't even concentrate on the list of things I needed to buy for the house, as Mabel's and Daniel's cases kept flashing through my mind. I was dying to get out and do something. I wondered if anyone had spoken to the firemen who were called on the night Mabel's parents died. Might they have seen anything strange? Since Mabel's parents' house had only been on Eleventh Street, and thus within easy walking distance of my home, the fire engine would probably have come from the Jefferson Market fire station, at the bottom of Patchin Place. And nobody could object to my stretching my legs that far.

I had just moved on to Daniel's case and was going through the list of victims again, trying to find anything they had in common, when to my delight, I heard a door slamming across the street and saw Sid and Gus heading in my direction. My mother-in-law responded to the knock on the front door and I heard her say, "No visitors today, I'm afraid. She overdid things yesterday and isn't feeling at all well."

That was too much for me. I got up from the sofa and went to the door. "That doesn't include my friends, Mother Sullivan. What I need now is cheering up, and I'm sure they can do just that. Do we have any coffee left in the pot?"

She shot me an angry look, but she let Sid and Gus come in and stalked off to the kitchen.

"Not what you'd call a warm welcome," Sid said in a low voice. "Is she really banning all visitors, or is it just we who are persona non grata? I have the feeling she disapproves of us."

"She was just doing what she thought was best for me," I said, just in case she was listening. "I really didn't feel well this morning. I also had a horrible dream last night. Maybe Gus can interpret it for me. I've actually had it a couple of times before."

"When did you start having it?" Gus asked.

"After the accident. When I was lying in the hospital."

"So it's not a long-term problem you've been dealing with."

"No." I took a deep breath, making myself recall the details of the dream. "I'm lying in a dark, confined space, and I can hear water dripping and there is a horrible rumbling all around me, and I know I have to get out before it's too late."

Gus looked at me and smiled. "I don't think that one is too hard to interpret, Molly. You were in a train crash. Didn't you say you passed out and when you came to your senses there were people lying on top of you? And I'm sure the rumbling was the motor of the train still running nearby. You're just reliving a moment of great terror, the way Mabel is."

"I suppose so," I said, "although in my dream it feels as if I'm underground, and I can't breathe properly."

"You were buried under bodies in the train, so your brain is playing with the notion of being buried," Gus said. "Now, what I want you to do, the next time you dream it, is to take control of it. Visualize a square of light in one corner and say to yourself, 'Why, there is a way out after all.'"

"One can really do that in a dream?" I asked.

"Oh, yes. And it's very effective. If you wake up after the nightmare, you make yourself go back to sleep, fall back into the dream, only this time you make it have a positive outcome. You face the monster. You stop the horse from running away with you. I'm told it really does work."

"I'll try," I said. "And of course it would make sense that I'm dreaming about my terror in the train crash."

"And you know you have to get out in a hurry because the car is hanging over the edge and might fall," Sid said.

"You're right." I beamed at both of them. "I feel so much better now."

We looked up as Mrs. Sullivan came in carrying a tray with coffee cups and cookies.

"That's very kind of you, Mrs. Sullivan," Gus said. "But you should have called us. There was no need for you to carry it through yourself."

"Oh, it was no trouble," she said as she put the tray down on the low table.

"Won't you come and join us?" I asked.

"No, thank you, dear. I've the lunch to prepare and I want young Bridie to keep up with her lessons. I've set her some arithmetic to do. She's not too keen on long division."

"We'd be happy to help with Bridie's lessons, wouldn't we, Sid?" Gus asked.

"No, thank you kindly. I'd rather do it myself," My mother-in-law said quickly. And she made a hasty retreat. Sid and Gus looked at each other and started to laugh.

"Obviously we'd be a corrupting influence on young Bridie," Sid muttered. She looked around. "So where is the divine Liam today?"

"Just went down for his morning nap," I said. "He's been playing so hard with Bridie that for once he was exhausted. Otherwise he resists naps these days."

"We were considering going back to see Mabel Hamilton today," Gus said, "and we wondered if you wanted to come with us. But, given the circumstances, you'd better not go anywhere today. We'll have to report back to you."

"Do you think Mabel will want to see you again so soon?" I asked. "She became so agitated yesterday. Will she be prepared to discuss her dreams this time?"

"Maybe not," Gus said. "But she might have dreamed again last night and written it down. I also wanted to pursue what she said about sleepwalking. That might be significant."

Sid looked at me as she put down her coffee cup. "Yesterday you started to ask her something about sleepwalking, Molly. What were you going to say?"

"I was about to suggest that she might have gone into her parents' room and knocked over a lamp in her sleep, or even tried to light the gas, and, being asleep, when something went wrong and flames shot up, she'd gotten out down the fire escape without waking." Then I shook my head. "But that's not possible, is it? She'd wake if she saw flames."

"I suppose it might be possible," Gus said. "If she is prone to episodes of deep sleepwalking. I gather such sufferers can do amazing things without waking. But that still doesn't explain why her parents didn't leap up immediately once they were conscious of the flames."

"I thought of that too," I said. "And also, I didn't want to lay an additional burden on Mabel by suggesting she might have caused the fire in her sleep. But I'm as curious as you are about why the parents didn't escape. Something must have prevented them. And if they were found in their beds, it really does suggest that someone had drugged them or even killed them first."

Gus sighed. "So you are really in agreement with that beastly detective, and believe that Mabel killed her parents and then started the fire to cover up her deed?"

"Not necessarily," I said. "We have to examine the possibility that somebody else killed her parents."

"But there were only two maids and a cook in the house, and one of them also was killed in the fire. The other two were burned."

"Then we have to consider an intruder," I said. "Daniel says he'll try to suggest that the bodies should be exhumed and an autopsy take place. But you could do something for me if you go to see Mabel today—you could find out her father's profession. Whether he had any known enemies, or feuds within the family. Ask tactfully, please, but we need to know whether Mrs. Hamilton suspects that someone had a reason to see Mabel's parents dead."

Sid looked up excitedly as she put down her coffee cup. "So what you are suggesting is that Mabel might have witnessed her parents' murder. And what she saw was so horrible that she has shut the memories of it deep inside her head?"

"I am considering that it could be a possibility," I said.

"The snake." Sid looked at Gus. "Is it possible she really did see a snake? Someone brought a poisonous snake into the room and induced it to bite both parents?"

"How horrible." Gus shivered. "Can snakes be trained to bite on command? Wouldn't the parents have woken and cried out if a great snake had struck at them?"

"If someone else was in the room," I began, trying to picture the scene, "he could have repositioned their bodies in their beds before he set the room on fire."

"But that leaves another question," Sid said. "If Mabel saw this, why didn't he kill her too?"

"He didn't see her," Gus suggested. "She tiptoed away and escaped down the fire escape. Perhaps she feigned sleep so he wouldn't harm her. Perhaps she really passed out with terror."

I looked at Gus and nodded. "That sounds possible," I said. "And I had another idea. I wonder if anybody ever questioned the firemen. Did they see anybody running away? Or anything else they thought of as unusual?"

"When firemen are summoned to a fire, Molly, their one thought is to put it out," Sid said. "They don't automatically play detective like you. If someone was hiding in the bushes or walking away casually down the street, or even standing there watching the flames, they'd never have noticed."

"You're probably right." I sighed. "But all the same, I think I'll go and talk to them. Just in case."

❧ Sixteen ❧

I thought about taking a walk to the fire station, or even seeing if I felt up to taking Bridie to see her relatives, but my mother-in-law was adamant that I should not move all day. I was fed my lunch and sent back to bed. Sid and Gus returned later that afternoon, just as I was waking from a nap. I heard thunderous knocking on the front door, then Sid's voice and my mother-in-law saying in a firm and disapproving voice, "She's asleep. I'm afraid you'll have to come back later."

I tried to sit up and get out of bed rapidly, but these were things that still could not be done in a hurry without a good deal of pain. I had just swung my legs over the side of the bed when I heard the front door close again and watched Sid and Gus crossing Patchin Place to their own front door. Although I was dying of curiosity, I forced myself to wash my face and tidy my hair before I went downstairs.

"I suppose that knocking at the front door woke you?" Mrs. Sullivan said. "It was those two ladies from across the street pestering you again. You'd think they'd nothing better to do than come bothering you all day."

"But they were coming to report on a visit they had just made," I said. "I asked them to. And they don't bother me. I welcome their company."

"If you say so." Mrs. Sullivan sniffed. "Are we expecting your man home tonight at a reasonable hour?"

I smiled. "You were married to a policeman. You know that one can never expect him home at any hour. One is grateful when he arrives."

"That's the truth," she said. "Many's the night I've paced up and down the hallway, listening for the sound of his footsteps. Why Daniel had to follow his father into such a dangerous profession I'll never know. We sent him to Columbia for that very reason—so that he could become a lawyer or something equally safe and respectable. But no, he couldn't wait to graduate and join his father in the police force."

"A man has to do what he loves and what he has a talent for," I said, and in my head I asked: *Why couldn't a woman likewise do what she loved and had a talent for?* Why did we all have to accept that our lot was to be wives and mothers and to want nothing more? And it crossed my mind again that my nightmare might have something to do with being trapped in domesticity.

"Where is Liam?" I asked. And before she could answer, Liam came tottering out from the kitchen. He had a jammy mouth, and I suspected that his grandmother had been baking jam tarts.

"Mama." He gave me a beaming smile.

"Well, look at you, my precious," I said. "Aren't you having a good time? You've Bridie to play with and Grandma to make you good things to eat."

"Did you finish that tart then?" Mrs. Sullivan asked. "You're not having another one now. It will spoil your supper. Come on, let's clean up your face before you wipe it off on your mother's nice dress."

She swept him off to the kitchen. I followed.

"There is tea in the pot," she said. "And the tarts are fresh from the oven."

"You're spoiling us. You really shouldn't go to all this trouble." I reached across to take a tart.

"It's no trouble. It's good to have someone to look after." She wiped a protesting Liam's face, then set him down.

"I thought we might have a small celebration for Liam's birthday tomorrow," I said. "Seeing that it's Sunday and there is a slight chance that Daniel might have the afternoon free."

"I'll bake him a cake then." She looked quite pleased. "And some little sandwiches, do you think?"

"And Sid and Gus said they'd bring some food over with them."

"Oh, so they are coming too." She gave me a cold stare.

"Of course. They are Liam's aunties. They've been very good to us."

She sniffed. "If you say so." She turned to go back to the kitchen table, then looked back at me. "Oh, and what Mass do you go to to-morrow?"

Oh, Lord. I had forgotten that Sunday for her meant attendance at Mass. She never missed, like the good Catholic that she was.

"It's seven thirty at St. Joseph's on the square, I believe," I said. "But if you don't mind, I'll not join you this time. It takes me a while to get ready at the moment and all that kneeling and standing is a bit much for me."

"Of course," she said. "Bridie and I will go. And Daniel too, if he's home."

"I think I'll pay a visit across the street before suppertime," I said, "And I'll take Liam with me. His aunties love to see him and they were asking after him earlier."

"Just as you wish." Her face had become a stony mask. "If you really think it's wise and you are up to it."

"It's only a few yards across the street," I said. "I'm sure I'll be just grand." I turned to Liam. "Shall we go and see Auntie Sid and Gus?" I asked, and he set off instantly with determined steps for the front door before I'd finished the sentence. I picked him up and we crossed the street.

Gus looked delighted as she opened the front door. "Well, here you are," she said. "We thought you were to be kept away from us for the rest of the day. And you've brought our favorite man too. Molly's here, Sid," she called. "And our favorite young man too."

She took Liam from me and carried him down the hall at a great rate into the kitchen, where Sid was stirring something mysterious over the stove.

"It's couscous," Gus said as I peered at the pot. "We're having a Moroccan evening. We might even belly dance later. You're welcome to join us."

"Well, I won't want to join you in the belly dancing," I replied with a wry smile. "It still hurts me to stand up straight, let alone wiggle my middle."

"Oh, you poor thing. Of course. Sit down. I'll get you a pillow," Gus said. "Or would you be more comfortable in one of the armchairs in the sitting room?"

"No, I'm just fine here." I sat on one of the straight-backed kitchen chairs. "I do better sitting upright."

"You heard we were turned away from your house earlier?" Sid asked.

"I heard the knocking and then my mother-in-law's voice," I said. "But it takes me so long to get up at the moment that you'd gone again by the time I could come down the stairs. But I'm dying of curiosity, so wild horses wouldn't keep me away. So, did you go to see Mabel? Did you learn anything?"

Gus put some pots and pans on the floor for Liam to play with, then came to sit beside me. "We learned lots."

"Did you ask about her father's profession?" I asked.

"We did. And he was a senior clerk in his father-in-law's bank. He had hoped to be made a partner when he married Susan, but that never happened. But he was described as the sort of man who got along with everybody and didn't make enemies."

"Well, that doesn't sound promising, does it?" I said. "Nobody can have a grudge against a bank clerk. And apparently no family feud?"

"We had to ask that rather cautiously," Sid said, "because after all, Mrs. Hamilton is family. But she insisted that he was a likable sort, welcome at family gatherings, and that his father-in-law had finally come around to accepting him. There was even talk that he might be promoted to better things."

"So Mrs. Hamilton couldn't come up with anyone who might have done this foul thing?"

"She was quite annoyed that we even suggested it," Sid said. "We pointed out that you had asked the question, and you were used to dealing with criminal cases."

"But I'll tell you one thing, Molly," Gus said. "Mabel had another dream last night. Her aunt said she was whimpering and cowering in the corner when she found her. But she did write it down when she woke up."

"Was it the snake again?"

"It was. But this time she said the snake grew white hands. And the hands had long, pointed fingernails. And they were really sharp. And she held her breath and the snake didn't see her this time."

"How horrible," I said. "What can that mean—the snake growing fingers?"

"I don't know," Gus said. "I feel hopelessly out of my depth with this, Molly. It's all very well to have been taught that when we dream of being naked we're feeling vulnerable. That makes sense. But a snake that grows hands with long fingernails? I have no idea where to start. I do hope we get a letter back from Professor Freud soon and he can make some recommendation for us. This girl clearly needs help badly, and I'm afraid I can't give it to her."

Sid came over to join us. "I suggested to Gus that the snake might be Mabel's own evil side—intentions and impulses she can't control. Perhaps the hands were her hands, reaching out to do something terrible."

"Holy Mother of God," I muttered. "I just pray you aren't right there, Sid."

"This is where my smattering of alienist training is now revealed as hopelessly inadequate," Gus said. "I'm thinking of approaching the school of medicine at the university and seeing if they now teach the diseases of the mind."

"Wait a minute," I said. "There is always Dr. Birnbaum. Did you ever meet him? I don't think so. He's also an alienist who trained with Freud in Vienna, but he's been in America for several years now."

"So he won't have been involved in the study of dreams," Gus said. "All of that research is quite recent."

"But he is a proper alienist," Sid said. "That's something. How do you know him, Molly?"

"He was called in to treat a woman when I was staying at a mansion on the Hudson once," I said. "I've asked him for help several times since then. But I haven't been in contact with him for two years now. He's often out of the city, lecturing around the States. Would you like me to see if he's here at the moment?"

Sid looked at Gus. "It can't do any harm, can it? You said you needed a trained alienist."

"I suppose so," Gus agreed. I could tell she was torn. She really wanted to prove that she had the ability to solve this case, while her sensible side told her that she didn't. Then she nodded firmly. "Yes, that might be a good thing to do, Molly. A real alienist will know what should be done with Mabel, even if he can't interpret her dreams."

"And he may well have been reading up on Freud's latest research," Sid said. "The professor has published a book on the subject, hasn't he? So your Dr. Birnbaum might even have developed an interest in dream psychology himself. Yes, I definitely think we should contact him, Molly. Should we write him a letter, do you think?"

"He lives close by," I said. "Or he did when I last visited him. Would you like me to go and set the stage for you?"

"That would be a good idea," Gus said. "Better than receiving a letter from two crazy women out of the blue." And she smiled.

"Oh, and I also came to tell you that I thought we should celebrate Liam's birthday tomorrow, seeing that it's Sunday," I said. "There's a chance Daniel might have an afternoon off, or at least be able to get away for a while."

"Lovely." Gus beamed. "We'll bring some food with us. And champagne. We have to have champagne."

"Liam's a little young for champagne," I said, and they laughed.

"No, the champagne's for us, silly," Sid said. "To celebrate the fact that you've made it through a tumultuous year, and to drink to better times ahead."

"Amen to that," I said. "But you don't need to go to any trouble."

"You know we love parties. We live for parties," Sid said. "And we love spoiling Liam. You should see what we've got him for his birthday! Such fun."

I shook my head. "You're too good to us. And I'll apologize in advance for my mother-in-law. She'll be polite but distant."

Sid looked at Gus and they grinned. "She doesn't approve of us. We know. We're used to it. But you approve of us. So does Liam. That's all that matters."

❦ Seventeen ❦

So now I had to seek out Dr. Birnbaum, and I hoped I'd be able to do it in the morning, before we started preparing for Liam's party. I was pretty sure my mother-in-law would want to do all the preparation herself anyway, which would give me time to slip away. It felt good to be involved in Sid and Gus's case, rather than a passive observer. The only difficulty would be escaping the house against the wishes of my mother-in-law. I realized that I was sounding like one of those females I so despised, a meek little woman under her mother-in-law's thumb, but I knew she'd complain to Daniel, and I didn't want him upset or worried at this difficult time. And I did acknowledge that I had not returned to full health by a long way. What with dreams at night and my aching ribs and head by day, I was not up to running all over the city.

Luckily Dr. Birnbaum lived only a couple of streets away, and the next day dawned bright and clear with a crisp hint of fall about it. I heard Mother Sullivan and Bridie leaving for Mass, and Daniel himself left soon after, promising to be home at least for an hour or two in the afternoon. I got up, dressed, and to put everyone in a good mood, I cooked us all a grand breakfast. It was ready and on the table as they came in through the door.

"You shouldn't have been doing all that work," Mother Sullivan said. "You're supposed to be resting."

"It was the least I could do after everything you're doing for us," I replied. "And how hard is it to fry bacon, especially now I've a nice new stove."

"I'm not so sure about that gas myself," Mother Sullivan said. "I'm quite expecting it to explode every time I light the match. Give me a good old-fashioned range any day."

We ate breakfast, and I was wondering how I could find an excuse to visit Dr. Birnbaum when my mother-in-law herself looked up and said, "That child has been cooped up in the house too long. He needs to be out in the fresh air. Do you think that Bridie is big enough to take him for a walk in his buggy down to the park?"

Bridie jumped up eagerly. "I am big enough," she said.

"I don't know about that, Bridie, love," I said. "It's difficult to push a buggy over cobbles, and along these sidewalks where there are so many people. Why don't I come with you? I'm sure I can walk as far as Washington Square. You can do most of the pushing, but it would be good for me to get some fresh air too." I turned to my mother-in-law. "Won't you join us? It will be delightful to sit in the square on a day like this."

Mrs. Sullivan shook her head. "I have to bake Liam's birthday cake. And I thought I'd make some little scones too."

"Come for a walk with us and I'll help you later," I said. "Besides, my neighbors have said they'll be bringing food as well."

I could tell by her expression that was the wrong thing to say. "I doubt that their food will be suitable for the child, and after all, it is his birthday we're celebrating. And I had my walk to and from Mass this morning."

Suitably reprimanded, I went to get Liam ready and to put on my hat and gloves.

When we had Liam dressed for an outing and safely strapped into his buggy, we set off. I was glad that Bridie was eager to push, as the bumping of a buggy over the cobbles would certainly have been uncomfortable for me. She did a grand job, and I only took hold of the handle to help her when we had to cross Sixth Avenue and then Waverly Place into Washington Square. The square had been Liam's favorite outing last spring, before we'd had to leave the city in a hurry, but we hadn't been back since, and I wondered if he would remember it. But I watched him leaning forward in his buggy making excited noises as he saw the fountain and the bigger children playing there.

We sat on one of the benches, watching the colorful tapestry of life going on there. Bridie looked wistfully at a group of girls, turning a jump rope and chanting as they ran in and out, one by one. I remembered what Mrs. Sullivan had suggested about her going to school, and decided it would be an excellent idea. She needed companionship of her own age, not to be shut away in the country with an old woman. I just hoped that Daniel would agree when I had time to put it to him.

Liam, meanwhile, was fascinated and watched intently as the bigger boys played noisy games. Some of them were running with iron hoops, others engrossed in a battle of spinning tops, just like the boys at home. Yet others were kicking a can around, shouting to each other in high childish voices that were on the verge of breaking. There was such an assortment of people in the park. Families dressed in their Sunday best. Old Italian women, head to toe in black with scarves around their heads, walking on the arms of old men with impressive nicotine-stained mustaches. The boys who were playing kick the can were unwashed and unkempt—part of the general ragtag of unwanted children, earning a crust as crossing sweepers or even petty thieves, but enjoying a carefree game the way children do everywhere.

That brought my thoughts to the street urchin who had delivered that last message to police headquarters, and my own idea to use Bridie's cousins as my spies. They lived in one of the tenements, if they hadn't been kicked out of yet another place for unruly behavior and not paying their rent.

"Bridie," I said as if the idea had just come to me. "You know what I've been thinking? I think we should probably pay a visit to your father's cousin Nuala."

"Cousin Nuala?" she looked up, horrified. "But she's horrible."

"I agree she's not the nicest person in the world," I said, "but they are your only relatives and they would want to see you once if you were in town."

"Do we have to tell them?" She was chewing her lip. "They need never know I'm here."

"I'll come with you," I said. "Just a quick social call. And I was also thinking that perhaps they might have had news of your father and brother, and not known your address to contact you."

Her face lit up then. "Do you think so? All right, let's go then."

I felt a great stab of guilt that I was putting her through this for my own devious ends. I almost called it off, then and there, but it occurred to me that they actually might have had news of Seamus and not been able to pass it along to Bridie. Of course it might not be good news, but it was always better to know, wasn't it?

"We'll have to wait a few more days," I said. "I don't think I'm up to taking a trolley yet."

This conversation was interrupted by a squawk of frustration from Liam, still strapped in his buggy but itching to get down to touch the fountain or join the bigger boys.

"You're not getting out here yet, young man," I said. "You have to wait until you can walk better. You'll fall on the gravel and hurt your hands and get dirty."

I stood up, deciding it was probably time to move on. He started to bawl as we pushed him away, and kept it up until we passed under the arch and began walking along Waverly Place to the Hotel Lafayette, where Dr. Birnbaum had rooms—or had had rooms the last time I had sought him out. That must have been two years ago now. But

I had been in this hotel since then . . . and the full, vivid memory of my night here after the fire came back to me. The terror, the grief, the terrible insecurity and belief that nothing would ever be right again all flooded through me once more as I stood in the foyer, now so tranquil and genteel with its wicker furniture and potted plants. Liam had been sitting contentedly in his buggy until we came through the door, but suddenly he let out a wail and held out his arms to come to me.

"Mama!" he cried. So he remembered too. I unbuckled his straps. "It's all right, Bridie," I said. "I'll hold him." And I took him into my arms.

"Can I help you, ma'am?" the clerk asked. He recognized me at the same moment that I realized he was the man who had taken care of us on that black night. "Mrs. Sullivan, isn't it?" He smiled. "It is good to see you again in better circumstances. I trust that all is well now?"

"Absolutely, thank you. I have just moved back into my house."

"I am so glad to hear it. We were so worried about you at that dreadful time."

"You were all very kind," I said. I shifted Liam onto my hip. He had calmed down but was clinging to me like a baby monkey.

"So what can I do for you today?" he asked.

"I'm wondering if Dr. Birnbaum might be available?" I asked.

"I believe he just stepped out," the clerk said. "Would you care to leave him a message?"

"Thank you. I'll do that," I said. I handed Liam to Bridie, who immediately took him over to the window to show him the pigeons on the sidewalk outside.

The clerk found me paper, pen, and ink, and I carried them over to one of the low wicker tables. I had barely started to write when the doorman opened the door and Dr. Birnbaum himself came in. He was looking a little older and more portly than when I last saw him, but he still cut a dapper figure with his neatly trimmed blond beard and well-cut jacket. He stopped in surprise when he saw me.

"Miss Murphy—I mean, Mrs. Sullivan—what a pleasant surprise," he said in his crisp German-accented English. "You have come to bid me farewell?"

I stood up and shook his outstretched hand. "Farewell? You are going on another trip?"

"I am going home," he said. "I have just been to bid good-bye to friends. I sail in two days."

"Oh, that's too bad," I said.

He shrugged. "I decided I had been away from Germany long enough. I miss my family. And I find that research in Europe is proceeding at a great pace without me. I stagnate here in America, Mrs. Sullivan, while great advances in the study of the mind are being made in Europe. I must be part of them."

"Of course you must," I said. "But it's most unfortunate that you are leaving at this very moment. I came to see you, hoping that you could help me in a distressing matter."

He shook his head. "My dear Mrs. Sullivan. It seems that every time we meet you are investigating a distressing matter. You are still pursuing your career as a detective?" he asked. "I thought that you put that phase of your life behind you when you married."

"I did. This is really on behalf of friends."

Dr. Birnbaum looked around. "Very well. I am not sure how I can be of help to you, but if I can give advice, I will do so. I have a few minutes before my next appointment. Shall we take a cup of coffee together? Anton, could you bring us coffee? We can sit here, out of the way, beside the potted palms."

I looked over at Bridie and Liam. "I must keep an eye on my son," I said. "He's quite a handful at the moment."

"You have a child now. My congratulations. He looks like a fine, strapping boy," Dr. Birnbaum said. "We will have Anton bring him a cookie. I find that usually works wonders in keeping children quiet." He smiled. "One learns a lot in the study of human nature."

We walked together to a group of chairs around a table in the window of the hotel. Dr. Birnbaum pulled one out for me and sat beside me. "This problem you have? I take it that it has something to do with my field of expertise?"

"It does." And I gave him the full story of Mabel and the fire and her dreams. "The problem is," I finished, "that we just don't know. Is it possible that she killed her parents and then set fire to their room? She seems such a sweet and delicate child and was clearly fond of them."

"You say your friend is trying to interpret her dreams?"

"We thought that maybe her dreams would give us a clue as to what really happened that night and what memories she had locked away."

He stroked his beard in a characteristic gesture. "My dear Mrs. Sullivan, this is indeed perplexing, and if I were staying here longer I should be intrigued to visit this young girl for myself."

"Could you not find time to see her once before you go?" I asked.

He shook his head. "My ship sails in two days and I have much business to take care of before I go. Besides, psychiatry is not the same as magic. One session with her would not produce any great revelations. It usually takes weeks of work and building confidence before results can be seen. But this friend of whom you speak. She is a trained alienist?"

"She studied the interpretation of dreams this summer with Dr. Freud," I said.

He shook his head. "But she is a qualified doctor?"

"No, I'm afraid she's an enthusiastic amateur," I said.

"*Mein Gott.* This is not the sort of situation to be taken lightly. You are dealing with a fragile mind here. The wrong approach could snap a tormented mind like this. And if your friend makes a wrong interpretation of the dreams, if she fails to pick up a crucial key—what then?"

"I agree with you, Doctor, which is why I sought you out."

The coffee had arrived and he poured in a generous amount of cream, stirred it, then took a delicate sip from his cup before wiping the line of cream from his mustache with his handkerchief. "Is there no one else your friend can turn to here?" he asked.

"She didn't think that doctors in America were taking the study of dreams seriously."

"That is true." He took a macaroon from the dish and nibbled at it, again dabbing at imaginary crumbs. "There are even doctors in America who believe the study of psychology is the same as hocus-pocus. I am afraid treating the mentally sick here is still thought of the same way as the biblical driving out of demons. I could maybe find time to write letters for you, though. There are certain forward-thinkers I have encountered in my travels around the country. . . . "

"There is an element of haste here, I'm afraid," I said. "The police are involved. A brash young lieutenant thinks the girl is faking amnesia and wants to find her guilty of killing her parents and setting fire to their house. He has threatened to have her locked away in the Tombs until her memory returns."

"*Mein Gott.* This is barbaric. It must not be allowed," Dr. Birnbaum said, raising his voice to the extent that Bridie and Liam looked up from their cookies. "You must explain to this man that amnesia after an event of great trauma is not unheard of. If the child witnessed her parents being burned to death, if she tried to save them but was not able to, of course her mind would refuse to acknowledge that such a thing ever happened."

"I've tried explaining," I said. "Unfortunately he's not the sort of man who listens, especially to a woman."

Dr. Birnbaum nodded. "I wish I could help you."

"My friend has written to Professor Freud in Vienna to ask for advice," I said, "but naturally it will take time for the letters to reach Vienna, and for us to receive a reply."

Dr. Birnbaum stroked his beard again. "There might be somebody you could turn to. I recall that Dr. Otto Werner was here in New York earlier this year. I read about his visit in a scholarly journal. A brilliant young man from Munich, they say, who has been doing ground-breaking work with Professor Freud in Vienna. I don't know if he is still here or if he has returned home. I wrote to him once at the New York address I had been given for him, inviting him to dine with me, but I received no reply. So I have to assume that he is no longer here. He would have been able to help you. Freud thought highly of him."

"Dr. Otto Werner," I said, memorizing the name. "I'll mention this to my friends and see if they can track him down."

"I understand that he has specialized in the study of the criminally insane," he said. "He would be a useful witness if you feel the police might unjustly accuse this girl of a criminal act."

"At least we would know one way or the other," I said. "That's the hard part. Daniel says he's encountered murderers who seemed sweet and gentle. And we still can't explain how Mabel was found outside the house, apparently unscathed by the fire."

"You may never know." He sighed. "But at least someone like Dr. Werner would have the training to ask the right questions." He put down his coffee cup, then looked up sharply at me. "These dreams. It is always the same scenario, the same symbols?"

"There is always the snake," I repeated what Mabel had said. "A giant snake that looms over her."

"That is a typical monster representation for many people—the snake, symbol of evil and death. I would suggest it was the embodiment of her terror."

"So you don't think that understanding her dreams can necessarily unlock her memories?"

"I'm afraid not." He stood up and extended his hand to me. "Now, I'm afraid I must take my leave of you. I have much to do—the carter will be coming for my trunks, and I still have many items to pack. One accumulates so much after a prolonged stay, don't you agree?"

"Yes, I'm sure. But one more thing. Do you happen to still have Dr. Otto Werner's address in New York?"

He reached into his breast pocket and pulled out a slim diary. He flicked through it. "Alas, no," he said. "I think I discarded it when I last changed notebooks, since he had not answered my letter. But I recall it was not too far from here. Maybe on Ninth Street—close to Astor Place?"

"Thank you," I said. "You've been most kind. My friends can ask at the university. They should know if an eminent scientist is still in the city."

"I wish you luck with your endeavors." He gave me a very Germanic bow, clicking his heels together.

"And I wish you bon voyage," I said.

Eighteen

I strode out, feeling annoyed and frustrated as we headed for home. If only I had sought out Dr. Birnbaum a few days earlier. Then at least he could have seen Mabel. He could have given us some suggestions. But now we were completely in the dark and going nowhere. And Dr. Birnbaum had indicated that dreaming about monster images was to be expected after a traumatic event, and it didn't need interpreting after all. What's more, he'd said that Gus could be doing more harm than good to Mabel. I wondered how she would feel about that, and whether she'd be able to walk away. I wondered if I'd be able to walk away, knowing that Mabel was in danger from the brash lieutenant as well as from her dreams.

I hadn't realized how fast I was walking until Bridie tugged at my skirt. "I can't keep up with you," she said, "and Liam is getting bounced around like a sack of potatoes."

I smiled and slowed down. "I'm sorry," I said. "I've got a lot on my mind."

"The girl who wasn't burned in the fire?" she said. "You thought that doctor would help her, and he's not going to?"

"Exactly." Then I remembered Mrs. Sullivan's stern warning about involving Bridie in this kind of conversation. "But don't worry." I tried to sound bright. "I'm sure Miss Walcott will find another doctor who can treat Mabel and make her well again."

"I hope so," Bridie said. "I bet she's feeling scared right now. I would be. It's hard when bad things happen to people in your family and you can't do anything to stop them."

I knew she was thinking of her own father and brother, and again I felt guilty that I might be raising false hopes by taking her to see her cousins.

"Watch out, Molly." Bridie yanked back the buggy as an automobile came careering toward us at an ungodly speed, making horses neigh in terror in their shafts. It was all that the cabby could do to quieten one of them. I dreaded to think what would happen if automobiles ever became commonplace. Our lives would not be safe crossing the street. But Liam, his father's son in every way, clapped his hands and made *brmm brmm* noises, a delighted look on his face.

As we neared the impressive gothic structure of the Jefferson Market building with its rough stone turrets, I realized that this would be a good chance to question the firemen. It was a Sunday morning, there were no fires. They'd be bored and eager to chat.

"Bridie," I said. "Do you think you can push the buggy back to my house by yourself from here? I just want to pop across the street to the market building."

"But there's no market on Sundays," she said, eyeing the deserted area with its empty pallets and blowing straw.

"No, I don't need to buy vegetables," I said. "I need to have a word with a man—at the police station there," I added, as I was sure the news would go straight back to Mrs. Sullivan. "I'm just sending a message to my husband, to remind him about Liam's birthday party."

Even mother-in-laws couldn't find fault in that, could they?

I watched Bridie pushing the buggy down Patchin Place, then I crossed the street. Two firemen were polishing the bright red engine. Another was grooming one of the horses. I went up to them.

"I'm sorry to disturb you," I said, "but I'm wondering if your engine was called out to a fire on Eleventh Street about a month ago. Two people were burned to death in their beds."

"Oh, that one? Pretty bad, wasn't it?" One of the firemen glanced across at his mate. "You were at Eleventh Street, weren't you, Abe?"

"The one at the beginning of August?" he said. "I sure was. One of the worst I've ever handled. Flames raging out of that place like the fires of hell. And those poor folks burned in their beds. Charred beyond recognition, they were." He looked across at his fellow fireman. "You feel so bad when you can't do your job and save them, don't you?"

The other man shook his head. "I heard there was no way. Those flames weren't natural."

He looked at me with interest. "Relatives of yours, were they, ma'am?"

"Good friends," I said. "And their poor little girl is left an orphan."

"Oh, yes, the little girl," the one called Abe said. "Ernie Howes was the one who found her. I remember him shouting out, 'There's a kid here. She's unconscious. I can't wake her.' And we thought she'd inhaled smoke. But you know what? There wasn't a mark on her. No soot. No burns. Nothing. It was the strangest thing. We had to get her out of that garden in a hurry as the bushes were already beginning to catch on fire. And when Ernie was carrying her out, she wakes up suddenly and doesn't know where she is, and asks for her parents."

"You didn't encounter anyone else there, did you?" I asked.

"Only the two servants who escaped. They were in a pretty bad way and we had them taken to St. Vincent's."

"But nobody else, maybe running away from the fire, or hanging around, watching it?"

They looked at me strangely then.

"You always get a crowd watching a fire," the first one said. "But running away? Are you trying to suggest the fire was started on purpose?"

"Isn't that possible? Didn't you say the flames were unnaturally fierce?"

He sucked in through his teeth. "Yeah. Maybe. But to answer your earlier question. When we're on our way to a fire, that's all we're thinking about. Horses at a flat-out gallop. Ringing that bell like crazy and the blood pounding in your head. You don't have time to notice anything else."

That pretty much summed it up. They wouldn't have had time to notice any clues. I could go to the ruins of the house myself, I supposed. But I doubted I would find anything there to show who might have started that fire. I remembered the ruins of my own house, and how it was impossible to find anything among the rubble. The only thing I had learned was that the firemen had had to carry Mabel out of the back garden in a hurry, as the bushes were already starting to burn. If she had killed her parents and started a fire, would she have stayed where she would also be in danger of being burned?

I was halfway down Patchin Place when something the fireman had said struck me. The fire had been at the beginning of August. It couldn't possibly be Daniel's missing murder, could it? I toyed with this notion all the way home. If only I could somehow prove that the crime was carried out by an intruder, then I could save Mabel. I wasn't at all sure how I could do this, but I'd give it a darned good try!

Now that I had some small campaign plan, I felt better as I went into the house. Mother Sullivan looked up from the kitchen table, her apron and hands covered in flour.

"Ah, there you are," she said. "I became worried when you were gone so long."

"We met an old friend who is sailing home to Germany this week," I said.

"To Germany? My, but you have an assortment of diverse friends."

"He's a doctor I met during my detective work," I said. "A doctor of the mind. An alienist."

"Really?" She brushed flour from her apron. "Too bad he's sailing for home, or he could have helped those friends of yours with their problem."

Sometimes she was rather too astute.

"Whatever you're baking smells wonderful," I said.

"It's just a few more jam tarts, since they seem to be Liam's favorites." She smiled at him. "Not that he can really eat them yet, but he does love sucking out the jam."

I put Liam into his high chair and mashed some carrots for his meal. Bridie begged to feed them to him, so I took the opportunity to slip across the street to Gus and Sid. I found Sid at the stove, cooking feverishly, while Gus was surrounded by textbooks in the German language.

"Drat and blast," she was saying as I came into the kitchen, "what does *gewalt* mean again? I know *wald* is forest, but I don't see how a forest fits into this sentence."

"I'll look it up for you." Sid went over to an enormous dictionary. "Really, German is such an annoying language," she said as she flicked through pages. "Too many words. Here we are. *Gewalt*. Violence. Force."

"Ah, that makes more sense." Gus looked up at me and smiled. "I'm trying to continue my studies, but it's not easy because all of the books are in German. Any luck with your doctor?"

"I found him, but he's returning to Germany in two days," I said.

"How frustrating. So near and yet so far," Gus said. "Did he have any advice for us?"

"He said the snake image might just be the universal monster of our nightmares, the embodiment of her fear that night, and he warned against trying to read too much into Mabel's dreams. He also stressed that she needs the help of a trained alienist if she is suffering from amnesia."

"We know that," Gus said testily. "But the question is where to find one."

"He did mention the name of a German doctor who had been working with Freud but came over here earlier this year. A Dr. Otto Werner."

Gus looked at Sid with an excited expression on her face. "We heard that name, didn't we? Do you remember at that little wine cellar, someone said it was too bad we weren't in New York, or we could have entertained Dr. Werner while he was visiting America. They spoke highly of him. He's supposed to be brilliant. Did your doctor know where we might find him?"

"He didn't. He said he had invited Dr. Werner to dinner once and not received a reply, so he concluded the doctor had left the city and was traveling around the States. And he'd since disposed of the address. He thought it might be somewhere near Astor Place."

"Someone must know where he is," Sid said, slapping a fist against her palm as if she was itching for action. "If he's speaking to learned societies, then the professors at the university here will know of him. We'll go and ask tomorrow."

"Let's hope he hasn't already returned home to Europe," Gus said. "That would be just our luck."

"No negative thoughts allowed," Sid said firmly. "Remember what else we learned in Vienna. If you voice your negative thoughts, you invite them in and turn them into reality."

"I know. And if you repeat positive images they will become reality. All right: we are going to find Dr. Werner and make Mabel well. We are going to find Dr. Werner and make Mabel well."

"How many times do you have to repeat it?" I asked, laughing.

"As many as it takes."

"Is this based on a scientific principle?" I asked.

"Certainly. There are promising results in the field of hypnosis for curing ailments of the mind," Gus said. "And this is a type of self-hypnosis. If you say something often enough, you believe it."

"Amazing," I said. "What will they think of next?"

"So we won't go see Mabel again until we know if we can trace this Dr. Werner," Sid said. "Molly is quite right in what she's told us. Mabel is in a fragile state. We must be careful not to say or do the wrong thing."

"I'm concerned that Lieutenant Yeats will say or do the wrong thing," I said. "I hope that Daniel can intervene or pull rank or whatever they do in the police force, but Daniel's got so much on his plate himself at the moment."

"Still looking into a string of murders, you say?" Sid asked. "Any progress?"

"Not that I know of."

"Then you should help him, Molly. Whether he likes it or not."

"I happen to have a few ideas," I said, and we exchanged a smile. "I'd better return home, I suppose. I slipped away while Bridie was feeding Liam his lunch."

"What a lovely girl she's turned out to be," Sid said. "A great help to you, Molly. You should keep her with you, if your mother-in-law can spare her."

"My mother-in-law actually suggested the same thing," I said. "She wants Bridie to be able to continue her education and go to school, and have a chance to meet other children."

Sid smiled. "Well, there's a turn-up for the books. So much for training her to be a maid."

"It's been quite clear to me for some time that Bridie wasn't destined to be anyone's maid," I said. "Mrs. Sullivan has been raising her to be a young lady."

"We'll see you around four then, shall we?" Sid asked. "If this wretched chicken liver pâté cools properly by then. It's too liquid at the moment. I know I shouldn't have put so much brandy in it."

"Is that for Liam's birthday party?" I asked. "He is only one, Sid."

"We have to eat too, don't we? I've some lovely smoked salmon and some petit fours from the French bakery."

I hesitated. "Uh, maybe you'd better leave those at home," I said. "I don't want to be ungrateful or anything, but my mother-in-law has been baking cakes all morning, and she'd see it as a slight if you came with store-bought cakes."

"Point taken," Sid said. "Never mind. We're supposed to be going to an art exhibition this evening, to honor a friend of Ryan's. We'll take them along to that. Starving artists will wolf them down in a trice."

I went home and helped prepare the dining table with a lace cloth Sid and Gus had loaned me, then made some ham and cucumber sandwiches. The table was laden with food by the time I dressed Liam in his new sailor suit and brought him into the parlor. There was no sign of Daniel, but Sid and Gus arrived promptly on the stroke of four, Sid carrying a tray covered in a white cloth and Gus with her arms full of brightly wrapped packages.

"Here we are. Our contributions to the feast," Sid said. She stood the bottle of champagne, wrapped in a cloth, on the table, then tried to find space for several exotic-looking dishes. "Pâté. Smoked salmon sandwiches. And some small Moroccan lamb kebabs with a yogurt sauce."

I could see my mother-in-law's face. Pâté and Moroccan lamb were outside her sphere of experience. "You didn't have to go to all this trouble," she said. "As you can see, we've plenty to eat for this many people."

"No trouble at all," Sid said with a smile. "We love to cook and experiment with different foods. It just happens that we're in a Moroccan phase right now, isn't that right, Gus."

"We've quite taken to it," Gus said. "We're actually thinking of taking a trip and renting camels and crossing the Sahara."

"Mercy me." Mrs. Sullivan patted her chest as if to quieten her heart.

"Other women have done it, so why not us?" Sid said. "Our mantra is living life to the full."

I'm not sure where this conversation would have led if Daniel had not burst in through the front door at that moment. "Where's my birthday boy?" he demanded, and he swung Liam up into the air, making him squeal with delight.

The party had officially started. Daniel was persuaded to open the champagne, and we toasted Liam's birthday. Then we sat and ate. Even my mother-in-law had to admit that Sid's chicken liver pâté was delicious and the smoked salmon sandwiches were perfect. Sid and Gus in turn praised Mrs. Sullivan's scones. Then she went into the kitchen and returned with the birthday cake in a festive paper wrapper, with one lit candle on top. We showed Liam how to blow it out, which he enjoyed so much he wanted to do it again. Then I cut the cake and we all got a slice. Liam was allowed for once to tear his apart with his hands. It was a light sponge with butter cream and jam in the middle, and the adults enjoyed it equally. After we were stuffed with food, we wiped the worst of the jam and crumbs from Liam and sat him on the rug to open Sid and Gus's presents.

The first one was a drum. Sid showed him how to bang with the drumsticks, and he took to it so much that he had to be persuaded to put it down and open the second one. This was a wind-up monkey that turned cartwheels. Liam was mystified and rather scared as it came toward him. He headed rapidly for me and stood, holding onto my skirt. But the third gift was also a big success—a big ball with stripes of different colors on it. Liam immediately picked it up and wanted to run off with it.

"You've been far too generous," Daniel said to Sid and Gus. "I feel guilty that we've had no time to buy a present for our son yet, but you have more than made up for it."

"He's our only nephew," Sid said. "We had a splendid time at FAO Schwarz choosing the toys, didn't we, Gus."

"We did. We were laughing so loudly that we got black looks from the store assistants," Gus said. "I'm glad to see they are a big success."

"I'm not so sure about the drum," Daniel said, as Liam returned to it and started beating on it loudly. "That may be put away for special occasions."

"Like when his father is at work," Sid said.

We laughed until I said, "Which he is, most of the time these days."

"You're still investigating the same case, Captain Sullivan, are you?" Gus asked innocently.

"I am. And it's proving to be very difficult." He held up a hand to forbid any further discussion. "But let's not spoil my son's birthday and talk about gloomy matters." He got up. "Come on, boy. Let's go into the hall and see how well you can kick the ball to your father."

After Sid and Gus were gone, we sat at the kitchen table, sipping at a last glass of champagne.

"Well, that was a good day, wasn't it?" I said.

"It was," Daniel agreed. "The tyke loved his gifts, didn't he?"

"And his cake." I laughed. "He had more on his face than went into his mouth."

Daniel reached over and took my hand. "Let's hope there are now more good days to come, Molly."

Almost on cue, there was a knock at the front door. "Sid and Gus probably found another present for Liam," I said, smiling as I went to answer it. Instead, a skinny young constable stood there, red-faced and panting as if he had been running.

"Is Captain Sullivan here?" he asked.

"Yes, he is, but . . . " I began.

"Tell him we got another note," the constable said.

Daniel was into the hallway in an instant. "Another note? When?"

"Delivered not five minutes ago, sir. I ran all the way like you told me to." The constable handed over an envelope to Daniel, who opened it and read it, scowling. Then he looked up. "And do we have any idea who delivered it? Was someone posted outside headquarters on the watch?"

"Yes, sir. It was a young kid, about eight years old. He was asked who gave the note to him, and he said it was a bigger boy, who'd told him that he'd give him a dime if he went to police headquarters and back in less than five minutes."

"A bigger boy, huh?" Daniel was still frowning. "He thinks ahead, doesn't he, this one? There could be a whole chain of boys, making it impossible to trace." He folded the note again. "Very well, Dobson. Wait a second and I'll come with you."

He turned back to me and put a hand on my shoulder. "Sorry, my dear. I have to go."

"Another note?" I asked. "What did it say?"

He shot me a warning look. Policemen aren't supposed to discuss threatening notes with their wives. "I don't know when I'll be back," he said. "Don't wait up for me. I'm glad we managed to have Liam's celebration before this." He gave me a wry smile. "So much for good days, huh?"

❧ Nineteen ❧

I n spite of Daniel's instruction not to wait up for him, I undressed but lay in bed staring at the ceiling, listening to the noises of the city night and worrying. What did the note say? Was it a specific threat to somebody? To Daniel himself? If Daniel was the one element that linked all the killings, then maybe he was now in danger— and if this was the last murder and the killer wanted to go out in a big way, then would Daniel be somehow involved in his horrible scheme? I sat up, seeing the streetlamps making small pools of light in the darkened alleyway. I knew what being a policeman's wife would involve when I married him, but it had never hit home more strongly than this year . . . when our whole lives started to unravel.

I heard a clock on a distant church strike eleven, and almost im-mediately I heard brisk footsteps coming up Patchin Place toward me. I watched Daniel's head of unruly black curls as he walked up to our front door, then the sound of his closing it quietly behind him. I got up and tiptoed downstairs. He looked up.

"What are you doing awake?"

"I couldn't sleep, worrying about you."

"I'm all right," he said. "It's the people I'm supposed to protect that I worry about. What use am I if I can't do my job properly."

"You do do your job properly, my love," I said, going over to wrap my arms around his waist. "Nobody works harder than you do."

"I haven't managed to stop the murders or find the killer, have I?"

I didn't have an answer for that one. "Has there been a report of another murder?" I asked cautiously.

He shook his head. "Not yet," he said.

"So what did the note say, or can't you tell me?"

He reached into his pocket. "I have it here. We've had it checked for fingerprints, but of course there are none. He is always meticulous." He opened the note and spread it on the kitchen table. I leaned over to read. It said, *Have you forgotten about me? Did you think I'd go quietly back to my grave? Saving the best for last. Going out with a bang.*

"'Going out with a bang,'" I said. "That sounds as if he's planning an explosion."

"It does. And the part about going quietly to his grave. What does he mean by it?"

"You said he could be acting on behalf of somebody else. Somebody dead. Seeking vengeance for them. But maybe he's pretending to be someone else—someone who died."

"What do you mean?" Daniel looked at me suspiciously.

I shrugged, realizing as I formed the thought that it sounded silly. "Maybe he sees himself as a masked avenger, a character from a storybook, righting wrongs."

"Righting wrongs?" Daniel asked angrily. "What can a sweet mentally defective woman have done wrong? Or an elderly judge's wife? You might say they led blameless lives. And how did he know them?" He looked up at me, frowning. "Who is he, Molly? What kind of man?"

When I didn't answer he went on, "Sometimes I think that I believe him, that he is some kind of supernatural being. We still haven't come up with any rational explanation for that train crash. Engineer and signalman are both sticking to their stories. Each swears by the disk he saw on the front of the train. It doesn't make sense."

I weighed whether I should share with him my own little plan to visit Nuala and use her boys to find out which urchin delivered the messages, but I sensed that he wasn't in the mood to accept help from anybody, especially not his wife. I looked at him tenderly. "Come to bed now," I said. "Nothing will be solved at this time of night, and you need a proper night's sleep."

"You're right. I need all the strength I can get. I'll have to report to the commissioner again tomorrow. He's losing patience with me."

"Things will look brighter in the morning," I said. "Maybe it will be the day for a wonderful breakthrough. Finally, the one thing will materialize that makes it all fall into place."

"Hmmph," he said grumpily, but he allowed me to lead him up the stairs.

Daniel went to work at first light. In spite of the ever-present ache in my ribs, I decided I would risk taking Bridie to see her relatives. It was a case of doing all I could to help Daniel at the moment, and getting a description of the killer might be the one small breakthrough he needed.

I was prepared for the look of disapproval I received when I told my mother-in-law that I'd be taking Bridie to see her relations. It was only right that she should pay a visit, seeing that she was in the city, I said.

"Are you sure you're up to it?" she asked, eyeing me with a worried frown. "They live on the Lower East Side, don't they? All those people jostling you around can't be good for you."

"I'll be fine," I said. "I've decided that my ribs ache whether I'm sitting at home or out doing something, so I'd rather keep myself busy."

"Well, take a hansom cab then," she said. "It's too far to walk and you'll not want to risk a crowded trolley."

I laughed, realizing how little she knew of the city. "You'd not get a cab down most of those streets," I said. "All those pushcarts make it impossible. Besides, I think I prefer not to be jolted around over the cobbles. I'll walk across to Ninth Street and we'll take the Third Avenue El. There's a stop right there at Fulton Street where Nuala works."

"The elevated?" Her face grew wary. "My dear, are you sure you want to face that again so soon?"

"Don't worry. There are no curves on this track," I said, sounding more carefree than I felt. I wished she hadn't brought that up. I wished she hadn't reminded me that Daniel suspected I was the intended target of the crash. In which case someone could be watching me and plotting when to strike again. It made staying home and not getting involved in Daniel's business seem like such a safe alternative. But I had pushed myself into things I didn't want to do before. And I wanted to catch this man as much as Daniel did.

"Bring me your hairbrush and let's do your hair, Bridie," I said. "You need to look respectable when we meet your relatives."

Bridie had been holding Liam and handed him to me when he started to cry. I, in turn, handed him to Daniel's mother. "Would you mind looking after him for a little while?" I said. "I really don't want to bring him with me to that part of the city. Too much disease always going around there."

"Of course," she said. "And you're in no condition to carry him." She looked down at him fondly. "Come on, my darling. You and I will see if there are any of those jam tarts left in the larder."

And off he went quite happily with his grandmother, without a single look back at me.

I put on my hat and took Bridie's hand as we stepped out into bright sunshine. It was warm for September, and I wasn't looking forward to facing the heat and noise of the Lower East Side. But there was no going back now, even though Bridie looked about as unenthusiastic as I felt.

"I don't like those boys, my cousins," she said. "They are rough, and they tease me."

"I don't like them much either," I said, giving a conspiratorial wink. "But we'll do our duty and not stay long."

"Do you think Cousin Nuala might have news of my dada?" she asked.

"I don't know, my darling. But it's worth seeing her, just on the off chance, isn't it?"

"Yes." She nodded, convincing herself. "I'd do anything to know if they're all right."

We climbed the steps to the Third Avenue El station. As the train came rumbling in I had a moment of anxiety. Could I really get on board without worrying that something would happen to me? I looked up and down the platform, but there were only a few housewives on their way from shopping, mothers with young children, and nobody who looked furtive or threatening. I wished I had taken more notice of the man who knocked into me, making me miss that train. It might have been a complete coincidence, but as a detective I'd learned not to believe in coincidences. The train came to a halt and I ushered Bridie on board, then hauled myself up. As we moved off, I tried to picture the man. He'd been young, I was sure. Cap or hat? What kind of jacket? I closed my eyes, but all that came back to me was a blur of running feet. Dark hair. Dark jacket. But not a businessman. A student? Yes, possibly more like a student. Which of course made sense— a student, late for his next class and not even aware that he had bumped me as he dashed for an empty compartment. However, this also made me think of Simon Grossman, and a killer who was brazen enough to drop cyanide into his coffee. Could students and their activities have something to do with this crime after all? Was someone playing a cruel joke on Daniel?

The moment we disembarked from the El, I could tell where we were by the smell. As we walked down Fulton Street, the odor of the fish market wafted toward us until it grew overwhelming.

"What's that horrible smell?" Bridie demanded. "Do we have to go this way?"

"It's the fish market at the bottom of Fulton Street," I said. "And this is actually where we're heading."

"I thought we were going to visit Cousin Nuala," she said peevishly.

"We are. I don't know her current address, but I do know that she works at the fish market."

Ahead of us was the fish market, facing the piers. Not an unattractive building, with its gabled roof and cupolas to let in light, while the tower and cables of the Brooklyn Bridge soared above it, unnaturally large and out of proportion with the hovels and small ships below. I took out my handkerchief and handed it to Bridie. "Put that over your nose and mouth. I sprinkled on eau de cologne this morning."

We negotiated the forecourt, with its barrows of fish constantly passing to and fro and crates of fish being loaded onto wagons and drays. Then we were inside, in the gloomy darkness, with the full richness of the smell of dead fish around us. Underfoot was slippery with scales and blood. I picked up my skirt and went forward cautiously. I thought I remembered where Nuala had been working before, but when I got there I couldn't spot her.

"Yes, ma'am. What can I do for you?" A large man in a blood-spattered apron loomed up out of the gloom. Presumably the foreman, making sure nobody slacked off or received visitors.

"I'm looking for Nuala O'Grady. I believe she works here."

"Used to work here," he said. "Don't work here no more."

"I see. Would you happen to know where I can find her now? Her little cousin is visiting New York and wants to see her."

He took in Bridie's lace-trimmed dress and pink-and-white complexion. "Her cousin?" He sounded skeptical.

I was growing impatient. "Yes, her father's cousin, actually. Could you tell me where I might find her home address?"

He shrugged. "Wouldn't know. People move around a lot. Get kicked out of one apartment. Find another."

"Look, it's very important that I find her," I said. "Did she get a job somewhere else?"

"Nah. She don't work no more. Her boys take care of her. A lady of leisure, that's what she is." And he laughed.

"So you can't actually help me?"

"Would if I could," he said, shrugging. "Sorry."

"Well, that was a waste of time," I said as we came out and stood breathing in the fresh breeze that came up the East River.

"Can we go home now?" Bridie asked expectantly.

"We must make an effort to find them." I stood thinking. I remembered that they had been thrown out of their old house on Cherry Street. I knew Finbar, Nuala's no-good husband, had lost his job as a bouncer at a tavern, on account of his drinking. But knowing Finbar, he'd still be drinking somewhere, wouldn't he? I'd try the local taverns.

We walked up Water Street, staying away from the crazy commerce on the waterfront and stopping off at every tavern we saw. At the third one, the Irish Harp, we were rewarded. Ladies were not allowed inside but I was able to pass a message via the bouncer at the front door, and eventually someone shouted, "Finbar, get your drunk and lazy carcass out here. There's a lady wants to speak to you."

And Finbar emerged. Bridie shrank back and hid herself behind my skirts. Indeed he was a frightening figure—his face shrunk to a skeleton of skin and bone, eyes hollow, hair matted and unwashed, and clothes half hanging off him.

"Whatta you want?" he growled.

"Finbar, it's Molly," I said. "And your cousin Bridie."

A leering smile crossed his face. "Little Bridie," he said. "Sweet little Bridie." And he reached out a hand to touch her. She flinched away.

A thought flashed across my mind that maybe he had tried to molest her when she lived with them. He had certainly tried it with me. Not that he'd gotten very far.

"Finbar, where are you living? Bridie's come to see Nuala and the boys."

"She throws me out every day," he said, now sounding weepy. "Doesn't want me around the house. Says I'm underfoot and a no-good bag of bones."

"The address, Finbar," I insisted.

"Fifty-eight James Street. Not far from the Bowery," he managed to get out with great effort. "Top floor."

Naturally, I thought. People like Finbar were always given the top floor, up all those stairs nobody else wanted to climb. I thanked him, and against my better judgment I put fifty cents into his hand. He beamed, wept, and bowed. "God bless you, lady. God bless you," he called after me as we walked away.

The tenement on James Street was, if anything, worse than the one where they had first lived on Cherry. The hallway was dark, and dank, and smelled of urine and cabbage and drains. The one sink that was the water supply for the whole building was now full of filthy water. We started to climb the stairs, one flight, then the next. By the third, my ribs were aching and it hurt me to breathe. As I stopped to catch my breath, a door opened and a woman's face poked out. Her unkempt hair stuck out at all angles, and she looked around with wild eyes. "Brendan?" she demanded. "Is that you?"

Then she saw me and scowled. "What do you want? We don't need no do-gooders around here."

"I'm looking for Nuala O'Grady," I said. "I'm told she lives on the top floor."

"What's she done now? Those boys of hers been getting in trouble again?"

"Just a friendly visit," I said.

"'Friendly'? You call that old cow friendly?" She scooped up a snotty-nosed baby that was attempting to crawl out of the door and shut it behind her.

Bridie looked at me, wide-eyed, and said nothing. I took her hand and we went up the last flights in silence. As I tapped on the door I was transported back to my first day in New York, almost five years ago, when I had stood outside Nuala's door on the top floor of a similarly disgusting tenement. The door was flung open, and the doorway filled with Nuala's enormous bulk. Just as she had done the first time, Nuala now looked at me with loathing. "Well, would you look what the cat's brought in," she said.

"And top of the morning to you too, Nuala," I replied. "A fine greeting for your young relative whom I've brought to see you."

Her face softened then. "Well, look at you, Bridie, love. My, aren't you growing into a fine young woman. And where did you get those clothes? Fancy, aren't they? Did herself buy them for you, now that she's a policeman's wife?" She jerked her head to indicate me, but refused to call me by name.

"Mrs. Sullivan made them for me," she said. "I live with her."

"Mrs. Sullivan?"

"My mother-in-law. She's kindly taken Bridie in and is educating her," I explained for her.

"Well, how about that?" she said. She stepped aside. "I suppose you'd better come in."

The inside was as sorry as the last place they'd lived. One threadbare armchair, a scrubbed table with benches made of planks over blocks, a couple of saucepans hanging over the sink, and the smell of frying and unwashed bodies.

"Sit yourselves down then," she said. "I'll be making the tea."

We sat.

"Bridie's anxious to hear if you've any news of her father," I said. "She herself has heard nothing, and naturally she's very worried."

"We did hear, a little while back," she said. "Himself met a man at the tavern who had come back from the canal. Said he couldn't stick it out. Said no amount of money was worth enduring that hellhole.

He'd caught yellow fever but recovered—one of the lucky ones, I suppose. Anyway . . . " I held my breath and didn't dare glance at Bridie. "Anyway, he'd come across Seamus and young Shamey."

"And they were both alive and well?"

"At the time he saw them, yes. He said it was an out-of-the-way, godforsaken place, days by mule from anywhere."

I turned to Bridie. "There, you see, my love. They are still all right. But they have no way to send you letters."

She nodded, her eyes still full of hope and fear at the same time.

The kettle boiled, and Nuala squeezed her bulk around the table to pour the water into the teapot.

"I see you're not working at the fish market any longer," I said. "Has Finbar found a better job that you're able to stay home?"

"Himself? That lazy, good-for-nothing bag of bones?" she half spat. "He's no job at all and drinks any money he can lay his hands on. No, it's my boys. They are making money, doing odd jobs for certain influential people." She didn't mention that the influential people was really one person—Monk Eastman, leader of one of the city's most powerful and brutal gangs. And I wasn't going to let on that I knew.

"How very nice," I said. "Are any of them here? I have a little job myself that needs doing, and I could use a smart boy."

"Malachy's out, doing something," she said, "and James is in school. He's the studious one. But I sent young Thomas down to bring us some oysters for our tea. The boat comes in from the marshes about this time, but you have to be quick. He should be back anytime now."

She handed us chipped and grubby cups, and we sipped politely.

"Last time I saw you, you were in the family way," she said.

"That's right. I've now a fine boy a year old. Liam."

"Boys." She sniffed. "Boys only bring you grief. Would that God had given me a girl like young Bridie here. She looks like butter wouldn't melt in her mouth. Is that right, Bridie? You're a good girl, aren't you?"

"Yes, Cousin Nuala," she said. "I try to be."

"You see. Doesn't give you a day's grief in her life. Boys, on the other hand, are always coming home dirty and bloody and . . . "

As if on cue we heard steps running up the stairs, and Thomas burst in. He was about to say something but stopped when he saw us.

"So you're back," Nuala said. "And where are my oysters?"

"I was too late. Some man pushed in front of me and took the last, and when I said something he threatened to punch me in the nose or push me off the dock." I could tell now that he had been crying. Tears had streaked the dirt on his cheeks.

"You've got to learn to stand up for yourself like your brother Malachy," she said. "You tell him who the man was, and no doubt someone will teach him a lesson he won't forget in a hurry. Malachy has a real protector now, and that applies to you too."

"Yes, Mah," he said. He smiled shyly at Bridie. He was probably a year older than her but hardly any taller. As fat as his mother was, he looked as if he never got a good meal.

"This is your cousin Bridie come to visit," I said. "And you remember me? Molly? I stayed with you once, and then you came and stayed with me."

"I know," he said. "Hello, Bridie. It's grand to see you looking so fine."

"Thank you, Thomas." She looked down, suddenly shy too.

"Thomas," Nuala said. "This lady might have an errand for you."

"That's right, Thomas," I said. "I need you to find a boy for me. This boy delivered a message to police headquarters on Mulberry Street."

"Is he in trouble?" Thomas asked, frowning.

"Not at all. He did nothing wrong. It's just that the man who gave him the note to deliver might have done something wrong, and we have to find him before he can hurt more people. It's no use if grownups ask questions, because the boys won't rat on each other. But you can tell the boy that the police won't question him. They'll leave him alone. We just need a description of the man who paid him . . . and paid him well, I suspect." I paused, then, taking a risk, I said, "Whatever the man paid him, I'll pay you."

"Is that a fact?" Thomas's face lit up. "All right. I'll do it. Tell me all about it."

I told him everything I knew, leaving out the fact that this man had murdered a whole list of people. No sense in scaring him. Thomas told me his brother could help him put the fear of God into the boys and get them to fess up. This wasn't what I'd had in mind, but I saw it could be useful. Nobody willingly crossed someone connected to the Eastmans.

As Bridie and I made our way down the stairs and took in a breath of good sea air, we both gave a sigh of relief.

"I don't think you wanted me to visit my relatives at all," Bridie commented as we made our way back along Fulton Street to the El station. "I think you wanted the boys to do that job for you, and you needed an excuse to visit them."

I looked down at her sweetly innocent face and smiled. "You are becoming too sharp for your years, young lady."

We walked on. "I wish I could live with you, Molly," she said. "I don't remember my real mother very well. I know she was kind and gentle and had a soft voice, but I don't really remember her. So you're the only mother I've got."

Before I could answer she went on, "I know that I should keep on with Mrs. Sullivan, because she's been so good to me and she's lonely up there, all alone."

I wanted to tell her the plans in store for her, but as I hadn't discussed the matter with Daniel yet, I had to stay silent. "You know I'd love to have you here with me, anytime," I said, "but you're right. Mrs. Sullivan has been good to you. Your father wanted us to find you a place as a maid, you know. Mrs. Sullivan took you in, started to train you for domestic service, and then became fond of you. Now you're turning into a young lady."

"I know," she said. "I've been very lucky." There was a long silence, and then she said, "You know sometimes I have bad thoughts."

"Bad thoughts? You?"

She nodded. "Sometimes I hope that my father won't come back, because I don't want to go back to living how we did, with Cousin Nuala. Then I'd really have to be a servant, wouldn't I?"

I looked down at her worried little face. "I don't think we'd let you go back to living with Nuala now," I said. "Even if your father returns soon, he won't want to be bothered with a young girl. He'll be happy someone else is taking care of her welfare."

I saw her face light up. "You think so?"

"What would Seamus know about raising a young woman?" I said.

"I don't think Cousin Nuala knows much about it either," she added with a grin.

❊❦ Twenty ❦❊

We had only just arrived home when Sid and Gus called to say they were starting their search for Dr. Werner and asked if I wanted to go with them, but I refused this time. Frankly, I was exhausted by that simple little jaunt to Nuala's. And I'd have been no use, having no experience of universities or medical schools.

So I stayed home, waiting and worrying. Maybe it would all go smoothly, I thought. The commissioner couldn't expect Daniel to work miracles. But it seemed I was wrong. Daniel came home in a foul mood, just as we were finishing our supper.

"Another long session with the commissioner," he said as he strode toward us down the hall, the sound of his heavy tread echoing up from the stairwell and the newly painted walls. "He wants to know why I haven't caught this guy yet, and how much longer he is expected to sanction having men stationed around the city watching prominent people and landmarks and generally being on high alert. It's costing too much in overtime hours, and he wants results." Daniel stomped through to the kitchen, sat, and began to unlace his boots. "He asked me if this man is finished with his killing spree or planning to strike again. As if I know. Does he think I'm a seer or a fortune-teller? How can anyone know the man's mind, if we don't know whom we're dealing with?"

He kicked off one boot and it fell with a clatter. "I could tell him nothing. I felt like a fool. Then I made the mistake of telling him that the only link we can find between the murders is that the notes were all addressed to me." The other boot joined its mate on the floor. "He didn't like that at all. Thought I was making too much of myself. To him I'm one of a hundred policemen. The killer could have picked my name at random—out of a newspaper, maybe."

He pushed the boots out of the way and drew his chair up to the table. "And then he said he wished the murderer had chosen some-one with a few more detecting skills, and we might have the case solved by now. "

"The cheek of it!" I said. "You're one of their top detectives. Youn-gest man to be made captain. How dare he?"

"He dares because he's the commissioner of police and in two years' time, someone else will be elected to the position." Daniel rested his elbows on the table and dropped his chin into his hands. "And then comes the kicker. He's suggesting adding another officer to 'assist' me."

"Well, I suppose it can't hurt at this stage, can it?" I said. "Two heads are better than one and you can't be everywhere at once."

I saw immediately that I'd said the wrong thing. "'It can't hurt'?" he demanded. "It damned well can hurt!"

I heard an intake of breath from his mother. "Daniel, such lan-guage," she said. "There are women and children present."

"Sorry, Mother," he muttered. "But you must understand my frus-tration. I've been pushed to snapping point over this." He slapped one fist against the other. "This second officer who is to 'assist' me will be the commissioner's spy, handpicked by him. Everything I do will be reported back instantly. For all I know, someone at the top is looking for a way to shove me aside. And when I am making no progress, how is that going to look?"

"Then tell him you think it's a great idea to assign another detective to the case, but you'd like to choose someone you can work with," I suggested.

"One does not tell the commissioner anything. The man enjoys his power. He's a trumped-up Tammany puppet, and he knows no more about police work than young Bridie here." He looked from me to his son, who was sitting in his high chair, watching wide-eyed at his father's outburst. "I tell you, Molly," Daniel said, "this may be the end of my career if something doesn't happen soon."

I got up and put a hand on his shoulder. "You're a good detective, Daniel. I'm sure everyone who matters knows that. And you're dealing with a case that isn't giving you any tangible leads. In a city this size, if someone wants to carry out random murders, how are you supposed to stop them?"

I heaped a plate with his favorite stew and put it in front of him. "Get that down you. You'll feel better. I'll wager you haven't eaten all day."

"Probably haven't. Can't remember," he said, already tucking into the steaming plate. "Thanks."

"Your mother made the stew. You can thank her," I said. There was so much more I wanted to say, but I wasn't going to risk it with Mrs. Sullivan sitting across the table. Instead I cleared away our dishes and started to wash up.

It wasn't until Liam was safely tucked in bed and the dinner was cleaned up that I came into the back parlor to see Daniel sitting at his desk. He looked up and held out a hand to me. "Sorry I was in such a foul mood earlier," he said.

"With justification," I said. "I'd have been hopping mad myself if I'd been insulted like that." I went over and saw he'd been writing names on a sheet of paper. "What are you doing?"

"What you suggested. Trying to remember any cases in which I was instrumental in bringing about a death penalty. I really can't think of any that fit the bill, though."

"Maybe it wasn't even the death penalty. If you had someone shut away for life, that could be considered similar to a living death, couldn't it? A loved one could blame you for taking away a brother or father." Then I tapped him excitedly on the arm. "Or, better yet. You've been a policeman for fifteen years. What if you had someone convicted for life, or a long sentence, but it was commuted for good behavior, and the man is now finally free? Maybe he's a quiet and brooding sort, and all these years he's been plotting revenge against you."

Daniel licked his lips. "You might have something there, Molly. It's worth looking into anyway. I'll have my sergeant get in touch with Sing Sing and find out who might have been released recently. Then we can see if any of them ring a bell." He gave me a weak smile. "Well, that's something to go on, isn't it?"

I decided to pluck up my courage and maybe get my head bitten off. "Daniel, I know you haven't wanted me to get involved in any of your police work in the past," I said. "But you said yourself that you are stumped. I'm wondering how you would feel if I did a little poking around myself. I thought I could visit the next of kin of the murder victims."

He held up his hand. "Oh, no, Molly. I'm sure you mean well and want to help, but I'd never hear the last of it if word got back to the commissioner that I was so desperate I'd had to use my wife."

"Hold your horses a moment," I said. "The people I interview need not know who I am. I could find some pretext, so they wouldn't know I was your wife."

"What sort of pretext?" he asked, still suspicious.

"It would be different for each one, wouldn't it? I'd be a newspaper reporter, doing a piece on the dangers of trolley cars in Brooklyn. I could easily pass as a female student who was a friend of Simon Grossman. I'll think of others as I go."

"But what would be the point, Molly? Do you think that I and my men haven't asked every conceivable question? Haven't looked into their backgrounds, their connections thoroughly?"

"I'm sure you have," I said. "But I'm a woman and a civilian and therefore not a threat. Women chat to other women. I could talk to the servants in the richer houses. There may be things that haven't come out yet, or things that nobody would want to tell to the police. And maybe it would just take one small detail . . . "

"In case you've forgotten, you're in no condition to go running all over the city," he said. I could tell that he was torn. He didn't want me getting involved. His pride was railing against it, as well as his caution at putting me into possible danger.

I decided to add my trump card. "In case *you've* forgotten, Daniel Sullivan, I am already involved in this. You believe that the killer might have had me in mind when he derailed that train, don't you?"

"*If* he derailed the train. We're still not quite able to believe it, and we've still no proof to hint that it wasn't simply human error."

"But if he did, then I'm already involved. If he's scheming to get at me, then I want to get him first, don't you understand?"

He drummed his fingers on his desktop. "But I want you to take time to heal, Molly. Not tax yourself at the moment."

"I know that. But time is of the essence here, isn't it? We're racing against the clock and against another possible murder."

There was a long silence. Then he said, "You're a good detective, Molly. I've never said that you weren't. But this is a tremendous risk . . . my career . . . "

"You yourself just said that your career might be in jeopardy if you can't solve this case. So what have you got to lose?"

He sighed. "You're right. What have I got to lose at this stage?"

"So I have your blessing? You know I don't like going behind your back."

"I've noticed," he said with a grin. Then he reached out and took my hand, pulling me closer to him. "You have my blessing. But if anyone finds out what you've been doing, I shall deny all knowledge of it. Oh, and, Molly, nothing stupid or risky, understand? You can ask questions, but no climbing in through windows, or any other reckless behavior."

I put on my most demure smile. "Daniel Sullivan—when have I ever engaged in reckless behavior?"

"I could name about a hundred occasions," he said, "but I hope you'll remember that you're older and wiser now, and you have a husband and child to consider."

"Don't worry," I said. "I'll be the soul of decorum."

"I'll believe that when I see it," he said.

✿ Twenty-one ✿

The next day I meant to begin my own investigation, visiting the victims' relatives, but when I got up and dressed I realized I just didn't feel up to facing more public transportation and crossing the bridge to Brooklyn. Daniel went off to work early in the morning and came back at night tired, frustrated, and with little to report. They had been through a list of long-term prisoners who had recently been released from Sing Sing, as well as prisoners who had died in custody, and none of them had been cases that Daniel had investigated. Back to square one.

Sid and Gus came over to report on their search for Dr. Otto Werner—so far without success. Gus said that she had been met with patronization bordering on rudeness from professors at the university medical school. One thought the whole branch of psychiatry had no medical basis or future. Another had no time for women outside the kitchen (or presumably the bedroom, Sid had added). And none of them had met Dr. Otto Werner.

"We must look into learned societies," Gus said. "Perhaps there is a society dedicated to the study of dreams, or the study of the mind."

"Quite possible," I said, "and there are also German clubs in the city. If I were a single man, far from home, I'd want a place where I could speak my own language and eat my own food."

"Brilliant idea, Molly." Gus beamed. "And the German consulate. Presumably he'll have checked in with them. And we should receive a reply from Professor Freud any day now. We just have to be patient."

Gus sighed. "It's hard to be patient when a young girl's life and sanity are at stake. Perhaps I will dare to visit her again, in case she has had a more detailed dream."

So they had their quest and I had mine. The only piece of positive news was that Lieutenant Yeats had agreed to exhume the bodies of Mabel's parents, in the hope that he could find out what had killed them.

"I had a talk with him," Daniel reported, when he arrived home that night. "As you say, he's a cocky young devil. He thinks he has enough to put the girl in the dock without any autopsy. And the way he told it, Molly, I can see his reasoning. The fire definitely started in the parents' bedroom. They can't tell if an overturned lamp caused it. The lamp's glass was shattered, but then it would have exploded in the fire. It's possible that some kind of fire starter may have been used, because the area surrounding the parents' beds burned the most fiercely."

"How awful. Yeats is suggesting that someone deliberately poured something flammable around their beds?"

Daniel nodded. "Gasoline perhaps. It looks that way."

"So we're definitely looking at a murder here?"

"Yeats thinks so. And his other point that your friends might not want to hear is that the parents' window was open, and the fire escape had been activated. Now the girl's room was close to the stairs. If the fire had started and she had awoken, smelling smoke or seeing flames, she could have run down the stairs to safety. But we know that she didn't do that, because the front door was locked. The servants got out through the kitchen door, and they didn't see her. If Mabel had gone into her parents' room and seen it already burning, there was no way she could have passed their bed and crossed the room without showing at least some sign of having been in a fire. It might even have been impossible to have reached the window after the fire started."

"So we have to conclude that she was in her parents' room before the fire, and that she got out down the fire escape before the fire took hold," I said.

"That's what we have to conclude, Molly. I trust your friends are no longer attempting their mumbo jumbo on the girl?"

"It's not mumbo jumbo," I said angrily. "Gus trained with *the* expert on the interpretation of dreams. But she admits herself that this is beyond her capabilities. They have written to Vienna for advice and are trying to trace one of Freud's fellow doctors who has been in America giving lectures. He was known to be in New York earlier this year. Gus has been asking about him at the university, but with no luck so far. When they receive an answer to their letter, let's hope we know more."

"A sad case," Daniel said. "But it's not the first time I have seen a young person, an apparently sane and devoted child, calmly murder a parent. Maybe they had forbidden her to do something she liked, and she acted in a fit of anger. Emotions run so high at that stage of life."

I shook my head. "I still can't believe it of Mabel. She seems such a gentle, delicate little thing. And if she had caused the fire herself, would she still find the event so traumatic?"

"She may have regretted it instantly, but it was too late to stop it," Daniel said. "Young people act so much on impulse. I know I did. Didn't you?"

I smiled. "I didn't have much chance to act on impulse in a cottage in Ireland. We were miles from anywhere, and there was nothing worth doing anyway, apart from letting a boy walk me part of the way home from a dance. Besides, by Mabel's age I had a father and three young brothers to take care of, and that was a full-time job."

He nodded with understanding. "Anyway, thank God this girl is not your problem," he added. "And let's hope that Gus Walcott is sensible enough to know her own limitations."

"I told you she has admitted the case is beyond her scope and is seeking out an alienist who might have studied the interpretation of dreams. We've been recommended a Dr. Otto Werner from Munich who is highly regarded and was known to be in New York earlier this year."

Daniel stroked his chin. "Otto Werner. That name rings a bell. I've come across it recently. He might have testified as an expert witness on some court case I attended."

"You wouldn't know where to find him, would you?"

"If he did appear in court, his address would be in the records somewhere. I'll ask one of the clerks to look it up for you."

"Thank you. That would be grand. We need something to start going right, don't we?"

He nodded, staring out past me, through the window at the darkened street. "Although you should realize that bringing in an expert to treat your young girl might not help her cause, Molly." He turned back to me and held my gaze. "He might be able to prove that she did kill her parents. He might return her to sanity and bring back the full memory of what happened. There are many possible outcomes, not all of them good."

"I know that. But it's a risk that has to be taken. Didn't you yourself say that it's better to know the truth than to not know?"

"I did." He got up and walked across to the window, pulled back the lace curtain, and stared out—something I noticed he had done several times since we'd moved back to the house. And I realized that he would never feel completely safe here again, never feel that he could protect his family after what had happened to us.

I went over to him, and ran my hand down his stubbly cheek. "It will be all right, Daniel. We will be all right. Don't worry."

He sighed and let me lead him away.

"There is one thing that crossed my mind," I said tentatively. "The fire was at the beginning of August. Could it possibly be your missing murder?"

"You're saying the fire was started by an intruder? Isn't that just grasping at straws to get your girl off the hook? I know you want to think she's innocent, but . . . "

"Hold your horses there, Daniel Sullivan." I put a warning hand on his lapel. "I'm just saying it's a remarkable coincidence that it fits into your killer's pattern. It's something we should consider."

"I'd need some sort of evidence before I considered it," he said. "Where was the note? He is a creature of habit, after all."

"Maybe it got lost in the mail, or it was given to a small boy who failed to deliver it," I suggested.

"Maybe." He sighed again. "I wish I could find just one morsel of truth in the case of my note writer. Four months, and I am none the wiser."

"I'll start visiting the victims' relatives tomorrow," I said. "Maybe something will come to light. And Nuala's sons may actually find the boy who delivered the notes. We may get a description of your killer."

Again he stared out past me, as if he was trying to see something in the darkness—maybe that figurative light at the end of the tunnel. "At this moment I'm feeling pretty low. Even if we catch him, he's such a cunning devil that we'd have a tough time pinning any of the crimes on him."

"He'll make one mistake in the end," I said. "They always do. You've always said that yourself, haven't you? He's so cocky that he won't be as careful. Like using an urchin to deliver his note. We'll find the right boy and get a good description."

Daniel looked at my face and managed a weak smile. "I'm glad you're so optimistic, Molly. You need optimism for both of us at this moment."

I didn't tell him that I was no more optimistic than he, but just clinging to shreds of hope that some good would come from my own plans.

The next morning I awoke early, resolved to tackle the first names on Daniel's list of victims' relatives that day. On the trolley over the Brooklyn Bridge, I tried to come up with a good reason to give for my visit, one that wouldn't link me to Daniel. I decided I was working for a ladies' magazine, doing an article on the dangers of electric trolleys. I alighted from just such a vehicle, and watched a large lady with a shopping basket over her arm have to sprint across the street as the trolley I had been riding took off again, ringing its bell furiously.

I stood on the sidewalk and opened my list of fatalities again to check the address:

May 10. Dolly Willis. 285 Flushing Avenue, Brooklyn. (Feebleminded woman of 62. Lived with her sister. Pushed into the path of a speeding trolley.)

Note said: "Trolley and Dolly rhyme. A fitting end this time."

One thing that struck me now was that the murderer knew her name. Had he only learned it when someone in the crowd peered down at her body and exclaimed, "Why, that's Dolly Willis!"? Or had he known it all along, meaning that this wasn't a random killing after all? For some reason, had Dolly Willis had to die?

When I had studied the list in my bedroom the night before, it had come to me what an enigmatic individual we were dealing with. In almost every case I'd handled during my life as a detective, some pattern had started to emerge—a method of killing, a motive, even a time of day or a place. Here there was nothing. No clue, no link. Just notes addressed to *Captain Daniel Sullivan.* I continued along the street until I stood across from Dolly's house. It was a small wooden structure, like the rest of the houses on the block. It looked as if it could do with a good coat of paint, but was otherwise a nice enough little place. As I watched, a trolley passed, going rather fast, followed by a carriage and an automobile. Dolly had indeed lived on a dangerous street. It struck me that Molly also rhymed with trolley, as he had written on the note.

Had he killed people in ways that rhymed? I wondered. But I couldn't make anything of Simon and cyanide or Marie and arsenic so I quickly abandoned that theory. I did, however, look very carefully both ways before I crossed the street myself. The idea that I had been the intended target in the train crash was still at the back of my mind. Maybe the murderer had been shadowing me ever since, waiting for the right moment. Then I told myself that this was foolish. He could have brushed against me and stabbed me on crowded Fulton Street yesterday. He could even have come in through my open bedroom window and . . . I stopped, shuddering at the thought, and pushed it from my mind.

On the corner, two houses from where Dolly had lived, was a small general store. I decided I might do well to glean some information before I visited Dolly's sister. I went in and asked for a pad of writing paper. The woman behind the counter smiled as she handed it to me. "Pleasant day for this time of year, isn't it?" she said.

"It is indeed," I replied. "Sometimes I think that fall is the best time in this part of the world."

"You're not from here yourself, I can tell," she said.

"No. I've been in the city nearly five years now. And yourself?"

"Born in Germany but brought over here as a baby," she said. "It's a good life compared to what we left, isn't it?"

"It is," I said. "If you can just stay out of the way of those trolleys zooming up and down your street."

"Aren't they the very devil himself," she said. "We had an old lady knocked down by one of them this spring. Knocked down and killed, she was, and a sweet old thing that never said a wrong word in her life."

"I read about it in the paper," I said. "Wasn't she a bit mentally defective?"

"Simple, she was. Not crazy, just simple. Mind like a child. Easily led. But always had a big smile when you spoke to her. Her sister used to send her out to do the errands, and she'd hand me a piece of paper with the shopping list on it. Couldn't read, you see." She gave me a conspiratorial smile. "I'd sometimes slip a candy or two into her bag. She was very fond of her candy."

The shop was still empty. I leaned closer. "There was some talk that she didn't step out in front of the trolley, she was pushed."

The woman shook her head. "That's what I heard too. But who would do a thing like that? Only maybe if someone was in a hurry and jostling to get to the front of the crowd. Leastways I never heard that anyone saw anything. Only the poor dear woman lurching forward, right under the wheels of that trolley. I heard the screams and looked up, and by then it was all over, of course."

"You didn't see anyone running away or acting strangely, then?"

She shook her head. "I did not. They were all clustered around her, trying to help her, but of course it was too late. I heard one man say 'Let me through, I'm a doctor.' But he couldn't do anything."

"Her sister must have been devastated," I said.

"She was. Still is, poor dear. They were so close, those two—Dolly just worshipped her sister. Relied on her for everything. And now poor Miss Willis is all alone. I feel so bad for her when she comes in here, lingering on to talk to me because she's nobody else to talk to. Gave up everything for that sister of hers—had a good job, you know. Well treated, with a fine family."

"Really?" I said.

"Oh, yes. An influential family in Manhattan. She was head parlor maid there. Then she came into some money, and left the job to look after her mother and sister."

I might have stayed longer, but several customers entered at once, so I thanked the shopkeeper and left. Not that I had learned anything from our little chat, I thought. Maybe I was rusty and needed to ask better questions.

I paused outside Miss Willis's house and took a deep breath. It had been a while since I'd been a detective, prying into other people's secrets, and it's amazing how soon one gets out of practice. I repeated my opening remarks to myself in my head before I knocked on the door.

It was opened by a middle-aged woman with a colorless face, her hair, streaked with gray, was drawn back in a severe bun. She was dressed in black and she looked warily at me.

"Yes? Can I help you?" she asked.

"I'm sorry to disturb you, Miss Willis," I said, and saw her react to my knowledge of her name, "but I'm a reporter with a ladies' magazine in Manhattan and I'm doing an article on how to keep the family safe in the modern city. I was in the corner shop and I happened to hear that your own poor sister was knocked down by a trolley car. So I wondered if I could take a moment of your time. It's just the sort of danger we want to warn mothers about. Next time it could be their child, couldn't it?"

"It could indeed." She peered out past me as we heard an approaching bell. "You've seen the speed they go at. It's not normal. It's not Christian. If you ask me, I believe the electricity was sent from the devil himself. I was so glad when old Mr. Cornelius refused to have it put into his own house. I expect Mr. Marcus had it done before his father's corpse was cold. Always one for change was Mr. Marcus."

"They were your employers?" I asked.

"They were indeed. And I couldn't have had a better master than old Mr. Cornelius. A proper gentleman in every sense of the word." She suddenly seemed to come to her senses and said, "Dear me, what must you be thinking, with me leaving you standing on the doorstep. Come in, do. I've just made a pot of coffee and it's warm on the hob."

"Thank you. You're very kind." I followed her down a little hallway smelling of furniture polish and into a spotlessly neat little back parlor. It was a product of the Victorian era, what we'd now consider old-fashioned—every inch decorated with china ornaments, potted ferns, even a wax flower arrangement under glass. The chairs were red velvet, now faded to a dull brown. I sat on one side of the fireplace while she went to fetch the coffee. On the mantel I noticed there was a photograph of the two sisters—a younger Miss Willis looking at the camera with haughty defiance, and beside her a softer, rounder-faced sister, slightly Oriental in appearance, giving the photographer a big, friendly grin.

"Here we are." Miss Willis returned. "I baked some gingerbread this morning. It used to be Dolly's favorite."

"How kind. And I'm most fond of gingerbread too," I said. "I take it that's your sister in the photograph on the mantelpiece?"

"That's right. When we were twenty-one."

"Oh. You were twins," I said.

"We were. Always did everything together. Made it my life's mission to take care of Dolly. But I couldn't protect her when she needed it." She didn't meet my eye as she handed me my coffee cup.

"I'm so sorry," I said. "What a senseless thing to have happened."

She nodded, lips pressed together. "She was always so careful crossing the street too. She did just like we told her. At the curb halt. Eyes left. Eyes right. Eyes left again. If all clear, quick march. She used to repeat that every time she stood at the curb."

"Maybe someone pushed her," I said, then added quickly, "by mistake, you know. Too eager to cross the road. And she lost her balance. I remember that someone nearly knocked me over on the train platform recently. He was in such a hurry to get to the first carriage."

"People have no manners these days," she said.

I realized that I couldn't ask her whether she suspected Dolly had been pushed deliberately, or whether she could think of anyone who wanted to do Dolly harm. It would be too cruel to put that thought into her head if it wasn't already there.

"What did the tram driver say?" I asked. "Did he see Dolly step out in front of him and try to stop?"

"He says he saw nothing. A crowd of people waiting to cross the street, and suddenly someone sprawling right under his wheels. He was quite shaken up about it—probably feeling guilty because he was going too fast, if you ask me."

"'Sprawling'? That really does sound as if she lost her balance and fell forward, doesn't it?" I said.

She handed me the plate of gingerbread and then said, "The police were here. They asked me if anyone might want to harm Dolly. What a terrible thing to say. Everyone loved Dolly. She didn't have a mean bone in her body."

I nodded in sympathetic understanding. "You don't have any unfriendly neighbors who might harbor a grudge? There are some really strange people in the world, aren't there?"

"Not our neighbors. I've known them all my life. Nobody moves much in this part of town. We're like a little village. Take care of each other. They were all so kind when my mother died, and now Dolly."

"When you worked as a maid, did you live away from home?" I asked, biting into deliciously moist gingerbread.

"I did. I didn't really want to leave them, but I wasn't qualified for anything but domestic service and I was lucky with my employer. I was with Mr. Cornelius for twenty-five years. I saw his younger son born and his poor wife die. I really felt part of that family. We all did. So it came as a shock to leave . . . not that I didn't want to come home, but all the same . . . "

"I thought—the lady at the corner shop told me that you had come into money. That's why you came home."

"Well, yes, that's true," she said. "Mr. Cornelius did leave me a nice legacy when he died, and I probably would have left my position anyway, but it came as a shock, Mr. Marcus telling me that my services were no longer required. He didn't put it as bluntly as that, you understand, but he said he was going to have the whole house refurbished and simplify his lifestyle, and he didn't want so many servants. So he was getting rid of me—me who had looked after him most of his life after his mother died. I can tell you that hurt. Such a selfish, arrogant young man he grew up to be."

"I'm sorry," I said. "It must have been really hard for you, losing your employer and your job."

"Oh, I'm not complaining," she said. "I have a tidy little sum from Mr. Cornelius. Mr. Marcus couldn't take that away from me if he tried.

If there was one thing Mr. Cornelius knew, it was how to tie up money properly. Well, he would, wouldn't he, seeing as he'd been a banker all his life."

We talked a little about the other dangers I was supposedly writing about—the dangers of electricity, and I told her the story about the woman whose lamp fell into the bathtub and electrocuted her. She shook her head in disbelief. "I'm just glad I'm not raising a family in these troubled times," she said. "They talk about progress, but it seems to me it just brings more heartache and grief."

I thought it was time for me to leave and I stood up, placing my cup and plate back on the tray. "You've been very kind to give me your time," I said.

"Not at all," she said. "The house seems awful quiet without Dolly here. Always singing, she was, in that funny little high voice of hers. Sometimes when I close my eyes I can still hear it."

She escorted me to the front door. I tried to think if there was anything else I could ask her. I couldn't imagine that she had pushed her own sister. Neither had anyone else from her neighborhood, apparently. Everyone loved Dolly. The only note of disquiet was Miss Willis's bitterness at having been cast out by her employers after so many years of service. Mr. Marcus—she had said he was the arrogant one. But surely he could have nothing to do with the death of a simple soul.

"Your former employers," I said. "They lived in Manhattan?"

"Oh, yes. A fine big house on the Upper East Side. But I heard Mr. Marcus let it out, or sold it, and went to live in the Dakota building in one of those fancy apartments. That's the way things go, isn't it? You build a legacy for your children, and they don't appreciate it. I wouldn't be surprised if he didn't run his father's bank into the ground. Never was good with money as a young man. Still, that's not my concern, is it? Nothing to do with me what he does anymore."

✂ **Twenty-two** ✂

"A h, there you are, just in time for lunch," Mother Sullivan greeted me as I returned to Patchin Place, hot, tired, and aching. "Had a nice walk? Did you find anything?"

"Find anything?" I looked at her cautiously, wondering what she meant, and whether she had gleaned information from listening in to my chats with Daniel.

"I thought you were on the hunt for more items for the kitchen," she said. "I mentioned that we could do with a bigger mixing bowl and an egg whisk. It's too tiring to make a good custard without an egg whisk."

"Oh, no," I said. "I didn't go shopping this morning. I don't really feel up to facing the crowded stores yet. I'm scared I might get bumped into and injure myself further."

"So where did you go?" she asked, pointedly. "Just out for a walk, was it, because you were gone a long time."

I could have told her it was none of her business, but there was no sense in antagonizing her. Besides, she was being good to us, doing virtually all the cleaning and cooking, when at home she had a maid who did such things for her.

"I went to visit an old woman I'd promised to see," I said. "She lives all alone since her sister died." I'd found it was always best to stay as close to the truth as possible.

She followed me down the hall after I had hung up my hat and put my gloves on the hallstand. "If it was a social call you could have taken Bridie with you. Old people are often cheered by the sight of a young face."

I turned then to look at her, forcing myself to bite my tongue. "It was a call I'd told Daniel I'd make," I said.

She stared at me for what seemed like an eternity. "From my experience it doesn't pay to try to get involved in your husband's work," she said. "It's not a job for a woman, especially not for a young mother like yourself."

"I'm not getting involved in his work," I replied testily. My feet were hurting me, my side was aching, and my head was starting to throb again. "Chatting with a lonely old lady is something a woman can do better than a man."

"I see." She said no more but went back to peeling potatoes. I had no doubt she'd have something to say to Daniel about my expedition. I just hoped that wouldn't make him decide to forbid me any future visits. Not that I'd probably make any difference to his investigation. Miss Willis had not told me anything that gave new insight into what had happened to Dolly—except that the new master of the household where she'd worked had dismissed her after his father died. But what that had to do with a simple old lady being pushed under a trolley car, I failed to see.

When Daniel came home that evening, I waited until we had eaten dinner and were alone in the back parlor before I gave him a full report.

"If she had been unjustly fired from her job, then surely she would have been the one pushing someone under a trolley," he said, half joking. "Besides, she wasn't unjustly fired. She inherited a legacy. I suspect her new employer was just being kind—giving her a little nudge, knowing that she didn't need to work anymore and suspecting she was only staying on out of loyalty."

"You could be right," I said, having not considered this.

"Old ladies always like something to complain about," he said.

"You're right about that too," I said, thinking that his mother would no doubt tell him I should not go running around. He smiled, reading my thoughts.

"And I've something to report to you and your friends. They exhumed the bodies today. They were badly charred. I don't know if a pathologist can glean anything from such a body, but I will tell you one thing. Photographs were taken at the scene, and also when the bodies were removed to the morgue. They were both lying on their backs with their arms crossed over their chests, as if laid out for a burial. They were definitely either dead or heavily drugged before that fire started."

"And there was no obvious sign of how they died?" I asked. "No stab wound or bullet?"

"It wouldn't be easy to tell that definitely just from observation," he said. "Maybe when the autopsy is conducted we might find evidence of stabbing or a bullet, but I think not."

"And suffocation?" I asked. "If someone had put a pillow over their heads as they slept?"

He looked at me again with amusement. "I don't know if you've ever tried to suffocate somebody, but you have to be strong. They would wake up and struggle."

"So a young girl like Mabel would definitely not have been strong enough to do that."

"I think it's unlikely. But she could have administered some kind of poison—although I can't surmise what that would have been, when the bodies showed no signs of distress. Something quick-acting like cyanide, and the body convulses in agony. Something like arsenic and there would have been prior distress, vomiting . . . " He paused again.

"I can't believe I'm having this conversation with my wife. It's not exactly normal drawing room talk, is it?"

"You know that not many wives can help their husbands with insights into a difficult case," I said. "And you'd be bored if I related everything Liam had done all day and my annoyance with the dressmaker."

He laughed, and I noticed how much I liked the way his eyes crinkled at the sides when the lines of worry were removed from his face.

"A sleeping draft would be the most obvious," I said, as this new thought struck me. "If her parents had such a preparation on hand, she could have mixed it into their evening hot milk."

"You realize you're coming up with a scenario that makes her look guilty," Daniel said. "If we find out from the servants that either parent took sleeping powders, and we determine that there were cups near the bed, then I'm afraid Yeats will have your young lady locked up and prosecuted."

"Oh, dear," I said. "I just hope that Sid and Gus can find this Dr. Werner soon, and he can help unlock the girl's dreams. My heart tells me she is innocent, Daniel. I'm sure there is more to this than we are seeing right now."

I lay awake that night, weighing the events of the day—poor little Mabel and whether I believed her capable of killing her parents, and Miss Willis, grieving for a simpleminded sister. *Who might have sneaked up behind an elderly woman and shoved her in front of a trolley?* I wondered. But I couldn't come up with any answers. I could have concluded that Dolly would have inherited her sister's legacy some day and someone else wanted to inherit, except that the note writer had gone on to murder a strange variety of other people. I toyed with the idea that someone thought he was doing Miss Willis a favor, ridding her of a mentally incompetent sister. But one would only have to have witnessed her grief-stricken face to know that she loved Dolly and missed her.

Although I didn't say anything to Daniel, I found that the journey to Brooklyn had taken its toll on me. My side ached. My head ached. And when I finally drifted off to sleep, I went straight back to that dream. The narrow dark room. The sound of rumbling that shook every fiber of my body, and the terror that I couldn't move. Couldn't breathe.

Daniel shook me awake. "You were moaning in your sleep again," he said.

"It was that same dream. Trapped in the narrow room and the horrible rumbling."

"You're trying to do too much, Molly. We should have listened to my mother and let her take care of you while you recover. No more rushing all over town. It's not going to get us anywhere. My men and I have already asked every question you asked." He wrapped a protective arm around me. "Go back to sleep," he whispered. "I'm here. I won't let anything bad happen to you."

The next morning I had wanted to go visit Simon Grossman's family, and then Mrs. Daughtery's son, but my head still ached slightly and I had to admit, reluctantly, that Daniel and his mother were right. I still needed time to heal. And there was probably nothing they could reveal that had not already been revealed to the police. I was sitting on the sofa, watching Bridie teaching Liam how to operate his new toy monkey, when there was a tap at the front door. Bridie went to answer it and I heard Sid's voice asking if I was home.

"Show them in, Bridie," I called, and Sid and Gus came into the parlor, their faces alight with excitement.

"We've found him, Molly," Gus exclaimed, perching on the sofa beside me. "We've located Dr. Werner. You were right when you suggested the German consulate. We went to see the consul. At first he was sure that Dr. Werner had gone home earlier this year. He said that Dr. Werner had not attended a soiree for the ambassador, who was a friend of his, so he concluded he was no longer in New York.

But then he added that he was much in demand as a speaker and could well have been visiting another American city. So he gave us the last address he had for the doctor. It was not far from here as you had suggested—on Ninth Street close to Astor Place. We went there and nobody was home, but a neighbor confirmed that she had seen the doctor coming and going recently—always in a hurry, she said. A busy man and a little curt in his ways. Never wanting to pass the time of day with more than a nod and a 'Good morning.'"

"So we wrote him a letter," Sid continued. "We explained the situation and Gus mentioned her own experience studying with Professor Freud and how his colleagues had spoken highly of him, and we asked him to call on us at his earliest convenience."

"Well, that's good news," I said. "I have been worrying about Mabel." I glanced at Bridie, who was sitting on the carpet with Liam again, but all ears. "Bridie, would you please go and ask Mrs. Sullivan if she would be kind enough to put the coffeepot on for us? I'm sure these two ladies have enough time to stay for a cup of coffee."

Bridie got up and nodded before running down the hall.

"She's such a sweet girl," I said. "And so good with Liam." I waited until I heard her high little voice in the kitchen before I continued softly. "They have had the bodies of Mabel's parents exhumed, and it appears that they were somehow drugged before their room was set on fire. They were laid out as if for burial."

"How awful," Gus said. "Surely they can't think that Mabel . . . "

"It will depend on what kind of drug they find during an autopsy, I suppose. If it was a simple sleeping powder, then I'm afraid the police will think . . . "

"Don't." Gus shivered. "You've seen her, Molly. She is so clearly distressed by what happened. She can't have had anything to do with it. I could believe she knocked over a lamp when she was sleepwalking, but deliberately drugging her parents, laying them out, and then setting fire to them? No. I'll not believe that of her."

"I don't believe it either," I said. "But I'm being realistic. Lieutenant

Yeats is young and keen and wants to make a name for himself with a sensational case."

"Can't Daniel intervene?" Sid asked.

I shook my head. "He is so busy with his own case, and besides, he has to tread carefully these days. He is not in favor with the commissioner."

"Can't you help him, Molly?" Sid asked.

"I wish I could. I just don't see what I can do that hasn't already been done. And I have to admit that I'm not feeling up to par yet. I'm still getting headaches and I had another of my horrible dreams last night."

Gus wagged an excited finger at me. "We'll tell Dr. Werner about that too. He might be able to help you as well as Mabel."

"We don't want to bother the doctor with my small problems," I said. "It will be enough if he can help Mabel. I'm sure I'll feel better as the bump on my head goes away."

"I hope he will come," Gus said. "It didn't sound, from what we've heard, that he is the most congenial of men."

"I would think that his professional curiosity would make him want to see Mabel," Sid said. "And if he doesn't come soon, we'll lurk on Ninth Street and catch him unawares."

We all laughed at that, and I began to feel a little better about everything.

❈ Twenty-three ❈

A s the day progressed I felt a little better. Mrs. Sullivan took Liam and Bridie with her to do the shopping, leaving me with strict instructions that I was to stay put and do nothing. But I couldn't abide the emptiness of being in the house alone. I decided to see if Sid and Gus were at home. I was crossing the street when I heard the sound of the fire engine in the distance, its bell clanging madly. I stared down Patchin Place, thinking about the fire that killed the Hamiltons and wondering how it might fit in to Daniel's case. But nothing came to mind beyond the fact that it fit the timeline. It was, as Daniel had said, grasping at straws to save Mabel.

Gus welcomed me, saying they were glad to have something to take their minds off Dr. Werner. They hadn't been able to settle down enough to do anything all morning. She sent Sid off to make us some Moroccan mint tea, which had currently taken the place of coffee in their household. I had just taken a sip when there was a sharp rap at their front door. Sid went to answer it and we heard her say, "Dr. Werner? How very good of you to come so quickly. Please do come in. We're just having coffee." And she led him through to the conservatory, beaming as if she was displaying a prize pet.

"Dr. Otto Werner," she announced. "May I present Miss Walcott, and Mrs. Sullivan?"

He gave us what only could be described as a supercilious stare, clicking his heels and giving a perfunctory bow to Gus, and then eyeing her with interest before doing the same to me. He was a thin, dark-haired man with a well-trimmed beard and a monocle in one eye, meticulously attired and reminding me in a way of a dark version of Dr. Birnbaum. I made a note to ask Gus whether all German and Austrian doctors paid so much attention to their appearance.

"I come because you request it," he said in clipped and heavily accented English. "But I must tell you that my time in New York now is at an end. I take the ship home to the fatherland. My task here is complete."

"Oh, that's a great pity," Gus said, "because your help and expertise are desperately needed."

"There are many doctors in New York, are there not?" he said, giving another curt nod as Sid put a cup of coffee in front of him. "Why is it so important that you seek me out and summon me?"

"Because you are an expert on dream psychology," Gus said.

He raised an eyebrow then, making the monocle move up and down. "Who is telling you this?"

"As I wrote to you in my note, I studied this year in Vienna with Professor Freud," Gus said. "Your colleagues mentioned your name several times. They spoke highly of your research."

"*Ach*, so," he said. "You have worked with my colleagues in Vienna. This is good. You wish to consult me on a tricky case? I will be glad to give you my opinion."

"I wish you to see a young girl. A troubled young girl, plagued by terrible nightmares," Gus said. "I feel certain that unlocking the symbols of her dreams is the only way to help her."

"Of what does she dream? A recurring symbol?"

"Yes. She says there is always a snake. A giant snake looming over her."

"*Ach.* This is not so hard," he said. "She is of what age?"

"Fourteen," Gus replied.

He nodded. "This is a common dream at the time of female development, no? The snake? The male symbol? She fears being consumed by her own sexuality, and being dominated by a male."

"I would agree with you, Dr. Werner, except she has been through a traumatic event," Gus said. "Her house burned down with her parents in it. She was found unharmed in the garden and remembers nothing of that night. But her dreams are full of terror. I am sure something terrible happened that night that she can't remember."

"Naturally something terrible happened—a fire that consumes the house and kills her parents. What could be more terrible? And you say that she escapes, unharmed? Well, then I suggest that the snake could represent her guilt. She feels she could have saved them. Have done more. And her guilt consumes her."

"Oh," Gus said, considering this. "You may be right. She clearly adored her parents. Perhaps she wanted to help, but was driven back by the fire."

"Exactly. You see. Not so complicated after all." He permitted himself a tight-lipped smile.

"But I would still be very grateful if you could spare a minute to visit her," Gus said. "She lives in the city."

"I really do not think . . . ." he began. "My ship. It sails in a few days. There is much to do."

"It seems that everyone is heading home to Germany at the moment," I said. "Another colleague of yours, Dr. Birnbaum, was also sailing home this week."

"Birnbaum? I am not acquainted with this name," he said.

"He also trained in Vienna with Freud," I said, "but he has been in this country for several years now."

"Then it is sad that our paths did not cross either here or in Vienna. I should have welcomed the chance to converse in my own language. It tires one to always have to think of the correct English word."

"Your English is very good," Gus said.

"One improves with time, but I still do not speak it naturally."

I had to agree with that. His accent was still strong, and the words were delivered with such staccato force that it was almost painful to listen to him. I found myself thinking that I would not have wanted to listen to one of the lectures he had apparently been giving all over the country.

"Perhaps you will be on the same ship as Dr. Birnbaum," I said. "Then you two can chat about your research all the way across the Atlantic."

"That would be a pleasure." He looked at me critically. "You are also a student of psychology, *meine Frau?*"

"No. I'm a wife and mother," I said. "Just a friend and neighbor of these ladies. I live across the street."

"A charming street it is indeed," he said. "It is good to live a tranquil life."

Sid chuckled. "Molly hardly lives a tranquil life. Her husband is a policeman, and she was recently in that horrible train crash."

"The train crash? *Mein Gott,* what a calamity this was. This train driver—he should be punished for driving so fast." He turned the full force of his stare on me again. "You were lucky that you escaped unhurt, *meine Frau.*"

"Hardly unhurt. She cracked her ribs and had a concussion," Gus said. "She's still getting headaches. And bad dreams."

"No, really. I am fine. Mending quickly," I said, laughing off her concern.

"You have seen a doctor for this?"

"Yes, at the hospital. Ribs have to heal themselves, so I understand."

"But the headaches." He made a tut-tutting noise. "One does not trifle with a blow to the head. I could perhaps prescribe something to relieve the pain and help you sleep, if you wish?"

"Thank you, it's very kind of you when you're so busy," I said. "But I'm sure the local dispensary could also . . . "

"It is no problem." He waved an elegant hand at me. "It will take but a minute. I will have a messenger deliver it to you. You say your house is opposite this one?"

"Yes, number nine. Thank you very much. You're very kind," I said.

"This young girl, Dr. Werner," Gus said. "Would you not at least see her? A recommendation from you would mean a lot to the family."

"Her name?"

"Her name is Mabel Hamilton. She is living with her aunt on East Twentieth Street, near Gramercy Park."

"Mabel Hamilton." He spoke the words carefully, as if Mabel was a name he had never heard before. "Very well. I will grant your request and see Fraulein Mabel." He pronounced it May Bell. "We could go now, if you wish, since I have no appointment before this afternoon."

"I'll go and summon a cab," Sid said.

Much as I was brimming with curiosity, I could find no good reason to ask to join them. And there would not be room for me in the cab. Besides, my mother-in-law would be returning from her shopping soon, and I had promised not to go rushing all over the city. So reluctantly I took my leave, watching them walk down Patchin Place to find their cab.

I went about my morning tasks, waiting impatiently. I had just finished feeding Liam his midday meal, and was wiping a face liberally plastered with carrot, when Gus came to the front door.

"I knew you'd want a full report, Molly," she said. "I'm sorry you couldn't go with us, but frankly it was rather embarrassing to be crowded into a cab with Dr. Werner, having just met him. I don't think he expected both of us to come with him, and he clearly found it distasteful to be sitting so close to two women. Rather amusing, actually. He's very effete, wouldn't you say?"

"Certainly doesn't have what you'd call a bedside manner," I said. "Although that was kind of him to offer to prescribe me something for my headaches, wasn't it?"

"He was very kind to Mabel too," Gus said. "Surprisingly so. I thought he'd be remote and professional, but he spoke to her kindly but firmly, as one would to a dog whose trust one was gaining. He asked us all to leave the room, so I can't tell you what was said, but when he came out, he looked grave and said that he had been wrong. She was profoundly disturbed and in danger of losing her sanity. He regretted he was leaving so soon, and said that treatment would probably take months with a highly skilled alienist. Unfortunately, he knew of nobody in America who possessed these skills. However, he mentioned a clinic in Switzerland where a colleague of his was doing great work, and where he could also be available to supervise her treatment."

"In Switzerland?" I asked. "That's a long way from home."

"He praised it highly—the mountain air, the healthy food, the outdoor life. They would all contribute to making Mabel receptive to treatment and restoring her to full health."

"I suppose she has inherited money," I said. "What did her aunt think?"

"She was rather startled by the whole thing. She wanted time to think it over. I don't think she cared for Dr. Werner. After he had gone, she said there was something about him she didn't take to. Maybe he was just too supercilious. And Mabel was agitated after seeing him too. I think she overheard what he said about the clinic in Switzerland. So we'll have to wait to find out what happens next."

As I tucked Liam into his crib for his afternoon nap, I thought over what Gus had just told me. At least Dr. Werner had discerned that the girl was deeply troubled and needed an alienist to bring her back to sanity. His testimony should prevent Lieutenant Yeats from arresting her at the moment. And if she was taken to Switzerland, then she would be out of the grasp of the American law. So that would be a good thing. However . . . I paused, considering. Switzerland. So far away. So different from her home and everything she was used to. How would she handle the loneliness and isolation, and who would take her there? Not Mrs. Hamilton, with her four lively sons and a husband to look after. Surely there was a suitable clinic closer to home—in the countryside, out of the city, where her family could visit her, and the attendants spoke her own language. And if no qualified alienist could be found, then her family's money could pay for one to come across from Vienna.

I decided to suggest this to Sid and Gus when I saw them again. I realized Mabel would be in danger from Yeats if she were closer to home, but I thought the testimony of a qualified doctor would prevent him from doing anything until she was cured. And in the meantime, she would be one less worry on my mind. I paused and told myself firmly that I was wrong to be worrying about her in the first place. She wasn't my concern. Mrs. Hamilton had asked for assistance from Gus, not from me. And yet, as always, I wanted to know the truth. Somebody had drugged or killed Mabel's parents and then set fire to their room. Who hated them enough to do that? And if Lieutenant Yeats didn't stretch his investigation beyond Mabel, who would ever find the cold-blooded murderer who was walking free?

I was tempted to visit the Hamilton household myself, to talk to the servants who had escaped from the burning house, but I realized it would be more sensible to wait—not just so that my own recovery could continue, but so the autopsy could be performed and might reveal a substance that was used to drug Mabel's parents.

Liam whined and wriggled in his crib, bringing me back to reality and the claims of everyday life. "Time to sleep," I said gently and patted his back, humming his favorite lullaby. His eyes fluttered closed. His thumb came into his mouth and he lay there, looking like a cherub from an old painting. So sweet. So vulnerable. It was hard to believe that he'd grow into a boisterous, noisy youngster like Mrs. Hamilton's sons, or a tough and scruffy lad like Nuala's boys. I wondered if Thomas had had any success in finding out who had paid a boy to deliver the note to the police headquarters.

I sighed with frustration. There was so much I wanted to do. I wanted to help Daniel with his investigation (and I must confess, I wanted to find something that the police had somehow overlooked, as much for my own satisfaction as to help my husband). I wanted to help solve Mabel's case too. But I was no longer a detective. I was a wife and a mother, and I was recovering from injuries. I would have to be patient. And patience was a virtue I had never really learned.

I tried not to think. I tried to play with my son and with Bridie. We built towers of blocks and knocked them down. Liam's laughter echoed through the house and did me a power of good. But I had another bad dream that night and hoped that Dr. Werner would find time to send me some medicine, as he had promised. I remembered he had expressed concern and said that concussions should not be taken lightly. Perhaps I should be heeding his warning and not filling my head with worries. It turned out that Mabel too had another dream that night. Mrs. Hamilton sent around a note to Sid and Gus the next morning.

When Gus came to my front door just as we were finishing breakfast, I thought it would be to say that she had just bought croissants from the French bakery and I was invited to coffee. Instead, she held only an envelope in her hand, and her face was full of concerned animation.

"Listen, Molly," Gus said. The envelope in her hands flapped in the wind that swirled down our small backwater. "This just arrived from Minnie Hamilton." She removed a sheet of paper from the envelope and tried to hold it steady while she read. "She says that Mabel had a terrifying dream last night. They heard her screams and she was cowering in the corner, saying 'Why is the world upside down?' and 'Why does it smell so sweet?' When they woke her up she looked at them and said, 'The snake spoke to me. He spoke to me.'

"Mrs. Hamilton asked her, 'What did he say?'

"'He said, "You are mine."'"

❧ Twenty-four ❧

id came out to join us and we debated what the words might mean, but we could come up with no reasonable explanations. "'Why is the world upside down?'" Sid said. "Well, her world is upside down now, isn't it?"

"And I wonder what might have smelled sweet?" Gus asked.

"They did find her curled up in the back garden," I said. "Maybe she found herself among some sweet-smelling flowers and was surprised to find herself there."

"That's good, Molly." Gus nodded. "But the snake saying, 'You are mine.' That is definitely disturbing."

"We've talked of the snake representing her own darker thoughts, haven't we?" Sid ventured. "Could this be hinting that her evil nature is taking over?"

"How horrible," Gus said. "Don't let's think that of Mabel. I want another explanation."

"I feel so sorry for her, living with these dreams for so long now," I said. "I've had bad dreams that are not nearly as terrifying just since the accident, and I find them most distressing. Hers have gone on for how long? Over a month, wasn't it?"

"Since the beginning of August," Sid said.

Gus looked at my face. "What is it, Molly? You've thought of something?"

"No, nothing really," I muttered. "Nothing important." Because of course I couldn't tell them that this fire and Mabel's parents' deaths might have been caused by the same man Daniel was after.

But how then did it explain Mabel's miraculous escape unscathed, not down the stairs, but out through the fire escape? Was I just wishing her to be innocent because of her sweet and innocent appearance?

I returned home, and we were in the middle of having tea at four o'clock when the front door was thrown open violently, sending a gust of wind down the hall.

"Mercy me, who can that be?" Mother Sullivan asked, half rising from her chair.

"Only me," Daniel called back. He came into the kitchen, looked around the table, and nodded with satisfaction. "I see I've timed my arrival perfectly. Mother's made one of her seed cakes."

"Sit down, boy, and I'll find you a cup," she said, going to the shelf before I could do or say anything.

"I won't say no," he replied. "As usual I had no time for lunch, and I've just come from the morgue. I walked all the way to get that smell out of my nostrils."

"It never really goes away, does it?" I said. "I didn't think I'd be able to stand it the first time."

"Children—we're at the table," Mrs. Sullivan exclaimed, as she banged Daniel's cup and saucer down firmly onto the table. "Your conversation would turn the stomachs of half of New York. I'm just glad you don't move among the Four Hundred, or you'd be banned from their company for life with such talk."

Daniel chuckled. "My wife was not made for drawing room chatter," he said. He cut himself a large slice of cake and took a bite, nodding with satisfaction.

"What are you doing home so early?" I asked. "Don't tell me they've given you an afternoon off?"

"They haven't. I came straight from the morgue because I thought you and your friends would want to know."

"If the talk's to be about morgues and dead bodies, could you please carry it on in another room?" Mother Sullivan said. "I wish to enjoy my tea."

"I don't want to hear about dead bodies either," Bridie said. "I'll have nightmares."

Daniel got up. "Very well. Come along, Molly. Into the study."

I followed him and he closed the door behind us. "Very interesting autopsy," he said.

"Of the Hamilton girl's parents?"

He nodded. "I wangled myself an invitation, since the pathologist is an old friend of mine. Yeats declined to attend. I think he felt it would offend his delicate nature." He grinned.

"And you found something?"

"It's not conclusive yet. It will need further testing, but my pathologist friend worked in South America as a young doctor. He thinks the muscle tissue shows evidence of curare having been administered."

"Curare?" The word meant nothing to me.

"It's a poison made from vines in South America. The natives tip their arrows with it and fire it at animals they are hunting. It doesn't kill the animal, but it paralyzes it so that they can dispatch it at their leisure."

"How horrible. How would anyone get his hands on curare, unless he too had been to South America?"

"I understand that there is some interest in it now among the medical community. Experiments are being done to see if it can be used as a possible anesthetic," he said.

I stood still, staring past him into the backyard, where the wind was swirling fallen leaves, trying to make sense of this. "So the doctor thinks that someone injected Mabel's parents with curare, and then set fire to their bedroom?"

"It would seem that way."

"But that means . . . " I paused, letting the full horror of this sink in, "that they could have been awake but paralyzed as they were burned to death. That's monstrous, Daniel." I put my hand up to my mouth, breathing deeply before I could say the next words. "And it's all too possible that Mabel witnessed this. No wonder it has driven her to the brink of madness—to watch one's parents burned, and to know you can do nothing to help them."

"It doesn't bear thinking about, does it?" he said, looking at me with tender concern.

"Now you have to believe what I suggested—that the man who set the fire is the same one you are seeking," I said. "To kill in this manner. This man is a fiend and must be stopped."

"I suppose I must agree that the fiendish nature of these murders might possibly indicate the same man. But I still come back to the absence of a note."

"Perhaps he did send a note, and it got lost in the mail," I suggested. "Perhaps he went to post the note at the main post office and noticed your men, watching, and lost his nerve."

"Then why not have it delivered by hand, as the last two have been?"

"I don't know," I said. "But one thing makes me very happy. It now doesn't seem likely that Mabel killed or drugged her parents and set their room on fire. There is no way that a young girl could get her hands on this curare or know how to administer it."

"Then let's hope the evidence is conclusive," Daniel said. "For your sake as well as hers."

I sank onto the nearest chair as if the burden of all this knowledge was suddenly too much for me. "What happens to Mabel now?" I asked. "Would it be right to try and bring her memory back? Or would the memory of that scene be too much to bear?"

"I'm not an alienist," he said. "We'd need to get a professional opinion. But if it would help identify a killer, then I'm afraid it would have to be done, whatever the consequences to her sanity might be."

"Poor child," I said. "I can't decide whether it would be better to know the truth or to continue to be haunted by these nightmares."

"In the end it's always better to know," Daniel said. "But we'll do nothing in a hurry, I promise you that."

"There is another thing that we can be thankful for," I said. "It means that this crime is now part of your investigation, doesn't it? You'll take over and Lieutenant Yeats will no longer be able to torment Mabel."

"I expect he'll still be involved," Daniel said, "but now working under me."

"Which means he can't do anything without your permission. No dragging Mabel off to the Tombs, or even threatening it."

He nodded, holding out his hand to pull me to my feet. "All the same, he comes with powerful friends in the right places, Molly. I'm highly aware of that. The commissioner may be glad that he now has someone to report on my failings."

"You'll solve the case and they'll all be impressed," I said, slipping my arm through his. "This may be the one link that we needed to start to make sense of this."

"As always I admire your optimism," he said, "but it does give me more people to question, and a renewed drive to stop this man. If he is capable of such heartless evil, then he can't be allowed to kill again."

We went back to the kitchen then and enjoyed the rest of our tea without a single mention of unsuitable subjects. I felt unreasonably happy and energized—happy that Mabel did not have a hidden dark side, and energized that I had been able to fill in one piece of the puzzle. Although, we hadn't proven the connection yet, and how a staid middle-class couple could be linked to the simple woman and the student was still a complete enigma.

"You must interview the Hamiltons' former servants, Daniel," I said, as he prepared to return to work. "Find out if the Hamiltons had any enemies or secrets. Servants always know everything. I did have Sid and Gus ask Mrs. Minnie Hamilton, Mabel's current guardian, if she could think of anyone who might have wished them harm, but she couldn't. She said that Bertie was an affable, harmless sort of fellow, devoted to his family, without any vices that she knew of."

When Daniel had gone, I took out a map of New York and stuck pins in the sites where the murders had occurred. But I saw no pattern to them at all. They weren't equal distance apart, they didn't share the circumference of a circle around a given point. Nothing. Completely random. I got up and paced the room. I could no longer keep out of this. Now that I suspected what the same monster had done to Mabel's parents, and how Mabel was suffering because of it, I had to do whatever I could to help find him. My trip to Brooklyn had revealed no new clues, as far as I could tell. No links to the other deaths. But I should still go forward with my plan to visit the next of kin of the other victims. Perhaps one of them would reveal something that gave us the link we needed. As to my own aches and pains, I'd grin and bear them.

It seemed as if I had an immediate affirmation of my decision, because right after I had made it, we had another visitor. It was Dr. Werner, standing on my doorstep in his immaculate black suit and tall black hat, monocle in his eye. "Mrs. Sullivan." A nod and click of the heels punctuated this. "I am passing through the area so I come to deliver the mixture I had promised. It should help ease the headaches and help you sleep."

"You're very kind, Doctor," I said. "Thank you. What do I owe you?"

He held up a hand. "Consider it a gift from me. I am glad to help. Take it right before bedtime, as it will make you sleepy."

I took the bottle from him. "My friends are also grateful that you saw Mabel Hamilton," I said. "It now seems that she witnessed something so shocking that she had blocked it from her conscious mind." I wasn't sure how much of this Daniel would want me to reveal, and his findings had also not yet been confirmed.

"This young lady must be treated with the utmost delicacy," Dr. Werner said slowly, deliberately. "Her memory must not be forced, do you understand? She must be given time to heal."

"Perhaps you would be good enough to write a note to that effect, that her aunt can show to the police. The young officer in charge of the case has been threatening to lock her up to make her remember."

"But that is unthinkable. Barbaric," he said. "It must not be allowed. The child can only heal in peace and serenity. Away from this place. I recommend a fine clinic in Switzerland. I could personally supervise her treatment there. But her family, they do not like to send her away. I fear for her, Mrs. Sullivan. And I will be happy to report my findings and recommendations to your ignorant police." Then he clicked his heels again in that very Germanic way. "I have taken enough of your time. I bid you adieu." And he strode off.

I went inside and put the bottle carefully on the mantel in my bedroom, out of the reach of small hands. Now that I had it, I wasn't at all sure I wanted to take it. If it made me too sleepy, would I hear Liam if he woke and cried in the middle of the night? I decided to take only a fraction of the dose tonight and see what effect it had.

❧ Twenty-five ❧

I was conscious of dreaming, but this time they were pleasant dreams. I was floating in a sea of colors, and I was warm and I could fly. I came to slowly, like a diver coming to the surface from deep water, as I felt myself being shaken.

"Molly, are you all right?" Daniel's voice was demanding from far away.

"Is something wrong?" I asked, forcing my eyes open.

"No, but it's past eight o'clock. You never sleep this late, and Liam had been crying for you. My mother is feeding him breakfast. She told me to let you sleep, but I wasn't sure . . ."

"I took a little of the medicine Dr. Werner prescribed for my headaches," I said. "I had lovely dreams. Perhaps I needed to catch up on a good sleep."

"Perhaps you did." He patted my shoulder. "I must be off now."

I sat up, feeling the world sway uneasily. "I'm sorry. I didn't make your breakfast."

"It's all right. My mother made me oatmeal, eggs, and ham so I'm well fortified. I'll see you later, then."

I still felt strange and disconnected as I washed and came downstairs. Did I want a medicine that put me so soundly to sleep, albeit to pleasant dreams instead of nightmares? I decided I'd rather have the headaches. I slapped cold water on my face and told myself to buck up, as I had big plans for today. Mother Sullivan looked concerned and disapproving when I told her I had things to do and asked if she could watch Liam for me.

"Off gallivanting again? You've been told to rest, my girl."

"I know, but there are things I've been putting off that really must be done."

"Then let me take care of them for you," she said.

I shook my head. "I'm afraid you can't. There are some people I have to visit."

"Part of Daniel's work again?" she said. "Has he actually asked for your help, or will he see it as interference?"

"It's just a few small details I might be able to find for him," I said. "He really has so much on his plate at the moment."

"If you think you're up to it, and he'll appreciate your—" she had been about to say "interference," I'm sure, but she swallowed back the word and said "help" instead. And she turned her back on me.

To be honest, I wasn't sure I was up to it, but I gave Liam a big kiss, hugged Bridie, and smiled in a confident manner as I went to find my hat and set off. My plan was to visit Simon Grossman's family. And if I still had energy after that, I'd go to see the judge.

I had just reached the end of Patchin Place and was about to hurl myself into the busy stream of pedestrians around the Jefferson Market when someone called my name, and I saw a boy forcing his way through the crowd, running toward me. It was Thomas, Nuala's son.

"Miss Molly," he called and came to a halt beside me, panting as if he'd run a long way. "I'm glad I caught you."

"I'm glad too, Thomas. Have you found out anything for me?"

"I have," he said. "The kids who sweep the crossings on the Bowery not far from Mulberry said that a skinny little runt had been boasting that some guy gave him a whole dollar to deliver a letter. So I found the kid and he took a bit of persuading . . . " he gave me a gap-toothed grin, "but I told him he'd be in trouble from my brother, who's a Junior Eastman, if he didn't talk. So he looked scared then, and said it was a young guy, skinny, tall, and dressed like he could be a student. He said he didn't believe the guy was the sort who'd part with a whole dollar and he thought the bill might be fake, but then the guy gave him four quarters."

"Did he say how he spoke? Where he might have come from?"

"He said he spoke real refined. That's why he thought he was a student, 'cos it ain't too far from the university where the guy met him."

"A student," I said. "I see. Anything else you can tell me about him?"

"He said the guy had good boots. He was shabby looking, but his boots were good. And he seemed nervous and wanting to be away from there."

I reached into my purse and took out a dollar bill. "This one is real, I promise you, Thomas," I said. "You did good work. Thank you."

"Anytime, Miss Molly," he said. "If you want any errands run, just ask me."

I couldn't think of anything else he might do for me, but I promised I'd call on him if I was in need. I watched him swagger off with a whole dollar in his pocket. Then I continued on my way to Washington Square. Was it significant that the person who had paid the urchin to deliver a note had looked like a student? Perhaps there was a connection to the university after all. Then I had a thought that pricked my balloon of optimism. The man Daniel was seeking was clever and cocky. The student had probably only been one in a chain of delivery boys. The writer of the note had probably paid the student to deliver it. The student had gotten cold feet as he approached police headquarters and decided to pay a street child to do his dirty work instead. I was no nearer to the truth.

I stood looking across Washington Square, where students stood in clusters or headed to class, books tucked earnestly under their arms, and my gaze fell onto Fritz's café. The person who paid a street boy to deliver the note to police headquarters had been young, and skinny, and looked like a student. A student—responsible for such diverse crimes? It didn't make sense. I toyed with what I had suggested before, that some kind of secret society, a modern-day Hellfire Club, was responsible for the killings. Somehow I couldn't make myself believe it. Then I decided on a more plausible explanation. Students are always hard up. Some, like Simon Grossman, have run up gambling debts they can't tell their parents about. Maybe there was a puppet master responsible for these crimes, paying a student, or students, to do his bidding. And Simon, essentially honorable, had refused and threatened to go to the police, and had been silenced with cyanide.

I looked up as spatters of rain fell onto me. I realized I should have brought a brolly with me, but I wasn't going to waste time going home now. I was energized by the thought of having something positive to tell Daniel. And I'd also mention my earlier visit to Fritz's café, where it was hinted that Simon had run afoul of Italians with his gambling debts.

So I ignored the threat of rain and was passing the fire station when I heard someone calling me. It was Abe, one of the firemen.

"You were the lady who asked me about the fire on Eleventh Street," he said. "You asked if there was anything strange or unusual. Well, I thought about it, and I remembered something. The little girl had something in her hand when I saw her carried away."

"What sort of something?" I asked.

"Paper," he said. "A piece of paper."

"And what happened to it?" I asked.

He shrugged. "Don't know. The whole roof fell in just about then and I had no time to think."

My heart beat faster. Was it possible there had been a note after all, clutched in the sleeping girl's hand? I thanked him, and instead of going to the El station I walked up Sixth Avenue to Eleventh Street. The skeleton of Mabel's burned house was a sorry sight. Two blackened box trees outside what had once been front steps leading to a front door. The rest was little more than a pile of rubble. I tried to pick my way around, but realized this was too much for me. I couldn't risk falling again in my present condition. But I would tell Daniel when I saw him that there might, indeed, have been a note.

So I resumed my former mission and went across to catch the Third Avenue El up to Thirty-second Street, where Simon Grossman had lived with his parents. It was in the respectable Murray Hill neighborhood and the house itself was a pleasant brownstone, like the others in the block, but was distinguished by having a brass plate beside the door, advertising *L. Grossman, Physician.*

Now I hesitated. If I went up the front steps and knocked at the front door, presumably it would be answered by the doctor's receptionist, and I'd have to make up an excuse for why I had come. I tried to think of an illness I could feign. Then suddenly I realized I couldn't do this. When I had been a detective I had been a single woman, alone in the city and living by my wits. Now I was married with a child of my own. Simon had been the apple of his father's eye. I simply couldn't question Dr. Grossman about who might have wanted to see him dead. I had no right to open old wounds. I could picture all too well how I would feel if anything terrible had happened to Liam and some inquisitive female came to quiz me about it. I was sure Daniel would have done a thorough job. Surely he'd found out about Simon's gambling debts and the Italian connection, and he would have already looked into them. But as I'd said to the young men in the café, dropping cyanide into a coffee cup was not their mode of operation. A knife between the ribs as Simon walked home late at night would do the job efficiently, with less risk of being caught. My second theory of a puppet master, making students do his dirty work, seemed more plausible. And I was certain Simon's parents would know nothing about that.

Having come this far, I really didn't want to walk away empty-handed. If there was any hint of gossip, the servants would know of it, and I'd found it was usually easier to get servants to talk. I went around the corner to see if there was a servant's entrance at the back of the house, but could find no other way in. So I was forced to walk away. In truth I was rather disgusted with myself that I had not been able to face Simon's parents, or even to have questioned a servant. I was becoming soft and sentimental since I'd had a child. I tried to focus my thoughts on the next person on the list. The judge's wife, poisoned with arsenic. And I realized that I lacked the gumption to go there either. What excuse could I give to a judge to get him to talk about his wife's death? Men in his position were skilled at sniffing out falsehoods and impostors. He'd see through any lame excuse in a minute, and I could hardly say that I was secretly helping the police to solve his wife's murder. Judges have connections, and if he complained about me to the commissioner, or another of Daniel's superiors, my husband would be in more trouble.

So the next person I could possibly question was Terrence Daughtery, the son of the woman who had been electrocuted in her bathtub. That involved a crosstown jitney, still horse-drawn and moving at a snail's pace. I realized it was quite probable he'd be at work at this hour and I'd be wasting my time, but when I tapped on the door of the unassuming house in Chelsea it was answered by a painfully thin man, pasty-faced and with soulful dark eyes, probably in his thirties or early forties. His hair was already receding, and he was wearing a black mourning suit that made him look even paler. He glanced at me warily.

"Can I help you?" he asked. He had a high, clipped, almost effeminate voice.

I decided to use the magazine ploy again. "I'm sorry to trouble you, Mr. Daughtery," I said. "My name is Mrs. Murphy. I work for a women's magazine, and I've been asked to write a piece on the dangers of the modern age, especially the introduction of electricity into the home. I understand that you have recently experienced a tragedy brought about by electricity. I wondered if you'd share your feelings with our readers, and perhaps be able to warn them."

He continued to stare, trying to size me up. "My feelings?" he said with bitterness in his voice. "What do you imagine my feelings are? I've lost the best mother in the world. She sacrificed everything to give me a good education. She took care of me through a long illness. And to die in this way . . . I still can't get over the unfairness of it."

"I'm really sorry," I said. "I can understand how painful it must be to talk about it. But if we can make one other family aware of the dangers of these newfangled household appliances, then at least some small good will come out if this tragedy, won't it?"

"I'm not sure that we can blame the lamp or electricity," he said. He looked up and down the street, then said, "I suppose you'd better come in. Mother would not have approved of chatting on the doorstep like common servants."

I followed him into a dark and gloomy room. It hadn't been dusted in a while, and I suspected it was only used for visitors, of whom there had been none recently. I sat on a faded brocade sofa, while he took the armchair by the fire. I noticed he didn't offer me any refreshment.

"Now," I continued. "You were just saying that one couldn't blame the lamp or the electricity for your mother's death. Am I wrong in thinking that a lamp fell into the bathtub full of water and electrocuted your mother?"

He winced as if I'd struck him. "That is correct," he said. "But the police indicated that it might not have been an accident. They suggested that an intruder might have done this foul thing, quite deliberately."

"Killed your mother, you mean? Why?"

He shrugged. "Why indeed? That's what I've been asking myself ever since that awful day. Who would have wanted to kill her?"

"How did someone get into the house while your mother was taking a bath?" I said. "Did she not lock the front door?"

"Always. She was afraid of being alone in the city. She always went to the front door with me as I left for work, stood and waved as I walked down the block, and then went inside and locked the door."

"So how did an intruder get in?"

Again that wince of pain. "She always opened the bathroom window when she took a bath, otherwise the room steamed up too much. She took a bath regularly on Wednesdays and Saturdays, to be ready for church on Sunday, you know. Always at eight o'clock, right after I left for work."

"And the bathroom is upstairs?"

He nodded. "It is. My mother had an indoor bathroom put in when we moved here after my father died. My mother was a very modern woman, Mrs. Murphy. She was forward-looking in her ways. That's why she jumped at the chance to have electricity installed in the house when it came to our part of the city. And look what it brought us." He squeezed his eyes shut, trying to stop tears.

"So do I understand that the police believe someone climbed in through an open upstairs window?"

"That's what they said. I find it quite amazing, myself. We have a small backyard, but the houses behind look onto our back windows. Anyone might have seen a person trying to climb up the wall."

"He came up the drainpipe, I suppose?"

"Drainpipe or the creeper. We've a creeper growing up the wall. That made it easier for him, damn him." Then he blinked and shot me an anguished look. "I do apologize for my language, Mrs. Murphy. It is only my intense suffering, I assure you. Mother would never have permitted . . . "

"I quite understand, Mr. Daughtery," I said. "No offense taken. So did the police have any suggestion as to why someone would have entered the house and killed your mother? Was it perhaps a burglar who saw you leave for work and assumed the house was empty? He climbed in and was startled to find your mother in her bath . . . and when she started to scream, he panicked and silenced her?"

"I suppose that might be plausible," he said. "I can't come up with any other reason."

"She had no enemies that you can think of?"

He looked shocked. "Mrs. Murphy, my mother wasn't always an easy woman. She could be critical of shoddy work. She sometimes fell out with the neighbors if they were too loud or behaved in a way she did not consider seemly, but one does not kill for such trivialities."

Of course he was right. One did not kill unless there was a really good reason.

"I'm surprised that nobody heard her screams through an open window," I said. "Did nobody hear her and summon the constable?"

"Nobody. The fiend must have silenced her instantly, when she was too terrified to scream."

"Have there been any other similar crimes in the neighborhood? Any burglaries through open windows? Any other murders?"

"None that I've heard of. And one always hears of murders, doesn't one?"

I stood up. "I shouldn't take up any more of your time, Mr. Daughtery. I realize now that you don't blame electricity for what happened. I was lucky to have caught you at home, wasn't I? I was in the neighborhood so I thought I'd just try to visit you, but in truth I expected you'd be at work. What sort of job do you do?"

He looked away from me. "I haven't been able to work since my mother died. I've completely lost my nerve, Mrs. Murphy. When I go out, I see the face of a murderer in everyone I pass."

"What was your profession until this?"

I could tell he appreciated the use of that word, rather than "job" "I received a first-class education, Mrs. Murphy," he said. "My mother scrimped and saved to send me to Princeton, where my father went. She wanted me to go into one of the professions, preferably law. But

I contracted rheumatic fever in my last year of college and it affected my heart. So I've had to take it easy ever since. I've been a private tutor for many years."

"To the same family?"

He smiled. "Children grow up. I find that I stay with one family for five years or so, then the children go on to school or college. I was with my current family for three years. Two charming little girls, aged eight and ten. But of course they had to find a new tutor when I couldn't return. So I'm not sure when I'll be ready to face the world again. Actually I'm thinking of moving out of the city, to a small town, where life isn't quite as dangerous." He paused, staring at the clock on the mantel that was now chiming eleven. "There have been too many tragedies, Mrs. Murphy. Too much evil. Life should not be full of tragedy and loss."

I held out my hand. "I wish you well, Mr. Daughtery. I hope you find peace in a new life."

He took my hand. His was moist and unpleasant, rather like touching a dead fish. "You are very kind, but nothing can ever bring back my mother. I have nothing to live for now."

I was deep in thought as I left Terrence Daughtery's house. I went around the house and tried to find a back alley where a man could have entered. But there was none. The tiny yards backed onto each other. Someone would have had to climb fences to reach the Daughterys' yard. And the houses faced each other, close enough together that an intruder ran a huge risk of being seen, or of his victim's screams being heard. Like all the other crimes it made no sense, and I found myself thinking that if there had not been an incriminating note sent to Daniel, I'd have suspected Terrence of getting rid of an overbearing mother. He certainly had the temperament to have snapped after being criticized one time too many. But there was the note claiming responsibility, and I didn't think that Terrence could have committed the other murders. He'd have lacked the gumption to walk through a crowded café and tip cyanide into a coffee cup, or to have climbed through a judge's wife's window and administered arsenic to her.

I started to walk faster and faster as my thoughts tumbled around. Poor old Dolly, whom everyone loved. Simon Grossman was also a likable sort of fellow whom everyone liked. But Dolly needed looking after, and Simon had secret vices. And Terrence adored his mother, but she was overbearing and critical and kept him under her thumb. And the judge's wife was a semi-invalid. Was it possible that our murderer thought he was doing good deeds and ridding the victims' dear ones of a burden? It was an intriguing thought, but I couldn't go along with it. The man who wrote those notes was vicious and arrogant and self-centered. He would not do good deeds. He would not even care how other people felt. If our suspicions were true, he had even made a train plunge to its doom in the hope of killing one person. And according to Daniel, that one person might have been me.

I looked around uneasily and walked a little faster. Was he watching me at this moment? I remembered the feeling of being followed as I made my way to the station to catch that fateful train. I felt no such prickling on the back of my neck now, but it did confirm that my sixth sense did warn me on occasion of imminent danger.

I came out to the bustle of Fifth Avenue just as the skies darkened and plump raindrops spattered down onto the sidewalk. I sighed. I knew I should have returned home for my brolly. Now I'd be well and truly soaked. I darted forward until I came to a portico, jutting out across the sidewalk. Other pedestrians had similar ideas, and we crowded in together as the rain turned into a deluge.

"Stand aside, please, ladies and gentlemen," a loud voice boomed. "You can't block the entrance. Our customers must be able to come in and out."

Through the crowd I saw that he was a military type, wearing some kind of uniform with a lot of braid. I wondered for a moment if we were standing outside a swank hotel, but couldn't think of one on this stretch of Fifth Avenue. Then someone in front of me shifted and

I could see in through the plate-glass windows. A marble floor. Mahogany desks and a counter with pigeonholes along one wall. It was a bank. Obviously a bank with affluent clients, I thought, if they could employ such an imposing doorman.

I wondered if Mabel's mother's father owned such a bank, and if Mabel's father had been one of those serious young men in frock coats who sat at their desks, scribbling away, surreptitiously glancing at the owner's daughter as she swept past him, not aware of his existence. *How had he won her heart?* I wondered. Thunder rumbled nearby and there was a flash of lightning, making a child standing close by scream.

"It's all right, my pet," a woman said. "It's only lightning. It can't hurt us under here."

I felt as if I'd been hit by a bolt of lightning myself, because I had just realized something. Old Miss Willis had said that her former employer had owned a bank. We had a connection.

✂❦ Twenty-six ❦✂

I waited impatiently for Daniel, but he didn't come home for dinner. I put Liam to bed and read a story with Bridie. Daniel's dinner was rapidly drying out in the oven, and still he didn't come. In the end tiredness won out, and I got ready for bed. I was half asleep when I heard the front door shut quietly and then his footsteps creeping up the stairs.

"Not asleep?" he asked, noticing that I hadn't turned out the gas lamp on the wall.

"I waited up for you," I said.

"You shouldn't have done that. I grabbed a bite to eat at an Italian place on Mulberry. I'm acquiring quite a taste for spaghetti and meat-balls. You'll have to learn how to cook it." He grinned as he sat on the bed and started to unlace his boots.

"I stayed awake because I've come up with something." I sat up, propping myself up with pillows. "First of all, I might have come up with proof that the Hamiltons' murder was linked to the others. One of the firemen remembered seeing Mabel carried away with a piece of paper clutched in her hand. I tried to look at the burned house, but I decided it was too dangerous for me to be clambering over burned-out ruins."

"Very wise," Daniel said. "But that's certainly interesting."

"And there's more," I said, inching toward him down the bed. "I was reminded today that Mabel Hamilton's father worked in his father-in-law's bank."

"That's right. Her mother was Susan Masters. Of Deveraux and Masters—important merchant bankers."

"It didn't occur to me before," I went on, excitedly now, "but Miss Willis mentioned that her former employer owned a bank. It's our first connection, isn't it?"

"A tenuous one," Daniel said. "There are plenty of banks in the city, and I don't really see what Miss Willis's former employer had to do with her sister's death. Did the Willis woman mention her employer's name?"

"She did. But called him Mr. Cornelius. So not the same bank, but at least we're in the same field for once."

He looked up at me sharply. "Cornelius Deveraux?"

"Oh." I sat up straight, staring at him as I digested this. "You are suggesting that Cornelius was his first name?"

"It's not a very usual name, is it? And two banks owned by someone called Cornelius really would be strange."

I was trying to recall all the details of my conversation with Miss Willis. "His son was called Marcus, I believe."

"Then we are talking about the same person. Marcus Deveraux. He inherited when his father was killed, years ago. I remember him now. Arrogant little prig he was too."

"So there is a real connection," I said. "We finally have a real connection, Daniel."

"Or a remarkable coincidence." He still didn't look as excited as I felt.

"I don't believe in coincidences. You must go and see Marcus Deveraux first thing tomorrow."

"You are suggesting that Marcus Deveraux might somehow be behind this?"

"As the killer?" I paused to consider this, as that hadn't been what I'd meant at all. "No, probably not," I said. "It doesn't seem that a man who owns a bank would have any reason to kill the sister of a former employee—although he did fire her after his father died. Why would he do that?"

"I thought we discussed this and concluded he probably thought he was doing her a favor—he knew of her loyalty, and he wanted to make sure that she had the freedom to enjoy her inheritance."

"And yet you called him an arrogant little prig. And from the way Miss Willis described him, he didn't sound like a particularly kind-hearted person." I was warming to my subject now. "And Mabel's aunt and uncle would know if there was any kind of feud or falling out between Marcus Deveraux and his partner's daughter. Maybe . . . " I wagged an excited finger. "Listen, Daniel. Maybe there was some provision in the partnership that left everything, including Mr. Masters's share, to Marcus Deveraux if Susan died. Maybe that was the real murder—the one he wanted to accomplish and disguised with the other, random killings. That's why there was no note at the beginning of August."

"I'm glad you don't work for the police department," Daniel said, half smiling. "You've built yourself a perfect scenario to have Marcus Deveraux hauled in and arrested."

"Well?"

"All on supposition, Molly. We've investigated these murders quite thoroughly—except for the Hamilton couple, and we're still working on that—but no mention, no hint of Marcus Deveraux came up when we spoke to friends and family."

"You see!" I said excitedly. "You're still working on the Hamilton case. Perhaps you haven't asked the right questions yet. Before you speak to Marcus Deveraux, you can see Mabel's aunt and the family lawyer, and find out whether the Masters's fortune would go to Marcus Deveraux if Susan and her father died. Then you'd have a motive."

"What about the other murders? Can you come up with a motive for them?" He looked almost amused. "If you have nailed Marcus Deveraux as your suspect, then why would he want to shut a butcher in his meat safe? Because he delivered bad meat?"

"You don't ever take me seriously," I snapped. I was tired and it had been a long day, and I had been so excited at the thought of providing the missing link for my husband.

The smile left his face instantly. "On the contrary. I do take you seriously, and you have come up with a link that none of us found. But the link could have been through anyone at the bank—a disgruntled employee, for example. We can't jump on Marcus Deveraux because he is now one of the partners."

"There's something else I found out today," I said. "Another link, if you will."

"You're full of surprises," he said.

"Listen." I wagged at finger warningly at him. "I found out who paid a street child to deliver that note to your headquarters."

Now he looked genuinely impressed, and surprised. "You did? How?"

"I have my methods," I said. "And my spies."

"Ah. Nuala's brood. The little Eastmans."

"Exactly. And the person was a young man who looked like a student, according to Thomas."

"Like a student? Then he was probably being paid to deliver it himself."

"That's what I thought," I said, "but there's something else. Listen, Daniel. The other day I went to the café where Simon Grossman was poisoned. Two things were obvious: one, that it would be relatively easy to put a few drops of poison into a coffee cup while a group at a table was in deep discussion, and two—that most people there were regulars, and students. An outsider who was not one of them would have been noticed. I certainly was as soon as I entered."

"Ah, but you're a pretty woman. Young men notice such things."

"Thank you for the compliment, sir," I said, "but I think the same would have been true for any stranger, especially one walking between tables to find Simon Grossman."

"So what are you implying by this?"

"That the person who put the cyanide into Simon Grossman's drink must not have stood out. He must have looked like one of them. Another student."

I saw the spark in his eyes. "Ah. So you're saying that students might be being used by somebody to do his dirty work?"

"Exactly. Students are always short of money. They always have things they don't want their parents to know about. Someone rich and powerful—someone like Marcus Deveraux—could use them to carry out his plans." I paused, swinging my legs over the side of the bed now and facing him. "Whoever committed most of these crimes had to be agile enough to climb up the side of a building and in through a window."

"You're right," he said. "It would have to have been someone agile and daring."

"So you'll interview Marcus Deveraux?"

"I will. Since his partner's daughter has been murdered, I'll have a valid reason to talk to him."

Something just struck me as he talked and I watched his face. "You called him an arrogant little prig. Do you know him? Is he young?"

"No, he must be mid-thirties by now. Around my age. I met him long ago."

"How did you know him? Was he at Columbia with you or something?"

"No. I had to question him when I was investigating his father's death. I was newly promoted to detective and probably looked too young to do the job, and he was horribly patronizing to me, even though he was certainly no older."

"His father's death? His father was murdered?" I almost shouted out the words.

Daniel was frowning now. "We were never sure if it was murder or just a horrible accident, but the person we thought might have done it wouldn't cooperate with us, and claimed he had nothing to do with it."

"Who was this person?"

"Edward Deveraux, the younger son."

"The younger son." I stared at him. "There was a younger son who was involved in a murder, Daniel? And you haven't considered that he might be part of your investigation?'

I realized I had been yelling.

"Hold your horses!" Daniel put out a hand and touched my shoulder as I tried to stand up. "We've only just figured out this minute that this could have anything to do with the Deveraux family."

"Thanks to me," I couldn't resist adding.

"Thanks to you," he agreed. "But until now, until we considered the murder of the Hamilton couple a part of this same crime spree, the Deveraux name would never have come up."

"But it has now, and you have the most likely suspect—someone who killed his father, Daniel."

"He always claimed he was innocent," Daniel pointed out.

"Could he have been innocent?"

"Hardly. The court didn't think so at the time. He was a strange, twisted individual, antisocial, reclusive. He had quarreled with his father that morning and said, 'It's time you died, old man.' Later, raised voices were heard coming from the father's study, then Edward was found with blood all over him. Pretty conclusive, wouldn't you say, when there were only servants in the house apart from him?"

"So where is he now?" I was so excited I could hardly breathe.

"He was found not guilty by reason of insanity and sent to an institution for the criminally insane for life. I believe, because his family had clout and money, that it was agreed he could be locked in a private institution out in the country."

"We've got it, Daniel." I stood up now and wrapped my arms around his neck. "It's him. Edward Deveraux. He felt he was unjustly accused, and he's escaped and is punishing those involved."

"We would have been notified if he had escaped. And I always understood that the facility was quite secure—out in the Catskill Mountains, with a high wall around it. But I have to agree that we may have a perfect suspect. I'll talk to Marcus Deveraux first thing tomorrow. He'd have been notified if his brother had escaped. We should have been too. Of course the department may have been, and the news somehow never was reported to me. I wasn't the lead officer at the time, and old Boyle has retired. If Edward Deveraux has escaped, it will just be a question of finding him in a city of a million people."

❧ Twenty-seven ❧

I n the morning, Daniel was gone at first light. Part of me wanted to wait home to see if he would bring me any news, but the other part wanted to find out what connection the various other victims might have had to Edward Deveraux and his father's murder. Daniel's mother simply rolled her eyes when I told her I'd be going out again.

"And I thought I was called to look after an invalid," she said. "Here you are running around like a mad thing. Well, I won't be responsible if you have a relapse. And I won't be staying on to help you either. I've my own life to lead, you know."

I went over and kissed her on the cheek. "I know you have, and I'm truly grateful," I said. "Believe me, I do still hurt and I should be resting, but this is just too important. Thanks to what I've found out, Daniel might be closer to solving a case that has kept him baffled for months."

She stared at me, then said, "And if you're a smart girl, you'll not go rubbing that in. You'll let him think it was all his work and let him take the credit. That's the way to keep a happy marriage."

"And it's what you did with Daniel's father?" I asked, smiling now.

"Jesus, Mary, and Joseph," she said. "I would no more have dreamed of helping out in his police work than of flying to the moon. No, he left his cases behind at the front door and we never discussed them. I provided the safe and happy home that he could look forward to each evening. That was my job."

"I try to do that too," I said, "and usually Daniel keeps his police work from me. But it was a piece of luck that that young girl Sid and Gus were asked to help was actually tied in to the crime that has stumped Daniel for so long. It opened a chink in a door that may lead somewhere." I put a hand on her shoulder. "So I can't stop now. There is a very dangerous man at large, and if I can help in my small way to catch him, I will." Then I checked myself. "That is, if you're willing to look after your grandson for one more day."

She smiled then. "It's not as if I have much to do. Young Bridie has taken him over as her personal charge. He only wants her now to feed and change him." She glanced down the hall to see if Bridie was in earshot. "Have you had a chance to ask Daniel yet about what we discussed?"

"I haven't, I'm afraid." I shook my head. "Whenever we meet the conversation has been entirely about police matters. But I think it's a splendid idea, so I don't see any reason why he won't go along with it." I saw Liam starting to totter out of the kitchen, with Bridie in hot pursuit.

"I should go," I said, and I snatched up my hat from the hallstand before Liam could decide that he wanted his mother rather than Bridie after all.

The weather had turned bleak and blustery after yesterday's rain, and I battled with my brolly as the wind threatened to turn it inside out after I dismounted from the streetcar in Brooklyn. On the ride over the East River, I had decided to come clean with Miss Willis, now that I had nothing to hide. I didn't think she'd have gone out on such a disagreeable day, and I was right. She opened the front door, wrestling with it as the wind threatened to snatch it out of her hands, and stared at me in surprise.

"Why, it's the lady from the magazine, isn't it? Fancy seeing you again. What could you be wanting now?"

"I'm sorry to trouble you again, Miss Willis," I said, "but if I could just come in for a minute, I've something really important to ask you."

"Very well." She didn't look too sure. "Although I can't see what else I could tell you about my poor sister that hasn't already been said."

This time she didn't offer me coffee and cake. The small parlor felt damp and cold, and I suspected that in weather like this she herself stayed in the kitchen, where the stove gave off continued warmth. I know that's what I would have done.

I took a deep breath. "Miss Willis," I said. "I wasn't quite honest with you before. I was actually helping the police to find out who pushed your sister, but I wasn't allowed to tell you that."

"I see." She was staring at me, wide-eyed. "You're a lady policeman?"

I smiled at the term. "Just helping out. Not official. But we think we might have found out something important. You used to work for the Deveraux family, is that right?"

"Yes, I told you that before."

She hadn't, but I wasn't going to contradict her. "Tell me about Edward Deveraux."

"Young Edward?" I could tell this threw her completely off guard. "He was a strange little boy—lonely, always had his head in a book, and would look at you in that odd way when you spoke to him. Anyway, his big brother went off to school and then college, but they kept Edward at home, with a tutor, saying he was too delicate. Personally I thought that was a mistake. I thought he might have turned out all right if he'd had to mix with other boys. But I expect they knew what they were doing."

"And he didn't get along with his father?"

"His father despised him, and made it obvious too. Mr. Cornelius was a big, blustering sort of man, and he couldn't abide what he thought to be weakness. I felt sorry for little Edward when he was small. His mother pampered him—well, spoiled him, if you ask me. But then she died and he had no one, really. You could see that he shrank more and more into himself. Stayed locked away in his room, reading and doing all kinds of nasty experiments. If his father hadn't constantly criticized and belittled him, I think things might have turned out differently."

"You mean his father's death? Do you think Edward was responsible for that?"

"I know he was." She nodded. "I heard them shouting. 'You disgust me,' his father said. 'I expected more from you.' I couldn't hear any more of the exact words because the study door was closed. Well, I went on with my cleaning, and then a little later I looked up and Edward was standing there. He had a dazed look on his face, and his hands were all covered in blood. And he said, 'He's dead, Mary. My father is dead.' And then he started to laugh. It was horrible."

"What happened after that?" I asked gently, because I could see that the memory distressed her.

"The police came, of course, and they took him away. I had to give evidence at the trial, and the way he looked at me, it turned my blood." She shut her eyes, then took a deep breath. "They didn't execute him, which was a blessing. He was ruled not guilty by reason of insanity. That's what the judge said. So they locked him away, poor soul."

"And where is he now? Still locked away?"

"I'm sure he is. He was sentenced to be locked away for life, and you can't cure insanity, can you? Mr. Marcus inherited and sold the big family place and I was let go, so I don't know anything more about the family these days."

I paused, collecting my thoughts, because the next thing was hard for me to say. "Miss Willis, if Edward Deveraux had escaped . . . "

"Escaped?" Her hand went up to her expansive bosom. "You mean he got out of that place?"

"We don't know. If he had escaped, do you think he might have come looking for you?"

"Why would he want to see me again? I was always kind to the little chap—sneaked him an extra cookie when his father had been yelling at him—but we were never close. He never let anybody get close to him."

I went on, slowly, carefully. "I was wondering if he might look you up to punish you."

Now she really looked agitated. "To punish me? What for? I never did a thing to him."

"You gave evidence at his trial. You helped lock him away."

"I had to," she said, with anguish in her voice. "The judge summoned me and made me swear on the Bible that I'd tell the truth. So I told them exactly what I told you." She stopped, her mouth open. "Are you telling me that he came looking for me, to kill me?"

"And killed your sister by mistake, perhaps?"

She shook her head. "How could that be? Nobody could mistake me for Dolly. Take a look at the photograph. We looked quite different. She was a round, dumpy little thing, with that moon face, God bless her."

"Perhaps he asked in the neighborhood about Miss Willis, and someone saw your sister and pointed her out as Miss Willis. He hadn't seen you in years, maybe he thought it was you."

She was still shaking her head. "I just don't see how and why. It doesn't make sense. And if he then found out he'd killed my sister by mistake, why not come back for me?"

I couldn't answer that one. Why not, indeed?

"So they think he's escaped, do they?" Her voice quivered a little now. "When will they be sure of that? Because I'd need to be locking my door if what you say is true."

"We should know today, Miss Willis, and we'll make sure someone passes on the information to you instantly. But I think I can assure you that you're safe. If he hasn't come after you by now, he's probably not going to."

"Well, that's a relief." Her hand went to her breast again. "But I still can't see why he wanted to punish me. Like I said, I was always kind to him. Felt sorry for him, you know. And he'd understand that I had no choice but to testify to what I'd seen and heard. That judge was a very forceful man."

"What was his name? Do you remember?'

"I'll never forget it. He had this severe frown on his face and he said, 'I am Judge Ellingham. We are here to see justice done.'"

Judge Ellingham, whose wife had died of arsenic poisoning. The pieces of the puzzle were finally falling into place.

✿ Twenty-eight ✿

I thanked Miss Willis, reassured her to the best of my ability, then boarded the crowded trolley again. I couldn't wait to get back to Terrence Daughtery. I hoped that he wouldn't have chosen this as the moment to go out, and was glad when the rain picked up, making the going very unpleasant.

"Mrs. Murphy!" he exclaimed when he opened the door a crack and peered out. "What on earth brings you back here, and on such a wild day? I thought we'd concluded our conversation yesterday."

"I have to ask you one question, Mr. Daughtery," I said. "Were you at anytime a tutor to the Deveraux family?"

He looked astonished. "Why, yes. I tutored Edward Deveraux for several years, until . . ."

"Until he killed his father?"

He winced as if a spasm of pain had shot through his body. "No, I left the year before that. He had reached the age of eighteen, and frankly, he was such a bright boy that I told his father there was nothing more I could teach him. Edward really belonged in a university. But his father wouldn't hear of it. Do you know what he said? He said it would be a waste of money, since, in his words, 'Whoever would want to employ him?'"

Then wind swirled and spattered raindrops from the porch over-hang, making him realize I was still standing outside. "Dear me. Most rude of me. Please, come in. I'll make some coffee."

I followed him inside, this time to a small, warm kitchen. He put on a kettle before he turned to me and said, "May I ask what interest you have in Edward Deveraux?"

"It's possible that he has something to do with your mother's death," I said.

His mouth dropped open, then he frowned. "Are you suggest-ing . . . but that's impossible. They took him away and locked him up. I wrote to him for a while. He wrote back . . . long, rambling let-ters about science experiments he was conducting. He didn't seem particularly unhappy. It wasn't one of those dreadful state institutions, you understand. They let him have access to books, and he was used to being shut away on his own. But there was always someone guard-ing his door. He can't have escaped, surely? One would have heard if he'd escaped."

"The police are finding out today whether he might have escaped," I said.

The kettle boiled and Terrence poured boiling water over the cof-fee grounds. The enticing aroma filled the kitchen, making me real-ize how cold and miserable I had become.

When he had finished pouring, he put the kettle back on the hob and looked up at me. "You can't possibly think that he killed my mother."

"I'm afraid we have to consider the possibility."

He closed his eyes tightly, as if not allowing pain to enter. "No! No, I won't believe it. Edward and I were friends," he said. "I was the only person he trusted. The only person he could talk to."

"Did you give evidence at his trial?"

Another spasm of pain crossed his face. "I had to. I was called as a witness and they asked me lots of questions about his mental state. I knew it sounded very bad for Ed, but I had to tell the truth, didn't I?"

"What sort of things did they ask you?" I asked, then nodded as he put a cup of coffee in front of me.

"Whether I had witnessed abnormal behavior. And of course I had to say yes, I had. He did experiments on insects and small animals. He seemed to delight in inflicting pain. He cut himself sometimes and would sit, watching the blood run." He saw me give an involuntary shudder, then added, "Yes, Edward Deveraux was definitely not normal, but in spite of everything I was fond of him, and I thought he was of me. I can't believe he would have killed my mother. I simply can't believe it."

But I believed it as I left his house. Terrence Daughtery had said that Edward had delighted in inflicting pain. What more pain could he have caused than killing Terrence's mother, or Mary Willis's sister, or presumably Judge Ellingham's wife? Now I only hoped they could catch him quickly, before he did any more damage.

I wasn't sure what to do next. If Edward had been bent on inflicting pain, he had taken revenge by killing the nearest and dearest of those he thought had betrayed him. In which case Dr. Grossman must also have somehow been involved in Edward Deveraux's trial, and been punished by the killing of his only son. Which led me to think about the Hamiltons. Who was being punished by killing Susan and Albert Hamilton? Surely not Mabel, who wasn't even born when Edward killed his father and was shut away for life. Maybe Mr. Masters, his late father's partner? Had Mr. Masters too testified at the trial? Had Susan been an adored only child? But why would her husband have had to die as well, when presumably he had no connection to Edward or the murder of Cornelius Deveraux?

I decided that Daniel could find out what connection Dr. Grossman might have had to Edward Deveraux, and instead went to see Minnie Hamilton. I had to know how Susan Hamilton fitted into the picture.

Minnie Hamilton looked flustered and a little unkempt when I was shown into her drawing room.

"Oh, Mrs. Sullivan, I wasn't expecting visitors," she said. "I'm afraid two of the boys are down with some kind of grippe, and I was up all night with them."

"I'm very sorry to hear that," I said. "How are they now?"

"Much better, thank you; in fact, Frank has been insisting he feels well enough for a pork chop, and doesn't want gruel and broth." She bade me sit, clearing away magazines and a toy automobile from the sofa. "If you've come to see Mabel, I'm afraid this might not be a good time. She's been so upset lately, what with the police and then the doctor."

"I hope she won't be disturbed by the police any longer, now that it has been established that she couldn't have killed her parents."

She gave a disgusted sniff. "As if anyone could have believed that in the first place. A sweeter child you'd never see. And she worshipped them both. But I gather that your own husband is now taking over the investigation. Thank God for that."

"I didn't come to see Mabel," I began. "I came about a different matter. I wondered what you could tell me about Edward Deveraux."

Her head shot up in surprise. "Edward Deveraux? What an extraordinary question. Why should I know anything about him, apart from the name? I believe I met him once. He must have been at Susan's wedding, but then you probably heard what happened soon after that. He killed his father and was sent to an institution. Locked away for life."

"I wondered what possible connection he might have had to your sister-in-law and brother-in-law."

"None at all, apart from the family business partnership with Susan's father," Mrs. Hamilton started to say, then I could see that she had thought of something. "There was one thing," she said. "He used to be sweet on Susan. More than that. Obsessed with her, perhaps. Susan never said much, she was not the most open of individuals and

250

didn't confide easily, but I got the impression that she had been afraid of Edward Deveraux and abhorred his advances." She glanced toward the door, then leaned closer to me, lowering her voice. "In fact, I always suspected that contributed to her decision to accept Bertie's proposal so suddenly. It was a complete change of heart. She'd shown no interest in him before, and then suddenly she had him invited to a party she was attending, and just like that they were engaged."

"I see." I paused to digest this. "You think she wanted to get out of a life in which she had to socialize with the Deveraux family? Or was it worse than that? Do you suspect that Edward actually forced himself upon her?"

She could not meet my gaze. "I've always wondered," she said. "She was such a delicate, sheltered little thing. I think it quite possible that he had at least tried to molest her."

"You don't think that Mabel might be his child?" I blurted out the words without giving due thought.

She looked shocked. "My dear Mrs. Sullivan, certainly not. Mabel was born a year after they married. And she resembles my husband's family in facial features. Would you mind telling me why you are digging up this painful subject just now?"

"Because it's possible that Edward Deveraux might have been responsible for the death of Mabel's parents."

"But he was sent to an insane asylum," she exclaimed. "And that was years ago. Long forgotten."

"Not for a man who had nothing to do but brood," I said. "I may be quite wrong and I'm sorry if I've upset you, but I want to find out the truth as soon as possible, and it seems as if the fire was one in a long string of deaths, all linked to Edward Deveraux."

"How extraordinary," she said. "How did he get out? That's what I'd like to know."

"We'll find out more soon. My husband is looking into it today." I stood up, ready to take my leave. "I'll make sure you are informed as soon as the police know any more."

I thanked her then and came out into chilly autumn rain. If Edward Deveraux had killed Mabel's parents, had she seen him? Had he seen her? In which case, why had he not killed her too?

I was so excited by what I had discovered that I had to find Daniel right away. I forced my way onto a crowded El train, oblivious for once to the ache in my side, then disembarked at Canal Street and ran all the way to Mulberry Street.

"Captain Sullivan," I gasped to the young constable manning the front desk. "I have to speak with Captain Sullivan right away. It's urgent."

"He's upstairs in his office, ma'am," he said, "but I don't think that at this moment . . . "

I never heard the end of the sentence, as I was already running up the stairs. I think he called out behind me but I didn't stop. I opened the frosted glass door to Daniel's office and burst in. He was sitting at his desk and swiveled around, startled.

"Daniel, I've got it." I gasped, hardly able to get the words out. "The pieces to the puzzle. They all fit. I had to come and tell you right away."

"Molly, you can't just come barging in here to share minute household details, however thrilled you are with them," he said in a horribly patronizing tone. "I have work to do, and as it happens, I'm in the middle of an important meeting right now."

I looked around then and noticed for the first time a distinguished older man, not wearing a police uniform but a well-cut suit, sitting behind the door. Daniel turned to address him. "I'm really sorry, sir. My wife doesn't usually intrude in this manner. She's been quite upset since our home was burned down in the spring, as you can imagine, and is now able to be optimistic for the first time as she refurnishes our house." Daniel stood up and took my arm. "Let me escort you downstairs again, my dear, and I'll look forward to hearing all the details of your exciting shopping expedition when I get home."

He shot the man a look befitting an exasperated husband as he led me firmly out into the hall, then propelled me rapidly down the stairs and out into the street. I said nothing, but my anger reached boiling point as we came out into the open air, the rain now falling harder.

"How dare you humiliate me like that," I burst out as soon as we were outside. "Why did you have to treat me as if I was a simpering imbecile, when I've only come because I have vital information that will solve your apparently unsolvable case."

"I'm sorry, Molly," he said, his voice scarcely louder than a whisper, "but that was the assistant commissioner. He is no fonder of me than his superior, for the same reason—because I am not under the thumb of Tammany Hall, and can't be bought. They would both love to find an excuse to demote me or remove me, and discovering that my wife was working on a major crime would do the trick beautifully for them." He put his hand on my shoulder. "That's the reason for the charade up there. I had to make him think . . . well, you know."

"That I was an ordinary housewife whose interests didn't stretch beyond decorating fabrics for new pillows?" I demanded, still not quite able to quieten my disgust.

"Exactly. I was in the middle of being grilled."

"About the case? Then you can march back in triumphantly and tell them that it's all but solved. Daniel, I went to see Miss Willis again . . . "

"You went to question her without asking me first?" His voice now had a sharp edge to it.

"I had to. It was a matter of urgency. Besides, it's a free country, isn't it? I can visit anyone I want on a social call."

"I suppose you can, but . . . " he started to say, but I cut him off.

"And she made me start to see that everything ties in to Edward Deveraux. He felt betrayed because she had to testify at his trial. As did Terrence Daughtery, and the judge at that trial was Judge Elling-ham, and listen to this—Edward was obsessed with Susan Hamilton, and may even have tried to molest her. Don't you see? It's just a question of catching Edward Deveraux again."

"Not quite as simple as that," Daniel said.

"What do you mean?"

"Molly, I went to see Marcus Deveraux this morning as you suggested, and he told me that his brother is dead."

❧ Twenty-nine ❧

I stared at him blankly for a second, then shook my head. "Edward can't be dead. He's clever, Daniel. His tutor said he has a brilliant brain. He would have faked his death and then escaped. He would have fooled them, just as he's fooled you for so long."

"Just not possible," Daniel said. "According to his brother's account, Edward was allowed to walk around the grounds, supervised, of course. Then, without warning, he climbed up on a parapet and threw himself off a footbridge onto the rocks below. The doctor with him managed to climb down instantly, but Edward had suffered massive head injuries and was already dead."

"Oh, I see," I said. "And there could be no mistake? The doctor actually saw his body?"

"So did several medical workers who came to help bring him up from the creek bed. And so did his brother when he was lying in his casket."

"Oh." I felt like a deflating balloon. "But it all fitted together so perfectly. Edward Deveraux was the one thing that all these people had in common. When did this happen?"

"This spring."

I moved aside as a pushcart came rattling over the cobbles, its owner shouting out in Italian and the enticing smell of roasting corn on the cob reached my nostrils.

"That must mean that his death propelled someone else to seek revenge on his behalf, Daniel," I said, formulating the idea in my head as I spoke. "Someone felt he was wrongly accused or shouldn't have been sent to an institution, and he now wants to punish those who put Edward away. What impression did you get of his brother, Marcus?"

"Exactly the one I had when I interviewed him after his father's death all those years ago. Pompous. Arrogant. Patronizing, although he couldn't quite be as rude to a police captain as he was to a young detective."

"And what were his feelings for his brother, do you think?"

"If you're speculating that he might have committed the murders on his brother's behalf, then you would be quite wrong. He clearly despised his brother. He called him a useless piece of flotsam. He said the family trust had been paying for the private institution all these years. . . . 'Just to keep that poor excuse for a man alive,' as he put it."

Two constables came out of the front door, putting on helmets as they stepped into the rain. They saluted Daniel, murmuring "Good day, sir," as they passed. Daniel glanced up at the building. "I must get back. I don't want to annoy the old man further. We'll discuss this tonight, Molly." His hand on my shoulder squeezed tightly. "And believe me, I'm grateful for all that you've done. We must be getting closer to an answer. As you say, it has to be someone connected to Deveraux in some way." Then he kissed me on the cheek and ran back up the steps and into the building.

I made my way home.

"Just look at you now. Like a drowned rat," Mrs. Sullivan commented as I came in the door.

"It was too windy for my brolly to be of any use," I said, removing a sodden hat from my wet hair.

"Take those wet things off, and I've warmed some of that stew for you," my mother-in-law said in a firm voice. I did as she instructed, then came into a kitchen where a steaming bowl of stew awaited me. I ate, gratefully. Afterward I took her advice again and went up for a rest. On my way, I peeked in at Liam, who was sleeping in his crib, his face angelic and his impossibly long eyelashes sweeping his cheek. I stood there, looking down at him, overwhelmed with love and then feeling guilty that I had spent so little time with him recently. I tip-toed out and lay on my own bed, listening to the rain drumming on the roof. I closed my eyes and tried to sleep, but my head was too full of disturbing thoughts. Edward Deveraux had been described as a lonely little boy, stuck at home with a tutor rather than being al-lowed to go to school and play with other boys. His mother, who spoiled him, had died. His brother despised him and was glad he was dead. So who cared enough about him to seek revenge on his be-half? Then a picture came into my mind—a thin, pale face with hol-low eyes, not unlike the way Edward Deveraux had been described. Another lonely misfit . . . Terrence Daughtery.

Had he been closer to Edward than he chose to admit? He had said that Edward did experiments with animals and insects. Had Ter-rence shown him how to do those things? Had they done them together—two similar lonely young men? Or had he used Edward as an excuse to create a string of murders, all seeming to be tied to Ed-ward himself . . . to accomplish the one murder he wanted—that of his mother? I toyed with this idea. We had discussed before the pos-sibility that the random string of murders was to hide the one mur-der that mattered. Terrence seemed desolate and grieving after his mother's death. But I had been told she was overbearing. What if he had finally had enough of being dominated and planned her demise? Of course he would feel tremendous remorse afterward, or Terrence Daughtery might just be a very good actor, feigning grief so that no-body ever suspected him.

The more I thought about it, the more sense it made. I had

wondered before why nobody heard his mother scream, which she surely would have done if a strange man had come into her bathroom. She would have been indignant if her son had come in. She would have ordered him out, but would not have screamed. I couldn't wait to tell Daniel tonight when he came home.

I must have drifted off to sleep, because I was back in the underground dark place, unable to move with the rumbling all around me. I jerked myself awake and lay there, my heart racing. What could possibly be the meaning of this dream? I wondered if Dr. Werner were still here in New York and if he could perhaps help me. He was supposed to be an expert on this, according to Gus, however little I had liked his handling of poor Mabel. Perhaps things were done differently in Germany and Austria and doctors were stern, unsympathetic characters over there. I'd have to ask Gus when I next saw her. . . .

I was just in the middle of this thought when there was a knock at my front door. I looked down from my window to see Sid and Gus standing there. I rose from my bed and ran down the stairs to open the door to them before my mother-in-law could tell them I was resting and send them away.

"Molly, dear, how are you feeling?" Sid asked. "I hope we didn't disturb your nap."

"I'm well on the road to recovery, thank you," I said. "Come on in."

"We won't stay," Gus said, stepping just over the threshold to get out of the rain. "We're going to see Minnie Hamilton. The letter we hoped for has just arrived from Professor Freud in Austria. You remember I wrote to him, telling him about Mabel and asking him for a recommendation? Well, he's kindly written back." She held up a letter written in a strange, foreign script. To me it looked as if a spider had crawled into the inkwell and then across the page. "And listen to what he says," she continued. "I'll translate as best I can, since I'm still not an expert at reading German handwriting. Anyway, I got the gist of it. He says that he believes Dr. Otto Werner might still be in America, and if he is, then he could recommend no man more highly for the job. He says Dr. Werner's insights into the workings of the subconscious mind are brilliant, especially in the new field of the interpretation of dreams."

"You see," Sid chimed in. "We found the right man, half by chance. So we're going back to see him again, and we'll show him the letter from Professor Freud. That will undoubtedly do the trick and make him realize that he is the only one who can help Mabel. And the more we thought about it, the more it made sense to do as Dr. Werner suggested and have him take Mabel to the clinic in Switzerland, where he can work with her. Of course she can't be cured in a few days. We were silly to think that she could."

"Sid thought that maybe I should volunteer to go with her, since I speak German and have the freedom to travel," Gus said. "I wouldn't want to leave Sid alone too long. Just enough to see Mabel safely settled in."

"That's really good of you, Gus," I said. "I'd feel happier if you were with Mabel. And I'd also feel happier if she were safely far away from New York."

"Why is that?" Gus asked.

"Because I think we're dealing with a dangerous man who has killed many times. I think he killed her parents, and her life may also be in danger." As I said the words, I wondered if Daniel had a photograph of Terrence Daughtery, and if showing it to Mabel might reawaken the memories she had suppressed.

"Do you now know who killed Mabel's parents?" Sid asked sharply.

"We may," I said. "And if she recognized the photograph, that would be proof, wouldn't it?"

"We'd have to ask Dr. Werner about that first," Gus said. "We don't know if seeing the man who killed her parents would be too much for her delicate mental state."

"Of course," I said.

"I just hope we're in time, and Dr. Werner hasn't already sailed home to Germany," Sid said. "He told us he was leaving in a few days, didn't he?"

"If he's sailed already and is going back to Professor Freud in Vienna, then all is not lost. Maybe I can take Mabel over to meet him in Switzerland," Gus said.

"In any case, please warn Mrs. Hamilton to watch Mabel carefully and keep the doors locked," I said. "This man may not have realized initially that he was seen. He is extremely cunning and clever."

"We'll warn her to take all precautions," Sid said, "and taking her out of the country seems the obvious thing to do."

We parted company, they to the Hamiltons' residence and I to retrieve a crying baby from his crib. He had obviously heard his beloved aunts' voices and was incensed that he wasn't being brought down to see them. I placated him with a rusk and some milk, and he cheered up completely when Bridie came into the kitchen holding his treasured new ball.

I helped prepare the evening meal and waited impatiently for Daniel to return home. He came just before seven, his jacket and hat drenched with rain.

"Absolutely pouring out there now," he said.

"Didn't you take an umbrella?" his mother asked, helping him off with his jacket before I could do so.

"Too much trouble. You can't move quickly through crowded streets with an umbrella," he said.

She sighed. "You two are as bad as each other. Both going to come to a sorry end catching pneumonia, if you want my opinion."

"I expect we'll survive." Daniel gave me a cautious smile as he came into the kitchen, not sure whether my wrath had completely subsided. "Where's Liam? In bed already?"

"He just went up. Bridie's reading him a story," I said.

"That girl is turning into a proper little nursemaid," he said. "Too bad we can't keep her."

I glanced at Daniel's mother.

"It's strange you should say that," she said, "because I was just tell-ing Molly that the child needs a more normal life than she gets all alone with me and Martha. She needs to go to a proper school and mix with children her own age. So if you're willing to keep her for a while, then I'm willing to sacrifice her—for her own good and for yours."

Daniel turned to me. "That might not be a bad idea. What do you think, Molly?"

"You know I've always loved Bridie," I said. "I think it would be a grand idea."

"Then we'll give it a try, if you're sure you can spare her," Daniel said.

So one good thing was going to happen, at last.

"Let's go up and say good-night to the boy, shall we?" Daniel put an arm around my shoulder.

As we walked up the stairs he whispered, "I'm really sorry about what happened earlier today. I hope you understood."

"Of course," I said. "I didn't want to bring trouble on you, and I would never have come, but I thought that what I'd found was so im-portant."

"I wish you had really solved it for us," Daniel said.

"I've been thinking since," I said, "and I've come up with someone else who might be the kind of person to carry out these murders. Ter-rence Daughtery. He was Edward's tutor."

"The tutor?" Daniel frowned. "What motive would he have had for killing all those people?"

"Two possible motives come to mind." I leaned against the banis-ter at the top of the stairs. "He might possibly have been fonder of Edward than he admitted. Maybe a real bond developed between them in those days. He might have felt guilty that his testimony helped put Edward away for life, and then when he heard that Edward had died, he decided to avenge him. Or . . . and this seems more likely . . . " I leaned closer to Daniel, just in case his mother was listening at the

261

bottom of the stairs, "he was secretly planning to murder his domi-neering mother, and he used the other murders to make them seem tied somehow to Edward Deveraux. Perhaps he hadn't even heard that Edward had died. Perhaps he wanted to pin them all on him."

Daniel stood staring at me, a frown creasing his forehead as he considered this.

"It would explain why his mother never screamed," I went on. "She would have screamed if a strange man had entered her bathroom, and neighbors would have heard that scream."

Daniel was still frowning. "Let me think about this," he said.

A loud cry came from Liam's room as he heard Daniel's voice. "Dada!" he yelled.

Daniel gave me a smile. "We'll discuss it later. More urgent mat-ters call." Then he walked through into Liam's nursery. "How's my boy?" he called in his booming voice.

Bridie beamed when we told her the plans for her over the dinner table, then she tried to look sad when she turned to Mrs. Sullivan. "I'll miss staying with you," she said. "Will you be all right without me?"

"Heavens, child, I've lived alone for a long while now," Mrs. Sul-livan said.

"And of course you're welcome to stay with us anytime you want," I said in what I hoped was a convincing manner. "And we'll all come up to you in the summer."

So that was settled, and I couldn't have been more happy. It wasn't until we were alone in the bedroom that I had a chance to discuss more urgent matters with Daniel.

"I've been thinking about what you said." He looked up at me as he unbuttoned his shirt. "Terrence Daughtery. He certainly does seem to be the type—antisocial, under his mother's thumb, young, smart, agile . . . " He paused. "But who would go to all that trouble to avenge a friend, or to commit so many murders to cover up one valid one?"

"A person who was mentally unstable? Who had too much time on his hands?" I suggested.

He sighed as he took the studs from his collar and hung his shirt on the high-backed chair. "We'll bring him in for questioning. He seems the sort who might crumble under the threat of the Tombs."

"And I've asked Sid and Gus to warn Mrs. Hamilton to take good care of Mabel," I said. "You never know—he may not have realized he was seen when he killed her parents, and he may now decide to get rid of her too."

"Possibly." Daniel nodded. "In which case you should be extra vigilant too, my darling. We still don't know whether that train crash was designed to finish you off, and he might be annoyed you are still running around."

"I don't think so," I said. "I sat in his parlor twice. I drank his coffee."

Daniel shook his head as if he found me hard to believe. "One of these days you'll come to a sticky end," he said. "You have to learn to be careful. Or better still, you have to learn to act like a mother and wife, and not like an investigator."

"I didn't have any idea that Terrence Daughtery might himself be involved when I went to visit him," I said. "And besides, it was my investigation that finally put the pieces together for you in a case that has been stalled for months."

"I suppose I have to agree with that," he said, "but I'm only concerned with keeping you safe. I don't want to lose you."

I came over and wrapped my arms around his neck, feeling the warmth of his bare flesh against my fine cotton nightgown, and I felt a desire I hadn't known for weeks shoot through me. Daniel felt it too and his lips came hard against mine. "Will those ribs of yours mind too much if we take this a little further?" he whispered, breathing heavily as he lowered me onto the bed.

"I think we'll risk it and see," I whispered back.

Much later, when I was lying against Daniel's shoulder and we were both drifting off into satisfied sleep, a thought came to me.

"Daniel? Are you asleep?"

He grunted.

"Something's just struck me. Where do Dr. Grossman and the butcher who was locked in his meat safe come into this?"

"I've been thinking about that," he answered. "I believe Dr. Grossman was the expert witness who testified at the trial as to Edward Deveraux's mental state and urged for a verdict of insanity."

"But the butcher? Did he supply meat to the Deveraux family? Or the cleaver with which Edward's father was killed?"

Daniel sighed. "And here I was, drifting into a delightful sleep," he grunted. "The butcher. Good question. The information we have on him says that he only came to the city recently from somewhere upstate. I'll have to look into that tomorrow. But the father wasn't killed with a cleaver. He was hit over the head with a blunt object—from behind, mark you. Just the sort of thing a sneaky person like Edward would do." He pulled me closer to him. "Now, for heaven's sake, go to sleep. We'll know more in the morning."

❧ Thirty ❧

The next morning I awoke to sunlight streaming in. I could hear Daniel humming to himself as he shaved in the bathroom. *Today is the day*, I thought. We're going to solve everything. Daniel's going to be a hero at the police department, and all will be well.

I dressed and went downstairs to make him coffee and fry him eggs, for once beating his mother to it. She nodded with approval when she came into the kitchen. "That's more like it," she said. "Acting like a good wife for once, not rushing all over the place and putting yourself in harm's way."

I smiled sweetly and didn't answer. Clearly I was becoming more circumspect with age. After we had breakfasted and fed and bathed Liam, I decided we should go for a walk. Liam had been cooped up for a couple of days and needed fresh air, and truly it was too nice a day to stay inside. We strapped him into the buggy and off we went, Bridie trotting beside me like an obedient puppy. It felt as if the city had been spring-cleaned after the rain—everything sparkled and the sky was a clear blue arc as if made of spun glass. Sparrows fluttered, twittering around puddles. A carriage, going past at full speed, sent up a curtain of muddy spray that just missed us.

We went into Washington Square, still unpopulated at this hour apart from an old gardener attempting to rake up soggy leaves.

"Where are we going?" Bridie asked.

"Just for a walk," I said. "I'm afraid the swings are still too wet to swing on."

"I'm getting too old for things like that," she said. "I'm a proper mother's helper now, aren't I?"

I put my arm around her. "Oh, sweetheart, we're not keeping you here with us to be a mother's helper," I said. "Although you've certainly got a way with Liam, and I do appreciate the help. But we want you to enjoy your childhood while you can. It won't be long before you're a young lady. So anytime you feel like swinging on the swings, you do it."

She smiled, half embarrassed.

"I tell you what," I said. "Why don't I treat us to a hot chocolate at the Viennese pastry shop on Broadway?"

This suggestion met with no resistance and off we went. Bridie sipped delightedly at her hot chocolate, and Liam couldn't wait for me to cool each spoonful for him. But I'm afraid my brain was racing again. Being in the Viennese coffee shop was stirring up unwanted thoughts: Mabel going to Switzerland. Mabel possibly still being in danger. Daniel worried that I was still in danger. I glanced out of the window. Was someone stalking me, watching me at this moment?

"Rubbish," I said out loud, making Bridie look up. I grinned. "Just talking to myself," I said. I had been all over the city. There had been plenty of chances to push me in front of a speeding automobile or to put cyanide in my coffee. And yet our murderer had promised to go out with a bang. What did that mean? When was he planning his finale?

Suddenly I felt I should be doing something. Daniel would be interviewing Terrence Daughtery and the butcher's wife. But I wanted to know more about Edward Deveraux. I wanted to find out if he and his tutor had been close. I wanted to talk to Marcus Deveraux. I waited, attempting to hide my impatience, while Bridie savored the last drops of her chocolate. Then we walked back, in a way that seemed painfully slowly, with Bridie lingering to look in store windows, and then spending even more time stopping to pet dogs and smile at other children. I was tempted to suggest that Bridie could take Liam home by herself, but I remembered another occasion when a baby had been kidnapped from his pram. All too easy to do, and if someone wanted to get back at Daniel, what better way than to take his son? So I delivered them safely to the front door, told Mrs. Sullivan that I had a couple of errands to run, and disappeared before she could protest.

The Broadway trolley took me down to Wall Street, and I stopped a rather grand-looking businessman in a frock coat and topper to ask him where I might find Deveraux and Masters bank. It wasn't as impressive looking as some of the buildings that I passed, but there was a doorkeeper in a dark green livery and he halted me at the entrance. "May I help you?" he asked.

"I'd like to speak to Mr. Deveraux himself," I said. "It's a rather urgent matter."

I could see him sizing up the cut of my clothes, my still-Irish accent, and evaluating whether I might be a client or even worthy of admission. Grudgingly, he opened the door for me and let me step into a dark foyer, all mahogany and green marble. It smelled slightly musty and dusty, the way old libraries do. And there was no sign of clients, just several clerks, scribbling away at desks.

"Please wait here," the doorman said, and he signaled to a balding man sitting at the closest desk. "This lady would like to speak with Mr. Deveraux," he said in hushed tones.

The balding man raised an eyebrow. "Do you have an appointment, ma'am?"

"No, but it is a matter of some urgency, concerning his brother," I said.

This took him completely by surprise. "His brother? Did you not know that his brother is dead?"

"I am well aware of that. If I could just have a minute of Mr. Deveraux's valuable time, I've come about a matter that needs to be settled."

I could see him trying to work out what important matter concerning Edward Deveraux might concern me.

"Mr. Deveraux is extremely busy. However I'll see if . . . " He started toward a flight of marble steps, sweeping rather grandly up to a gloomy landing. I waited, listening to the scratching of pens and the occasional cough. I decided I was prepared to barge up those steps myself if necessary, but he returned quite quickly. "Mr. Deveraux is prepared to see you for a moment. This way please." And he went before me back up the steps, then tapped on a mahogany door and ushered me into a large, bright office. It faced away from the street, letting in sunlight and giving a glimpse of the East River. It had a thick pile carpet and the walls were lined with books—it was clearly designed to impress potential clients.

A large man in a well-tailored black suit was sitting at a polished desk. He looked up frowning as I came in, then a smile crossed his face. "I know you," he said. "The lady from the train."

I recognized him too now. "You were the one who saved my baby," I said. "I'm eternally grateful, Mr. Deveraux."

"I only did what any decent man would have done," he said. "And if you've just come back to thank me, that really wasn't necessary."

I smiled, thinking how I might make use of this unforeseen connection.

"What a terrible business," he went on. "I hope the young fellow was unharmed?"

"Luckily he came away without a scratch, thanks to you," I said.

"As I did myself," he said. "Luck of the devil, I call it." And he smiled, making him look suddenly younger. I realized then that he must be under forty. Not much older than Daniel. "And you yourself?" he continued. "I hope that you were also unharmed?"

"I came away relatively unscathed," I said. "Bruised ribs and a bump on the head. But compared to some poor people, I count myself blessed."

"It was an unmitigated outrage," he went on. "I take that train to work every morning and nothing has ever happened before. Someone should be held accountable—either the engineer or the signalman, and of course they are each blaming the other. But someone routed that train on the wrong track. We were just fortunate that the whole thing didn't plunge down to destruction, weren't we?"

I stood there, staring at him, because I had just realized something. "It wasn't me," I blurted out. "It was you."

"I beg your pardon?" he looked confused.

"Mr. Deveraux," I began tentatively. "It's just possible that someone planned that train crash to kill you."

"To kill me?" He laughed, a little nervously. "What are you talking about?"

"I believe my husband came to see you yesterday. Captain Sullivan?"

"He asked me about my brother. I told him Edward was dead. He seemed surprised."

"There is no doubt that your brother died, I suppose?"

"None at all. I saw his body. Not a pretty sight. He'd thrown himself onto rocks, you know—face first. But it was Ed all right. No question about it. Besides, one of the medical staff was with him and witnessed the whole thing. He was horribly shaken by it and felt guilty that he hadn't seen it coming. I must say I was rather of the same opinion. I pointed out that I paid them a considerable sum of money to keep my brother safe." He toyed with the fountain pen on his desk, spinning it around on the polished surface, then he looked up suddenly. "So what exactly is this all about?"

"I don't know how much more Captain Sullivan told you," I went on, "but there have been several murders in the city this summer, all of them somehow linked to your brother and his trial."

"But that's absurd. Linked to my brother? How?"

"It appears that someone has wanted to punish those who helped put your brother into the asylum. All of those killed had a dear one who had testified at the trial, or in some way betrayed your brother. Someone might have felt he had been treated unjustly."

"Treated unjustly?" His voice rose angrily. "The boy was a poor, twisted specimen. He'd never have made anything of himself. Always a liability to the family. The institution was the best possible place for him." He paused, frowning. "Who could possibly want to avenge my brother?"

"I wondered if you might have any idea about that."

"He had no friends. Other boys found him strange and repulsive, as I did."

"What about his tutor? Were they ever close?"

This clearly surprised him. "I was away at school and then college, of course." He paused, considering. "Close? Are you implying unnaturally close?" He was scowling now. "I remember the tutor—another weakling, wasn't he? Strange feminine sort of individual. Liked poetry. I suppose it might have been possible that he and Ed . . . but passionate enough about him to want to kill people who had harmed Ed? That would imply insanity of the worst kind."

"Possibly," I said.

He tipped his chair back, eyeing me. I noticed then that he had not invited me to sit. "You said that the train wreck might have been orchestrated with the intention of killing me?"

"It's possible. The murderer has been sending notes to my husband, gloating over the deaths. He seemed to take responsibility for the train crash."

"But that's absurd," he said again. "Was he driving the train?"

"No, but somebody changed the disk on the front of the locomotive, indicating it was a Sixth Avenue train, not a Ninth. That could have been done at a station when no one was looking."

"Well, I'll be damned." He shot me a half-apologetic look for using the word. "But that's ridiculous. Who would plan the destruction of a whole train full of people in the hope of killing one man? It's insane."

"We have to assume this individual is not quite sane," I said. "I wouldn't have believed it except that he sent a note, boasting, before it happened, then another after it had apparently not succeeded to his liking."

He was rubbing his chin now, clearly upset. "I just can't believe what you're saying. Surely anyone who wanted to kill me could wait around a dark corner and stab me. More certain than hoping a train crashes."

We stared at each other. Outside his window I heard the mournful toot of a tugboat on the East River. Then I asked, "Mr. Deveraux, is it possible that any other attempts have been made on your life?"

"Not that I'm aware of." He frowned suddenly. "Wait. Now that I think of it, there was one horrible incident. Not my life, but my dogs'. Earlier this year someone killed my dogs. Threw them poisoned meat. I complained to the police but nothing was ever done. You talked about this person wanting to punish. To inflict pain. I was dashed fond of those dogs."

"When was this?"

"Beginning of May."

"Then he started small and moved up to killing people," I said.

"And this man is still at large?" He was scowling again now. "What is your husband doing about it? If it's the tutor, arrest the blighter, for God's sake. Make him talk. I hear that the police have their ways of getting a confession."

"I believe my husband will be bringing him in for questioning today, so we may soon know the truth. But in the meantime, you might still be in danger. I'd advise you to be wary, Mr. Deveraux."

"Thank you for the warning, Mrs. Sullivan. I appreciate your taking the time to come and see me. Although how one can protect oneself from a monster who wrecks trains, I don't know."

I felt relieved, almost elated, as I came out of the building. I hadn't been the one targeted after all. It had been Marcus Deveraux. And Daniel would have arrested the tutor by now, and we could all breathe easier. I went home and resumed my wifely duties, ironing my husband's shirts and feeding my son his midday meal.

We had only just begun to eat when Daniel himself came in.

"This is a nice surprise," I said, getting up to greet him. "What are you doing home at this hour?" The question ended warily, because I had just remembered that his job was in jeopardy.

"I came to see if you'd like to go on a little trip with me tomorrow," he said.

"A trip—where?"

"Up to a place called Woodstock."

"What for? What's at Woodstock?"

"Not exactly in Woodstock. A couple of miles outside it, apparently. It's a private institution for the insane, where Edward Deveraux was locked away. I thought I should take a look for myself, and I'd appreciate another pair of sharp eyes."

"Of course, I'd love to come," I said. "Where is it?"

"In the Catskill Mountains, halfway up the Hudson River. We'll get off the train at Kingston, and I've telegraphed the local police to have some form of transportation waiting for us." He turned to his mother. "You can handle the boy for a day, can't you, Mother?"

Daniel's mother had already risen to her feet when he came in and was busy loading food onto a plate for him. She put it onto the table and indicated that he should sit and eat. As usual he complied, pulling out a chair and sinking onto it.

"She's been handling him ever since she arrived," I answered for her. "An absolute godsend. And Bridie's a big help."

"I expect we'll manage all right," Mrs. Sullivan said evenly as she put a glass of water next to her son's place. "Only I'm not sure it's wise taking Molly on a jolting train ride after what she's been through."

"I'll be fine," I said. "Almost healed." Of course I really wanted to go and would never have admitted to the ache that still nagged at my side. I sat down again opposite Daniel as he took a bite of his meat pie. "But why now? Has something new transpired?"

"Remember you asked about the butcher?" His face was alight as he looked up at me. "And we couldn't think what connection he could possibly have to Edward Deveraux?"

I nodded.

"I told you he only came to the city a year ago? And that he married a new wife recently? He ran a butcher's shop in Kingston. And the woman he married so recently had been employed at the asylum near Woodstock as a nurse. She and Edward Deveraux had not exactly seen eye to eye. Apparently she had ruined one of his experiments and made him keep his room tidy. He told her once that she'd be sorry."

"I see. And what can be gained from going to the asylum in person?"

"I'm not sure, but I think we should speak with the doctor in charge and verify the facts of Deveraux's death for ourselves, don't you?"

"More importantly, did you bring in the tutor?" I asked. "Were you able to establish a connection between him and Edward Deveraux? Had he visited the asylum?"

Daniel gave me an apologetic grin. "The tutor, I fear, is no longer our prime suspect. At the exact time that several of the murders took place, he was sitting with two little girls on the other side of the city, instructing them in their ABCs. Their mother confirmed it."

"Oh," I said. "Then who the deuce are we looking for?"

Daniel shrugged. "The only other person with a close connection to Edward Deveraux was his brother, Marcus, and there was certainly no love between them. He doesn't seem the type to avenge anyone's death."

I took a deep breath, because I wasn't sure I should be telling him. "I went to see Marcus Deveraux this morning," I said.

A spasm of surprise and annoyance crossed his face. "What made you do that?"

"I had to meet him for myself. To get an impression of him and of his brother."

"Molly, that was highly irregular. I hope you didn't say you were working with the police?"

"Hold your horses, Daniel, and don't scowl like that," I said. "As it happened I had a perfect excuse. Remember that I told you a man on my train carriage had saved Liam when we fell from the tracks? It was him, Daniel. Marcus Deveraux. He recognized me instantly, and of course I made it appear that I had come to thank him in person."

"Smart of you." He nodded approval.

I was about to go on that I had warned him he might be in danger, and that the train crash might have been aimed at killing him, but I thought that might be overstepping things. "And he certainly had no love for his dead brother. I think he actually said that the world was better off without him. He couldn't think of anybody who might have been close enough to his brother to want to avenge him. According to Marcus he had no friends."

"Then the answer must lie at the insane asylum," Daniel said. "It's possible that he formed a close attachment to another inmate there . . . maybe one who was due to be released."

I nodded. "Yes, that would make sense. But are people released from places like that?"

"We'll have to see, won't we? It could even be one of his minders, I suppose, but I find that hard to believe. In my experience, people who work in places like that are heartless sort of individuals who don't want to get close to their charges. And that butcher's wife certainly fit the bill. Hard as nails, I'd say. I wouldn't have wanted to be married to her."

I stared past Daniel and down the hall, thinking. "If someone decided to avenge Edward Deveraux's death by punishing those who had found him guilty, then they must have believed he was wrongly accused."

"He may have convinced some unbalanced person of that," Daniel said, "but there was no question of his guilt. He was alone in the house with his father at that moment, apart from old and reliable servants. If I remember correctly, the servants heard an argument going on, and the father said Edward was a disgrace to the family, or something similar. Then Edward came out of the study with blood all over him and laughed when he said his father was dead. How could he have been innocent?"

I nodded. "Maybe he felt he was justified, if his father had insulted him, or even was planning to send him away somewhere, if he felt Edward was an embarrassment to the family."

"I don't suppose we'll ever know now. But it was one of my first cases, and I was keen and determined to do the right thing, and I was in no doubt that he was guilty." Daniel took another bite of the pie and nodded approval at his mother. "This is good," he added.

❧ Thirty-one ❧

S o we were going to take a trip up the Hudson to a place called Woodstock. Personally I couldn't see what good it would do. Edward Deveraux had thrown himself from a bridge there many months ago. But the chance to have a day out with my husband was not to be missed. And just possibly, we might learn something that would fill in a still-missing piece of the puzzle. We were in luck. The day dawned bright and clear. Liam waved bye-bye quite happily as we set off. I had expected to depart from Grand Central Terminal, as the Hudson River trains I had taken before left from that station. Instead, Daniel said that we were to take the West Shore Line. The trains were less frequent, but at least we'd be on the right side of the river and not have to take a ferry, which would be dependent on the weather and the whims of the boatman.

So we started with a ferry instead, and took it across from the Hudson piers to the terminus of the West Shore Railroad in Jersey City. Actually it was more pleasant to leave from this station, as trains from Grand Central went through a long tunnel under Manhattan, and no matter how tightly the windows were closed, the carriage always ended up smelling of smoke. On our right the great river gleamed, moving lazily toward the Atlantic. A string of barges loaded with coal made their way downstream. A pleasure steamer with paddles turning and flags flying moved against the current. It was a jolly scene and it felt almost like a holiday outing, until I reminded myself that in New York City there was still a man who had promised to kill at least once more . . . and it was possible that his target was Marcus Deveraux.

We halted at unfamiliar stations—Teaneck, West Nyack—while across on the east bank I caught glimpses of places I did recognize. Irvington, Tarrytown . . . many of them carried memories for me of an unpleasant episode during my pregnancy—I'd been working on a case, which took me to a mansion on the hill and a convent where girls were treated so badly. The river narrowed, rushing wildly between steep banks. We passed West Point and the military academy perched on the bluff above the river. The country was wild now on our side as we continued northward. At last we came to Kingston. It looked like a prosperous riverside town, with a long main street of whitewashed and painted shops and the obligatory white church with a tall steeple. The young police officer sent to meet the train seemed so overawed at the visit of a New York City police captain that he could only answer Daniel's questions in monosyllables. He had come with a police wagon and driver, and after a courtesy call at the Kingston police department, we set off in the direction of Woodstock.

"Do the police not yet have any automobiles?" Daniel asked as we bumped and lurched along a muddy road, shaded by trees already starting to display their autumn foliage.

"Wouldn't be much point, sir," our young guide replied. "Always getting stuck in the mud. No paved roads around here yet, though I hear they have them around New York City now."

It was lovely wooded countryside, and we crossed over one rushing stream after another, sometimes on stone bridges, sometimes wooden. When the land opened up we had fleeting glimpses of the mountain range beyond. The air smelled fresh and sweet, tinged with wood smoke. After living in the city it was delightful, making me forget for a moment the serious import of our visit. I was jerked back to reality when we came into Woodstock and arrived at the little police station there. They had been warned of our coming, and Daniel went inside to speak with the officer who had been called out to Edward Deveraux's death. I, of course, was not invited to join him, so I went for a stroll up the main street and treated myself to a cup of coffee and a cake at the Copper Kettle café.

Daniel appeared again, helped me up onto the wagon, and off we went.

"Waste of time there," he said. "The man found nothing to contradict what we've already been told. Clear case of suicide while of unsound mind. The doctor had already signed the death certificate when the policeman arrived at the scene."

We continued on in silence, the horse's hoofs muffled where leaves had already fallen on the wet earth. A mile out of town the road started to climb. We were moving into the Catskill Mountains now, and the road snaked up the side of a hill with a rock wall on one side of us. Then at the top of the climb, we came to tall iron gates in the middle of a brick wall. The wall itself must have been ten feet high and was topped with shards of broken glass. The gates looked faceless and formidable. We rang a bell and waited. I noted there was no plaque or sign of any kind to indicate what lay behind that wall. At last one of the gates swung open, and we were admitted by a gatekeeper. The house itself stood among lawns, built of solid gray stone and looking surprisingly elegant, like a manor house I might have seen in Ireland. Then I noticed the bars on the windows. They were ornamental bars, quite attractive, but bars nonetheless. So it was a prison, even if it was in pleasant surroundings.

As we pulled up outside the front door, an elderly man with a shock of white hair came down the steps to greet us. "Captain Sullivan." He held out his hand. "I am Dr. Piper, head of this facility. Good of you to come in person, although I don't know what we can do to help you."

He looked at me with interest until Daniel introduced me.

"Ah, you make an excuse to give the little lady a trip into the country," he said, smiling as he took my hand. "That's nice."

Daniel glanced at me as I went to open my mouth, then said hastily, "On the contrary. My wife is a former detective and I value her powers of observation." I could have kissed him.

"A former detective. Well, I never." Dr. Piper raised an eyebrow. "Although I am not sure that there are any clues for you to follow here, Madam Sherlock Holmes." And he chuckled. "Please come in." He led us across a marble entrance hall with a wide flight of polished steps leading up to the floor above. From somewhere at the back of the building I could hear a piano being played.

"That's Alice Gorman," he said. "She was studying to be a concert pianist until she drowned her children in their bathtub. She practices every day and occasionally gives us a concert."

"So the inmates are allowed to intermingle?" Daniel asked.

"Those who are not considered a danger to themselves or others. And we allow them the niceties to make life bearable, if appropriate. There was no reason that Alice should not bring her piano."

He opened a door and led us into a pleasant study with chintz-covered armchairs and a big untidy desk. He indicated that I should take the chair in the bay window. I noticed that this window had no bars on it, but looked out across the lawn to the tree-covered hillside above.

"And Edward Deveraux? Did he intermingle?" Daniel asked, taking a seat across from the doctor.

"Edward was not the most sociable of beings. He brought his books with him and kept to himself. Always reading and doing experiments. I discussed them with him sometimes. Really quite a brilliant brain in some ways. So keen to know about scientific advances."

"Did he form any special attachments with any of the other inmates?" Daniel asked.

Dr. Piper frowned. "We prefer to call them patients here, Captain Sullivan. They all suffer from a deficiency of the brain that has made them not responsible for their actions. And no, Edward kept himself aloof from other patients here. Not that they are allowed to meet often in a social capacity, but Edward rarely wanted to be sociable even when they had a chance—he chose not to attend when Alice gave a concert, for example."

"And what about the staff here? Did Mr. Deveraux have a particular staff member who looked after him?"

"That would be Annie Peters," he said. "She left us last year to get married. We were sorry to lose her."

"Annie Peters. She married the butcher," Daniel said.

Dr. Piper nodded. "That's right. Such a tragedy that he was killed, after she had found happiness at such a late stage of her life."

"So she was the one who had the most dealings with Edward Deveraux?" I asked. My brain was leaping ahead. Had she become fond of him? Formed an attachment to him? Married the butcher for his money, perhaps? And then found a way to get rid of him while avenging Edward's death?

"Yes, she was his attendant," Dr. Piper said, then added "much to Edward's disgust. He found her stupid and annoying. She tidied up things he was working on. She made him wash and change his clothes." He smiled. "I think he grew a beard just to spite her, because she always insisted that he shave. Then, of course, he refused to comb his beard."

I was glad I hadn't voiced my thoughts. So there was no love lost between Edward and Annie Peters. Apparently nobody here would have cared about Edward enough to be his champion and avenger.

"Tell me about the day he died," Daniel said.

Dr. Piper sighed. "Such a tragic waste. I blame myself, of course."

"Yourself?" Daniel's voice was sharp.

"I was his doctor, responsible for the state of his mind. I should have seen that he was troubled, perhaps contemplating suicide, but he gave no indication of it. None at all. In fact he had seemed quite cheerful in the preceding days. He seemed to be looking forward to meeting this distinguished doctor. He read all he could of the doctor's papers. He even neatened up his appearance, which surely he would not have done had he been contemplating suicide. Spruced himself up properly." Dr. Piper got up and walked over to the window, standing beside me to look out, as if re-creating a scene in his mind. "He had recently become interested in ornithology. We have many fascinating birds in this part of the country. A pair of binoculars was sent to him and he spent long hours at his window, studying the birds and making notes on them. He made a fine scrapbook. He also asked that any dead birds found on the property be brought to him to dissect, but of course we couldn't comply with this request, since it would have involved sharp instruments, and our patients are not allowed knives of any sort."

"So he took up bird-watching," Daniel said. "And he was allowed outside to do this?"

"Our patients are encouraged to take a daily walk, accompanied by an attendant, of course."

"You don't worry about a patient overpowering his attendant and escaping?"

Dr. Piper shook his head emphatically. "Our grounds are completely surrounded by the wall, and there is no way to escape. The attendant always carries a whistle. Edward was permitted to take his binoculars and watch his birds. We found it a positive activity."

"On the day he died, you were walking with him?"

"No, not I. We had a distinguished doctor visiting us, and it transpired that he was also a keen ornithologist. Edward wanted him to see the hawk's nest he had recently discovered, so they went out together. They went to the upper part of our property, where the hawk's nest was located in a tall pine tree. A stream crosses that corner of the estate—"

"And the inmates cannot escape via this stream?" Daniel asked.

"Impossible. It enters as a waterfall down a sheer rock face and exits through a culvert with bars over it. Perhaps you would like to see for yourself?" He turned to me. "I am afraid it may be a little muddy after the rain we've just had. If you'd prefer to stay here?"

"I'd like to come too," I said. "I grew up in Ireland. I'm used to rain and mud."

The doctor let us out of a side door and we crossed the lawn. It was indeed muddy and I cursed my pointed heels that sank in, making it hard for me to keep up with striding men. On the other side, a path rose through a forest of oaks and conifers. Our footsteps made no sound on the carpet of leaves and needles. The cry of a hawk made me jump. There was an eerie watchfulness to the woods, and I glanced back over my shoulder as if someone might have been following us. Ahead I could hear the sound of running water, and we came to a rocky clearing where an ornamental stone bridge spanned the stream. We couldn't see the water until we walked onto the bridge and stood, looking down to where the stream danced swiftly over a series of cascades in a miniature gorge.

"Pretty, isn't it?" Dr. Piper said. "Very picturesque. In the old days I gather this was considered a local beauty spot, and tourists came from miles around to visit it. Now, of course, nobody sees it but us."

"So it was from this bridge that Deveraux threw himself?" Daniel stood at the edge of the bridge, looking down.

"It was." Dr. Piper sighed. "They stood here, and Edward pointed up at the rock face and the tree with the nest in it. Then while the doctor was looking up, Edward suddenly threw the strap of the binoculars around the doctor's neck and tried to strangle him. They struggled and fell to the ground. The doctor was relatively young and fit and was able to free himself from Edward's hold on him. But before he could get back to his feet, Edward climbed onto the parapet and threw himself, spread-eagled, to the rocks below."

He paused, staring down at the stream. "You have to understand," he said quietly, "that it was a late spring this year. The snow and ice above had not yet melted. There was only a mere trickle of water coming down, and the rocks were exposed. He was killed instantly.

It was horrible to behold. Dr. Werner managed to climb down to him, at considerable risk to himself, and in spite of the injuries he had sustained, but . . . "

"Wait a minute," I interrupted. "Did you say Dr. Werner?"

"That's right. He was visiting this country from Vienna, and knowing him to be a leading expert in the field of deviations of the brain, I invited him to come and see our patients. You have perhaps heard of him?"

"Dr. Otto Werner?" I said. "Yes. I have met him in New York."

"A fine man," Dr. Piper said with warmth. "And so distressed by what happened. He was lucky to come away with his life. His throat was so bruised he could hardly speak. We begged him to stay and recuperate but he wanted to go straight to a hospital in the city—he was worried about damage to his vocal cords."

Daniel looked at me. "Dr. Werner, isn't he the man who was treating the Hamilton girl?"

"Yes," I said. "Daniel, we must get back to New York immediately."

As we talked I had been looking around, trying to picture the scene—the doctor looking up at the hawk's nest, the strap coming suddenly around his neck, him falling backward onto the rocky surface. It was lucky he was not knocked out by hitting his head on one of those rocks, I thought.

"I didn't think that Dr. Werner was still in New York," the doctor said. "I understood that he was planning to sail home last spring."

"No, he's still here," I said, "but leaving this week, if he hasn't already sailed."

"I don't know what else he can tell you about Edward Deveraux's death, or how those facts can assist you in solving a crime," Dr. Piper said. "He gave a full report to local police, and of course other members of our staff were on the scene almost immediately. Anyone who accompanies a patient onto the grounds is always equipped with a whistle. As soon as Dr. Werner remembered the whistle and had the strength to blow it, other staff members rushed to his aid. Several of our male attendants climbed down to help him bring Edward up from the streambed. It wasn't easy, as you can imagine. Of course it was already too late to save him. As I said before, he had died instantly."

I shifted from foot to foot, impatient to get back to New York. As I looked around, my eyes moving from the rushing stream to the rocky hillside, I caught a glimpse of something sparkling from the gorge. Curious, I went closer. It appeared to be a small mirror, lodged halfway down in a clump of bushes growing from the rock wall. I was about to point it out to Daniel, but he had already started to walk away.

✥❀ Thirty-two ❀✥

The train seemed to move at a snail's pace.

"This is a remarkable coincidence," Daniel said.

I had been weighing the facts on the slow ride back to the station, trying to see them impartially.

"Perhaps not so remarkable," I replied. "I suppose as one of the leaders in his field it was natural that he would be invited to see the patients at such an institution. And, as an expert on dreams, he was the one recommended by Professor Freud to treat Mabel."

"It just seems strange that Edward Deveraux's name never came up in conversation," Daniel said.

"How would Dr. Werner know that Mabel was in any way connected to the Deveraux family? Sid and Gus found him and took him to see the girl at her aunt's house. All the same, I don't usually believe in coincidence, and neither do you."

"You know where this Dr. Werner lives, do you?"

"Sid and Gus do. But he may no longer be in the city. When we last saw him, he had his passage booked on a liner sailing to Germany. He said he was looking forward to going home after being away for so long."

"So he will not be treating the Hamilton girl after all?"

"He suggested that her relatives send her to a clinic in Switzerland, where he will have time to treat her. He said cases like hers could not be rushed."

"I can see that," Daniel said. "All the same, I don't know whether we can allow her to leave the city. She is our one witness, if she ever recovers her memory."

"I don't think she wants to go, actually," I said. "I wouldn't, if I felt alone and vulnerable and I was currently safe in the bosom of my family."

Daniel nodded. "So Dr. Werner wasn't able to interpret her dreams? Neither was your friend Augusta?"

I sighed. "He seemed to think that the snake in her dreams was a common symbol for a young girl going through puberty. Apparently most of our dreams symbols are connected to sex, according to Professor Freud."

We had been talking in low voices but there was a horrified intake of breath from the stout matron sitting opposite us, obviously the type who enjoys eavesdropping. I realized that polite society did not condone the mention of any bodily function. It certainly didn't condone the mention of sex. I looked at Daniel, and we exchanged a grin as the woman pretended to concentrate on her knitting.

"I'm just wondering whether today was essentially a waste of time and police money," Daniel said as we neared the end of our journey and the Manhattan skyline appeared on our left across the Hudson. "True, we learned that Dr. Werner was there when Deveraux killed himself, and that is indeed an unexpected and interesting fact. But it was also confirmed that Edward Deveraux was essentially a loner who developed no close friends or confidants. Certainly nobody who would have killed for him."

"I wonder why he suddenly decided to attack Dr. Werner, after so many years of docility?" I said.

Daniel shrugged. "Maybe the doctor's questions probed too near to the bone for Deveraux's liking, Dr. Werner may have gotten Deveraux to admit something he didn't want to face. Werner is a leading alienist, after all."

"And when Edward Deveraux realized he'd confessed something he should have kept quiet about, he decided to silence the doctor."

"Or . . . " Daniel paused, waving a finger as he thought. "Maybe Deveraux had decided to end his life, and killing an eminent alienist before he died was to be his last defiance. I've seen it often enough— I'm going to go, but I'm going to take you with me."

"That makes sense too," I said. "I hope Dr. Werner hasn't already left New York. He may have his own thoughts on Edward's motive."

"I must go to headquarters when we get into the city," Daniel said. "Let's hope I'm not now in more trouble for wasting police money on a useless jaunt. Can you visit your friends and find out Dr. Werner's address for me?"

"Of course. And should I bring it to you at Mulberry Street?"

"Probably not," Daniel said. "If we happened to bump into the assistant commissioner again, I don't think that would go down well. I may have to put off visiting Werner until later."

"How much time do we have, Daniel?" I could feel the urgency building up inside me. "He's leaving any moment now. We have to speak to him first."

Daniel shrugged. "Is it that crucial?"

"Of course it is. We need every detail of what transpired between him and Edward, everything Edward might have said to him. There has to be come vital insight that we've all missed. And Dr. Werner may have seen Mabel Hamilton again. She may have revealed something to him that will make sense to us."

"Maybe." Daniel didn't sound as enthusiastic as I felt he should be. Myself, I couldn't wait to talk to the doctor. I felt he must be able to shed light on some aspect of this complicated thread. I was already standing up as the train pulled into the Jersey terminus.

We rode the ferry across to Manhattan, then Daniel set off in one direction for Mulberry Street while I went home to Patchin Place. My motherly instinct told me I should stop in first to see that Liam was all right, then I reminded myself that my mother-in-law was perfectly capable. Bridie never let him out of her sight, and besides, it was still in the middle of his afternoon naptime. And I was anxious to get Dr. Werner's address so that Daniel could question him. Actually I would have liked to talk to the doctor myself, but I knew that would not go down well with Daniel and the New York police.

I tapped on Sid and Gus's door and was relieved when I heard footsteps coming down the hall toward me. They were rarely home on fine days. Sid opened the door, which was also unusual, as Gus seemed to be the designated greeter.

"Molly!" She looked almost startled to see me.

"I'm sorry. I hope I'm not disturbing something. If you have visitors, I could go away and come back later."

"No. You'd better come in. You may be able to help, since you have more experience with this kind of thing than we do." She almost yanked me inside and shut the door, taking me through to the drawing room, which was in itself unusual, as they lived in the kitchen and conservatory most of the year. As I came in I saw two people sitting together on the sofa. One was Gus and the other was Minnie Hamilton. Gus was holding her hand, which surprised me even further.

"Oh, Molly, it's you. Thank God," Gus said as they looked up at me.

"What's wrong? What's happened?" I asked.

"Sit down, do. We'll need your help," Gus said.

I perched on an upright chair across from them.

"It's Mabel," Mrs. Hamilton said. "She's gone."

"Gone? Where? Did you decide to send her to Europe after all?"

Minnie Hamilton shook her head, and I could see she had been crying. "Just gone. When I went into her room this morning she wasn't there. I let her sleep as late as she likes, because her nights are so often disturbed. But when she wasn't awake by ten I decided to peek in on her. There was no sign of her. I don't understand it. Where can she be? Did she decide to run away and slip out during the night?"

"Is there any reason she might have wanted to run away?" I asked.

"I thought she felt safe with us," Minnie said. "But she was upset when we talked of sending her to Switzerland. She should have known we'd never do anything like that against her will."

"Where might she go if she ran away?" I asked. "Has she friends in the city?"

"No bosom friends that I know of. She attended an academy for young ladies on the Upper East Side and must have had friends there, but nobody has come to visit her since the tragedy, apart from her schoolmistress."

"Was she fond of this teacher?" I asked. "Might she have run to her?"

"Mabel didn't seem particularly overjoyed to see her. Thanked her politely for coming, but seemed relieved when she went again."

"Was her bedroom window open?" I asked.

Minnie Hamilton's eyebrows shot up. "You don't think she'd have climbed out of her window? I know there is a creeper on the back wall of the house, but it would be foolish . . . "

"Have you spoken to the police yet?" I asked.

"No. Not yet. I was in such a tizzy. Frankly I didn't know what to do."

"We must tell them right away," I said. "It's possible she's been kid-napped."

"Kidnapped? By the man who killed her parents?" Minnie put her hand to her mouth. "I never thought . . . I never believed. You're right. I must tell the police right away."

"Tell me. Has she seen Dr. Werner again?"

"A couple of days ago. He came to the house briefly to say good-bye, and to give us his address in Germany and the name of the clinic in Switzerland. He said he would make all the arrangements if we changed our minds and decided to send her."

"Did he say when he was sailing?"

"I believe it was yesterday."

"That's too bad," I said. "Daniel very much wanted to speak with him." I was about to add that the doctor had been connected to Edward Deveraux, but then I remembered I had kept the details of the case from Sid and Gus, at Daniel's request. "I should probably take down his address anyway," I added. "Although I can't see what good it would do now. Daniel will have to wait and write to him when he is back in Vienna. How annoying."

Gus stood up. "I'll find his address for you," she said. "I'm only sorry he couldn't do more for Mabel on the spot. These alienists are always so cautious. I just wish I was more experienced and had been able to do more. I still feel that Mabel's dreams are the key to all of this."

"Has she had any more dreams with vivid symbols in them recently?" I asked.

Minnie shook her head. "It's always the snake."

❧ **Thirty-three** ❧

I sat at their writing desk and wrote Daniel a note, telling him that Mabel had vanished and he needed to send men to start looking for her immediately. I also wrote down Dr. Werner's address, but added that I understood he had sailed for Germany yesterday. Then I decided I would deliver the note myself, even if I incurred Daniel's wrath. So I set out for Mulberry Street, noting as I walked that I was feeling the effects of a long day on a jolting train and wagon. But my own small ailments were of no importance compared to a missing girl. The tension that had been growing inside me all day had now reached the point of explosion. Mabel had been kidnapped, I was sure of it— kidnapped by the monster who killed her parents.

I forced my way through the crowds on Mulberry, dodging around pushcarts and playing children until I came to police headquarters. The same young officer was manning the desk, and I saw wary recognition in his eyes. He had probably gotten an earful for allowing me upstairs the last time I came.

"I need to speak with Captain Sullivan immediately," I said. "Could you go and fetch him for me? Just tell him that Mabel has been kidnapped."

"I'm sorry, I can't do that, ma'am," he replied, and when I was about to explode he added quickly, "Captain Sullivan's not here. He came in about half an hour ago, was only here a few minutes, then left again."

"Did he say where he was going?"

"I wouldn't ever ask a captain where he is going," the young man replied. "But he seemed in a great hurry."

I sighed. "Then please give him this letter the moment he comes back. Tell him it's very important. A matter of life and death."

He took it from me. "I will, ma'am."

I lingered, but there was nothing else to say or do. I wondered if somehow the police had been told about Mabel, or—and I felt a sudden chill gripping at my stomach—her body had been found. I wanted to do something useful, to help, to be involved, but I couldn't think what. Then I decided that at least I could go to the shipping offices, and confirm that Dr. Werner had indeed left New York. That would be useful without interfering.

I threw caution to the winds and took a cab to the Hudson piers from which the ocean liners departed. No German liner was docked there at the moment, only a smaller steamship called, inappropriately, *Queen of the Amazon*, and the French liner *La Lorraine*, on which I had sailed earlier this year. She evoked no fond memories, and I walked past her to where a board announced sailings for the month. There I saw that the *Deutschland*, a ship of the Hamburg-Amerika line, had indeed sailed yesterday. I found their offices and asked whether a Dr. Otto Werner had been on the passenger list.

A very correct German clerk looked for me. Yes, indeed, he said. Dr. Otto Werner had been on the passenger list. I gave a sigh. That was that, then. Now we'd never know exactly what had transpired between him and Edward Deveraux. I thanked the clerk and was about to walk to the door when he called after me, "*Fraulein*. I have a message here that it appears Dr. Werner did not sail after all. He was checked in on board, but his cabin was never occupied. He must have changed his mind at the last minute."

"Thank you," I said. I left. A blustery wind swept in from the Atlantic, bringing with it the promise of more rain. I held onto my hat as I walked along West Street, deciding what to do next. I should go home, I supposed. Resume my wifely duties and leave the hunt for Mabel to Daniel and his men. Then I started to wonder why Dr. Werner had changed his mind at the last minute. Was it possible he saw the *La Lorraine* in port, and decided it would make more sense to sail into France if he was finally heading for Vienna? There was a shipping agency nearby, advertising everything from cruises to the Bahamas for forty-seven dollars, to sailings to Canada and England. *Your shipping needs taken care of,* said the sign. *Let us whisk you to Europe in the lap of luxury.*

A bell jangled as I went inside.

"I wonder if a Dr. Werner was recently in here, and booked a crossing on the *La Lorraine*?" I asked.

The man behind the counter ran a finger down a ledger. "No, madam. There is nobody of that name on board."

Was it possible he'd chosen another ship? "So he never came into this office? Tall, thin man, with hollow eyes and a trimmed black beard? Rather pale complexion. Probably wearing a black suit and a monocle?"

The clerk shook his head. "I don't believe . . ."

"Wait," said a young sandy-haired clerk looking up from his desk. "A man like that was in here, a couple of weeks ago. But he didn't have a monocle."

"With a strong German accent?"

"No. He was American. Nicely spoken. He booked two tickets for himself and his daughter on the *Queen of the Amazon*, sailing to South America tomorrow. What was his name?" He paused, thinking. "That's it. I remember. Mr. Edwards."

I left, my heart pounding. My mind was toying with a preposterous idea. *Don't be ridiculous,* I told myself. There were plenty of tall, thin men sporting black beards in New York City. And a Mr. Edwards taking his daughter on a journey to South America was just yet another coincidence. But I had to make sure. I had to see for myself whether Dr. Werner had left his residence or not. I was planning to hail another hansom cab. I started walking through the narrow streets of the dock area without seeing any sign of a cab, and I was beginning to get annoyed when I recognized the shape of City Hall in the distance ahead of me. I could certainly find a cab there, I thought, and hurried forward. Then I noticed the subway station. I had used the Métro often enough in Paris, but still hadn't conditioned myself to think of the subway as a good mode of transportation in New York.

I went down the steps to an elegant foyer with a glass-domed roof, more like a museum than a train station. But I had no time or inclination to study architecture today. I paid for a ticket and went down the steps to the platform. Almost immediately I heard the rumble of a train. It thundered into the station. People got out. I climbed aboard and in no time at all found myself at Astor Place. Just across Broadway, past Wanamaker's department store, was Ninth Street. I stopped outside number 18. Heavy drapes were drawn across the windows. It had that closed, unlived-in look to it. I couldn't bring myself to go and knock on the front door. That would definitely be something I left for Daniel, but I walked slowly past on the other side of the street, then waited on the corner until I saw a woman coming toward me with a laden shopping basket. When she was about to go into a house almost directly across from Dr. Werner's, I approached her.

"Excuse me," I said.

She stopped and turned back to me.

"That house over there. Would you happen to know if it's empty right now? We're looking for a place around here to rent, and someone told me the former tenant had moved out."

"That's right," she said. "I guess he must have gone by now. I heard he was returning to Europe and I haven't seen him for the past day or so. If you're wanting to rent it, it's a Mr. Michelson who owns several of the houses on this street. You'll find his offices on Broadway."

"Thank you," I said. "Do you think anyone could let me in now to look around, since I'm in the area, and very keen to snap up a good house? It's in good condition, would you say?"

"I couldn't tell you that," she replied. "There's been a gentleman living there alone these past months. Mrs. Hallinan at number twenty-four used to clean for him, and kept it nice and neat. But then one day he fired her—he didn't give a reason—and since then he must have been looking after himself. I've yet to see a gentleman who knows how to cook and clean, so I'm wondering about the state of the place. Probably nothing a good dose of elbow grease can't cure."

"Perhaps he sends out his laundry and takes his meals at a nearby café," I said. "Some gentlemen like their privacy, particularly academic types."

"I never saw the laundry cart stop at his house," she said.

"What sort of man was he—friendly?" I felt bold enough to go on now.

"To start with, yes, he was pleasant enough. He spoke English with a strong accent, mind you, but you could understand him all right. But then one day he completely ignored me, and since then he's hardly managed a civil nod if I bid him good day. Good riddance, I say. I like my neighbors to be friendly, don't you? I hope you do move in here. You've a nice open face. Are you married with little ones? We could do with more children on this street."

"I've a baby boy," I said. "My husband's with the police."

"Perfect." She beamed at me. "I'm Mrs. Rogers."

"Sullivan," I said, and we shook hands. I felt like a fraud as she closed her door, leaving me standing on the deserted street.

I felt so excited I was shaking now. Dr. Werner, who had been described as "a fine man," and recommended by none other than

Professor Freud, was initially friendly to his neighbors, but then he had recently become abrupt and rude. My preposterous idea now seemed to take on shape and reality. And Edward Deveraux had grown a beard. Mabel was in terrible danger. I couldn't wait to find Daniel and tell him this. They were probably staying in one of those harbor-front rooming houses, close to the ships. I was about to walk away when I noticed one of the drapes was not completely drawn across the front window of number 18. I glanced both ways before I crossed the street, went up to the window, and tried to peer inside. Now that I had chatted with Mrs. Rogers about renting the place, I had a perfect excuse for nosiness. It was quite dark inside and I could see almost nothing, just the indistinct shapes of furniture under sheets. It certainly looked as if the place had been shut up and was no longer occupied.

My nose picked up the smell—sweet, cloying, and somehow familiar—a fraction of a second before everything went black.

❦ Thirty-four ❦

I opened my eyes to darkness. I was lying in a dark and confined space. It smelled damp and musty. As I lay there, I heard a rumbling sound that set objects rattling, and I could feel it in my bones. I knew exactly where I was. I was in the place of my dream. But I was definitely not asleep. And unlike in my dream, I could move. I turned my head. I noticed a faint chink of light coming from under a door. And when the rumbling came again, I identified it. I was in the basement of number 18, and the new subway line ran close by.

That sweet, cloying smell was still in my nostrils, and I recognized it too. Chloroform. I had encountered it before. And the murderer had obviously used it on Mabel the night he killed her parents, making her ask "Why does it smell so sweet?" in her dream. I was about to sit up when I heard movement outside the door. The handle turned. I lay still and closed my eyes. Light flooded in from beyond the door. From under my lashes I watched the tall, thin figure come into the room. He came right up and stood there, looking down at me. He bent over me. I could sense his breath on me. And I knew that he had been Mabel's snake, probably wearing a mask of some sort, bending over her to see if she was asleep. I willed myself not to twitch or

297

move a muscle, keeping my breathing slow and regular. Then I saw that he held something in his hand. It was a syringe, and I knew then what he planned to do, and why I hadn't been able to move in my dream.

He bent low over me, and I couldn't tell whether he wanted to make sure I was still under the influence of the chloroform, or whether he was gloating over having taken me so fortuitously. He felt my arm, then to my horror, he started to lift up my skirt. I had not expected this behavior from him, until I realized that I was wearing a wool jacket, too thick to plunge a needle through, and he was going for my thigh instead. I waited, watching my skirt lifted higher and higher. I could hear his breathing quicken as if this act excited him. He raised the syringe, positioning the needle. I summoned all my strength and without warning, delivered a mighty kick to his midsection. I must have struck lucky or had more force than I expected, because he doubled over, gasping, and the needle flew from his hand, clattering to the stone floor. I leaped up, going after it. Although he was still gasping he lunged at me. I kicked the needle across the floor, threw myself after it, and bent to pick it up. He grabbed at me but only got hold of my skirt. I wrenched myself away. I heard a ripping sound, unnaturally loud in that confined and echoing space, and he came away with torn muslin in his hand as my own hand closed around the syringe.

I stood up, triumphant, as I turned to face him. He stopped short and took a step away from me, still holding his middle and gasping for breath.

"Well, Mr. Edward Deveraux, we meet at last," I said.

"How did you know?" he asked. "How did you find out?"

"People don't often change their personality," I said. "Dr. Piper spoke warmly of Dr. Werner. He called him 'a fine man.' But the Dr. Werner I met was a curt and unpleasant individual, with no bedside manner. And all the murders were so clearly linked to Edward Deveraux, it made sense that you were alive somewhere. Then I realized that you planned your escape as soon as you heard that Dr. Werner was coming to visit the institution, and you realized he resembled you in build and appearance. You started growing a beard. You developed an interest in birds because he was a keen bird-watcher. You took him for a walk to the one part of the estate where you could kill him easily. When he looked up for the hawk's nest, you hit him over the head with a rock, switched clothes with him, then hurled him down onto the rocks—having first smashed in his face so that he would not be recognized. Dr. Piper mentioned that you had trimmed your beard in anticipation of the doctor's arrival. You smeared yourself with mud and blood to indicate a struggle, and so that the facial differences between you would not be noticed, and you double-checked the placing of the monocle in the little mirror you carried for that purpose—am I correct?"

He was looking at me with narrowed eyes, like a snake. "You're intelligent, for a woman," he said. "Too bad I didn't get rid of you in that train crash."

"Who were you aiming for—Marcus or me?" I felt surprisingly calm now, feeling the coldness of the glass syringe against my palm.

"Marcus, of course, but when I found you were on board, well, you were an added treat. Too bad you didn't take the sleeping mixture I left for you at the hospital, or we wouldn't be having this conversation."

"That was you? Funny. I sensed danger then. I often do. I'm Irish. We have the sixth sense."

"Do you sense danger now, Mrs. Sullivan?" he asked. "You should."

"I believe I'm the one with the power at this moment, Mr. Deveraux," I said. My voice sounded more confident that I really felt. "I know what's in this syringe. You were planning to do to me what you did to Mabel's parents, weren't you?"

"Not exactly," he said. "I set fire to them. But I rigged up this house to explode after I leave. It was a sort of small-scale practice for the real thing. I like to get my details right. Everything has to work smoothly. And by the time the house goes up, Dr. Werner will have been at sea for two days."

"You've failed in one little detail," I said. "The ship radioed that you were not on board. And I also happened to find out that a Mr. Edwards was sailing to South America with his daughter. Couldn't you have come up with a more creative name?"

His eyes narrowed. "You might have the syringe, but in case you haven't noticed, I'm closer to the door. There's no way out of here, you know, and once I've set the timer, there is no stopping it. You'll hear the ticking until *boom*. It will be too late."

He smiled then. It was the smile of evil, such as I had rarely seen before.

"Why has it been so important to you to ruin so many lives?" I said. "Once you escaped from the asylum, you could have taken the next boat to Europe, and nobody would ever have found you."

"Because those people sentenced me to a life of hell," he said. "That stupid maid and my own tutor who gave evidence against me, that doctor who certified me as insane, the ridiculous judge, trying to be nice. They deserved to be punished."

"You deserved to be punished for killing your father, surely?"

"But I didn't kill my father. That's the whole point. I went into his study, stumbled over his body, and came running out to get help. But I was so much in shock that I started laughing. And I had blood on my hands. And I was the strange one, the pitiful one. Nobody believed me. So they all deserved to die. Just as you will die now because your husband was bent on convicting me."

As he talked he had been inching toward the door. Suddenly he leaped through the doorway and went to close the door. I flung myself at the door and sank the needle into his hand, pushing hard on the plunger. I heard him cry out as the door slammed shut with me inside. I stood there, again in darkness, my heart pounding. Would a small amount of curare in his hand be enough to incapacitate him?

How long before it worked? Long enough for him to escape and activate the switch?

I tried to turn the doorknob. The door resisted. I shoved with all my might, and it inched open. I saw that Edward Deveraux's paralyzed body had been blocking it. He was lying like a broken puppet, his head and limbs at odd angles, his eyes wide open and staring at me. I gave him the briefest of glances as I stepped over him, then ran past him up a flight of steep steps, and opened a door into the passage.

"Mabel!" I yelled. "Mabel, where are you?"

Had he silenced her with curare? I ran from room to room, but they all lay in dusty silence. I pulled off one dust sheet after another, hoping to find her lying beneath one of them, but I didn't. At least I knew now that he wouldn't have killed her. He had rescued her from the house. He was planning to take her to South America. He believed, or wanted to believe, that she was his daughter.

I made it up to the very top of the house. The upper floor was empty and bare. I came down again. Surely he wouldn't have left her in a hotel room near the docks, unless he had drugged her heavily? I had no idea how long the effects of curare lasted. As I stood in the front hall, I noticed wires running along the floor to the front door. He had booby-trapped the house. Then a chilling thought came into my head. Had he had time to turn on the timer before he collapsed? Where was it? Could I disable it again, or would touching it only set it off? I went down the steps cautiously and was relieved to see him still lying there. I followed the wires down the cellar steps and found what had to be the bomb. There was an alarm clock attached to it and it was ticking. Did that mean . . . ?

I knew I had to get out now, but I couldn't risk leaving Mabel here. I opened one door leading to a coal storage area. Then another containing a broom closet. Then at the back, there was a door that was locked, with the key still in it. I turned the key and came into a room lit by a high grating. A shaft of light fell onto a bed where a pale body lay. I ran over to her.

"Mabel? It's me. Mrs. Sullivan."

To my intense relief she opened her eyes, and I saw recognition in them.

"I've come to get you out of here," I said.

"Where is he? He'll find us."

"He's lying unconscious at the moment, but we must be quick." I noticed then that he had tied her to the bed frame. I fumbled with the knots, cursing at the amount of time I was taking, wondering if maybe this bed was also somehow rigged to explode if she tried to escape. At last she was free and stood up, tentatively rubbing her limbs.

"It was awful," she said in a trembling voice. "It was him, wasn't it? He was the snake in my dream. I realized as soon as he came to my bedroom again. He bent over me and I knew. He was wearing something over his face before—a black mask, I think, so that all I could see were slits of eyes. Like snake's eyes. Then he put something over my face, like he did the time before." She looked at me, her blue eyes wide and terrified. "I used to go into my mother's room when I had a bad dream. I'd curl up on the daybed in the corner. I saw him. I saw him come in the window, and he held something in his hand. I saw the whole thing, but I was too scared to move or cry out. When he was pouring some stuff around their beds, he noticed me."

"And he carried you to safety down the fire escape," I said. "Come on, let's see if we can get out of here."

Edward was still lying on the floor, his eyes wide and staring. I went and stood over him. I couldn't resist it. "I'm taking Mabel now," I said. "She wasn't your daughter, you know. What an absurd notion."

Then I ran up the steps after Mabel, who was heading for the front door.

"Don't touch it," I shouted, making her leap away. "It may have been rigged to explode. He's got some kind of bomb downstairs. Let's see if there are wires connected to the windows." There weren't. We

slid one up, and soon we were both standing on the street, to the surprise of two passing women.

I grabbed the first constable I could find. "Get Captain Sullivan
immediately," I told him. "Tell him Edward Deveraux is at Eighteen
Ninth Street, but tell him not to break down the door. The house
may be rigged to explode."

He looked at me strangely, as if I might be off my head. "I'm his
wife, Mrs. Sullivan," I said, frustration building inside me. "I've just
been held prisoner there, as has this young woman. Go on, man. Move.
Do you want the whole street to go up? Do you want a murderer to
go free?"

He shot me a scared look and ran off.

"Come on," I said to Mabel. "Let's take you home."

❦ Thirty-five ❦

W ell, here you are," Mrs. Sullivan said as I came in. "Just in time for the little one's supper. He's been no trouble at all. Have you had a nice day out?"

"It's been interesting," I said, and I went over to give Liam a kiss.

"Is Daniel not with you?" She looked around.

"No. He has police work to do," I said. "We may have caught the man he's been looking for."

"Well, that's good. All's well that ends well," she replied.

I couldn't tell her of my own fear—that Edward Deveraux would awake and escape, or that he would somehow make the house explode with Daniel in it. I sat, tense as a coiled watch spring, unable to eat, until he came home at ten.

"Thank God," he and I both said at the same time, falling into each other's arms.

"Did you catch him? He didn't escape, did he? He was still there in the house where I left him? I sent the constable to find you. I told him how urgent it was."

"Edward Deveraux didn't escape," Daniel said. "We were too late.

He'd set off some kind of explosive and it brought the house down, with him in it."

"I thought he'd set the timer on the bomb," I said. "He'd rigged the house with explosives, you know. I was terrified you'd open the front door and be blown up."

"He took you captive? You escaped?" he asked, holding my shoulders fiercely. "What possessed you to go anywhere near him? You knew what he was capable of."

"I didn't mean to go near him," I said. "I saw that he was planning to sail to South America on the *Queen of the Amazon* tomorrow, and I wanted to see whether he had left his house or not."

"So you went there? Are you crazy?"

"Of course I didn't. I'm not stupid, you know. I stood across the street and observed the house. I chatted with a neighbor. She said she hadn't seen him for a couple of days. Then I noticed one of his drapes was not quite closed, so I went to peek inside. That's when he must have chloroformed me."

"Why didn't you just tell the police and go home? Why take a risk yourself? You're lucky to be alive."

"I know that. I came to see you at Mulberry Street, risking your anger, but you weren't there. I left you a note. I thought I'd help by finding out if he had sailed yet, and when I found that a man matching his description was sailing for South America with his daughter, it began to dawn on me that Dr. Werner might be Edward Deveraux, and that he had Mabel with him. And I didn't think I was taking a risk by looking at the outside of a house in broad daylight to see if it was still occupied."

He was gazing at me with a kind of fierce tenderness. "Thank God you're all right," he said. "And Mabel too. If you hadn't released her, she might not have survived." He was still holding me, his fingers digging into my shoulders as if he wanted to make sure I was there and real.

"He was the snake in her dreams, Daniel," I said. "He carried her to safety when he torched her parents' house. He wanted to believe he was her father."

"And was he?"

"Of course not. Another of his delusions. But one thing he still swore, Daniel. He didn't kill his father. Edward came upon his father lying there, bent to help him, and got blood all over himself. Everything conspired against him to make him seem guilty, but he was wrongly accused. That's why he wanted revenge so badly."

"If he didn't kill his father, who did?"

"I'm thinking it had to be Marcus, didn't it? One of the servants heard the father saying 'You are a disgrace to this family.' And we know that Marcus has always had expensive tastes." Then I stopped and put my hand to my mouth. "Oh, Marcus," I said.

"What?"

"Remember Edward sent you the note about going out with a bang?"

"And he did."

"No." I shook my head. "He said the rigging of his house was just a small-scale practice for the big one."

"So what are you suggesting?"

"I'm suggesting that his final act of revenge would be to bomb the family bank."

Men were dispatched immediately, and they found a large quantity of explosives in the bank cellar and a timer set to go off at ten the next morning—the moment that the ship was to sail. It was dismantled safely, and Marcus Deveraux, when pressed sufficiently by the police, told the truth about what had happened the day his father died. A horrible accident, he said. His father was furious with his debts. He came right up to Marcus, yelling, threatening, waving a sheaf of bills in his face. Marcus pushed his father away because he felt so threatened. His father tripped over the edge of the rug, fell, and hit his head on the fender. Marcus could think of nothing but getting away. He climbed out through the window. When he heard that Edward had been accused he said nothing, deciding that his life was more valuable to the bank and the family's future than Edward's. But he paid a large sum for Edward to be housed humanely and well.

I related all this to Sid and Gus the next day while Liam played happily on their floor with their pots and pans.

"I still find this hard to believe," Gus said. "Think of it, Sid. We actually sat in a hansom cab with a murderer. With a man who had no compassion, no human feeling, and who took the most amazing risks. We are actually fortunate to be alive."

"Edward Deveraux had no reason to want to dispatch you," I said. "I think he must have wholeheartedly enjoyed the thrill of being asked to treat a patient whose infirmity he caused in the first place."

"The man certainly did like taking incredible risks," Sid said. "How could he possibly think he could pass himself off for the doctor? Did they look that similar?"

"In age, build, and coloring, yes. And if the facial features differed, it didn't matter. He made sure he smashed the doctor's face before he threw him down into the chasm, and he smeared his own face with blood and mud, claiming to be in distress from the strangulation attempt. It was mentioned that he could hardly talk. That way it wouldn't be noticed that his speech was different. And he claimed to be so upset by the whole thing that he refused to stay the night and departed immediately after giving his statement to the police. And the doctor wore a monocle. People are funny. They notice the little details, like the monocle and the beard. And if someone is clearly in distress, you don't look at him too hard. Edward knew his psychology, all right."

"I suppose he must have been brooding and plotting for years," Gus said. "And all that time dreaming about punishing those who had contributed to his wrongful conviction." She looked up from her coffee cup. "I blame his brother. How could one live with oneself, knowing that he had condemned an innocent man to a life in a mental institution?"

"I suppose one can understand," Sid said. "Marcus had a promising future. His brother didn't. Many young men might have done the same."

"And condemned his brother to a life that was no life?" Gus retorted. "I could never have lived with my conscience."

"Ah, but you are altruistic and tenderhearted," Sid replied. "Marcus was self-centered."

Gus handed me a plate of macaroons. "And I am fascinated to know that Mabel's dream all made sense," she said. "The snake. The long sharp fingers were the needle. I must write to Professor Freud. He'll be interested."

"And you can also tell him that there is such a thing as prophetic dreams," I said. "Dreams that come to us as warnings. I dreamed of the basement room where Edward put me, and I dreamed of being paralyzed, so that I was forewarned when he came in with that syringe of curare."

"Ah, but Molly, you're Irish. It's only Celts who can do things like that," Gus said. "I don't think that an Austrian professor will change his thinking to include you."

And we laughed. Liam, not understanding the joke, looked up from the floor and laughed too.

HISTORICAL NOTE

The crash of the Ninth Avenue Elevated train happened on September 11, 1905, exactly as I have described it. A Ninth Avenue train, traveling at a speed suitable for a straight track, was diverted to the Sixth Avenue curve. Its speed was too great, and it plunged down to the street below.

Both the locomotive driver and the signalman were interrogated, but both claimed innocence. The locomotive driver came under suspicion because there was union unrest, and they were planning a strike. He was briefly imprisoned, then released and fled the state, but died soon after.

So the cause of the train crash was never established. Except in my book.

And of course the excitement in the medical community caused by Sigmund Freud's treatise on the interpretation of dreams is also real.